KU-125-751

DEAD UNTIL DARK

CHARLAINE HARRIS

WHEELER
CHIVERS

This Large Print edition is published by Wheeler Publishing, Waterville, Maine USA and by BBC Audiobooks, Ltd, Bath, England.

Published in 2004 in the U.S. by arrangement with The Berkley Publishing Group, a member of Penguin Group (USA) Inc.

Published in 2004 in the U.K. by arrangement with Time Warner Books UK.

U.S. Hardcover 1-58724-630-9 (Softcover)
U.K. Hardcover 0-7540-6995-8 (Chivers Large Print)
U.K. Softcover 0-7540-6996-6 (Camden Large Print)

Copyright © 2001 by Charlaine Harris Schulz
A Southern Vampire Novel

All rights reserved.

This is a work of fiction. Names, characters, places, and incidents either are the product of the author's imagination or are used fictitiously, and any resemblance to actual persons, living or dead, business establishments, events, or locales is entirely coincidental.

The text of this Large Print edition is unabridged. Other aspects of the book may vary from the original edition.

Set in 16 pt. Plantin by Myrna S. Raven.

Printed in the United States on permanent paper.

British Library Cataloguing-In-Publication Data available

ISBN 1-58724-630-9 (lg. print : sc : alk. paper)

*My thanks and appreciation go to the people
who thought this book
was a good idea — Dean James, Toni L. P. Kelner
and
Gary and Susan Nowlin*

LEICESTER CITY LIBRARIES	
6 8403 98 976 1 387	
BBC AUDIOBOOKS	6.12.07
F	£15.99

LEICESTER CITY
LIBRARIES

1

I'd been waiting for the vampire for years when he walked into the bar.

Ever since vampires came out of the coffin (as they laughingly put it) four years ago, I'd hoped one would come to Bon Temps. We had all the other minorities in our little town — why not the newest, the legally recognized undead? But rural northern Louisiana wasn't too tempting to vampires, apparently; on the other hand, New Orleans was a real center for them — the whole Anne Rice thing, right?

It's not that long a drive from Bon Temps to New Orleans, and everyone who came into the bar said that if you threw a rock on a street corner you'd hit one. Though you better not.

But I was waiting for my own vampire.

You can tell I don't get out much. And it's not because I'm not pretty. I am. I'm blond and blue-eyed and twenty-five, and my legs are strong and my bosom is substantial, and I have a waspy waistline. I look good in the warm-weather waitress outfit Sam picked for us: black shorts, white T, white socks, black Nikes.

But I have a disability. That's how I try to think of it.

The bar patrons just say I'm crazy.

Either way, the result is that I almost never

have a date. So little treats count a lot with me.

And he sat at one of my tables — the vampire.

I knew immediately what he was. It amazed me when no one else turned around to stare. They couldn't tell! But to me, his skin had a little glow, and I just knew.

I could have danced with joy, and in fact I did do a little step right there by the bar. Sam Merlotte, my boss, looked up from the drink he was mixing and gave me a tiny smile. I grabbed my tray and pad and went over to the vampire's table. I hoped that my lipstick was still even and my ponytail was still neat. I'm kind of tense, and I could feel my smile yanking the corners of my mouth up.

He seemed lost in thought, and I had a chance to give him a good once-over before he looked up. He was a little under six feet, I estimated. He had thick brown hair, combed straight back and brushing his collar, and his long sideburns seemed curiously old-fashioned. He was pale, of course; hey, he was dead, if you believed the old tales. The politically correct theory, the one the vamps themselves publicly backed, had it that this guy was the victim of a virus that left him apparently dead for a couple of days and thereafter allergic to sunlight, silver, and garlic. The details depended on which newspaper you read. They were all full of vampire stuff these days.

Anyway, his lips were lovely, sharply sculpted,

and he had arched dark brows. His nose swooped down right out of that arch, like a prince's in a Byzantine mosaic. When he finally looked up, I saw his eyes were even darker than his hair, and the whites were incredibly white.

"What can I get you?" I asked, happy almost beyond words.

He raised his eyebrows. "Do you have the bottled synthetic blood?" he asked.

"No, I'm so sorry! Sam's got some on order. Should be in next week."

"Then red wine, please," he said, and his voice was cool and clear, like a stream over smooth stones. I laughed out loud. It was too perfect.

"Don't mind, Sookie, mister, she's crazy," came a familiar voice from the booth against the wall. All my happiness deflated, though I could feel the smile still straining my lips. The vampire was staring at me, watching the life go out of my face.

"I'll get your wine right away," I said, and strode off, not even looking at Mack Rattray's smug face. He was there almost every night, he and his wife Denise. I called them the Rat Couple. They'd done their best to make me miserable since they'd moved into the rent trailer at Four Tracks Corner. I had hoped that they'd blow out of Bon Temps as suddenly as they'd blown in.

When they'd first come into Merlotte's, I'd very rudely listened in to their thoughts — I know, pretty low-class of me. But I get bored like everyone else, and though I spend most of my time blocking out the thoughts of other people that try to pass through my brain, sometimes I just give in. So I knew some things about the Rattrays that maybe no one else did. For one thing, I knew they'd been in jail, though I didn't know why. For another, I'd read the nasty thoughts Mack Rattray had entertained about yours truly. And then I'd heard in Denise's thoughts that she'd abandoned a baby she'd had two years before, a baby that wasn't Mack's.

And they didn't tip, either.

Sam poured a glass of the house red wine, looking over at the vampire's table as he put it on my tray.

When Sam looked back at me, I could tell he too knew our new customer was undead. Sam's eyes are Paul Newman blue, as opposed to my own hazy blue gray. Sam is blond, too, but his hair is wiry and his blond is almost a sort of hot red gold. He is always a little sunburned, and though he looks slight in his clothes, I have seen him unload trucks with his shirt off, and he has plenty of upper body strength. I never listen to Sam's thoughts. He's my boss. I've had to quit jobs before because I found out things I didn't want to know about my boss.

But Sam didn't comment, he just gave me the wine. I checked the glass to make sure it was sparkly clean and made my way back to the vampire's table.

"Your wine, sir," I said ceremoniously and placed it carefully on the table exactly in front of him. He looked at me again, and I stared into his lovely eyes while I had the chance. "Enjoy," I said proudly. Behind me, Mack Rattray yelled, "Hey, Sookie! We need another pitcher of beer here!" I sighed and turned to take the empty pitcher from the Rats' table. Denise was in fine form tonight, I noticed, wearing a halter top and short shorts, her mess of brown hair floofing around her head in fashionable tangles. Denise wasn't truly pretty, but she was so flashy and confident that it took awhile to figure that out.

A little while later, to my dismay, I saw the Rattrays had moved over to the vampire's table. They were talking at him. I couldn't see that he was responding a lot, but he wasn't leaving either.

"Look at that!" I said disgustedly to Arlene, my fellow waitress. Arlene is redheaded and freckled and ten years older than me, and she's been married four times. She has two kids, and from time to time, I think she considers me her third.

"New guy, huh?" she said with small interest. Arlene is currently dating Rene Lenier, and though I can't see the attraction, she seems pretty satisfied. I think Rene was her second husband.

"Oh, he's a vampire," I said, just having to

share my delight with someone.

"Really? Here? Well, just think," she said, smiling a little to show she appreciated my pleasure. "He can't be too bright, though, honey, if he's with the Rats. On the other hand, Denise is giving him quite a show."

I figured it out after Arlene made it plain to me; she's much better at sizing up sexual situations than I am due to her experience and my lack.

The vampire was hungry. I'd always heard that the synthetic blood the Japanese had developed kept vampires up to par as far as nutrition, but didn't really satisfy their hunger, which was why there were "Unfortunate Incidents" from time to time. (That was the vampire euphemism for the bloody slaying of a human.) And here was Denise Rattray, stroking her throat, turning her neck from side to side . . . what a *bitch*.

My brother, Jason, came into the bar, then, and sauntered over to give me a hug. He knows that women like a man who's good to his family and also kind to the disabled, so hugging me is a double whammy of recommendation. Not that Jason needs many more points than he has just by being himself. He's handsome. He can sure be mean, too, but most women seem quite willing to overlook that.

"Hey, sis, how's Gran?"

"She's okay, about the same. Come by to see."

"I will. Who's loose tonight?"

"Look for yourself." I noticed that when Jason began to glance around there was a flutter of female hands to hair, blouses, lips.

"Hey. I see DeeAnne. She free?"

"She's here with a trucker from Hammond. He's in the bathroom. Watch it."

Jason grinned at me, and I marvelled that other women could not see the selfishness of that smile. Even Arlene tucked in her T-shirt when Jason came in, and after four husbands she should have known a little about evaluating men. The other waitress I worked with, Dawn, tossed her hair and straightened her back to make her boobs stand out. Jason gave her an amiable wave. She pretended to sneer. She's on the outs with Jason, but she still wants him to notice her.

I got really busy — everyone came to Merlotte's on Saturday night for some portion of the evening — so I lost track of my vampire for a while. When I next had a moment to check on him, he was talking to Denise. Mack was looking at him with an expression so avid that I became worried.

I went closer to the table, staring at Mack. Finally, I let down my guard and listened.

Mack and Denise had been in jail for vampire draining.

Deeply upset, I nevertheless automatically carried a pitcher of beer and some glasses to a raucous table of four. Since vampire blood was

13

supposed to temporarily relieve symptoms of illness and increase sexual potency, kind of like prednisone and Viagra rolled into one, there was a huge black market for genuine, undiluted vampire blood. Where there's a market there are suppliers; in this case, I'd just learned, the scummy Rat Couple. They'd formerly trapped vampires and drained them, selling the little vials of blood for as much as $200 apiece. It had been the drug of choice for at least two years now. Some buyers went crazy after drinking pure vampire blood, but that didn't slow the market any.

The drained vampire didn't last long, as a rule. The drainers left the vampires staked or simply dumped them out in the open. When the sun came up, that was all she wrote. From time to time, you read about the tables being turned when the vampire managed to get free. Then you got your dead drainers.

Now my vampire was getting up and leaving with the Rats. Mack met my eyes, and I saw him looking distinctly startled at the expression on my face. He turned away, shrugging me off like everyone else.

That made me mad. Really mad.

What should I do? While I struggled with myself, they were out the door. Would the vampire believe me if I ran after them, told him? No one else did. Or if by chance they did, they hated and feared me for reading the thoughts concealed in people's brains. Arlene had

14

begged me to read her fourth husband's mind when he'd come in to pick her up one night because she was pretty certain he was thinking of leaving her and the kids, but I wouldn't because I wanted to keep the one friend I had. And even Arlene hadn't been able to ask me directly because that would be admitting I had this gift, this curse. People couldn't admit it. They had to think I was crazy. Which sometimes I almost was!

So I dithered, confused and frightened and angry, and then I knew I just had to act. I was goaded by the look Mack had given me —as if I was negligible.

I slid down the bar to Jason, where he was sweeping DeeAnne off her feet. She didn't take much sweeping, popular opinion had it. The trucker from Hammond was glowering from her other side.

"Jason," I said urgently. He turned to give me a warning glare. "Listen, is that chain still in the back of the pickup?"

"Never leave home without it," he said lazily, his eyes scanning my face for signs of trouble. "You going to fight, Sookie?"

I smiled at him, so used to grinning that it was easy. "I sure hope not," I said cheerfully.

"Hey, you need help?" After all, he was my brother.

"No, thanks," I said, trying to sound reassuring. And I slipped over to Arlene. "Listen, I got to leave a little early. My tables are pretty

15

thin, can you cover for me?" I didn't think I'd ever asked Arlene such a thing, though I'd covered for her many times. She, too, offered me help. "That's okay," I said. "I'll be back in if I can. If you clean my area, I'll do your trailer."

Arlene nodded her red mane enthusiastically.

I pointed to the employee door, to myself, and made my fingers walk, to tell Sam where I was going.

He nodded. He didn't look happy.

So out the back door I went, trying to make my feet quiet on the gravel. The employee parking lot is at the rear of the bar, through a door leading into the storeroom. The cook's car was there, and Arlene's, Dawn's, and mine. To my right, the east, Sam's pickup was sitting in front of his trailer.

I went out of the gravelled employee parking area onto the blacktop that surfaced the much larger customer lot to the west of the bar. Woods surrounded the clearing in which Merlotte's stood, and the edges of the parking lot were mostly gravel. Sam kept it well lit, and the surrealistic glare of the high, parking lot lights made everything look strange.

I saw the Rat Couple's dented red sports car, so I knew they were close.

I found Jason's truck at last. It was black with custom aqua and pink swirls on the sides. He sure did love to be noticed. I pulled myself up by the tailgate and rummaged around in the bed for his chain, a thick length of links that he carried in case of a fight. I looped it and carried it pressed to my body so it wouldn't chink.

I thought a second. The only halfway private spot to which the Rattrays could have lured the vampire was the end of the parking lot where the trees actually overhung the cars. So I crept in that direction, trying to move fast and low.

I paused every few seconds and listened. Soon I heard a groan and the faint sounds of voices. I snaked between the cars, and I spotted them right where I'd figured they'd be. The vampire was down on the ground on his back, his face contorted in agony, and the gleam of chains crisscrossed his wrists and ran down to his ankles. Silver. There were two little vials of blood already on the ground beside Denise's feet, and as I watched, she fixed a new Vacutainer to the needle. The tourniquet above his elbow dug cruelly into his arm.

Their backs were to me, and the vampire hadn't seen me yet. I loosened the coiled chain so a good three feet of it swung free. Who to attack first? They were both small and vicious.

I remembered Mack's contemptuous dismissal and the fact that he never left me a tip. Mack first.

I'd never actually been in a fight before. Somehow I was positively looking forward to it.

I leapt out from behind a pickup and swung the chain. It thwacked across Mack's back as he knelt beside his victim. He screamed and jumped up. After a glance, Denise set about getting the third Vacutainer plugged. Mack's hand dipped down to his boot and came up shining. I gulped. He had a knife in his hand.

"Uh-oh," I said, and grinned at him.

"You crazy bitch!" he screamed. He sounded like he was looking forward to using the knife. I was too involved to keep my mental guard up, and I had a clear flash of what Mack wanted to do to me. It drove me really crazy. I went for him with every intention of hurting him as badly as I could. But he was ready for me and jumped forward with the knife while I was swinging the chain. He sliced at my arm and just missed it. The chain, on its recoil, wrapped around his skinny neck like a lover. Mack's yell of triumph turned into a gurgle. He dropped the knife and clawed at the links with both hands. Losing air, he dropped to his knees on the rough pavement, yanking the chain from my hand.

Well, there went Jason's chain. I swooped down and scooped up Mack's knife, holding it like I knew how to use it. Denise had been lunging forward, looking like a redneck witch in the lines and shadows of the security lights.

She stopped in her tracks when she saw I had Mack's knife. She cursed and railed and said terrible things. I waited till she'd run down to say, "Get. Out. Now."

Denise stared holes of hate in my head. She tried to scoop up the vials of blood, but I hissed at her to leave them alone. So she pulled Mack

18

to his feet. He was still making choking, gurgling sounds and holding the chain. Denise kind of dragged him along to their car and shoved him in through the passenger's side. Yanking some keys from her pocket, Denise threw herself in the driver's seat.

As I heard the engine roar into life, suddenly I realized that the Rats now had another weapon. Faster than I've ever moved, I ran to the vampire's head and panted, "Push with your feet!" I grabbed him under the arms and yanked back with all my might, and he caught on and braced his feet and shoved. We were just inside the tree line when the red car came roaring down at us. Denise missed us by less than a yard when she had to swerve to avoid hitting a pine. Then I heard the big motor of the Rats' car receding in the distance.

"Oh, wow," I breathed, and knelt by the vampire because my knees wouldn't hold me up any more. I breathed heavily for just a minute, trying to get hold of myself. The vampire moved a little, and I looked over. To my horror, I saw wisps of smoke coming up from his wrists where the silver touched them.

"Oh, you poor thing," I said, angry at myself for not caring for him instantly. Still trying to catch my breath, I began to unwind the thin bands of silver, which all seemed to be part of one very long chain. "Poor baby," I whispered, never thinking until later how incongruous that sounded. I have agile fingers, and I released his wrists pretty quickly. I wondered how the Rats had distracted him while they got into position to put them on, and I could feel myself reddening as I pictured it.

The vampire cradled his arms to his chest while I worked on the silver wrapped around his legs. His ankles had fared better since the drainers hadn't troubled to pull up his jeans legs and put the silver against his bare skin.

"I'm sorry I didn't get here faster," I said apologetically. "You'll feel better in a minute, right? Do you want me to leave?"

"No."

That made me feel pretty good until he added, "They might come back, and I can't fight yet." His cool voice was uneven, but I couldn't exactly say I'd heard him panting.

I made a sour face at him, and while he was recovering, I took a few precautions. I sat with my back to him, giving him some privacy. I know how unpleasant it is to be stared at when you're hurting. I hunkered down on the pavement, keeping watch on the parking lot. Several cars left, and others came in, but none came down to our end by the woods. By the movement of the air around me, I knew when the vampire had sat up.

He didn't speak right away. I turned my head to the left to look at him. He was closer than I'd thought. His big dark eyes looked into mine. His fangs had retracted; I was a little disappointed about that.

"Thank you," he said stiffly.

So he wasn't thrilled about being rescued by a woman. Typical guy.

Since he was being so ungracious, I felt I could do something rude, too, and I listened to him, opening my mind completely.

And I heard . . . nothing.

"Oh," I said, hearing the shock in my own voice, hardly knowing what I was saying. "I *can't hear you.*"

"Thank you!" the vampire said, moving his lips exaggeratedly.

"No, no . . . I can hear you speak, but . . ." and in my excitement, I did something I ordinarily would never do, because it was pushy, and personal, and revealed I was disabled. I turned fully to him and put my hands on both sides of his white face, and I looked at him intently. I focused with all my energy. *Nothing*. It was like having to listen to the radio all the time, to stations you didn't get to select, and then suddenly tuning in to a wavelength you couldn't receive.

It was heaven.

His eyes were getting wider and darker, though he was holding absolutely still.

"Oh, excuse me," I said with a gasp of embarrassment. I snatched my hands away and resumed staring at the parking lot. I began babbling about Mack and Denise, all the time thinking how marvelous it would be to have a companion I could not hear unless he chose to speak out loud. How beautiful his silence was.

". . . so I figured I better come out here to see how you were," I concluded, and had no idea what I'd been saying.

"You came out here to rescue me. It was brave," he said in a voice so seductive it would have shivered DeeAnne right out of her red nylon panties.

"Now you cut that out," I said tartly, coming right down to earth with a thud.

He looked astonished for a whole second before his face returned to its white smoothness.

"Aren't you afraid to be alone with a hungry vampire?" he asked, something arch and yet dangerous running beneath the words.

"Nope."

"Are you assuming that since you came to my rescue that you're safe, that I harbor an ounce of sentimental feeling after all these years? Vampires often turn on those who trust them. We don't have human values, you know."

"A lot of humans turn on those who trust them," I pointed out. I can be practical. "I'm not a total fool." I held out my arm and turned my neck. While he'd been recovering, I'd been wrapping the Rats' chains around my neck and arms.

He shivered visibly.

"But there's a juicy artery in your groin," he said after a pause to regroup, his voice as slithery as a snake on a slide.

"Don't you talk dirty," I told him. "I won't listen to that."

Once again we looked at each other in silence. I was afraid I'd never see him again; after all, his first visit to Merlotte's hadn't exactly been a success. So I was trying to absorb every detail I could; I would treasure this encounter and rehash it for a long, long time. It was rare, a prize. I wanted to touch his skin again. I couldn't remember how it felt. But that would be going beyond some boundary of manners, and also maybe start him going on the seductive crap again.

"Would you like to drink the blood they collected?" he asked unexpectedly. "It would be a way for me to show my gratitude." He gestured at the stoppered vials lying on the blacktop. "My blood is supposed to improve your sex life and your health."

"I'm healthy as a horse," I told him honestly. "And I have no sex life to speak of. You do what you want with it."

"You could sell it," he suggested, but I thought he was just waiting to see what I'd say about that.

"I wouldn't touch it," I said, insulted.

"You're different," he said. "What are you?" He seemed to be going through a list of possibilities in his head from the way he was looking at me. To my pleasure, I could not hear a one of them.

"Well. I'm Sookie Stackhouse, and I'm a waitress," I told him. "What's your name?" I thought I could at least ask that without being presuming.

"Bill," he said.

Before I could stop myself, I rocked back onto my butt with laughter. "The vampire Bill!" I said. "I thought it might be Antoine, or Basil, or Langford! Bill!" I hadn't laughed so hard in a long time. "Well, see ya, Bill. I got to get back to work." I could feel the tense grin snap back into place when I thought of Merlotte's. I put my hand on Bill's shoulder and pushed up. It was rock hard, and I was on my feet so fast I had to stop myself from stumbling. I examined my socks to make sure their cuffs were exactly even, and I looked up and down my outfit to check for wear and tear during the fight with the Rats. I dusted off my bottom since I'd been sitting on the dirty pavement and gave Bill a wave as I started off across the parking lot.

It had been a stimulating evening, one with a lot of food for thought. I felt almost as cheerful as my smile when I considered it.

But Jason was going to be mighty angry about the chain.

After work that night, I drove home, which is only about four miles south from the bar. Jason had been gone (and so had DeeAnne) when I got back to work, and that had been another good thing. I was reviewing the evening as I drove to my grandmother's house, where I lived. It's right before Tall Pines cemetery, which lies off a narrow two-lane parish road.

My great-great-great grandfather had started the house, and he'd had ideas about privacy, so to reach it you had to turn off the parish road into the driveway, go through some woods, and then you arrived at the clearing in which the house stood.

It's sure not any historic landmark, since most of the oldest parts have been ripped down and replaced over the years, and of course it's got electricity and plumbing and insulation, all that good modern stuff. But it still has a tin roof that gleams blindingly on sunny days. When the roof needed to be replaced, I wanted to put regular roofing tiles on it, but my grandmother said no. Though I was paying, it's her house; so naturally, tin it was.

Historical or not, I'd lived in this house since I was about seven, and I'd visited it often before then, so I loved it. It was just a big old family home, too big for Granny and me, I guess. It had a broad front covered by a screened-in porch, and it was painted white, Granny being a traditionalist all the way. I went through the big living room, strewn with battered furniture arranged to suit us, and down the hall to the first bedroom on the left, the biggest.

Adele Hale Stackhouse, my grandmother, was propped up in her high bed, about a million pillows padding her skinny shoulders. She was wearing a long-sleeved cotton nightgown even in the warmth of this spring night, and her bedside lamp was still on. There was a book propped in her lap.

"Hey," I said.

"Hi, honey."

My grandmother is very small and very old, but her hair is still thick, and so white it almost has the very faintest of green tinges. She wears it kind of rolled against her neck during the day, but at night it's loose or braided. I looked at the cover of her book.

"You reading Danielle Steele again?"

"Oh, that woman can sure tell a story." My grandmother's great pleasures were reading Danielle Steele, watching her soap operas (which she called her "stories") and attending meetings of the myriad clubs she'd belonged to all her adult life, it seemed. Her favorites were the Descendants of the Glorious Dead and the Bon Temps Gardening Society.

"Guess what happened tonight?" I asked her.

"What? You got a date?"

"No," I said, working to keep a smile on my face. "A vampire came into the bar."

"Ooh, did he have fangs?"

I'd seen them glisten in the parking lot lights when the Rats were draining him, but there was no need to describe that to Gran. "Sure, but they were retracted."

"A vampire right here in Bon Temps." Granny was as pleased as punch. "Did he bite anybody in the bar?"

"Oh, no, Gran! He just sat and had a glass of

red wine. Well, he ordered it, but he didn't drink it. I think he just wanted some company."

"Wonder where he stays."

"He wouldn't be too likely to tell anyone that."

"No," Gran said, thinking about it a moment. "I guess not. Did you like him?"

Now that was kind of a hard question. I mulled it over. "I don't know. He was real interesting," I said cautiously.

"I'd surely love to meet him." I wasn't surprised Gran said this because she enjoyed new things almost as much as I did. She wasn't one of those reactionaries who'd decided vampires were damned right off the bat. "But I better go to sleep now. I was just waiting for you to come home before I turned out my light."

I bent over to give Gran a kiss, and said, "Night night."

I half-closed her door on my way out and heard the click of the lamp as she turned it off. My cat, Tina, came from wherever she'd been sleeping to rub against my legs, and I picked her up and cuddled her for a while before putting her out for the night. I glanced at the clock. It was almost two o'clock, and my bed was calling me.

My room was right across the hall from Gran's. When I first used this room, after my folks had died, Gran had moved my bedroom furniture from their house so I'd feel more homey. And here it was still, the single bed and

27

vanity in white-painted wood, the small chest of drawers.

I turned on my own light and shut the door and began taking off my clothes. I had at least five pair of black shorts and many, many white T-shirts, since those tended to get stained so easily. No telling how many pairs of white socks were rolled up in my drawer. So I didn't have to do the wash tonight. I was too tired for a shower. I did brush my teeth and wash the makeup off my face, slap on some moisturizer, and take the band out of my hair.

I crawled into bed in my favorite Mickey Mouse sleep T-shirt, which came almost to my knees. I turned on my side, like I always do, and I relished the silence of the room. Almost everyone's brain is turned off in the wee hours of the night, and the vibrations are gone, the intrusions do not have to be repelled. With such peace, I only had time to think of the vampire's dark eyes, and then I fell into the deep sleep of exhaustion.

By lunchtime the next day I was in my folding aluminum chaise out in the front yard, getting browner by the second. I was in my favorite white strapless two-piece, and it was a little roomier than last summer, so I was pleased as punch.

Then I heard a vehicle coming down the drive, and Jason's black truck with its pink and aqua blazons pulled up to within a yard of my feet.

Jason climbed down — did I mention the truck sports those high tires? — to stalk toward me. He was wearing his usual work clothes, a khaki shirt and pants, and he had his sheathed knife clipped to his belt, like most of the county road workers did. Just by the way he walked, I knew he was in a huff.

I put my dark glasses on.

"Why didn't you tell me you beat up the Rattrays last night?" My brother threw himself into the aluminum yard chair by my chaise. "Where's Gran?" he asked belatedly.

"Hanging out the laundry," I said. Gran used the dryer in a pinch, but she really liked hanging the wet clothes out in the sun. Of course the clothesline was in the backyard, where clotheslines should be. "She's fixing country-fried steak and sweet potatoes and green beans she put up last year, for lunch," I added, knowing that would distract Jason a little bit. I hoped Gran stayed out back. I didn't want her to hear this conversation. "Keep your voice low," I reminded him.

"Rene Lenier couldn't wait till I got to work this morning to tell me all about it. He was over to the Rattrays' trailer last night to buy him some weed, and Denise drove up like she wanted to kill someone. Rene said he liked to have gotten killed, she was so mad. It took both Rene and Denise to get Mack into the trailer, and then they took him to the hospital in Monroe." Jason glared at me accusingly.

"Did Rene tell you that Mack came after me with a knife?" I asked, deciding attacking was the best way of handling this. I could tell Jason's pique was due in large part to the fact that he had heard about this from someone else.

"If Denise told Rene, he didn't mention it to me," Jason said slowly, and I saw his handsome face darken with rage. "He came after you with a knife?"

"So I had to defend myself," I said, as if it were matter-of-fact. "And he took your chain." This was all true, if a little skewed.

"I came in to tell you," I continued, "but by the time I got back in the bar, you were gone with DeeAnne, and since I was fine, it just didn't seem worth tracking you down. I knew you'd feel obliged to go after him if I told you about the knife," I added diplomatically. There was a lot more truth in that, since Jason dearly loves a fight.

"What the hell were you doing out there anyway?" he asked, but he had relaxed, and I knew he was accepting this.

"Did you know that, in addition to selling drugs, the Rats are vampire drainers?"

Now he was fascinated. "No . . . so?"

"Well, one of my customers last night was a vampire, and they were draining him out in Merlotte's parking lot! I couldn't have that."

"There's a vampire here in Bon Temps?"

"Yep. Even if you don't want a vampire for

your best friend, you can't let trash like the Rats drain them. It's not like siphoning gas out of a car. And they would have left him out in the woods to die." Though the Rats hadn't told me their intentions, that was my bet. Even if they'd put him under cover so he could survive the day, a drained vampire took at least twenty years to recover, at least that's what one had said on *Oprah*. And that's if another vampire took care of him.

"The vampire was in the bar when I was there?" Jason asked, dazzled.

"Uh-huh. The dark-haired guy sitting with the Rats."

Jason grinned at my epithet for the Rattrays. But he hadn't let go of the night before, yet. "How'd you know he was a vampire?" he asked, but when he looked at me, I could tell he was wishing he had bitten his tongue.

"I just knew," I said in my flattest voice.

"Right." And we shared a whole unspoken conversation.

"Homulka doesn't have a vampire," Jason said thoughtfully. He tilted his face back to catch the sun, and I knew we were off dangerous ground.

"True," I agreed. Homulka was the town Bon Temps loved to hate. We'd been rivals in football, basketball, and historical significance for generations.

"Neither does Roedale," Gran said from behind us, and Jason and I both jumped. I give

31

Jason credit, he jumps up and gives Gran a hug everytime he sees her.

"Gran, you got enough food in the oven for me?"

"You and two others," Gran said. Our grandmother smiled up at Jason. She was not blind to his faults (or mine), but she loved him. "I just got a phone call from Everlee Mason. She was telling me you hooked up with DeeAnne last night."

"Boy oh boy, can't do anything in this town without getting caught," Jason said, but he wasn't really angry.

"That DeeAnne," Gran said warningly as we all started into the house, "she's been pregnant one time I know of. You just take care she doesn't have one of yours, you'll be paying the rest of your life. Course, that may be the only way I get great-grandchildren!"

Gran had the food ready on the table, so after Jason hung up his hat we sat down and said grace. Then Gran and Jason began gossiping with each other (though they called it "catching up") about people in our little town and parish. My brother worked for the state, supervising road crews. It seemed to me like Jason's day consisted of driving around in a state pickup, clocking off work, and then driving around all night in his own pickup. Rene was on one of the work crews Jason oversaw, and they'd been to high school together. They hung around with Hoyt Fortenberry a lot.

"Sookie, I had to replace the hot water heater in the house," Jason said suddenly. He lives in my parents' old house, the one we'd been living in when they died in a flash flood. We lived with Gran after that, but when Jason got through his two years of college and went to work for the state, he moved back into the house, which on paper is half mine.

"You need any money on that?" I asked.

"Naw, I got it."

We both make salaries, but we also have a little income from a fund established when an oil well was sunk on my parents' property. It played out in a few years, but my parents and then Gran made sure the money was invested. It saved Jason and me a lot of struggle, that padding. I don't know how Gran could have raised us if it hadn't been for that money. She was determined not to sell any land, but her own income is not much more than social security. That's one reason I don't get an apartment. If I get groceries when I'm living with her, that's reasonable, to her; but if I buy groceries and bring them to her house and leave them on her table and go home to my house, that's charity and that makes her mad.

"What kind did you get?" I asked, just to show interest.

He was dying to tell me; Jason's an appliance freak, and he wanted to describe his comparison shopping for a new water heater in detail. I

33

listened with as much attention as I could muster.

And then he interrupted himself. "Hey Sook, you remember Maudette Pickens?"

"Sure," I said, surprised. "We graduated in the same class."

"Somebody killed Maudette in her apartment last night."

Gran and I were riveted. "When?" Gran asked, puzzled that she hadn't heard already.

"They just found her this very morning in her bedroom. Her boss tried to call her to find out why she hadn't shown up for work yesterday and today and got no answer, so he rode over and got the manager up, and they unlocked the place. You know she had the apartment across from DeeAnne's?" Bon Temps had only one bona fide apartment complex, a three-building, two-story U-shaped grouping, so we knew exactly where he meant.

"She got killed there?" I felt ill. I remembered Maudette clearly. Maudette had had a heavy jaw and a square bottom, pretty black hair and husky shoulders. Maudette had been a plodder, never bright or ambitious. I thought I recalled her working at the Grabbit Kwik, a gas station/convenience store.

"Yeah, she'd been working there for at least a year, I guess," Jason confirmed.

"How was it done?" My grandmother had that squnched, give-it-to-me-quick look with which nice people ask for bad news.

"She had some vampire bites on her — uh — inner thighs," my brother said, looking down at his plate. "But that wasn't what killed her. She was strangled. DeeAnne told me Maudette liked to go to that vampire bar in Shreveport when she had a couple of days off, so maybe that's where she got the bites. Might not have been *Sookie's* vampire."

"Maudette was a fang-banger?" I felt queasy, imagining slow, chunky Maudette draped in the exotic black dresses fang-bangers affected.

"What's that?" asked Gran. She must have missed *Sally-Jessy* the day the phenomenon was explored.

"Men and women that hang around with vampires and enjoy being bitten. Vampire groupies. They don't last too long, I think, because they want to be bitten too much, and sooner or later they get that one bite too many."

"But a bite didn't kill Maudette." Gran wanted to be sure she had it straight.

"Nope, strangling." Jason had begun finishing his lunch.

"Don't you always get gas at the Grabbit?" I asked.

"Sure. So do a lot of people."

"And didn't you hang around with Maudette some?" Gran asked.

"Well, in a way of speaking," Jason said cautiously.

I took that to mean he'd bedded Maudette

when he couldn't find anyone else.

"I hope the sheriff doesn't want to talk to you," Gran said, shaking her head as if indicating "no" would make it less likely.

"What?" Jason was turning red, looking defensive.

"You see Maudette in the store all the time when you get your gas, you so-to-speak date her, then she winds up dead in an apartment you're familiar with," I summarized. It wasn't much, but it was something, and there were so few mysterious homicides in Bon Temps that I thought every stone would be turned in its investigation.

"I ain't the only one who fills the bill. Plenty of other guys get their gas there, and all of them know Maudette."

"Yeah, but in what sense?" Gran asked bluntly. "She wasn't a prostitute, was she? So she will have talked about who she saw."

"She just liked to have a good time, she wasn't a pro." It was good of Jason to defend Maudette, considering what I knew of his selfish character. I began to think a little better of my big brother. "She was kinda lonely, I guess," he added.

Jason looked at both of us, then, and saw we were surprised and touched.

"Speaking of prostitutes," he said hastily, "there's one in Monroe specializes in vampires. She keeps a guy standing by with a stake in case one gets carried away. She drinks synthetic

36

blood to keep her blood supply up."

That was a pretty definite change of subject, so Gran and I tried to think of a question we could ask without being indecent.

"Wonder how much she charges?" I ventured, and when Jason told us the figure he'd heard, we both gasped.

Once we got off the topic of Maudette's murder, lunch went about as usual, with Jason looking at his watch and exclaiming that he had to leave just when it was time to do the dishes.

But Gran's mind was still running on vampires, I found out. She came into my room later, when I was putting on my makeup to go to work.

"How old you reckon the vampire is, the one you met?"

"I have no idea, Gran." I was putting on my mascara, looking wide-eyed and trying to hold still so I wouldn't poke myself in the eye, so my voice came out funny, as if I was trying out for a horror movie.

"Do you suppose . . . he might remember the War?"

I didn't need to ask which war. After all, Gran was a charter member of the Descendants of the Glorious Dead.

"Could be," I said, turning my face from side to side to make sure my blush was even.

"You think he might come to talk to us about it? We could have a special meeting."

"At night," I reminded her.

"Oh. Yes, it'd have to be." The Descendants usually met at noon at the library and brought a bag lunch.

I thought about it. It would be plain rude to suggest to the vampire that he ought to speak to Gran's club because I'd saved his blood from Drainers, but maybe he would offer if I gave a little hint? I didn't like to, but I'd do it for Gran. "I'll ask him the next time he comes in," I promised.

"At least he could come talk to me and maybe I could tape his recollections?" Gran said. I could hear her mind clicking as she thought of what a coup that would be for her. "It would be so interesting to the other club members," she said piously.

I stifled an impulse to laugh. "I'll suggest it to him," I said. "We'll see."

When I left, Gran was clearly counting her chickens.

I hadn't thought of Rene Lenier going to Sam with the story of the parking lot fight. Rene'd been a busy bee, though. When I got to work that afternoon, I assumed the agitation I felt in the air was due to Maudette's murder. I found out different.

Sam hustled me into the storeroom the minute I came in. He was hopping with anger. He reamed me up one side and down the other.

Sam had never been mad with me before,

and soon I was on the edge of tears.

"And if you think a customer isn't safe, you tell me, and I'll deal with it, not you," he was saying for the sixth time, when I finally realized that Sam had been scared for me.

I caught that rolling off him before I clamped down firmly on "hearing" Sam. Listening in to your boss led to disaster.

It had never occurred to me to ask Sam — or anyone else — for help.

"And if you think someone is being harmed in our parking lot, your next move is to call the police, not step out there yourself like a vigilante," Sam huffed. His fair complexion, always ruddy, was redder than ever, and his wiry golden hair looked as if he hadn't combed it.

"Okay," I said, trying to keep my voice even and my eyes wide open so the tears wouldn't roll out. "Are you gonna fire me?"

"No! No!" he exclaimed, apparently even angrier. "I don't want to lose you!" He gripped my shoulders and gave me a little shake. Then he stood looking at me with wide, crackling blue eyes, and I felt a surge of heat rushing out from him. Touching accelerates my disability, makes it imperative that I hear the person touching. I stared right into his eyes for a long moment, then I remembered myself, and I jumped back as his hands dropped away.

I whirled and left the storeroom, spooked.

I'd learned a couple of disconcerting things. Sam desired me; and I couldn't hear his thoughts as clearly as I could other people's. I'd had waves of impressions of how he was feeling, but not thoughts. More like wearing a mood ring than getting a fax.

So, what did I do about either piece of information?

Absolutely nothing.

I'd never looked on Sam as a beddable man before — or at least not beddable by me — for a lot of reasons. But the simplest one was that I never looked at anyone that way, not because I don't have hormones — boy, do I have hormones — but they are constantly tamped down because sex, for me, is a disaster. Can you imagine knowing everything your sex partner is thinking? Right. Along the order of "Gosh, look at that mole . . . her butt is a little big . . . wish she'd move to the right a little . . . why doesn't she take the hint and . . . ?" You get the idea. It's chilling to the emotions, believe me. And during sex, there is simply no way to keep a mental guard up.

Another reason is that I like Sam for a boss, and I like my job, which gets me out and keeps me active and earning so I won't turn into the recluse my grandmother fears I'll become. Working in an office is hard for me, and college was simply impossible because of the grim concentration necessary. It just drained me.

So, right now, I wanted to mull over the rush of desire I'd felt from him. It wasn't like he'd made me a verbal proposition or thrown me down on the storeroom floor. I'd felt his feelings, and I could ignore them if I chose. I appreciated the delicacy of this, and wondered if Sam had touched me on purpose, if he actually knew what I was.

I took care not be alone with him, but I have to admit I was pretty shaken that night.

The next two nights were better. We fell back into our comfortable relationship. I was relieved. I was disappointed. I was also run off my feet since Maudette's murder sparked a business boom at Merlotte's. All sorts of rumors were buzzing around Bon Temps, and the Shreveport news team did a little piece on Maudette Pickens' grisly death. Though I didn't attend her funeral, my grandmother did, and she said the church was jam-packed. Poor lumpy Maudette, with her bitten thighs, was more interesting in death than she'd ever been in life.

I was about to have two days off, and I was worried I'd miss connecting with the vampire, Bill. I needed to relay my grandmother's request. He hadn't returned to the bar, and I began to wonder if he would.

Mack and Denise hadn't been back in Merlotte's either, but Rene Lenier and Hoyt Fortenberry made sure I knew they'd threatened me with horrible things. I can't say I was seriously alarmed. Criminal trash like the Rats roamed the highways and trailer parks of

America, not smart enough or moral enough to settle down to productive living. They never made a positive mark on the world, or amounted to a hill of beans, to my way of thinking. I shrugged off Rene's warnings.

But he sure enjoyed relaying them. Rene Lenier was small like Sam, but where Sam was ruddy and blond, Rene was swarthy and had a bushy headful of rough, black hair threaded with gray. Rene often came by the bar to drink a beer and visit with Arlene because (as he was fond of telling anyone in the bar) she was his favorite ex-wife. He had three. Hoyt Fortenberry was more of a cipher than Rene. He was neither dark nor fair, neither big nor little. He always seemed cheerful and always tipped decent. He admired my brother Jason far beyond what Jason deserved, in my opinion.

I was glad Rene and Hoyt weren't there the night the vampire returned.

He sat at the same table.

Now that the vampire was actually in front of me, I felt a little shy. I found I'd forgotten the almost imperceptible glow of his skin. I'd exaggerated his height and the clear-cut lines of his mouth.

"What can I get you?" I asked.

He looked up at me. I had forgotten, too, the depth of his eyes. He didn't smile or blink; he was so immobile. For the second time, I relaxed into his silence. When I let down my guard, I could feel my face relax. It was as good as getting a massage (I am guessing).

"What are you?" he asked me. It was the second time he'd wanted to know.

"I'm a waitress," I said, again deliberately misunderstanding him. I could feel my smile snap back into place again. My little bit of peace vanished.

"Red wine," he ordered, and if he was disappointed I couldn't tell by his voice.

"Sure," I said. "The synthetic blood should come in on the truck tomorrow. Listen, could I talk to you after work? I have a favor to ask you."

"Of course. I'm in your debt." And he sure didn't sound happy about it.

"Not a favor for me!" I was getting miffed myself. "For my grandmother. If you'll be up — well, I guess you will be — when I get off work at one-thirty, would you very much mind meeting me at the employee door at the back of the bar?" I nodded toward it, and my ponytail bounced around my shoulders. His eyes followed the movement of my hair.

"I'd be delighted."

I didn't know if he was displaying the courtesy Gran insisted was the standard in bygone times, or if he was plain old mocking me.

I resisted the temptation to stick out my tongue at him or blow a raspberry. I spun on my heel and marched back to the bar. When I brought him his wine, he tipped me 20 percent. Soon after that, I looked over at his table only to realize he'd vanished. I wondered if he'd keep his word.

Arlene and Dawn left before I was ready to go, for one reason and another; mostly because all the napkin holders in my area proved to be half-empty. As I retrieved my purse from the locked cabinet in Sam's office, where I stow it while I work, I called good-bye to my boss. I could hear him clanking around in the men's room, probably trying to fix the leaky toilet. I stepped into the ladies' room for a second to check my hair and makeup.

When I stepped outside I noticed that Sam had already switched off the customer parking lot lights. Only the security light on the electricity pole in front of his trailer illuminated the employee parking lot. To the amusement of Arlene and Dawn, Sam had put in a yard and planted boxwood in front of his trailer, and they were constantly teasing him about the neat line of his hedge.

I thought it was pretty.

As usual, Sam's truck was parked in front of his trailer, so my car was the only one left in the lot.

I stretched, looking from side to side. No Bill. I was surprised at how disappointed I was. I had really expected him to be courteous, even if his heart (did he have one?) wasn't in it.

Maybe, I thought with a smile, he'd jump out of a tree, or appear with a poof! in front of me draped in a red-lined black cape. But nothing happened. So I trudged over to my car.

I'd hoped for a surprise, but not the one I got.

Mack Rattray jumped out from behind my car and in one stride got close enough to clip me in the jaw. He didn't hold back one little bit, and I went down onto the gravel like a sack of cement. I let out a yell when I went down, but the ground knocked all the air out of me and some skin off of me, and I was silent and breathless and helpless. Then I saw Denise, saw her swing back her heavy boot, had just enough warning to roll into a ball before the Rattrays began kicking me.

The pain was immediate, intense, and unrelenting. I threw my arms over my face instinctively, taking the beating on my forearms, legs, and my back.

I think I was sure, during the first few blows, that they'd stop and hiss warnings and curses at me and leave. But I remember the exact moment I realized that they intended to kill me.

I could lie there passively and take a beating, but I would not lie there and be killed.

The next time a leg came close I lunged and grabbed it and held on for my life. I was trying to bite, trying to at least mark one of them. I wasn't even sure whose leg I had.

Then, from behind me, I heard a growl. Oh, no, they've brought a dog, I thought. The growl was definitely hostile. If I'd had any leeway with my emotions, the hair would have stood up on my scalp.

I took one more kick to the spine, and then the beating stopped.

The last kick had done something dreadful to me. I could hear my own breathing, stertorous, and a strange bubbling sound that seemed to be coming from my own lungs.

"What the hell is that?" Mack Rattray asked, and he sounded absolutely terrified.

I heard the growl again, closer, right behind me. And from another direction, I heard a sort of snarl. Denise began wailing, Mack was cursing. Denise yanked her leg from my grasp, which had grown very weak. My arms flopped to the ground. They seemed to be beyond my control. Though my vision was cloudy, I could see that my right arm was broken. My face felt wet. I was scared to continue evaluating my injuries.

Mack began screaming, and then Denise, and there seemed to be all kinds of activity going on around me, but I couldn't move. My only view was my broken arm and my battered knees and the darkness under my car.

Some time later there was silence. Behind me, the dog whined. A cold nose poked my ear, and a warm tongue licked it. I tried to raise my hand to pet the dog that had undoubtedly saved my life, but I couldn't. I could hear myself sigh. It seemed to come from a long way away.

Facing the fact, I said, "I'm dying." It began to seem more and more real to me. The toads and crickets that had been making the most of the night had fallen silent at all the activity and noise in the parking lot, so my little voice came out clearly and fell into the darkness. Oddly enough, soon after that I heard two voices.

Then a pair of knees covered in bloody blue jeans came into my view. The vampire Bill leaned over so I could look into his face. There was blood smeared on his mouth, and his fangs were out, glistening white against his lower lip. I tried to smile at him, but my face wasn't working right.

"I'm going to pick you up," Bill said. He sounded calm.

"I'll die if you do," I whispered.

He looked me over carefully. "Not just yet," he said, after this evaluation. Oddly enough, this made me feel better; no telling how many injuries he'd seen in his lifetime, I figured.

"This will hurt," he warned me.

It was hard to imagine anything that wouldn't.

His arms slid under me before I had time to get afraid. I screamed, but it was a weak effort.

"Quick," said a voice urgently.

"We're going back in the woods out of sight," Bill said, cradling my body to him as if it weighed nothing.

Was he going to bury me back there, out of sight? After he'd just rescued me from the Rats?

I almost didn't care.

It was only a small relief when he laid me down on a carpet of pine needles in the darkness of the woods. In the distance, I could see the glow of the light in the parking lot. I felt my hair trickling blood, and I felt the pain of my broken arm and the agony of deep bruises, but what was most frightening was what I didn't feel.

I didn't feel my legs.

My abdomen felt full, heavy. The phrase "internal bleeding" lodged in my thoughts, such as they were.

"You will die unless you do as I say," Bill told me.

"Sorry, don't want to be a vampire," I said, and my voice was weak and thready.

"No, you won't be," he said more gently. "You'll heal. Quickly. I have a cure. But you have to be willing."

"Then trot out the cure," I whispered. "I'm going." I could feel the pull the grayness was exerting on me.

In the little part of my mind that was still receiving signals from the world, I heard Bill grunt as if he'd been hurt. Then something was pressed up against my mouth.

"Drink," he said.

I tried to stick out my tongue, managed. He was bleeding, squeezing to encourage the flow of blood from his wrist into my mouth. I gagged. But I wanted to live. I forced myself to swallow. And swallow again.

48

Suddenly the blood tasted good, salty, the stuff of life. My unbroken arm rose, my hand clamped the vampire's wrist to my mouth. I felt better with every swallow. And after a minute, I drifted off to sleep.

When I woke up, I was still in the woods, still lying on the ground. Someone was stretched out beside me; it was the vampire. I could see his glow. I could feel his tongue moving on my head. He was licking my head wound. I could hardly begrudge him.

"Do I taste different from other people?" I asked.

"Yes," he said in a thick voice. "What are you?"

It was the third time he'd asked. Third time's the charm, Gran always said.

"Hey, I'm not dead," I said. I suddenly remembered I'd expected to check out for good. I wiggled my arm, the one that had been broken. It was weak, but it wasn't flopping any longer. I could feel my legs, and I wiggled them, too. I breathed in and out experimentally and was pleased with the resulting mild ache. I struggled to sit up. That proved to be quite an effort, but not an impossibility. It was like my first fever-free day after I'd had pneumonia as a kid. Feeble but blissful. I was aware I'd survived something awful.

Before I finished straightening, he'd put his arms under me and cradled me to him. He leaned back against a tree. I felt very comfortable sitting on his lap, my head against his chest.

"What I am, is telepathic," I said. "I can hear people's thoughts."

"Even mine?" He sounded merely curious.

"No. That's why I like you so much," I said, floating on a sea of pinkish well-being. I couldn't seem to be bothered with camouflaging my thoughts.

I felt his chest rumble as he laughed. The laugh was a little rusty.

"I can't hear you at all," I blathered on, my voice dreamy. "You have no idea how peaceful that is. After a lifetime of blah, blah, blah, to hear . . . nothing."

"How do you manage going out with men? With men your age, their only thought is still surely how to get you into bed."

"Well, I don't. Manage. And frankly, at any age, I think their goal is get a woman in bed. I don't date. Everyone thinks I'm crazy, you know, because I can't tell them the truth; which is, that I'm driven crazy by all these thoughts, all these heads. I had a few dates when I started working at the bar, guys who hadn't heard about me. But it was the same as always. You can't concentrate on being comfortable with a guy, or getting a head of steam up, when you can hear they're wondering if you dye your hair, or thinking that your butt's not pretty, or imagining what your boobs look like."

Suddenly I felt more alert, and I realized how

much of myself I was revealing to this creature.

"Excuse me," I said. "I didn't mean to burden you with my problems. Thank you for saving me from the Rats."

"It was my fault they had a chance to get you at all," he said. I could tell there was rage just under the calm surface of his voice. "If I had had the courtesy to be on time, it would not have happened. So I owed you some of my blood. I owed you the healing."

"Are they dead?" To my embarrassment, my voice sounded squeaky.

"Oh, yes."

I gulped. I couldn't regret that the world was rid of the Rats. But I had to look this straight in the face, I couldn't dodge the realization that I was sitting in the lap of a murderer. Yet I was quite happy to sit there, his arms around me.

"I should worry about this, but I'm not," I said, before I knew what I was going to say. I felt that rusty laugh again.

"Sookie, why did you want to talk to me tonight?"

I had to think back hard. Though I was miraculously recovered from the beating physically, I felt a little hazy mentally.

"My grandmother is real anxious to know how old you are," I said hesitantly. I didn't know how personal a question that was to a vampire. The vampire in question was stroking my back as though he were soothing a kitten.

"I was made vampire in 1870, when I was

thirty human years old." I looked up; his glowing face was expressionless, his eyes pits of blackness in the dark woods.

"Did you fight in the War?"

"Yes."

"I have the feeling you're gonna get mad. But it would make her and her club so happy if you'd tell them a little bit about the War, about what it was really like."

"Club?"

"She belongs to Descendants of the Glorious Dead."

"Glorious dead." The vampire's voice was unreadable, but I could tell, sure enough, he wasn't happy.

"Listen, you wouldn't have to tell them about the maggots and the infections and the starvation," I said. "They have their own picture of the War, and though they're not stupid people — they've lived through other wars — they would like to know more about the way people lived then, and uniforms and troop movements."

"Clean things."

I took a deep breath. "Yep."

"Would it make you happy if I did this?"

"What difference does that make? It would make Gran happy, and since you're in Bon Temps and seem to want to live around here, it would be a good public relations move for you."

"Would it make you happy?"

He was not a guy you could evade. "Well, yes."

"Then I'll do it."

"Gran says to please eat before you come," I said.

Again I heard the rumbling laugh, deeper this time.

"I'm looking forward to meeting her now. Can I call on you some night?"

"Ah. Sure. I work my last night tomorrow night, and the day after I'm off for two days, so Thursday would be a good night." I lifted my arm to look at my watch. It was running, but the glass was covered with dried blood. "Oh, yuck," I said, wetting my finger in my mouth and cleaning the watch face off with spit. I pressed the button that illuminated the hands, and gasped when I saw what time it was.

"Oh, gosh, I got to get home. I hope Gran went to sleep."

"She must worry about you being out so late at night by yourself," Bill observed. He sounded disapproving. Maybe he was thinking of Maudette? I had a moment of deep unease, wondering if in fact Bill had known her, if she'd invited him to come home with her. But I rejected the idea because I was stubbornly unwilling to dwell on the odd, awful, nature of Maudette's life and death; I didn't want that horror to cast a shadow on my little bit of happiness.

"It's part of my job," I said tartly. "Can't be

helped. I don't work nights all the time, anyway. But when I can, I do."

"Why?" The vampire gave me a shove up to my feet, and then he rose easily from the ground.

"Better tips. Harder work. No time to think."

"But night is more dangerous," he said disapprovingly.

He ought to know. "Now don't you go sounding like my grandmother," I chided him mildly. We had almost reached the parking lot.

"I'm older than your grandmother," he reminded me. That brought the conversation up short.

After I stepped out of the woods, I stood staring. The parking lot was as serene and untouched as if nothing had ever happened there, as if I hadn't been nearly beaten to death on that patch of gravel only an hour before, as if the Rats hadn't met their bloody end.

The lights in the bar and in Sam's trailer were off.

The gravel was wet, but not bloody.

My purse was sitting on the hood of my car.

"And what about the dog?" I said.

I turned to look at my savior.

He wasn't there.

2

I got up very late the next morning, which was not too surprising. Gran had been asleep when I got home, to my relief, and I was able to climb into my bed without waking her.

I was drinking a cup of coffee at the kitchen table and Gran was cleaning out the pantry when the phone rang. Gran eased her bottom up onto the stool by the counter, her normal chatting perch, to answer it.

"*Hel*-lo," she said. For some reason, she always sounded put out, as if a phone call were the last thing on earth she wanted. I knew for a fact that wasn't the case.

"Hey, Everlee. No, sitting here talking to Sookie, she just got up. No, I haven't heard any news today. No, no one called me yet. What? What tornado? Last night was clear. Four Tracks Corner? It did? No! No, it did not! Really? Both of 'em? Um, um, um. What did Mike Spencer say?"

Mike Spencer was our parish coroner. I began to have a creepy feeling. I finished my coffee and poured myself another cup. I thought I was going to need it.

Gran hung up a minute later. "Sookie, you are not going to believe what has happened!"

I was willing to bet I would believe it.

"What?" I asked, trying not to look guilty.

"No matter how smooth the weather looked last night, a tornado must have touched down at Four Tracks Corner! It turned over that rent trailer in the clearing there. The couple that was staying in it, they both got killed, trapped under the trailer somehow and crushed to a pulp. Mike says he hasn't seen anything like it."

"Is he sending the bodies for autopsy?"

"Well, I think he has to, though the cause of death seems clear enough, according to Stella. The trailer is over on its side, their car is halfway on top of it, and trees are pulled up in the yard."

"My God," I whispered, thinking of the strength necessary to accomplish the staging of that scene.

"Honey, you didn't tell me if your friend the vampire came in last night?"

I jumped in a guilty way until I realized that in Gran's mind, she'd changed subjects. She'd been asking me if I'd seen Bill every day, and now, at last, I could tell her yes — but not with a light heart.

Predictably, Gran was excited out of her gourd. She fluttered around the kitchen as if Prince Charles were the expected guest.

"Tomorrow night. Now what time's he coming?" she asked.

"After dark. That's as close as I can get."

"We're on daylight saving time, so that'll be

56

pretty late." Gran considered. "Good, we'll have time to eat supper and clear it away beforehand. And we'll have all day tomorrow to clean the house. I haven't cleaned that area rug in a year, I bet!"

"Gran, we're talking about a guy who sleeps in the ground all day," I reminded her. "I don't think he'd ever look at the rug."

"Well, if I'm not doing it for him, then I'm doing it for me, so I can feel proud," Gran said unanswerably. "Besides, young lady, how do you know where he sleeps?"

"Good question, Gran. I don't. But he has to keep out of the light and he has to keep safe, so that's my guess."

Nothing would prevent my grandmother from going into a house-proud frenzy, I realized very shortly. While I was getting ready for work, she went to the grocery and rented a rug cleaner and set to cleaning.

On my way to Merlotte's, I detoured north a bit and drove by the Four Tracks Corner. It was a crossroads as old as human habitation of the area. Now formalized by road signs and pavement, local lore said it was the intersection of two hunting trails. Sooner or later, there would be ranch-style houses and strip malls lining the roads, I guessed, but for now it was woods and the hunting was still good, according to Jason.

Since there was nothing to prevent me, I drove down the rutted path that led to the clearing where the Rattrays' rented trailer had stood. I stopped my car and stared out the windshield, appalled. The trailer, a very small and old one, lay crushed ten feet behind its original location. The Rattrays' dented red car was still resting on one end of the accordion-pleated mobile home. Bushes and debris were littered around the clearing, and the woods behind the trailer showed signs of a great force passing through; branches snapped off, the top of one pine hanging down by a thread of bark. There were clothes up in the branches, and even a roast pan.

I got out slowly and looked around me. The damage was simply incredible, especially since I knew it hadn't been caused by a tornado; Bill the vampire had staged this scene to account for the deaths of the Rattrays.

An old Jeep bumped its way down the ruts to come to a stop by me.

"Well, Sookie Stackhouse!" called Mike Spencer. "What you doing here, girl? Ain't you got work to go to?"

"Yes, sir. I knew the Rat — the Rattrays. This is just an awful thing." I thought that was sufficiently ambiguous. I could see now that the sheriff was with Mike.

"An awful thing. Yes, well. I did hear," Sheriff Bud Dearborn said as he climbed down out of the Jeep, "that you and Mack and Denise didn't exactly see eye to eye in the parking lot of Merlotte's, last week."

58

I felt a cold chill somewhere around the region of my liver as the two men ranged themselves in front of me.

Mike Spencer was the funeral director of one of Bon Temps' two funeral homes. As Mike was always quick and definite in pointing out, anyone who wanted could be buried by Spencer and Sons Funeral Home; but only white people seemed to want to. Likewise, only people of color chose to be buried at Sweet Rest. Mike himself was a heavy middle-aged man with hair and mustache the color of weak tea, and a fondness for cowboy boots and string ties that he could not wear when he was on duty at Spencer and Sons. He was wearing them now.

Sheriff Dearborn, who had the reputation of being a good man, was a little older than Mike, but fit and tough from his thick gray hair to his heavy shoes. The sheriff had a mashed-in face and quick brown eyes. He had been a good friend of my father's.

"Yes, sir, we had us a disagreement," I said frankly in my down-homiest voice.

"You want to tell me about it?" The sheriff pulled out a Marlboro and lit it with a plain, metal lighter.

And I made a mistake. I should have just told him. I was supposed to be crazy, and some thought me simple, too. But for the life of me, I could see no reason to explain myself to Bud Dearborn. No reason, except good sense.

"Why?" I asked.

His small brown eyes were suddenly sharp, and the amiable air vanished.

"Sookie," he said, with a world of disappointment in his voice. I didn't believe in it for a minute.

"I didn't do this," I said, waving my hand at the destruction.

"No, you didn't," he agreed. "But just the same, they die the week after they have a fight with someone, I feel I should ask questions."

I was reconsidering staring him down. It would feel good, but I didn't think feeling good was worth it. It was becoming apparent to me that a reputation for simplicity could be handy.

I may be uneducated and unworldly, but I'm not stupid or unread.

"Well, they were hurting my friend," I confessed, hanging my head and eyeing my shoes.

"Would that be this vampire that's living at the old Compton house?" Mike Spencer and Bud Dearborn exchanged glances.

"Yes, sir." I was surprised to hear where Bill was living, but they didn't know that. From years of deliberately not reacting to things I heard that I didn't want to know, I have good facial control. The old Compton house was right across the fields from us, on the same side of the road. Between our houses lay only the woods and the cemetery. How handy for Bill, I thought, and smiled.

"Sookie Stackhouse, your granny is letting

you associate with that vampire?" Spencer said unwisely.

"You can sure talk to her about that," I suggested maliciously, hardly able to wait to hear what Gran would say when someone suggested she wasn't taking care of me. "You know, the Rattrays were trying to drain Bill."

"So the vampire was being drained by the Rattrays? And you stopped them?" interrupted the sheriff.

"Yes," I said and tried to look resolute.

"Vampire draining *is* illegal," he mused.

"Isn't it murder, to kill a vampire that hasn't attacked you?" I asked.

I may have pushed the naivete a little too hard.

"You know damn good and well it is, though I don't agree with that law. It is a law, and I will uphold it," the sheriff said stiffly.

"So the vampire just let them leave, without threatening vengeance? Saying anything like he wished they were dead?" Mike Spencer was being stupid.

"That's right." I smiled at both of them and then looked at my watch. I remembered the blood on its face, my blood, beaten out of me by the Rattrays. I had to look through that blood to read the time.

"Excuse me, I have to get to work," I said. "Good-bye, Mr. Spencer, Sheriff."

"Good-bye, Sookie," Sheriff Dearborn said. He looked like he had more to ask me, but couldn't think of how to put it. I could tell he wasn't totally happy with the look of the scene, and I doubted any tornado had shown up on radar anywhere. Nonetheless, there was the trailer, there was the car, there were the trees, and the Rattrays had been dead under them. What could you decide but that the tornado had killed them? I guessed the bodies had been sent for an autopsy, and I wondered how much could be told by such a procedure under the circumstances.

The human mind is an amazing thing. Sheriff Dearborn must have known that vampires are very strong. But he just couldn't imagine how strong one could be: strong enough to turn over a trailer, crush it. It was even hard for me to comprehend, and I knew good and well that no tornado had touched down at Four Corners.

The whole bar was humming with the news of the deaths. Maudette's murder had taken a backseat to Denise and Mack's demises. I caught Sam eyeing me a couple of times, and I thought about the night before and wondered how much he knew. But I was scared to ask in case he hadn't seen anything. I knew there were things that had happened the night before that I hadn't yet explained to my own satisfaction, but I was so grateful to be alive that I put off thinking of them.

I'd never smiled so hard while I toted drinks, I'd never made change so briskly, I'd never gotten orders so exactly. Even ol' bushy-haired Rene didn't slow me down, though he insisted on dragging me into his long-winded conversations every time I came near the table he was sharing with Hoyt and a couple of other cronies.

Rene played the role of crazy Cajun some of the time, though any Cajun accent he might assume was faked. His folks had let their heritage fade. Every woman he'd married had been hard-living and wild. His brief hitch with Arlene had been when she was young and childless, and she'd told me that from time to time she'd done things then that curled her hair to think about now. She'd grown up since then, but Rene hadn't. Arlene was sure fond of him, to my amazement.

Everyone in the bar was excited that night because of the unusual happenings in Bon Temps. A woman had been murdered, and it was a mystery; usually murders in Bon Temps are easily solved. And a couple had died violently by a freak of nature. I attributed what happened next to that excitement. This is a neighborhood bar, with a few out of towners who pass through on a regular basis, and I've never had much problem with unwanted attention. But that night one of the men at a table next to Rene and Hoyt's, a heavy blond man with a broad, red face, slid his hand up the leg of my shorts when I was bringing their beer.

That doesn't fly at Merlotte's.

I thought of bringing the tray down on his head when I felt the hand removed. I felt someone standing right behind me. I turned my head and saw Rene, who had left his chair without my even realizing it. I followed his arm down and saw that his hand was gripping the blond's and squeezing. The blond's red face was turning a mottled mixture.

"Hey, man, let go!" the blond protested. "I didn't mean nothing."

"You don't touch anyone who works here. That's the rule." Rene might be short and slim, but anyone there would have put his money on our local boy over the beefier visitor.

"Okay, okay."

"Apologize to the lady."

"To Crazy Sookie?" His voice was incredulous. He must have been here before.

Rene's hand must have tightened. I saw tears spring into the blond's eyes.

"I'm sorry, Sookie, okay?"

I nodded as regally as I could. Rene let go of the man's hand abruptly and jerked his thumb to tell the guy to take a hike. The blond lost no time throwing himself out the door. His companion followed.

"Rene, you should have let me handle that myself," I said to him very quietly when it seemed the patrons had resumed their conversations. We'd given the gossip mill enough grist for at least a couple of days. "But I appreciate you standing up for me."

"I don't want no one messing with Arlene's friend," Rene said matter-of-factly. "Merlotte's is a nice place, we all want to keep it nice. 'Sides, sometimes you remind me of Cindy, you know?"

Cindy was Rene's sister. She'd moved to Baton Rouge a year or two ago. Cindy was blond and blue-eyed: beyond that I couldn't think of a similarity. But it didn't seem polite to say so. "You see Cindy much?" I asked. Hoyt and the other man at the table were exchanging Shreveport Captains scores and statistics.

"Every so now and then," Rene said, shaking his head as if to say he'd like it to be more often. "She works in a hospital cafeteria."

I patted him on the shoulder. "I gotta go work."

When I reached the bar to get my next order, Sam raised his eyebrows at me. I widened my eyes to show how amazed I was at Rene's intervention, and Sam shrugged slightly, as if to say there was no accounting for human behavior.

But when I went behind the bar to get some more napkins, I noticed he'd pulled out the baseball bat he kept below the till for emergencies.

Gran kept me busy all the next day. She dusted and vacuumed and mopped, and I scrubbed the bathrooms — did vampires even need to use the bathroom? I wondered, as I chugged the toilet brush around the bowl.

Gran had me vacuum the cat hair off the sofa. I emptied all the trash cans. I polished all the tables. I wiped down the washer and the dryer, for goodness' sake.

When Gran urged me to get in the shower and change my clothes, I realized that she regarded Bill the vampire as my date. That made me feel a little odd. One, Gran was so desperate for me to have a social life that even a vampire was eligible for my attention; two, that I had some feelings that backed up that idea; three, that Bill might accurately read all this; four, could vampires even do it like humans?

I showered and put on my makeup and wore a dress, since I knew Gran would have a fit if I didn't. It was a little blue cotton-knit dress with tiny daisies all over it, and it was tighter than Gran liked and shorter than Jason deemed proper in his sister. I'd heard that the first time I'd worn it. I put my little yellow ball earrings in and wore my hair pulled up and back with a yellow banana clip holding it loosely.

Gran gave me one odd look, which I was at a loss to interpret. I could have found out easily enough by listening in, but that was a terrible thing to do to the person you lived with, so I was careful not to. She herself was wearing a skirt and blouse that she often wore to the Descendants of the Glorious Dead meetings, not quite good enough for church, but not plain enough for everyday wear.

I was sweeping the front porch, which we'd

66

forgotten, when he came. He made a vampire entrance; one minute he wasn't there, and the next he was, standing at the bottom of the steps and looking up at me.

I grinned. "Didn't scare me," I said.

He looked a little embarrassed. "It's just a habit," he said, "appearing like that. I don't make much noise."

I opened the door. "Come on in," I invited, and he came up the steps, looking around.

"I remember this," he said. "It wasn't so big, though."

"You remember this house? Gran's gonna love it." I preceded him into the living room, calling Gran as I went.

She came into the living room very much on her dignity, and I realized for the first time she'd taken great pains with her thick white hair, which was smooth and orderly for a change, wrapped around her head in a complicated coil. She had on lipstick, too.

Bill proved as adept at social tactics as my grandmother. They greeted, thanked each other, complimented, and finally Bill ended up sitting on the couch and, after carrying out a tray with three glasses of peach tea, my Gran sat in the easy chair, making it clear I was to perch by Bill. There was no way to get out of this without being even more obvious, so I sat by him, but scooted forward to the edge, as if I might hop up at any moment to get him a refill on his, the ritual glass of iced tea.

He politely touched his lips to the edge of the glass and then set it down. Gran and I took big nervous swallows of ours.

Gran picked an unfortunate opening topic. She said, "I guess you heard about the strange tornado."

"Tell me," Bill said, his cool voice as smooth as silk. I didn't dare look at him, but sat with my hands folded and my eyes fixed to them.

So Gran told him about the freak tornado and the deaths of the Rats. She told him the whole thing seemed pretty awful, but cut-and-dried, and at that I thought Bill relaxed just a millimeter.

"I went by yesterday on my way to work," I said, without raising my gaze. "By the trailer."

"Did you find it looked as you expected?" Bill asked, only curiosity in his voice.

"No," I said. "It wasn't anything I could have expected. I was really . . . amazed."

"Sookie, you've seen tornado damage before," Gran said, surprised.

I changed the subject. "Bill, where'd you get your shirt? It looks nice." He was wearing khaki Dockers and a green-and-brown striped golfing shirt, polished loafers, and thin, brown socks.

"Dillard's," he said, and I tried to imagine him at the mall in Monroe, perhaps, other people turning to look at this exotic creature with his glowing skin and beautiful eyes. Where would he get the money to pay with? How did he wash his clothes? Did he go into his coffin naked? Did he have a car or did he just float wherever he wanted to go?

Gran was pleased with the normality of Bill's shopping habits. It gave me another pang of pain, observing how glad she was to see my supposed suitor in her living room, even if (according to popular literature) he was a victim of a virus that made him seem dead.

Gran plunged into questioning Bill. He answered her with courtesy and apparent goodwill. Okay, he was a *polite* dead man.

"And your people were from this area?" Gran inquired.

"My father's people were Comptons, my mother's people Loudermilks," Bill said readily. He seemed quite relaxed.

"There are lots of Loudermilks left," Gran said happily. "But I'm afraid old Mr. Jessie Compton died last year."

"I know," Bill said easily. "That's why I came back. The land reverted to me, and since things have changed in our culture toward people of my particular persuasion, I decided to claim it."

"Did you know the Stackhouses? Sookie says you have a long history." I thought Gran had put it well. I smiled at my hands.

"I remember Jonas Stackhouse," Bill said, to Gran's delight. "My folks were here when Bon Temps was just a hole in the road at the edge of the frontier. Jonas Stackhouse moved here with his wife and his four children when I was a young man of sixteen. Isn't this the house he built, at least in part?"

I noticed that when Bill was thinking of the past, his voice took on a different cadence and vocabulary. I wondered how many changes in slang and tone his English had taken on through the past century.

Of course, Gran was in genealogical hog heaven. She wanted to know all about Jonas, her husband's great-great-great-great-grand-father. "Did he own slaves?" she asked.

"Ma'am, if I remember correctly, he had a house slave and a yard slave. The house slave was a woman of middle age and the yard slave a very big young man, very strong, named Minas. But the Stackhouses mostly worked their own fields, as did my folks."

"Oh, that is exactly the kind of thing my little group would love to hear! Did Sookie tell you . . ." Gran and Bill, after much polite do-si-do-ing, set a date for Bill to address a night meeting of the Descendants.

"And now, if you'll excuse Sookie and me, maybe we'll take a walk. It's a lovely night." Slowly, so I could see it coming, he reached over and took my hand, rising and pulling me to my feet, too. His hand was cold and hard and smooth. Bill wasn't quite asking Gran's permission, but not quite not, either.

"Oh, you two go on," my grandmother said, fluttering with happiness. "I have so many things to look up. You'll have to tell me all the local names you remember from when you were . . ." and here Gran ran down, not wanting to say something wounding.

"Resident here in Bon Temps," I supplied helpfully.

"Of course," the vampire said, and I could tell from the compression of his lips that he was trying not to smile.

Somehow we were at the door, and I knew that Bill had lifted me and moved me quickly. I smiled, genuinely. I like the unexpected.

"We'll be back in a while," I said to Gran. I didn't think she'd noticed my odd transition, since she was gathering up our tea glasses.

"Oh, you two don't hurry on my account," she said. "I'll be just fine."

Outside, the frogs and toads and bugs were singing their nightly rural opera. Bill kept my hand as we strolled out into the yard, full of the smell of new-mown grass and budding things. My cat, Tina, came out of the shadows and asked to be tickled, and I bent over and scratched her head. To my surprise, the cat rubbed against Bill's legs, an activity he did nothing to discourage.

"You like this animal?" he asked, his voice neutral.

"It's my cat," I said. "Her name is Tina, and I like her a lot."

Without comment, Bill stood still, waiting until Tina went on her way into the darkness outside the porch light.

71

"Would you like to sit in the swing or the lawn chairs, or would you like to walk?" I asked, since I felt I was now the hostess.

"Oh, let's walk for a while. I need to stretch my legs."

Somehow this statement unsettled me a little, but I began moving down the long driveway in the direction of the two-lane parish road that ran in front of both our homes.

"Did the trailer upset you?"

I tried to think how to put it.

"I feel very . . . hmmm. Fragile. When I think about the trailer."

"You knew I was strong."

I tilted my head from side to side, considering. "Yes, but I didn't realize the full extent of your strength," I told him. "Or your imagination."

"Over the years, we get good at hiding what we've done."

"So. I guess you've killed a bunch of people."

"Some." Deal with it, his voice implied.

I clasped both hands behind my back. "Were you hungrier right after you became a vampire? How did that happen?"

He hadn't expected that. He looked at me. I could feel his eyes on me even though we were now in the dark. The woods were close around us. Our feet crunched on the gravel.

"As to how I became a vampire, that's too long a story for now," he said. "But yes, when I was younger — a few times — I killed by accident. I was never sure when I'd get to eat again, you understand? We were always hunted, naturally, and there was no such thing as artificial blood. And there were not as many people then. But I had been a good man when I was alive — I mean, before I caught the virus. So I tried to be civilized about it, select bad people as my victims, never feed on children. I managed never to kill a child, at least. It's so different now. I can go to the all-night clinic in any city and get some synthetic blood, though it's disgusting. Or I can pay a whore and get enough blood to keep going for a couple of days. Or I can glamor someone, so they'll let me bite them for love and then forget all about it. And I don't need so much now."

"Or you can meet a girl who gets head injuries," I said.

"Oh, you were the dessert. The Rattrays were the meal."

Deal with it.

"Whoa," I said, feeling breathless. "Give me a minute."

And he did. Not one man in a million would have allowed me that time without speaking. I opened my mind, let my guards down completely, relaxed. His silence washed over me. I stood, closed my eyes, breathed out the relief that was too profound for words.

"Are you happy now?" he asked, just as if he could tell.

"Yes," I breathed. At that moment I felt that

no matter what this creature beside me had done, this peace was priceless after a lifetime of the yammering of other minds inside my own.

"You feel good to me, too," he said, surprising me.

"How so?" I asked, dreamy and slow.

"No fear, no hurry, no condemnation. I don't have to use my glamor to make you hold still, to have a conversation with you."

"Glamor?"

"Like hypnotism," he explained. "All vampires use it, to some extent or another. Because to feed, until the new synthetic blood was developed, we had to persuade people we were harmless . . . or assure them they hadn't seen us at all . . . or delude them into thinking they'd seen something else."

"Does it work on me?"

"Of course," he said, sounding shocked.

"Okay, do it."

"Look at me."

"It's dark."

"No matter. Look at my face." And he stepped in front of me, his hands resting lightly on my shoulders, and looked down at me. I could see the faint shine of his skin and eyes, and I peered up at him, wondering if I'd begin to squawk like a chicken or take my clothes off.

But what happened was . . . nothing. I felt only the nearly druglike relaxation of being with him.

"Can you feel my influence?" he asked. He

sounded a little breathless.

"Not a bit, I'm sorry," I said humbly. "I just see you glow."

"You can see that?" I'd surprised him again.

"Sure. Can't everyone?"

"No. This is strange, Sookie."

"If you say so. Can I see you levitate?"

"Right here?" Bill sounded amused.

"Sure, why not? Unless there's a reason?"

"No, none at all." And he let go of my arms and began to rise.

I breathed a sigh of pure rapture. He floated up in the dark, gleaming like white marble in the moonlight. When he was about two feet off the ground, he began hovering. I thought he was smiling down at me.

"Can all of you do that?" I asked.

"Can you sing?"

"Nope, can't carry a tune."

"Well, we can't all do the same things, either." Bill came down slowly and landed on the ground without a thump. "Most humans are squeamish about vampires. You don't seem to be," he commented.

I shrugged. Who was I to be squeamish about something out of the ordinary? He seemed to understand because, after a pause, during which we'd resumed walking, Bill said, "Has it always been hard for you?"

"Yes, always." I couldn't say otherwise, though I didn't want to whine. "When I was very small, that was worst, because I didn't know how to put up my guard, and I heard thoughts I wasn't supposed to hear, of course, and I repeated them like a child will. My parents didn't know what to do about me. It embarrassed my father, in particular. My mother finally took me to a child psychologist, who knew exactly what I was, but she just couldn't accept it and kept trying to tell my folks I was reading their body language and was very observant, so I had good reason to imagine I heard people's thoughts. Of course, she couldn't admit I was literally *hearing people's thoughts* because that just didn't fit into her world.

"And I did poorly in school because it was so hard for me to concentrate when so few others were. But when there was testing, I would test very high because the other kids were concentrating on their own papers . . . that gave me a little leeway. Sometimes my folks thought I was lazy for not doing well on everyday work. Sometimes the teachers thought I had a learning disability; oh, you wouldn't believe the theories. I must have had my eyes and ears tested every two months, seemed like, and brain scans . . . gosh. My poor folks paid through the nose. But they never could accept the simple truth. At least outwardly, you know?"

"But they knew inside."

"Yes. Once, when my dad was trying to decide whether to back a man who wanted to

76

open an auto parts store, he asked me to sit with him when the man came to the house. After the man left, my dad took me outside and looked away and said, 'Sookie, is he telling the truth?' It was the strangest moment."

"How old were you?"

"I must've been less than seven 'cause they died when I was in the second grade."

"How?"

"Flash flood. Caught them on the bridge west of here."

Bill didn't comment. Of course, he'd seen deaths piled upon deaths.

"Was the man lying?" he asked after a few seconds had gone by.

"Oh, yes. He planned to take Daddy's money and run."

"You have a gift."

"Gift. Right." I could feel the corners of my mouth pull down.

"It makes you different from other humans."

"You're telling me." We walked for a moment in silence. "So you don't consider yourself human at all?"

"I haven't for a long time."

"Do you really believe you've lost your soul?" That was what the Catholic Church was preaching about vampires.

"I have no way of knowing," Bill said, almost casually. It was apparent that he'd brooded over it so often it was quite a commonplace thought to him. "Personally, I think not. There is something in me that isn't cruel, not murderous, even after all these years. Though I can be both."

"It's not your fault you were infected with a virus."

Bill snorted, even managing to sound elegant doing that. "There have been theories as long as there have been vampires. Maybe that one is true." Then he looked as if he was sorry he'd said that. "If what makes a vampire is a virus," he went on in a more offhand manner, "it's a selective one."

"How do you become a vampire?" I'd read all kinds of stuff, but this would be straight from the horse's mouth.

"I would have to drain you, at one sitting or over two or three days, to the point of your death, then give you my blood. You would lie like a corpse for about forty-eight hours, sometimes as long as three days, then rise and walk at night. And you would be hungry."

The way he said "hungry" made me shiver.

"No other way?"

"Other vampires have told me humans they habitually bite, day after day, can become vampires quite unexpectedly. But that requires consecutive, deep, feedings. Others, under the same conditions, merely become anemic. Then again, when people are near to death for some other reason, a car accident or a drug overdose, perhaps, the process can go . . . badly wrong."

I was getting the creepies. "Time to change

the subject. What do you plan on doing with the Compton land?"

"I plan on living there, as long as I can. I'm tired of drifting from city to city. I grew up in the country. Now that I have a legal right to exist, and I can go to Monroe or Shreveport or New Orleans for synthetic blood or prostitutes who specialize in our kind, I want to stay here. At least see if it's possible. I've been roaming for decades."

"What kind of shape is the house in?"

"Pretty bad," he admitted. "I've been trying to clean it out. That I can do at night. But I need workmen to get some repairs done. I'm not bad at carpentry, but I don't know a thing about electricity."

Of course, he wouldn't.

"It seems to me the house may need re-wiring," Bill continued, sounding for all the world like any other anxious homeowner.

"Do you have a phone?"

"Sure," he said, surprised.

"So what's the problem with the workmen?"

"It's hard to get in touch with them at night, hard to get them to meet with me so I can explain what needs doing. They're scared, or they think it's a prank call." Frustration was evident in Bill's voice, though his face was turned away from me.

I laughed. "If you want, I'll call them," I offered. "They know me. Even though everyone thinks I'm crazy, they know I'm honest."

"That would be a great favor," Bill said, after some hesitation. "They could work during the day, after I'd met with them to discuss the job and the cost."

"What an inconvenience, not being able to get out in the day," I said thoughtlessly. I'd never really considered it before.

Bill's voice was dry. "It certainly is."

"And having to hide your resting place," I blundered on.

When I felt the quality of Bill's silence, I apologized.

"I'm sorry," I said. If it hadn't been so dark, he would have seen me turn red.

"A vampire's daytime resting place is his most closely guarded secret," Bill said stiffly.

"I apologize."

"I accept," he said, after a bad little moment. We reached the road and looked up and down it as if we expected a taxi. I could see him clearly by the moonlight, now that we were out of the trees. He could see me, too. He looked me up and down.

"Your dress is the color of your eyes."

"Thank you." I sure couldn't see him *that* clearly.

"Not a lot of it, though."

"Excuse me?"

"It's hard for me to get used to young ladies with so few clothes on," Bill said.

"You've had a few decades to get used to it," I said tartly. "Come on, Bill! Dresses have been

80

short for forty years now!"

"I liked long skirts," he said nostalgically. "I liked the underthings women wore. The petticoats."

I made a rude noise.

"Do you even have a petticoat?" he asked.

"I have a very pretty beige nylon slip with lace," I said indignantly. "If you were a human guy, I'd say you were angling for me to talk about my underwear!"

He laughed, that deep, unused chuckle that affected me so strongly. "Do you have that slip on, Sookie?"

I stuck out my tongue at him because I knew he could see me. I edged the skirt of my dress up, revealing the lace of the slip and a couple more inches of tanned me.

"Happy?" I asked.

"You have pretty legs, but I still like long dresses better."

"You're stubborn," I told him.

"That's what my wife always told me."

"You were married."

"Yes, I became a vampire when I was thirty. I had a wife, and I had five living children. My sister, Sarah, lived with us. She never wed. Her young man was killed in the war."

"The Civil War."

"Yes. I came back from the battlefield. I was one of the lucky ones. At least I thought so at the time."

"You fought for the Confederacy," I said

81

wonderingly. "If you still had your uniform and wore it to the club, the ladies would faint with joy."

"I hadn't much of a uniform by the end of the war," he said grimly. "We were in rags and starving." He seemed to shake himself. "It had no meaning for me after I became vampire," Bill said, his voice once again chilly and remote.

"I've brought up something that upset you," I said. "I am sorry. What should we talk about?" We turned and began to stroll back down the driveway toward the house.

"Your life," he said. "Tell me what you do when you get up in the morning."

"I get out of bed. Then I make it up right away. I eat breakfast. Toast, sometimes cereal, sometimes eggs, and coffee and I brush my teeth and shower and dress. Sometimes I shave my legs, you know. If it's a workday, I go in to work. If I don't go in until night, I might go shopping, or take Gran to the store, or rent a movie to watch, or sunbathe. And I read a lot. I'm lucky Gran is still spry. She does the wash and the ironing and most of the cooking."

"What about young men?"

"Oh, I told you about that. It's just impossible."

"So what will you do, Sookie?" he asked gently.

"Grow old and die." My voice was short.

He'd touched on my sensitive area once too often.

To my surprise, Bill reached over and took my hand. Now that we'd made each other a little angry, touched some sore spots, the air seemed somehow clearer. In the quiet night, a breeze wafted my hair around my face.

"Take the clip out?" Bill asked.

No reason not to. I reclaimed my hand and reached up to open the clip. I shook my head to loosen my hair. I stuck the clip in his pocket, since I hadn't any. As if it was the most normal thing in the world, Bill began running his fingers through my hair, spreading it out on my shoulders.

I touched his sideburns, since apparently touching was okay. "They're long," I observed.

"That was the fashion," he said. "It's lucky for me I didn't wear a beard as so many men did, or I'd have it for eternity."

"You never have to shave?"

"No, luckily I had just shaven." He seemed fascinated with my hair. "In the moonlight, it looks silver," he said very quietly.

"Ah. What do you like to do?"

I could see a shadow of a smile in the darkness.

"I like to read, too." He thought. "I like the movies . . . of course, I've followed their whole inception. I like the company of people who lead ordinary lives. Sometimes I crave the company of other vampires, though most of them lead very different lives from mine."

We walked in silence for a moment.

"Do you like television?"

"Sometimes," he confessed. "For a while I taped soap operas and watched them at night when I thought I might be forgetting what it was like to be human. After a while I stopped, because from the examples I saw on those shows, forgetting humanity was a good thing." I laughed.

We walked into the circle of light around the house. I had half-expected Gran to be on the porch swing waiting for us, but she wasn't. And only one dim bulb glowed in the living room. Really, Gran, I thought, exasperated. This was just like being brought home from a first date by a new man. I actually caught myself wondering if Bill would try to kiss me or not. With his views on long dresses, he would probably think it was out of line. But as stupid as kissing a vampire might seem, I realized that was what I really wanted to do, more than anything.

I got a tight feeling in my chest, a bitterness, at another thing I was denied. And I thought, Why not?

I stopped him by pulling gently on his hand. I stretched up and lay my lips on his shining cheek. I inhaled the scent of him, ordinary but faintly salty. He was wearing a trace of cologne.

I felt him shudder. He turned his head so his lips touched mine. After a moment, I reached to circle his neck with my arms. His kiss deepened, and I parted my lips. I'd never been kissed like this. It went on and on until I thought the whole world was involved in this kiss in the vampire's mouth on mine. I could feel my breathing speeding up, and I began to want other things to happen.

Suddenly Bill pulled back. He looked shaken, which pleased me no end. "Good night, Sookie," he said, stroking my hair one last time.

"Good night, Bill," I said. I sounded pretty quavery myself. "I'll try to call some electricians tomorrow. I'll let you know what they say."

"Come by the house tomorrow night — if you're off work?"

"Yes," I said. I was still trying to gather myself.

"See you then. Thanks, Sookie." And he turned away to walk through the woods back over to his place. Once he reached the darkness, he was invisible.

I stood staring like a fool, until I shook myself and went inside to go to bed.

I spent an indecent amount of time lying awake in bed wondering if the undead could actually do — it. Also, I wondered if it would be possible to have a frank discussion with Bill about that. Sometimes he seemed very old-fashioned, sometimes he seemed as normal as the guy next door. Well, not really, but pretty normal.

It seemed both wonderful and pathetic to me

that the one creature I'd met in years that I'd want to have sex with was actually not human. My telepathy limited my options severely. I could have had sex just to have it, sure; but I had waited to have sex I could actually enjoy.

What if we did it, and after all these years I discovered I had no talent for it? Or maybe it wouldn't feel good. Maybe all the books and movies exaggerated. Arlene, too, who never seemed to understand that her sex life was not something I wanted to hear about.

I finally got to sleep, to have long, dark dreams.

The next morning, between fielding Gran's questions about my walk with Bill and our future plans, I made some phone calls. I found two electricians, a plumber, and some other service people who gave me phone numbers where they could be reached at night and made sure they understood that a phone call from Bill Compton was not a prank.

Finally, I was lying out in the sun turning toasty when Gran carried the phone out to me.

"It's your boss," she said. Gran liked Sam, and he must have said something to make her happy because she was grinning like a Cheshire cat.

"Hi, Sam," I said, maybe not sounding too glad because I knew something had gone wrong at work.

"Dawn didn't make it in, cher," he said.

"Oh . . . *hell,*" I said, knowing I'd have to go

in. "I kind of have plans, Sam." That was a first. "When do you need me?"

"Could you just come in from five to nine? That would help out a lot."

"Am I gonna get another full day off?"

"What about Dawn splitting a shift with you another night?"

I made a rude noise, and Gran stood there with a stern face. I knew I'd get a lecture later. "Oh, all right," I said grudgingly. "See you at five."

"Thanks, Sookie," he said. "I knew I could count on you."

I tried to feel good about that. It seemed like a boring virtue. You can always count on Sookie to step in and help because she doesn't have a life!

Of course, it would be fine to get to Bill's after nine. He'd be up all night, anyway.

Work had never seemed so slow. I had trouble concentrating enough to keep my guard intact because I was always thinking about Bill. It was lucky there weren't many customers, or I would have heard unwanted thoughts galore. As it was, I found out Arlene's period was late, and she was scared she was pregnant, and before I could stop myself I gave her a hug. She stared at me searchingly and then turned red in the face.

"Did you read my mind, Sookie?" she asked, warning written in her voice. Arlene was one of the few people who simply acknowledged my ability without trying to explain it or categorizing me as a freak for possessing such an ability. She also didn't talk about it often or in any normal voice, I'd noticed.

"Sorry, I didn't mean to," I apologized. "I'm just not focused today."

"All right, then. You stay out from now on, though." And Arlene, her flaming curls bobbing around her cheeks, shook her finger in my face.

I felt like crying. "Sorry," I said again and strode off into the storeroom to collect myself. I had to pull my face straight and hold in those tears.

I heard the door open behind me.

"Hey, I said I was sorry, Arlene!" I snapped, wanting to be left alone. Sometimes Arlene confused telepathy with psychic talent. I was scared she'd ask me if she was really pregnant. She'd be better off buying an early home pregnancy kit.

"Sookie." It was Sam. He turned me around with a hand on my shoulder. "What's wrong?"

His voice was gentle and pushed me much closer to tears.

"You should sound mean so I won't cry!" I said.

He laughed, not a big laugh, a small one. He put an arm around me.

"What's the matter?" He wasn't going to give up and go away.

"Oh, I . . ." and I stopped dead. I'd never,

ever explicitly discussed my problem (that's how I thought of it) with Sam or anyone else. Everyone in Bon Temps knew the rumors about why I was strange, but no one seemed to realize that I had to listen to their mental clatter nonstop, whether I wanted to or not — every day, the yammer yammer yammer . . .

"Did you hear something that bothered you?" His voice was quiet and matter-of-fact. He touched the middle of my forehead, to indicate he knew exactly how I could "hear."

"Yes."

"Can't help it, can you?"

"Nope."

"Hate it, don't you, cher?"

"Oh, yes."

"Not your fault then, is it?"

"I try not to listen, but I can't always keep my guard up." I felt a tear I hadn't been able to quell start trickling down my cheek.

"Is that how you do it? How do you keep your guard up, Sookie?"

He sounded really interested, not as though he thought I was a basket case. I looked up, not very far, into Sam's prominent, brilliant blue eyes.

"I just . . . it's hard to describe unless you can do it . . . I pull up a fence — no, not a fence, it's like I'm snapping together steel plates — between my brain and all others."

"You have to hold the plates up?"

"Yes. It takes a lot of concentration. It's like

dividing my mind all the time. That's why people think I'm crazy. Half my brain is trying to keep the steel plates up, and the other half might be taking drink orders, so sometimes there's not a lot left over for coherent conversation." What a gush of relief I was feeling, just being able to talk about it.

"Do you hear words or just get impressions?"

"Depends on who I'm listening to. And their state. If they're drunk, or really disturbed, it's just pictures, impressions, intentions. If they're sober and sane it's words and some pictures."

"The vampire says you can't hear him."

The idea of Bill and Sam having a conversation about me made me feel very peculiar. "That's true," I admitted.

"Is that relaxing to you?"

"Oh, *yes*." I meant it from my heart.

"Can you hear me, Sookie?"

"I don't want to try!" I said hastily. I moved to the door of the storeroom and stood with my hand on the knob. I pulled a tissue from my shorts pocket and patted the tear track off my cheek. "I'll have to quit if I read your mind, Sam! I like you, I like it here."

"Just try it sometime, Sookie," he said casually, turning to open a carton of whiskey with the razor-edged box cutter he kept in his pocket. "Don't worry about me. You have a job as long as you want one."

I wiped down a table Jason had spilled salt on. He'd been in earlier to eat a hamburger and fries and down a couple of beers.

I was turning over Sam's offer in my mind.

I wouldn't try to listen to him today. He was ready for me. I'd wait when he was busy doing something else. I'd just sort of slip in and give him a listen. He'd invited me, which was absolutely unique.

It was kind of nice to be invited.

I repaired my makeup and brushed my hair. I'd worn it loose, since Bill had seemed to like that, and a darn nuisance it had been all evening. It was just about time to go, so I retrieved my purse from its drawer in Sam's office.

The Compton house, like Gran's, was set back from the road. It was a bit more visible from the parish road than hers, and it had a view of the cemetery, which her house didn't. This was due (at least in part) to the Compton house's higher setting. It was on top of a knoll and it was fully two-storied. Gran's house had a couple of spare bedrooms upstairs, and an attic, but it was more like half a top story.

At one point in the family's long history, the Comptons had had a very nice house. Even in the dark, it had a certain graciousness. But I knew in the daylight you could see the pillars were peeling, the wood siding was crooked, and the yard was simply a jungle. In the humid warmth of Louisiana, yard growth could get out of hand mighty quick, and old Mr. Compton had not been one to hire someone to do his yard work. When he'd gotten too feeble, it had simply gone undone.

The circular drive hadn't gotten fresh gravel in many years, and my car lurched to the front door. I saw that the house was all lit up, and I began to realize that the evening would not go like last evening. There was another car parked in front of the house, a Lincoln Continental, white with a dark blue top. A blue-on-white bumper sticker read VAMPIRES SUCK. A red and yellow one stated HONK IF YOU'RE A BLOOD DONOR! The vanity plate read, simply, FANGS 1.

If Bill already had company, maybe I should just go on home.

But I had been invited and was expected. Hesitantly, I raised my hand and knocked.

The door was opened by a female vampire.

She glowed like crazy. She was at least five feet eleven and black. She was wearing spandex. An exercise bra in flamingo pink and matching calf-length leggings, with a man's white dress shirt flung on unbuttoned, constituted the vampire's ensemble.

I thought she looked cheap as hell and most likely absolutely mouthwatering from a male point of view.

"Hey, little human chick," the vampire purred.

And all of a sudden I realized I was in danger. Bill had warned me repeatedly that not all vampires were like him, and he had moments when he was not so nice, himself. I couldn't read this creature's mind, but I could hear cruelty in her voice.

Maybe she had hurt Bill. Maybe she was his lover.

All of this passed through my mind in a rush, but none of it showed on my face. I've had years of experience in controlling my face. I could feel my bright smile snap on protectively, my spine straightened, and I said cheerfully, "Hi! I was supposed to drop by tonight and give Bill some information. Is he available?"

The female vampire laughed at me, which was nothing I wasn't used to. My smile notched up a degree brighter. This critter radiated danger the way a light bulb gives off heat.

"This little human gal here says she has some information for you, Bill!" she yelled over her (slim, brown, beautiful) shoulder.

I tried not to let relief show in any way.

"You wanna see this little thing? Or shall I just give her a love bite?"

Over my dead body, I thought furiously, and then realized it might be just that.

I didn't hear Bill speak, but the vampire stood back, and I stepped into the old house. Running wouldn't do any good; this vamp could undoubtedly bring me down before I'd gone five steps. And I hadn't laid eyes on Bill, and I couldn't be sure he was all right until I saw him. I'd brave this out and hope for the best. I'm pretty good at doing that.

The big front room was crammed with dark old furniture and people. No, not people, I realized after I'd looked carefully; two people, and two more strange vampires.

The two vampires were both male and white. One had a buzz cut and tattoos on every visible inch of his skin. The other was even taller than the woman, maybe six foot four, with a head of long rippling dark hair and a magnificent build.

The humans were less impressive. The woman was blond and plump, thirty-five or older. She was wearing maybe a pound too much makeup. She looked as worn as an old boot. The man was another story. He was lovely, the prettiest man I'd ever seen. He couldn't have been more than twenty-one. He was swarthy, maybe Hispanic, small and fine-boned. He wore denim cut-offs and nothing else. Except for makeup. I took that in my stride, but I didn't find it appealing.

Then Bill moved and I saw him, standing in the shadows of the dark hall leading from the living room to the back of the house. I looked at him, trying to get my bearings in this unexpected situation. To my dismay, he didn't look at all reassuring. His face was very still, absolutely impenetrable. Though I couldn't believe I was even thinking it, it would have been great at that point to have had a peek into his mind.

"Well, we can have a wonderful evening now," the long-haired male vampire said. He sounded delighted. "Is this a little friend of yours, Bill? She's so fresh."

I thought of a few choice words I'd learned from Jason.

"If you'll just excuse me and Bill a minute," I said very politely, as if this was a perfectly normal evening, "I've been arranging for workmen for the house." I tried to sound businesslike and impersonal, though wearing shorts and a T-shirt and Nikes does not inspire professional respect. But I hoped I conveyed the impression that nice people I encountered in the course of my working day could not possibly hold any threat of danger.

"And we heard Bill was on a diet of synthetic blood only," said the tattooed vampire. "Guess we heard wrong, Diane."

The female vampire cocked her head and gave me a long look. "I'm not so sure. She looks like a virgin to me."

I didn't think Diane was talking hymens.

I took a few casual steps toward Bill, hoping like hell he would defend me if worst came to worst, but finding myself not absolutely sure. I was still smiling, hoping he would speak, would move.

And then he did. "Sookie is mine," he said, and his voice was so cold and smooth it wouldn't have made a ripple in the water if it had been a stone.

I looked at him sharply, but I had enough brains to keep my mouth shut.

"How good you been taking care of our Bill?" Diane asked.

"None of your fucking business," I answered, using one of Jason's words and still smiling. I said I had a temper.

There was a sharp little pause. Everyone, human and vampire, seemed to examine me closely enough to count the hairs on my arms. Then the tall male began to rock with laughter and the others followed suit. While they were yukking it up, I moved a few feet closer to Bill. His dark eyes were fixed on me — *he* wasn't laughing — and I got the distinct feeling he wished, just as much as I did, that I could read his mind.

He was in some danger, I could tell. And if he was, then I was.

"You have a funny smile," said the tall male thoughtfully. I'd liked him better when he was laughing.

"Oh, Malcolm," said Diane. "All human women look funny to you."

Malcolm pulled the human male to him and gave him a long kiss. I began to feel a little sick. That kind of stuff is private. "This is true," Malcolm said, pulling away after a moment, to the small man's apparent disappointment. "But there is something rare about this one. Maybe she has rich blood."

"Aw," said the blond woman, in a voice that could blister paint, "that's just crazy Sookie Stackhouse."

I looked at the woman with more attention. I recognized her at last, when I mentally erased a few miles of hard road and half the makeup. Janella Lennox had worked at Merlotte's for two weeks until Sam had fired her. She'd moved to Monroe, Arlene had told me.

The male vampire with the tattoos put his arm around Janella and rubbed her breasts. I could feel the blood drain out of my face. I was disgusted. It got worse. Janella, as lost to decency as the vampire, put her hand on his crotch and massaged.

At least I saw clearly that vampires can sure have sex.

I was less than excited about that knowledge at the moment.

Malcolm was watching me, and I'd showed my distaste.

"She's innocent," he said to Bill, with a smile full of anticipation.

"She's mine," Bill said again. This time his voice was more intense. If he'd been a rattlesnake his warning could not have been clearer.

"Now, Bill, you can't tell me you've been getting everything you need from that little thing," Diane said. "You look pale and droopy. She ain't been taking good care of you."

I inched a little closer to Bill.

"Here," offered Diane, whom I was beginning to hate, "have a taste of Liam's woman or Malcolm's pretty boy, Jerry."

Janella didn't react to being offered around,

maybe because she was too busy unzipping Liam's jeans, but Malcolm's beautiful boyfriend, Jerry, slithered willingly over to Bill. I smiled as though my jaws were going to crack as he wrapped his arms around Bill, nuzzled Bill's neck, rubbed his chest against Bill's shirt.

The strain in my vampire's face was terrible to see. His fangs slid out. I saw them fully extended for the first time. The synthetic blood was not answering all Bill's needs, all right.

Jerry began licking a spot at the base of Bill's neck. Keeping my guard up was proving to be more than I could handle. Since three present were vampires, whose thoughts I couldn't hear, and Janella was fully occupied, that left Jerry. I listened and gagged.

Bill, shaking with temptation, was actually bending to sink his fangs into Jerry's neck when I said, "No! He has the Sino-virus!"

As if released from a spell, Bill looked at me over Jerry's shoulder. He was breathing heavily, but his fangs retracted. I took advantage of the moment by taking more steps. I was within a yard of Bill, now.

"Sino-AIDS," I said.

Alcoholic and heavily drugged victims affected vampires temporarily, and some of them were said to enjoy that buzz; but the blood of a human with full-blown AIDS didn't, nor did sexually transmitted diseases, or any other bugs that plagued humans.

Except Sino-AIDS. Even Sino-AIDS didn't

kill vampires as surely as the AIDS virus killed humans, but it left the undead very weak for nearly a month, during which time it was comparatively easy to catch and stake them. And every now and then, if a vampire fed from an infected human more than once, the vampire actually died — redied? — without being staked. Still rare in the United States, Sino-AIDS was gaining a foothold around ports like New Orleans, with sailors and other travelers from many countries passing through the city in a partying mood.

All the vampires were frozen, staring at Jerry as if he were death in disguise; and for them, perhaps, he was.

The beautiful young man took me completely by surprise. He turned and leapt on me. He was no vampire, but he was strong, evidently only in the earliest stages of the virus, and he knocked me against the wall to my left. He circled my throat with one hand and lifted the other to punch me in the face. My arms were still coming up to defend myself when Jerry's hand was seized, and his body froze.

"Let go of her throat," Bill said in such a terrifying voice that I was scared myself. By now, the scares were just piling up so quickly I didn't think I'd ever feel safe again. But Jerry's fingers didn't relax, and I made a little whimpering sound without wanting to at all. I slewed my eyes sideways, and when I looked at Jerry's gray face, I realized that Bill was holding his hand,

Malcolm was gripping his legs, and Jerry was so frightened he couldn't grasp what was wanted of him.

The room began to get fuzzy, and voices buzzed in and out. Jerry's mind was beating against mine. I was helpless to hold him out. His mind was clouded with visions of the lover who had passed the virus to Jerry, a lover who had left him for a vampire, a lover Jerry himself had murdered in a fit of jealous rage. Jerry was seeing his death coming from the vampires he had wanted to kill, and he was not satisfied that he had extracted enough vengeance with the vampires he had already infected.

I could see Diane's face over Jerry's shoulder, and she was smiling.

Bill broke Jerry's wrist.

He screamed and collapsed on the floor. The blood began surging into my head again, and I almost fainted. Malcolm picked Jerry up and carried him over to the couch as casually as if Jerry were a rolled-up rug. But Malcolm's face was not as casual. I knew Jerry would be lucky if he died quickly.

Bill stepped in front of me, taking Jerry's place. His fingers, the fingers that had just broken Jerry's wrist, massaged my neck as gently as my grandmother's would have done. He put a finger across my lips to make sure I knew to keep silent.

Then, his arm around me, he turned to face the other vampires.

"This has all been very entertaining," Liam said. His voice was as cool as if Janella wasn't giving him a truly intimate massage there on the couch. He hadn't troubled himself to budge during the whole incident. He had newly visible tattoos I could never in this world have imagined. I was sick to my stomach. "But I think we should be driving back to Monroe. We have to have a little talk with Jerry when he wakes up, right, Malcolm?"

Malcolm heaved the unconscious Jerry over his shoulder and nodded at Liam. Diane looked disappointed.

"But fellas," she protested. "We haven't found out how this little gal knew."

The two male vampires simultaneously switched their gaze to me. Quite casually, Liam took a second off to reach a climax. Yep, vampires could do it, all right. After a little sigh of completion, he said, "Thanks, Janella. That's a good question, Malcolm. As usual, our Diane has cut to the quick." And the three visiting vampires laughed as if that was a very good joke, but I thought it was a scary one.

"You can't speak yet, can you, sweetheart?" Bill gave my shoulder a squeeze as he asked, as if I couldn't get the hint.

I shook my head.

"I could probably make her talk," Diane offered.

"Diane, you forget," Bill said gently.

"Oh, yeah. She's yours," Diane said. But she

didn't sound cowed or convinced.

"We'll have to visit some other time," Bill said, and his voice made it clear the others had to leave or fight him.

Liam stood, zipped up his pants, gestured to his human woman. "Out, Janella, we're being evicted." The tattoos rippled across his heavy arms as he stretched. Janella ran her hands along his ribs as if she just couldn't get enough of him, and he swatted her away as lightly as if she'd been a fly. She looked vexed, but not mortified as I would have been. This was not new treatment for Janella.

Malcolm picked up Jerry and carried him out the front door without a word. If drinking from Jerry had given him the virus, Malcolm was not yet impaired. Diane went last, slinging a purse over her shoulder and casting a bright-eyed glance behind her.

"I'll leave you two lovebirds on your own, then. It's been fun, honey," she said lightly, and she slammed the door behind her.

The minute I heard the car start up outside, I fainted.

I'd never done so in my life, and I hoped never to again, but I felt I had some excuse.

I seemed to spend a lot of time around Bill unconscious. That was a crucial thought, and I knew it deserved a lot of pondering, but not just at that moment. When I came to, everything I'd seen and heard rushed back, and I gagged for real. Immediately Bill bent me over the edge of the couch. But I managed to keep my food down, maybe because there wasn't much in my stomach.

"Do vampires act like that?" I whispered. My throat was sore and bruised where Jerry had squeezed it. "They were horrible."

"I tried to catch you at the bar when I found out you weren't at home," Bill said. His voice was empty. "But you'd left."

Though I knew it wouldn't help a thing, I began crying. I was sure Jerry was dead by now, and I felt I should have done something about that, but I couldn't have kept silent when he was about to infect Bill. So many things about this short episode had upset me so deeply that I didn't know where to begin being upset. In maybe fifteen minutes I'd been in fear of my life, in fear for Bill's life (well — existence), made to witness sex acts that should be strictly private, seen my potential sweetie in the throes of blood lust (emphasis on lust), and nearly been choked to death by a diseased hustler.

On second thought, I gave myself full permission to cry. I sat up and wept and mopped my face with a handkerchief Bill handed me. My curiosity about why a vampire would need a handkerchief was just a little flicker of normality, drenched by the flood of my nervous tears.

Bill had enough sense not to put his arms around me. He sat on the floor, and had the grace to keep his eyes averted while I mopped myself dry.

"When vampires live in nests," he said suddenly, "they often become more cruel because they egg each other on. They see others like themselves constantly, and so they are reminded of how far from being human they are. They become laws unto themselves. Vampires like me, who live alone, are a little better reminded of their former humanity."

I listened to his soft voice, going slowly through his thoughts as he made an attempt to explain the unexplainable to me.

"Sookie, our life is seducing and taking and has been for centuries, for some of us. Synthetic blood and grudging human acceptance isn't going to change that overnight — or over a decade. Diane and Liam and Malcolm have been together for fifty years."

"How sweet," I said, and my voice held something I'd never heard from myself before: bitterness. "Their golden wedding anniversary."

"Can you forget about this?" Bill asked. His huge dark eyes came closer and closer. His mouth was about two inches from mine.

"I don't know." The words jerked out of me. "Do you know, I didn't know if you could do it?"

His eyebrows rose interrogatively. "Do . . . ?"

"Get —" and I stopped, trying to think of a pleasant way to put it. I'd seen more crudity this evening than I'd seen in my lifetime, and I didn't want to add to it. "An erection," I said, avoiding his eyes.

"You know better now." He sounded like he was trying not to be amused. "We can have sex, but we can't make children or have them. Doesn't it make you feel better, that Diane can't have a baby?"

My fuses blew. I opened my eyes and looked at him steadily. "Don't — you — laugh — at — me."

"Oh, Sookie," he said, and his hand rose to touch my cheek.

I dodged his hand and struggled to my feet. He didn't help me, which was a good thing, but he sat on the floor watching me with a still, unreadable face. Bill's fangs had retracted, but I knew he was still suffering from hunger. Too bad.

My purse was on the floor by the front door. I wasn't walking very steadily, but I was walking. I pulled the list of electricians out of a pocket and lay it on a table.

"I have to go."

He was in front of me suddenly. He'd done one of those vampire things again. "Can I kiss you good-bye?" he asked, his hands down at his sides, making it so obvious he wouldn't touch me until I said green light.

"No," I said vehemently. "I can't stand it after them."

"I'll come see you."

"Yes. Maybe."

He reached past me to open the door, but I thought he was reaching for me, and I flinched.

I spun on my heel and almost ran to my car, tears blurring my vision again. I was glad the drive home was so short.

3

The phone was ringing. I pulled my pillow over my head. Surely Gran would get it? As the irritating noise persisted, I realized Gran must be gone shopping or outside working in the yard. I began squirming to the bed table, not happy but resigned. With the headache and regrets of someone who has a terrible hangover (though mine was emotional rather than alcohol induced) I stretched out a shaky hand and grabbed the receiver.

"Yes?" I asked. It didn't come out quite right. I cleared my throat and tried again. "Hello?"

"Sookie?"

"Um-hum. Sam?"

"Yeah. Listen, cher, do me a favor?"

"What?" I was due to work today anyway, and I didn't want to hold down Dawn's shift and mine, too.

"Go by Dawn's place, and see what she's up to, would you? She won't answer her phone, and she hasn't come in. The delivery truck just pulled up, and I got to tell these guys where to put stuff."

"Now? You want me to go now?" My old bed had never held on to me harder.

"Could you?" For the first time, he seemed

to grasp my unusual mood. I had never refused Sam anything.

"I guess so," I said, feeling tired all over again at the very idea. I wasn't too crazy about Dawn, and she wasn't too crazy about me. She was convinced I'd read her mind and told Jason something she'd been thinking about him, which had caused him to break up with her. If I took that kind of interest in Jason's romances, I'd never have time to eat or sleep.

I showered and pulled on my work clothes, moving sluggishly. All my bounce had gone flat, like soda with the top left off. I ate cereal and brushed my teeth and told Gran where I was going when I tracked her down; she'd been outside planting petunias in a tub by the back door. She didn't seem to understand exactly what I meant, but smiled and waved anyway. Gran was getting a little more deaf every week, but I realized that was no great wonder since she was seventy-eight. It was marvelous that she was so strong and healthy, and her brain was sound as a bell.

As I went on my unwelcome errand, I thought about how hard it must have been for Gran to raise two more children after she'd already raised her own. My father, her son, had died when I was seven and Jason ten. When I'd been twenty-three, Gran's daughter, my Aunt Linda, had died of uterine cancer. Aunt Linda's girl, Hadley, had vanished into the same subculture that had spawned the Rattrays even be-

108

fore Aunt Linda had passed away, and to this day we didn't know if Hadley realizes her mother is dead. That was a lot of grief to get through, yet Gran had always been strong for us.

I peered through my windshield at the three small duplexes on one side of Berry Street, a run-down block or two that ran behind the oldest part of downtown Bon Temps. Dawn lived in one of them. I spotted her car, a green compact, in the driveway of one of the better-kept houses, and pulled in behind it. Dawn had already put a hanging basket of begonias by her front door, but they looked dry. I knocked.

I waited for a minute or two. I knocked again.

"Sookie, you need some help?" The voice sounded familiar. I turned around and shielded my eyes from the morning sun. Rene Lenier was standing by his pickup, parked across the street at one of the small frame houses that populated the rest of the neighborhood.

"Well," I began, not sure if I needed help or not, or if I did that Rene could supply it. "Have you seen Dawn? She didn't come to work today, and she never called in yesterday. Sam asked me to stop by."

"Sam should come do his own dirty work," Rene said, which perversely made me defend my boss.

"Truck came in, had to be unloaded." I turned and knocked again. "Dawn," I yelled.

"Come let me in." I looked down at the concrete porch. The pine pollen had begun falling two days ago. Dawn's porch was solid yellow. Mine were the only footprints. My scalp began to prickle.

I barely registered the fact that Rene stood awkwardly by the door to his pickup, unsure whether to stay or go.

Dawn's duplex was a one-story, quite small, and the door to the other half was just feet away from Dawn's. Its little driveway was empty, and there were no curtains at the windows. It looked as though Dawn was temporarily out of a neighbor. Dawn had been proud enough to hang curtains, white with dark gold flowers. They were drawn, but the fabric was thin and unlined, and Dawn hadn't shut the cheap one-inch aluminum blinds. I peered in and discovered the living room held only some flea-market furniture. A coffee mug sat on the table by a lumpy recliner and an old couch covered with a hand-crocheted afghan was pushed against the wall.

"I think I'll go around back," I called to Rene. He started across the street as though I'd given him a signal, and I stepped off the front porch. My feet brushed the dusty grass, yellow with pine pollen, and I knew I'd have to dust off my shoes and maybe change my socks before work. During pine pollen season, everything turns yellow. Cars, plants, roofs, windows, all are powdered with a golden haze.

The ponds and pools of rainwater have yellow scum around the edges.

Dawn's bathroom window was so discreetly high that I couldn't see in. She'd lowered the blinds in the bedroom, but hadn't closed them tightly. I could see a little through the slats. Dawn was in bed on her back. The bedclothes were tossed around wildly. Her legs were spraddled. Her face was swollen and discolored, and her tongue protruded from her mouth. There were flies crawling on it.

I could hear Rene coming up behind me.

"Go call the police," I said.

"What you say, Sookie? You see her?"

"Go *call the police!*"

"Okay, okay!" Rene beat a hasty retreat.

Some female solidarity had made me not want Rene to see Dawn like that, without Dawn's consent. And my fellow waitress was far beyond consenting.

I stood with my back to the window, horribly tempted to look again in the futile hope I'd made a mistake the first time. Staring at the duplex next door to Dawn's, maybe a scant six feet away, I wondered how its tenants could have avoided hearing Dawn's death, which had been violent.

Here came Rene again. His weatherbeaten face was puckered into an expression of deep concern, and his bright brown eyes looked suspiciously shiney.

"Would you call Sam, too?" I asked. Without

a word, he turned and trudged back to his place. He was being mighty good. Despite his tendency to gossip, Rene had always been one to help where he saw a need. I remembered him coming out to the house to help Jason hang Gran's porch swing, a random memory of a day far different from this.

The duplex next door was just like Dawn's, so I was looking directly at its bedroom window. Now a face appeared, and the window was raised. A tousled head poked out. "What you doing, Sookie Stackhouse?" asked a slow, deep, male voice. I peered at him for a minute, finally placing the face, while trying not to look too closely at the fine, bare chest underneath.

"JB?"

"Sure thing."

I'd gone to high school with JB du Rone. In fact, some of my few dates had been with JB, who was lovely but so simple that he didn't care if I read his mind or not. Even under to-day's circumstances, I could appreciate JB's beauty. When your hormones have been held in check as long as mine, it doesn't take much to set them off. I heaved a sigh at the sight of JB's muscular arms and pectorals.

"What you doing out here?" he asked again.

"Something bad seems to have happened to Dawn," I said, not knowing if I should tell him or not. "My boss sent me here to look for her when she didn't come to work."

"She in there?" JB simply scrambled out of

the window. He had some shorts on, cut-offs.

"Please don't look," I asked, holding up my hand and without warning I began crying. I was doing that a lot lately, too. "She looks so awful, JB."

"Aw, honey," he said, and bless his country heart, he put an arm around me and patted me on the shoulder. If there was a female around who needed comforting, by God, that was a priority to JB du Rone.

"Dawn liked 'em rough," he said consolingly, as if that would explain everything.

It might to some people, but not to un-worldly me.

"What, rough?" I asked, hoping I had a tissue in my shorts pocket.

I looked up at JB to see him turn a little red.

"Honey, she liked . . . aw, Sookie, you don't need to hear this."

I had a widespread reputation for virtue, which I found somewhat ironic. At the moment, it was inconvenient.

"You can tell me, I worked with her," I said, and JB nodded solemnly, as if that made sense.

"Well, honey, she liked men to — like, bite and hit her." JB looked weirded out by this preference of Dawn's. I must have made a face because he said, "I know, I can't understand why some people like that, either." JB, never one to ignore an opportunity to make hay, put both arms around me and kept up the patting, but it seemed to concentrate on the middle of

113

my back (checking to see if I was wearing a bra) and then quite a bit lower (JB liked firm rear ends, I remembered.)

A lot of questions hovered on the edge of my tongue, but they remained shut inside my mouth. The police got there, in the persons of Kenya Jones and Kevin Prior. When the town police chief had partnered Kenya and Kevin, he'd been indulging his sense of humor, the town figured, for Kenya was at least five foot eleven, the color of bitter chocolate, and built to weather hurricanes. Kevin possibly made it up to five foot eight, had freckles over every visible inch of his pale body, and had the narrow, fatless build of a runner. Oddly enough, the two K's got along very well, though they'd had some memorable quarrels.

Now they both looked like cops.

"What's this about, Miss Stackhouse?" Kenya asked. "Rene says something happened to Dawn Green?" She'd scanned JB while she talked, and Kevin was looking at the ground all around us. I had no idea why, but I was sure there was a good police reason.

"My boss sent me here to find out why Dawn missed work yesterday and hadn't shown up today," I said. "I knocked on her door, and she didn't answer, but her car was here. I was worried about her, so I started around the house looking in the windows, and she's in there." I pointed behind them, and the two officers turned to look at the window. Then they looked at each other and nodded as if they'd had a whole conversation. While Kenya went over to the window, Kevin went around to the back door.

JB had forgotten to pat while he watched the officers work. In fact, his mouth was a little open, revealing perfect teeth. He wanted to go look through the window more than anything, but he couldn't shoulder past Kenya, who pretty much took up whatever space was available.

I didn't want my own thoughts any more. I relaxed, dropping my guard, and listened to the thoughts of others. Out of the clamor, I picked one thread and concentrated on it.

Kenya Jones turned back to stare through us without seeing us. She was thinking of everything she and Kevin needed to do to keep the investigation as textbook perfect as Bon Temps patrol officers could. She was thinking she'd heard bad things about Dawn and her liking for rough sex. She was thinking that it was no surprise Dawn had met a bad end, though she felt sorry for anyone who ended up with flies crawling on her face. Kenya was thinking she was sorry she'd eaten that extra doughnut that morning at the Nut Hut because it might come back up and that would shame her as a black woman police officer.

I tuned in to another channel.

JB was thinking about Dawn getting killed during rough sex just a few feet away from him, and while it was awful it was also a little exciting and Sookie was still built wonderful. He wished he could screw her right now. She was so sweet and nice. He was pushing away the humiliation he'd felt when Dawn had wanted him to hit her, and he couldn't, and it was an old humiliation.

I switched.

Kevin came around the corner thinking that he and Kenya better not botch any evidence and that he was glad no one knew he'd ever slept with Dawn Green. He was furious that someone had killed a woman he knew, and he was hoping it wasn't a black man because that would make his relationship with Kenya even more tense.

I switched.

Rene Lenier was wishing someone would come and get the body out of the house. He was hoping no one knew he'd slept with Dawn Green. I couldn't spell out his thoughts exactly, they were very black and snarled. Some people I can't get a clear reading on. He was very agitated.

Sam came hurrying toward me, slowing down when he saw JB was touching me. I could not read Sam's thoughts. I could feel his emotions (right now a mix of worry, concern, and anger) but I could not spell out one single thought. This was so fascinating and unexpected that I stepped out of JB's embrace, wanting to go up to Sam and grab his arms and look into his eyes and really probe around in his head. I remembered when he'd touched me, and I'd shied away. Now he *felt* me in his head and though he kept on walking toward me, his mind flinched back. Despite his invitation to me, he hadn't known I would see he was different from others: I picked up on that until he shut me down.

I'd never felt anything like it. It was like an iron door slamming. In my face.

I'd been on the point of reaching out to him instinctively, but my hand dropped to my side. Sam deliberately looked at Kevin, not at me.

"What's happening, Officer?" Sam asked.

"We're going to break into this house, Mr. Merlotte, unless you have a master key."

Why would Sam have a key?

"He's my landlord," JB said in my ear, and I jumped.

"He is?" I asked stupidly.

"He owns all three duplexes."

Sam had been fishing in his pocket, and now he came up with a bunch of keys. He flipped through them expertly, stopping at one and singling it out, getting it off the ring and handing it to Kevin.

"This fits front and back?" Kevin asked. Sam nodded. He still wasn't looking at me.

Kevin went to the back door of the duplex, out of sight, and we were all so quiet we could hear the key turn in the lock. Then he was in the bedroom with the dead woman, and we could see his face twist when the smell hit him. Holding one hand across his mouth and nose, he bent over the body and put his fingers on her neck. He looked out the window then and shook his head at his partner. Kenya nodded and headed out to the street to use the radio in the patrol car.

"Listen, Sookie, how about going to dinner with me tonight?" JB asked. "This has been tough on you, and you need some fun to make up for it."

"Thanks, JB." I was very conscious of Sam listening. "It's really nice of you to ask. But I have a feeling I'm going to be working extra hours today."

For just a second, JB's handsome face was blank. Then comprehension filtered in. "Yeah, Sam's gotta hire someone else," he observed. "I got a cousin in Springhill needs a job. Maybe I'll give her a call. We could live right next door to each other, now."

I smiled at him, though I am sure it was a very weak smile, as I stood shoulder to shoulder with the man I'd worked with for two years.

"I'm sorry, Sookie," he said quietly.

"For what?" My own voice was just as low. Was he going to acknowledge what had passed between us — or rather, failed to pass?

"For sending you to check on Dawn. I should have come myself. I was sure she was just shacked up with someone new and needed a reminder that she was supposed to be working. The last time I had to come get her, she yelled at me so much I just didn't want to deal with it again. So like a coward, I sent you, and you had to find her like that."

"You're full of surprises, Sam."

He didn't turn to look at me or make any reply. But his fingers folded around mine. For a long moment, we stood in the sun with people buzzing around us, holding hands. His palm was hot and dry, and his fingers were strong. I felt I had truly connected with another human. But then his grip loosened, and Sam stepped over to talk with the detective, who was emerging from his car, and JB began asking me how Dawn had looked, and the world fell back into its same old groove.

The contrast was cruel. I felt tired all over again, and remembered the night before in more detail than I wanted to. The world seemed a bad and terrible place, all its denizens suspect, and I the lamb wandering through the valley of death with a bell around my neck. I stomped over to my car and opened the door, sank sideways into the seat. I'd be standing plenty today; I'd sit while I could.

JB followed me. Now that he'd rediscovered me, he could not be detached. I remembered when Gran had had high hopes for some permanent relationship between us, when I'd been in high school. But talking to JB, even reading his mind, was as interesting as a kindergarten primer was to an adult reader. It was one of God's jokes that such a dumb mind had been put in such an eloquent body.

He knelt before me and took my hand. I found myself hoping that some smart rich lady would come along and marry JB and take care of him and enjoy what he had to offer. She would be getting a bargain.

"Where are you working now?" I asked him, just to distract myself.

"My dad's warehouse," he said.

That was the job of last resort, the one JB always returned to when he got fired from other jobs for doing something lamebrained, or for not showing up, or for offending some supervisor mortally. JB's dad ran an auto parts store.

"How are your folks doing?"

"Oh, fine. Sookie, we should do something together."

Don't tempt me, I thought.

Someday my hormones were going to get the better of me and I'd do something I'd regret; and I could do worse than do it with JB. But I would hold out and hope for something better. "Thanks, honey," I said. "Maybe we will. But I'm kind of upset right now."

"Are you in love with that vampire?" he asked directly.

"Where did you hear that?"

"Dawn said so." JB's face clouded as he remembered Dawn was dead. What Dawn had said, I found on scanning JB's mind, was "That new vampire is interested in Sookie Stackhouse. I'd be better for him. He needs a woman who can take some rough treatment. Sookie would scream if he touched her."

It was pointless being mad at a dead person, but briefly I indulged myself by doing just that.

Then the detective was walking toward us, and JB got to his feet and moved away.

The detective took JB's position, squatting on the ground in front of me. I must look in bad shape.

"Miss Stackhouse?" he asked. He was using that quiet intense voice many professionals adopt in a crisis. "I'm Andy Bellefleur." The Bellefleurs had been around Bon Temps as long as there'd been a Bon Temps, so I wasn't amused at a man being "beautiful flower." In fact, I felt sorry for whoever thought it was amusing as I looked down at the block of muscle that was Detective Bellefleur. This particular family member had graduated before Jason, and I'd been one class behind his sister Portia.

He'd been placing me, too. "Your brother doing okay?" he asked, his voice still quiet, not quite as neutral. It sounded like he'd had a run-in or two with Jason.

"The little I see of him, he's doing fine," I answered.

"And your grandmother?"

I smiled. "She's out planting flowers this morning."

"That's wonderful," he said, doing that sincere head shake that's supposed to indicate admiring amazement. "Now, I understand that you work at Merlotte's?"

"Yes."

"And so did Dawn Green?"

"Yes."

"When was the last time you saw Dawn?"

"Two days ago. At work." I already felt exhausted. Without shifting my feet from the ground or my arm from the steering wheel, I lay my head sideways on the headrest of the driver's seat.

"Did you talk to her then?"

I tried to remember. "I don't think so."

"Were you close to Miss Green?"

"No."

"And why did you come here today?"

I explained about working for Dawn yesterday, about Sam's phone call this morning.

"Did Mr. Merlotte tell you why he didn't want to come here himself?"

"Yes, a truck was there to unload. Sam has to show the guys where to put the boxes." Sam also did a lot of the unloading himself, half the time, to speed up the process.

"Do you think Mr. Merlotte had any relationship with Dawn?"

"He was her boss."

"No, outside work."

"Nope."

"You sound pretty positive."

"I am."

"Do you have a relationship with Sam?"

"No."

"Then how are you so sure?"

Good question. Because from time to time I'd heard thoughts that indicated that if she didn't hate Sam, Dawn sure as hell wasn't real fond of him? Not too smart a thing to tell the detective.

"Sam keeps everything real professional at the bar," I said. It sounded lame, even to me. It just happened to be the truth.

"Did you know anything about Dawn's personal life?"

"No."

"You weren't friendly?"

"Not particularly." My thoughts drifted as the detective bent his head in thought. At least that was what it looked like.

"Why is that?"

"I guess we didn't have anything in common."

"Like what? Give me an example."

I sighed heavily, blowing my lips out in exasperation. If we didn't have anything in common, how could I give him an example?

"Okay," I said slowly. "Dawn had a real active social life, and she liked to be with men. She wasn't so crazy about spending time with women. Her family is from Monroe, so she didn't have family ties here. She drank, and I don't. I read a lot, and she didn't. That enough?"

Andy Bellefleur scanned my face to see if I was giving him attitude. He must have been reassured by what he saw.

"So, you two didn't ever see each other after working hours?"

"That's correct."

"Doesn't it seem strange to you that Sam Merlotte asked you to check on Dawn, then?"

"No, not at all," I said stoutly. At least, it didn't seem strange now, after Sam's description of Dawn's tantrum. "This is on my way to the bar, and I don't have children like Arlene, the other waitress on our shift. So it would be easier for me." That was pretty sound, I thought. If I said Dawn had screamed at Sam the last time he'd been here, that would give exactly the wrong impression.

"What did you do after work two days ago, Sookie?"

"I didn't come to work. I had the day off."

"And your plan for that day was — ?"

"I sunbathed and helped Gran clean house, and we had company."

"Who would that be?"

"That would be Bill Compton."

"The vampire."

"Right."

"How late was Mr. Compton at your house?"

"I don't know. Maybe midnight or one."

"How did he seem to you?"

"He seemed fine."

"Edgy? Irritated?"

"No."

"Miss Stackhouse, we need to talk to you more at the station house. This is going to take awhile, here, as you can see."

"Okay, I guess."

"Can you come in a couple of hours?"

I looked at my wristwatch. "If Sam doesn't need me to work."

"You know, Miss Stackhouse, this really takes precedence over working at a bar."

Okay, I was pissed off. Not because he thought murder investigations were more important than getting to work on time; I agreed with him, there. It was his unspoken prejudice against my particular job.

"You may not think my job amounts to much, but it's one I'm good at, and I like it. I am as worthy of respect as your sister, the lawyer, Andy Bellefleur, and don't you forget it. I am not stupid, and I am not a slut."

The detective turned red, slowly and unattractively. "I apologize," Andy said stiffly. He was still trying to deny the old connection, the shared high school, the knowledge of each other's family. He was thinking he should have been a detective in another town, where he could treat people the way he thought a police officer should.

"No, you'll be a better detective here if you can get over that attitude," I told him. His gray eyes flared wide in shock, and I was childishly glad I'd rocked him, though I was sure I would pay for it sooner or later. I always did when I gave people a peek at my disability.

Mostly, people couldn't get away from me fast enough when I'd given them a taste of mind reading, but Andy Bellefleur was fascinated. "It's true, then," he breathed, as if we were somewhere alone instead of sitting in the driveway of a rundown duplex in rural Louisiana.

"No, forget it," I said quickly. "I can just tell sometimes by the way people look what they're thinking."

He deliberately thought about unbuttoning my blouse. But I was wary now, back to my normal state of barricaded siege, and I did no more than smile brightly. I could tell I wasn't fooling him, though.

"When you're ready for me, you come to the bar. We can talk in the storeroom or Sam's office," I said firmly and swung my legs into the car.

The bar was buzzing when I got there. Sam had called Terry Bellefleur, Andy's second cousin if I recalled correctly, in to watch the bar while he talked to the police at Dawn's place. Terry had had a bad war in Vietnam, and he existed narrowly on government disability of some kind. He'd been wounded, captured, held prisoner for two years, and now his thoughts were most often so scary that I was extra special careful when I was around him. Terry had a hard life, and acting normal was even harder for him than it was for me. Terry didn't drink, thank God.

Today I gave him a light kiss on the cheek while I got my tray and scrubbed my hands. Through the window into the little kitchen I could see Lafayette Reynold, the cook, flipping burgers and sinking a basket of fries into hot oil. Merlotte's serves a few sandwiches, and that's all. Sam doesn't want to run a restaurant, but a bar with some food available.

"What was that for, not that I'm not honored," Terry said. He'd raised his eyebrows. Terry was redhaired, though when he needed a shave, I could tell his whiskers were gray. Terry spent a lot of time outside, but his skin never exactly tanned. It got a rough, reddened look, which made the scars on his left cheek stand out more clearly. That didn't seem to bother Terry. Arlene had been to bed with Terry one night when she'd been drinking, and she'd confided in me that Terry had many scars even worse than the one on his cheek.

"Just for being here," I said.

"It true about Dawn?"

Lafayette put two plates on the serving hatch. He winked at me with a sweep of his thick, false lashes. Lafayette wears a lot of makeup. I was so used to him I never thought of it any more, but now his eye shadow brought the boy, Jerry, to my mind. I'd let him go with the three vampires without protest. That had probably been wrong, but realistic. I couldn't have stopped them from taking him. I couldn't have gotten the police to catch up with them in time. He was dying anyway, and he was taking as many vampires and humans with him as he could; and he was already a killer himself. I told my conscience this would be the last talk we'd have about Jerry.

"Arlene, burgers up," Terry called, jerking me back into the here and now. Arlene came over to grab the plates. She gave me a look that said she was going to pump me dry at the first chance she got. Charlsie Tooten was working, too. She filled in when one of the regular women got sick or just didn't show. I hoped Charlsie would take Dawn's place full-time. I'd always liked her.

"Yeah, Dawn's dead," I told Terry. He didn't seem to mind my long pause.

"What happened to her?"

"I don't know, but it wasn't peaceful." I'd seen blood on the sheets, not a lot, but some.

"Maudette," Terry said, and I instantly understood.

"Maybe," I said. It sure was possible that whoever had done in Dawn was the same person who'd killed Maudette.

Of course, everyone in Renard Parish came in that day, if not for lunch, then for an afternoon cup of coffee or a beer. If they couldn't make their work schedule bend around that, they waited until they clocked out and came in on their way home. Two young women in our town murdered in one month? You bet people wanted to talk.

Sam returned about two, with heat radiating off his body and sweat trickling down his face from standing out in the shadeless yard at the crime scene. He told me that Andy Bellefleur had said he was coming to talk to me again soon.

"I don't know why," I said, maybe a tad sullenly. "I never hung around with Dawn. What happened to her, did they tell you?"

"Someone strangled her after beating on her a little," Sam said. "But she had some old tooth marks, too. Like Maudette."

"There are lots of vampires, Sam," I said, answering his unspoken comment.

"Sookie." His voice was so serious and quiet. It made me remember how he'd held my hand at Dawn's house, and then I remembered how he'd shut me out of his mind, known I was probing, known how to keep me out. "Honey, Bill is a good guy, for a vampire, but he's just not human."

"Honey, neither are you," I said, very quietly but very sharply. And I turned my back on Sam, not exactly wanting to admit why I was so angry with him, but wanting him to know it nonetheless.

I worked like a demon. Whatever her faults, Dawn had been efficient, and Charlsie just couldn't keep up with the pace. She was

129

willing, and I was sure she'd catch up with the rhythm of the bar, but for tonight, Arlene and I had to take up the slack.

I earned a ton of money in tips that evening and on into the night when people found out I'd actually discovered the body. I just kept my face solemn and got through it, not wanting to offend customers who just wanted to know what everyone else in town wanted to know.

On my way home, I allowed myself to relax a little. I was exhausted. The last thing I expected to see, after I turned into the little drive through the woods that led to our house, was Bill Compton. He was leaning against a pine tree waiting for me. I drove past him a little, almost deciding to ignore him. But then I stopped.

He opened my door. Without looking him in the eyes, I got out. He seemed comfortable in the night, in a way I never could be. There were too many childhood taboos about the night and the darkness and things that went bump.

Come to think of it, Bill was one of those things. No wonder he felt at ease.

"Are you going to look at your feet all night, or are you going to talk to me?" he asked in a voice that was just above a whisper.

"Something happened you should know about."

"Tell me." He was trying to do something to me: I could feel his power hovering around me, but I batted it away. He sighed.

"I can't stand up," I said wearily. "Let's sit on the ground or something. My feet are tired."

In answer, he picked me up and set me on the hood of the car. Then he stood in front of me, his arms crossed, very obviously waiting.

"Tell me."

"Dawn was murdered. Just like Maudette Pickens."

"Dawn?"

Suddenly I felt a little better. "The other waitress at the bar."

"The redheaded one, the one who's been married so often?"

I felt a lot better. "No, the dark-haired one, the one who kept bumping into your chair with her hips to get you to notice her."

"Oh, that one. She came to my house."

"Dawn? When?"

"After you left the other night. The night the other vampires were there. She's lucky she missed them. She was very confident of her ability to handle anything."

I looked up at him. "Why is she so lucky? Wouldn't you have protected her?"

Bill's eyes were totally dark in the moonlight. "I don't think so," he said.

"You are . . ."

"I'm a vampire, Sookie. I don't think like you. I don't care about people automatically."

"You protected me."

"You're different."

131

"Yeah? I'm a waitress, like Dawn. I come from a plain family, like Maudette. What's so different?"

I was in a sudden rage. I knew what was coming.

His cool finger touched the middle of my forehead. "Different," he said. "You're not like us. But you're not like them, either."

I felt a flare of rage so intense it was almost divine. I hauled off and hit him, an insane thing to do. It was like hitting a Brink's armored truck. In a flash, he had me off the car and pinned to him, my arms bound to my sides by one of his arms.

"No!" I screamed. I kicked and fought, but I might as well have saved the energy. Finally I sagged against him.

My breathing was ragged, and so was his. But I didn't think it was for the same reason.

"Why did you think I needed to know about Dawn?" He sounded so reasonable, you'd think the struggle hadn't happened.

"Well, Mr. Lord of Darkness," I said furiously, "Maudette had old bite marks on her thighs, and the police told Sam that Dawn had bite marks, too."

If silence can be characterized, his was thoughtful. While he was mulling, or whatever vampires do, his embrace loosened. One hand began rubbing my back absently, as if I was a puppy who had whimpered.

"You imply they didn't die from these bites."

"No. From strangulation."

"Not a vampire, then." His tone put it beyond question.

"Why not?"

"If a vampire had been feeding from these women, they would have been drained instead of strangled. They wouldn't have been wasted like that."

Just when I was beginning to be comfortable with Bill, he'd say something so cold, so vampirey, I had to start all over again.

"Then," I said wearily, "either you have a crafty vampire with great self-control, or you have someone who's determined to kill women who've been with vampires."

"Hmmm."

I didn't feel very good about either of those choices.

"Do you think I'd do that?" he asked.

The question was unexpected. I wriggled in his pinioning embrace to look up at him.

"You've taken great care to point out how heartless you are," I reminded him. "What do you really want me to believe?"

And it was so wonderful not to know. I almost smiled.

"I could have killed them, but I wouldn't do it here, or now," Bill said. He had no color in the moonlight except for the dark pools of his eyes and the dark arches of his brows. "This is where I want to stay. I want a home."

A vampire, yearning for home.

Bill read my face. "Don't pity me, Sookie. That would be a mistake." He seemed willing me to stare into his eyes.

"Bill, you can't glamor me, or whatever you do. You can't enchant me into pulling my T-shirt down for you to bite me, you can't convince me you weren't ever here, you can't do any of your usual stuff. You have to be regular with me, or just force me."

"No," he said, his mouth almost on mine. "I won't force you."

I fought the urge to kiss him. But at least I knew it was my very own urge, not a manufactured one.

"So, if it wasn't you," I said, struggling to keep on course, "then Maudette and Dawn knew another vampire. Maudette went to the vampire bar in Shreveport. Maybe Dawn did, too. Will you take me there?"

"Why?" he asked, sounding no more than curious.

I just couldn't explain being in danger to someone who was so used to being beyond it. At least at night. "I'm not sure Andy Bellefleur will go to the trouble," I lied.

"There are still Bellefleurs here," he said, and there was something different in his voice. His arms hardened around me to the point of pain.

"Yes," I said. "Lots of them. Andy is a police detective. His sister, Portia, is a lawyer. His cousin Terry is a veteran and a bartender. He substitutes for Sam. There are lots of others."

"Bellefleur . . ."

I was getting crushed.

"Bill," I said, my voice squeaky with panic.

He loosened his grip immediately. "Excuse me," he said formally.

"I have to go to bed," I said. "I'm really tired, Bill."

He set me down on the gravel with scarcely a bump. He looked down at me.

"You told those other vampires that I belonged to you," I said.

"Yes."

"What exactly did that mean?"

"That means that if they try to feed on you, I'll kill them," he said. "It means you are my human."

"I have to say I'm glad you did that, but I'm not really sure what being your human entails," I said cautiously. "And I don't recall being asked if that was okay with me."

"Whatever it is, it's probably better than partying with Malcolm, Liam, and Diane."

He wasn't going to answer me directly.

"Are you going to take me to the bar?"

"What's your next night off?"

"Two nights from now."

"Then, at sunset. I'll drive."

"You have a car?"

"How do you think I get places?" There might have been a smile on his shining face.

He turned to melt into the woods. Over his shoulder he said, "Sookie. Do me proud."

I was left standing with my mouth open.

Do him proud indeed.

4

Half the patrons of Merlotte's thought Bill had had a hand in the markings on the women's bodies. The other 50 percent thought that some of the vampires from bigger towns or cities had bitten Maudette and Dawn when they were out barhopping, and they deserved what they got if they wanted to go to bed with vampires. Some thought the girls had been strangled by a vampire, some thought they had just continued their promiscuous ways into disaster.

But everyone who came into Merlotte's was worried that some other woman would be killed, too. I couldn't count the times I was told to be careful, told to watch my friend Bill Compton, told to lock my doors and not let anyone in my house. . . . As if those were things I wouldn't do, normally.

Jason came in for both commiseration and suspicion as a man who'd "dated" both women. He came by the house one day and held forth for a whole hour, while Gran and I tried to encourage him to keep going with his work like an innocent man would. But for the first time in my memory, my handsome brother was really worried. I wasn't exactly glad he was in trouble, but I wasn't exactly sorry, either. I know that was small and petty of me.

I am not perfect.

I am so not-perfect that despite the deaths of two women I knew, I spent a substantial amount of time wondering what Bill meant about doing him proud. I had no idea what constituted appropriate dress for visiting a vampire bar. I wasn't about to dress in some kind of stupid costume, as I'd heard some bar visitors did.

I sure didn't know anyone to ask.

I wasn't tall enough or bony enough to dress in the sort of spandex outfit the vampire Diane had worn.

Finally I pulled a dress from the back of my closet, one I'd had little occasion to wear. It was a Nice Date dress, if you wanted the personal interest of whoever was your escort. It was cut square and low in the neck and it was sleeveless. It was tight and white. The fabric was thinly scattered with bright red flowers with long green stems. My tan glowed and my boobs showed. I wore red enamel earrings and red high-heeled screw-me shoes. I had a little red straw purse. I put on light makeup and wore my wavy hair loose down my back.

Gran's eyes opened wide when I came out of my room.

"Honey, you look beautiful," she said. "Aren't you going to be a little cold in that dress?"

I grinned. "No, ma'am, I don't think so. It's

pretty warm outside."

"Wouldn't you like to wear a nice white sweater over that?"

"No, I don't think so." I laughed. I had pushed the other vampires far enough back in my mind to where looking sexy was okay again. I was pretty excited about having a date, though I had kind of asked Bill myself and it was more of a fact-finding mission. That, too, I tried to forget, so I could just enjoy myself.

Sam called me to tell me my paycheck was ready. He asked if I'd come in and pick it up, which I usually did if I wasn't going to work the next day.

I drove to Merlotte's feeling a little anxious at walking in dressed up.

But when I came in the door, I got the tribute of a moment of stunned silence. Sam's back was to me, but Lafayette was looking through the hatch and Rene and JB were at the bar. Unfortunately, so was my brother, Jason, whose eyes opened wide when he turned to see what Rene was staring at.

"You lookin' good, girl!" called Lafayette enthusiastically. "Where you get that dress?"

"Oh, I've had this old thing forever," I said mockingly, and he laughed.

Sam turned to see what Lafayette was gawking at, and his eyes got wide, too.

"God almighty," he breathed. I walked over to ask for my check, feeling very self-conscious.

"Come in the office, Sookie," he said, and I

139

followed him to his small cubicle by the store-room. Rene gave me a half-hug on my way by him, and JB kissed my cheek.

Sam rummaged through the piles of paper on top of his desk, and finally came up with my check. He didn't hand it to me, though.

"Are you going somewhere special?" Sam asked, almost unwillingly.

"I have a date," I said, trying to sound matter-of-fact.

"You look great," Sam said, and I saw him swallow. His eyes were hot.

"Thank you. Um, Sam, can I have my check?"

"Sure." He handed it to me, and I popped it in my purse.

"Good-bye, then."

"Good-bye." But instead of indicating I should leave, Sam stepped over and smelled me. He put his face close to my neck and inhaled. His brilliant blue eyes closed briefly, as if to evaluate my odor. He exhaled gently, his breath hot on my bare skin.

I stepped out of the door and left the bar, puzzled and interested in Sam's behavior.

When I got home a strange car was parked in front of the house. It was a black Cadillac, and it shone like glass. Bill's. Where did they get the money to buy these cars? Shaking my head, I went up the steps to the porch and walked in. Bill turned to the door expectantly; he was sitting on the couch talking to Gran, who was perched on one arm of an old overstuffed chair.

When he saw me, I was sure I'd overdone it, and he was really angry. His face went quite still. His eyes flared. His fingers curved as if he were scooping something up with them.

"Is this all right?" I asked anxiously. I felt the blood surge up into my cheeks.

"Yes," he said finally. But his pause had been long enough to anger my grandmother.

"Anyone with a brain in his head has got to admit that Sookie is one of the prettiest girls around," she said, her voice friendly on the surface but steel underneath.

"Oh, yes," he agreed, but there was a curious lack of inflection in his voice.

Well, screw him. I'd tried my best. I stiffened my back, and said, "Shall we go, then?"

"Yes," he said again, and stood. "Good-bye, Mrs. Stackhouse. It was a pleasure seeing you again."

"Well, you two have a good time," she said, mollified. "Drive careful, Bill, and don't drink too much."

He raised an eyebrow. "No, ma'am."

Gran let that sail right on past.

Bill held my car door open as I got in, a carefully calculated series of maneuvers to keep as much of me as possible in the dress. He shut the door and got in on the driver's side. I wondered who had taught him to drive a car. Henry Ford, probably.

"I'm sorry I'm not dressed correctly," I said,

looking straight ahead of me.

We'd been going slowly on the bumpy driveway through the woods. The car lurched to a halt.

"Who said that?" Bill asked, his voice very gentle.

"You looked at me as though I'd done something wrong," I snapped.

"I'm just doubting my ability to get you in and out without having to kill someone who wants you."

"You're being sarcastic." I still wouldn't look.

His hand gripped the back of my neck, forced me to turn to him.

"Do I look like I am?" he asked.

His dark eyes were wide and unblinking.

"Ah . . . no," I admitted.

"Then accept what I say."

The ride to Shreveport was mostly silent, but not uncomfortably so. Bill played tapes most of the way. He was partial to Kenny G.

Fangtasia, the vampire bar, was located in a suburban shopping area of Shreveport, close to a Sam's and a Toys 'R' Us. It was in a shopping strip, which was all closed down at this hour except for the bar. The name of the place was spelled out in jazzy red neon above the door, and the facade was painted steel gray, a red door providing color contrast. Whoever owned the place must have thought gray was less obvious than black because the interior was decorated in the same colors.

I was carded at the door by a vampire. Of course, she recognized Bill as one of her own kind and acknowledged him with a cool nod, but she scanned me intently. Chalky pale, as all Caucasian vampires are, she was eerily striking in her long black dress with its trailing sleeves. I wondered if the overdone "vampire" look was her own inclination, or if she'd just adopted it because the human patrons thought it appropriate.

"I haven't been carded in years," I said, fishing in my red purse for my driver's license. We were standing in a little boxy entrance hall.

"I can no longer tell human ages, and we must be very careful we serve no minors. In any capacity," she said with what was probably meant to be a genial smile. She cast a sideways look at Bill, her eyes flicking up and down him with an offensive interest. Offensive to me, at least.

"I haven't seen you in a few months," she said to him, her voice as cool and sweet as his could be.

"I'm mainstreaming," he explained, and she nodded.

"What were you telling her?" I whispered as we walked down the short hall and through the red double doors into the main room.

"That I'm trying to live among humans."

I wanted to hear more, but then I got my first comprehensive look at Fangtasia's interior. Everything was in gray, black, and red. The walls were lined with framed pictures of every movie vampire who had shown fangs on the silver screen, from Bela Lugosi to George Hamilton to Gary Oldman, from famous to obscure. The lighting was dim, of course, nothing unusual about that; what was unusual was the clientele. And the posted signs.

The bar was full. The human clients were divided among vampire groupies and tourists. The groupies (fang-bangers, they were called) were dressed in their best finery. It ranged from the traditional capes and tuxes for the men to many Morticia Adams ripoffs among the females. The clothes ranged from reproductions of those worn by Brad Pitt and Tom Cruise in *Interview with the Vampire* to some modern outfits that I thought were influenced by *The Hunger.* Some of the fang-bangers were wearing false fangs, some had painted trickles of blood from the corners of their mouths or puncture marks on their necks. They were extraordinary, and extraordinarily pathetic.

The tourists looked like tourists anywhere, maybe more adventurous than most. But to enter into the spirit of the bar, they were nearly all dressed in black like the fang-bangers. Maybe it was part of a tour package? "Bring some black for your exciting visit to a real vampire bar! Follow the rules, and you'll be fine, catching a glimpse of this exotic underworld."

Strewn among this human assortment, like

real jewels in a bin of rhinestones, were the vampires, perhaps fifteen of them. They mostly favored dark clothes, too.

I stood in the middle of the floor, looking around me with interest and amazement and some distaste, and Bill whispered, "You look like a white candle in a coal mine."

I laughed, and we strolled through the scattered tables to the bar. It was the only bar I'd ever seen that had a case of warmed bottled blood on display. Bill, naturally, ordered one, and I took a deep breath and ordered a gin and tonic. The bartender smiled at me, showing me that his fangs had shot out a little at the pleasure of serving me. I tried to smile back and look modest at the same time. He was an American Indian, with long coal black straight hair and a craggy nose, a straight line of a mouth, and a whippy build.

"How's it going, Bill?" the bartender asked. "Long time, no see. This your meal for the night?" He nodded toward me as he put our drinks on the bar before us.

"This is my friend Sookie. She has some questions to ask."

"Anything, beautiful woman," said the bartender, smiling once again. I liked him better when his mouth was the straight line.

"Have you seen this woman, or this one, in the bar?" I asked, drawing the newspaper photos of Maudette and Dawn from my purse. "Or this man?" With a jolt of misgiving, I pulled out my brother's picture.

"Yes to the women, no to the man, though he looks delicious," said the bartender, smiling at me again. "Your brother, perhaps?"

"Yes."

"What possibilities," he whispered.

It was lucky I'd had extensive practice in face control. "Do you remember who the women hung around with?"

"That's something I wouldn't know," he replied quickly, his face closing down. "That's something we don't notice, here. You won't, either."

"Thank you," I said politely, realizing I'd broken a bar rule. It was dangerous to ask who left with whom, evidently. "I appreciate your taking the time."

He looked at me consideringly. "That one," he said, poking a finger at Dawn's picture, "she wanted to die."

"How do you know?"

"Everyone who comes here does, to one extent or another," he said so matter-of-factly I could tell he took that for granted. "That is what we are. Death."

I shuddered. Bill's hand on my arm drew me away to a just-vacated booth. Underscoring the Indian's pronouncement, at regular intervals wall placards proclaimed, "No biting on premises." "No lingering in the parking lot." "Conduct your personal business elsewhere." "Your patronage is appreci-

146

ated." "Proceed at your own risk."

Bill took the top off the bottle with one finger and took a sip. I tried not to look, failed. Of course he saw my face, and he shook his head.

"This is the reality, Sookie," he said. "I need it to live."

There were red stains between his teeth.

"Of course," I said, trying to match the matter-of-fact tone of the bartender. I took a deep breath. "Do you suppose I want to die, since I came here with you?"

"I think you want to find out why other people are dying," he said. But I wasn't sure that was what he really believed.

I didn't think Bill had yet realized that his personal position was precarious. I sipped my drink, felt the blossoming warmth of the gin spread through me.

A fang-banger approached the booth. I was half-hidden by Bill, but still, they'd all seen me enter with him. She was frizzy-haired and boney, with glasses that she stuffed in a purse as she walked over. She bent across the table to get her mouth about two inches from Bill.

"Hi, dangerous," she said in what she hoped was a seductive voice. She tapped Bill's bottled blood with a fingernail painted scarlet. "I have the real stuff." She stroked her neck to make sure he got the point.

I took a deep breath to control my temper. I had invited Bill to this place; he hadn't invited me. I could not comment on what he chose to do here, though I had a surprisingly vivid mental image of leaving a slap mark on this hussy's pale, freckled cheek. I held absolutely still so I wouldn't give Bill any cues about what I wanted.

"I have a companion," Bill said gently.

"She doesn't have any puncture marks on her neck," the girl observed, acknowledging my presence with a contemptuous look. She might as well have said "Chicken!" and flapped her arms like wings. I wondered if steam was visibly coming out of my ears.

"I have a companion," Bill said again, his voice not so gentle this time.

"You don't know what you're missing," she said, her big pale eyes flashing with offense.

"Yes, I do," he said.

She recoiled as if I'd actually done the slapping, and stomped off to her table.

To my disgust, she was only the first of four. These people, men and women, wanted to be intimate with a vampire, and they weren't shy about it.

Bill handled all of them with calm aplomb.

"You're not talking," he said, after a man of forty had left, his eyes actually tearing up at Bill's rejection.

"There's nothing for me to say," I replied, with great self-control.

"You could have sent them on their way. Do you want me to leave you? Is there someone else here who catches your fancy? Long

148

Shadow, there at the bar, would love to spend time with you, I can tell."

"Oh, for God's sake, no!" I wouldn't have felt safe with any of the other vampires in the bar, would have been terrified they were like Liam or Diane. Bill had turned his dark eyes to me and seemed to be waiting for me to say something else. "I do have to ask them if they've seen Dawn and Maudette in here, though."

"Do you want me with you?"

"Please," I said, and sounded more frightened than I'd wanted to. I'd meant to ask like it would be a casual pleasure to have his company.

"The vampire over there is handsome; he has scanned you twice," he said. I almost wondered if he was doing a little tongue biting himself.

"You're teasing me," I said uncertainly after a moment.

The vampire he'd indicated was handsome, in fact, radiant; blond and blue-eyed, tall and broad shouldered. He was wearing boots, jeans, and a vest. Period. Kind of like the guys on the cover of romance books. He scared me to death.

"His name is Eric," said Bill.

"How old is he?"

"Very. He's the oldest thing in this bar."

"Is he mean?"

"We're all mean, Sookie. We're all very strong and very violent."

"Not you," I said. I saw his face close in on

149

itself. "You want to live mainstream. You're not gonna do antisocial stuff."

"Just when I think you're too naive to walk around alone, you say something shrewd," he said, with a short laugh. "All right, we'll go talk to Eric."

Eric, who, it was true, had glanced my way once or twice, was sitting with a female vampire who was just as lovely as he. They'd already repelled several advances by humans. In fact, one lovelorn young man had already crawled across the floor and kissed the female's boot. She'd stared down at him and kicked him in the shoulder. You could tell it had been an effort for her not to kick him in the face. Tourists flinched, and a couple got up and left hurriedly, but the fang-bangers seemed to take this scene for granted.

At our approach, Eric looked up and scowled until he realized who the intruders were.

"Bill," he said, nodding. Vampires didn't seem to shake hands.

Instead of walking right up to the table, Bill stood a careful distance away, and since he was gripping my arm above my elbow, I had to stop, too. This seemed to be the courteous distance with this set.

"Who's your friend?" asked the female. Though Eric had a slight accent, this woman talked pure American, and her round face and sweet features would have done credit to a milkmaid. She smiled, and her fangs ran out, kind of ruining the image.

"Hi, I'm Sookie Stackhouse," I said politely.

"Aren't you sweet," Eric observed, and I hoped he was thinking of my character.

"Not especially," I said.

Eric stared at me in surprise for a moment. Then he laughed, and the female did, too.

"Sookie, this is Pam and I am Eric," the blond vampire said. Bill and Pam gave each other the vampire nod.

There was a pause. I would have spoken, but Bill squeezed my arm.

"My friend Sookie would like to ask a couple of questions," Bill said.

The seated vampires exchanged bored glances.

Pam said, "Like how long are our fangs, and what kind of coffin do we sleep in?" Her voice was laced with contempt, and you could tell those were tourist questions that she hated.

"No, ma'am," I said. I hoped Bill wouldn't pinch my arm off. I thought I was being calm and courteous.

She stared at me with amazement.

What the hell was so startling? I was getting a little tired of this. Before Bill could give me any more painful hints, I opened my purse and took out the pictures. "I'd like to know if you've seen either of these women in this bar." I wasn't getting Jason's picture out in front of this female. It would've been like putting a bowl of milk in front of a cat.

They looked at the pictures. Bill's face was blank. Eric looked up. "I have been with this one," he said coolly, tapping Dawn's picture. "She liked pain."

Pam was surprised Eric had answered me, I could tell by her eyebrows. She seemed somehow obligated to follow his example. "I have seen both of them. I have never been with them. This one," she flicked her finger at Maudette's picture, "was a pathetic creature."

"Thank you very much, that's all of your time I need to take," I said, and tried to turn to leave. But Bill still held my arm imprisoned.

"Bill, are you quite attached to your friend?" Eric asked.

It took a second for the meaning to sink in. Eric the Hunk was asking if I could be borrowed.

"She is mine," Bill said, but he wasn't roaring it as he had to the nasty vampires from Monroe. Nonetheless, he sounded pretty darn firm.

Eric inclined his golden head, but he gave me the once-over again. At least he started with my face.

Bill seemed to relax. He bowed to Eric, somehow including Pam in the gesture, backed away for two steps, finally permitting me to turn my back to the couple.

"Gee whiz, what was that about?" I asked in a furious whisper. I'd have a big bruise the next day.

"They're older than I am by centuries," Bill said, looking very vampirey.

"Is that the pecking order? By age?"

"Pecking order," Bill said thoughtfully. "That's not a bad way to put it." He almost laughed. I could tell by the way his lip twitched.

"If you had been interested, I would have been obliged to let you go with Eric," he said, after we'd resumed our seats and had a belt from our drinks.

"No," I said sharply.

"Why didn't you say anything when the fang-bangers came to our table trying to seduce me away from you?"

We weren't operating on the same wave level. Maybe social nuances weren't something vampires cared about. I was going to have to explain something that couldn't really bear much explaining.

I made a very unladylike sound out of sheer exasperation.

"Okay," I said sharply. "Listen up, Bill! When you came to my house, I had to invite you. When you came here with me, I had to invite you. You haven't asked me out. Lurking in my driveway doesn't count, and asking me to stop by your house and leave a list of contractors doesn't count. So it's always been me asking you. How can I tell you that you have to stay with me, if you want to go? If those girls will let you suck their blood — or that guy, for that matter — then I don't feel I have a right to stand in your way!"

"Eric is much better looking than I am," Bill said. "He is more powerful, and I understand sex with him is unforgettable. He is so old he only needs to take a sip to maintain his strength. He almost never kills any more. So, as vampires go, he's a good guy. You could still go with him. He is still looking at you. He would try his glamor on you if you were not with me."

"I don't want to go with Eric," I said stubbornly.

"I don't want to go with any of the fang-bangers," he said.

We sat in silence for a minute or two.

"So we're all right," I said obscurely.

"Yes."

We took a few moments more, thinking this over.

"Want another drink?" he asked.

"Yes, unless you need to get back."

"No, this is fine."

He went to the bar. Eric's friend Pam left, and Eric appeared to be counting my eyelashes. I tried to keep my gaze on my hands, to indicate modesty. I felt power tweaks kind of flow over me and had an uneasy feeling Eric was trying to influence me. I risked a quick peek, and sure enough he was looking at me expectantly. Was I supposed to pull off my dress? Bark like a dog? Kick Bill in the shins? Shit.

Bill came back with our drinks.

"He's gonna know I'm not normal," I said grimly. Bill didn't seem to need an explanation.

"He's breaking the rules just attempting to glamorize you after I've told him you're mine," Bill said. He sounded pretty pissed off. His voice didn't get hotter and hotter like mine would have, but colder and colder.

"You seem to be telling everyone that," I muttered. Without doing anything about it, I added silently.

"It's vampire tradition," Bill explained again. "If I pronounce you mine, no one else can try to feed on you."

"Feed on me, that's a delightful phrase," I said sharply, and Bill actually had an expression of exasperation for all of two seconds.

"I'm protecting you," he said, his voice not quite as neutral as usual.

"Had it occurred to you that I —"

And I stopped short. I closed my eyes. I counted to ten.

When I ventured a look at Bill, his eyes were fixed on my face, unblinking. I could practically hear the gears mesh.

"You — don't need protection?" he guessed softly. "You are protecting — me?"

I didn't say anything. I can do that.

But he took the back of my skull in his hand. He turned my head to him as though I were a puppet. (This was getting to be an annoying habit of his.) He looked so hard into my eyes that I thought I had tunnels

155

burned into my brain.

I pursed my lips and blew into his face. "Boo," I said. I was very uncomfortable. I glanced at the people in the bar, letting my guard down, listening.

"Boring," I told him. "These people are boring."

"Are they, Sookie? What are they thinking?" It was a relief to hear his voice, no matter that his voice was a little odd.

"Sex, sex, sex." And that was true. Every single person in that bar had sex on the brain. Even the tourists, who mostly weren't thinking about having sex with the vampires themselves, but were thinking about the fang-bangers having sex with the vampires.

"What are you thinking about, Sookie?"

"Not sex," I answered promptly and truthfully. I'd just gotten an unpleasant shock.

"Is that so?"

"I was thinking about the chances of us getting out of here without any trouble."

"Why were you thinking about that?"

"Because one of the tourists is a cop in disguise, and he just went to the bathroom, and he knows that a vampire is in there, sucking on the neck of a fang-banger. He's already called the police on his little radio."

"Out," he said smoothly, and we were out of the booth swiftly and moving for the door. Pam had vanished, but as we passed Eric's table, Bill gave him some sign. Just as smoothly, Eric eased from his seat and rose to his magnificent height, his stride so much longer than ours that he passed out the door first, taking the arm of the bouncer and propelling her outside with us.

As we were about to go out the door, I remembered the bartender, Long Shadow, had answered my questions willingly, so I turned and jabbed my finger in the direction of the door, unmistakably telling him to leave. He looked as alarmed as a vampire can look, and as Bill yanked me through the double doors, he was throwing down his towel.

Outside, Eric was waiting outside by his car — a Corvette, naturally.

"There's going to be a raid," Bill said.

"How do you know?"

Bill stuck on that one.

"Me," I said, getting him off the hook.

Eric's wide blue eyes shone even in the gloom of the parking lot. I was going to have to explain.

"I read a policeman's mind," I muttered. I snuck a look to see how Eric was taking this, and he was staring at me the same way the Monroe vampires had. Thoughtful. Hungry.

"That's interesting," he said. "I had a psychic once. It was incredible."

"Did the psychic think so?" My voice was tarter than I'd meant it to be.

I could hear Bill's indrawn breath.

Eric laughed. "For a while," he answered ambiguously.

We heard sirens in the distance, and without further words Eric and the bouncer slid into his car and were gone into the night, the car seeming quieter than others' cars, somehow. Bill and I buckled up hastily, and we were leaving the parking lot by one exit just as the police were coming in by another. They had their vampire van with them, a special prisoner transport with silver bars. It was driven by two cops who were of the fanged persuasion, and they sprang out of their van and reached the club door with a speed that rendered them just blurs on my human vision.

We had driven a few blocks when suddenly Bill pulled into the parking lot of yet another darkened strip mall.

"What — ?" I began, but got no further. Bill had unclipped my seat belt, moved the seat back, and grabbed me before I had finished my sentence. Frightened that he was angry, I pushed against him at first, but I might as well have been heaving against a tree. Then his mouth located mine, and I knew what he was.

Oh, boy, could he kiss. We might have problems communicating on some levels, but this wasn't one of them. We had a great time for maybe five minutes. I felt all the right things moving through my body in waves. Despite the awkwardness of being in the front seat of a car, I managed to be comfortable, mostly because he was so strong and considerate. I nipped his skin with my teeth. He made a sound like a growl.

"Sookie!" His voice was ragged.

I moved away from him, maybe half an inch.

"If you do that any more I'll have you whether you want to be had or not," he said, and I could tell he meant it.

"You don't want to," I said finally, trying not to make it a question.

"Oh, yes, I want to," and he grabbed my hand and showed me.

Suddenly, there was a bright rotating light beside us.

"The police," I said. I could see a figure get out of the patrol car and start toward Bill's window. "Don't let him know you're a vampire, Bill," I said hastily, fearing fallout from the Fangtasia raid. Though most police forces loved having vampires join them on the job, there was a lot of prejudice against vampires on the street, especially as part of a mixed couple.

The policeman's heavy hand rapped on the window.

Bill turned on the motor, hit the button that lowered the window. But he was silent, and I realized his fangs had not retracted. If he opened his mouth, it would be really obvious he was a vampire.

"Hello, officer," I said.

"Good evening," the man said, politely enough. He bent to look in the window. "You two know all the shops here are closed, right?"

"Yes, sir."

"Now, I can tell you been messing around a little, and I got nothing against that, but you two need to go home and do this kind of thing."

"We will." I nodded eagerly, and Bill managed a stiff inclination of his head.

"We're raiding a bar a few blocks back," the patrolman said casually. I could see only a little of his face, but he seemed burly and middle-aged. "You two coming from there, by any chance?"

"No," I said.

"Vampire bar," the cop remarked.

"Nope. Not us."

"Let me just shine this light on your neck, miss, if you don't mind."

"Not at all."

And by golly, he shone that old flashlight on my neck and then on Bill's.

"Okay, just checking. You two move on now."

"Yes, we will."

Bill's nod was even more curt. While the patrolman waited, I slid back over to my side and clipped my seat belt, and Bill put the car in gear and backed up.

Bill was just infuriated. All the way home he kept a sullen (I guess) silence, whereas I was inclined to view the whole thing as funny.

I was cheerful at finding Bill wasn't indifferent to my personal attractions, such as they were. I began to hope that someday he would want to kiss me again, maybe longer and harder, and maybe even — we could go further? I was trying not to get my hopes up. Actually, there was a thing or two that Bill didn't know about me, that no one knew, and I was very careful to try to keep my expectations modest.

When he got me back to Gran's, he came around and opened my door, which made me raise my eyebrows; but I am not one to stop a courteous act. I assumed Bill did realize I had functioning arms and the mental ability to figure out the door-opening mechanism. When I stepped out, he backed up.

I was hurt. He didn't want to kiss me again; he was regretting our earlier episode. Probably pining after that damn Pam. Or maybe even Long Shadow. I was beginning to see that the ability to have sex for several centuries leaves room for lots of experimentation. Would a telepath be so bad to add to his list?

I kind of hunched my shoulders together and wrapped my arms across my chest.

"Are you cold?" Bill asked instantly, putting his arm around me. But it was the physical equivalent of a coat, he seemed to be trying to stay as far away from me as the arm made possible.

"I am sorry I have pestered you. I won't ask you for any more," I said, keeping my voice even. Even as I spoke I realized that Gran hadn't set up a date for Bill to speak to the De-

161

scendants, but she and Bill would just have to work that out.

He stood still. Finally he said, "You — are — incredibly — naive." And he didn't even add that codicil about shrewdness, like he had earlier.

"Well," I said blankly. "I am?"

"Or maybe one of God's fools," he said, and that sounded a lot less pleasant, like Quasimodo or something.

"I guess," I said tartly, "you'll just have to find out."

"It had better be me that finds out," he said darkly, which I didn't understand at all. He walked me up to the door, and I was sure hoping for another kiss, but he gave me a little peck on the forehead. "Good night, Sookie," he whispered.

I rested my cheek against his for a moment. "Thanks for taking me," I said, and moved away quickly before he thought I was asking for something else. "I'm not calling you again." And before I could lose my determination, I slipped into the dark house and shut the door in Bill's face.

5

I certainly had a lot to think about the next couple of days. For someone who was always hoarding new things to keep from being bored, I'd stored enough up to last me for weeks. The people in Fangtasia, alone, were food for examination, to say nothing of the vampires. From longing to meet one vampire, now I'd met more than I cared to know.

A lot of men from Bon Temps and the surrounding area had been called in to the police station to answer a few questions about Dawn Green and her habits. Embarrassingly enough, Detective Bellefleur took to hanging around the bar on his off-hours, never drinking more alcohol than one beer, but observing everything that took place around him. Since Merlotte's was not exactly a hotbed of illegal activity, no one minded too much once they got used to Andy being there.

He always seemed to pick a table in my section. And he began to play a silent game with me. When I came to his table, he'd be thinking something provocative, trying to get me to say something. He didn't seem to understand how indecent that was. The provocation was the point, not the insult. He just wanted me to read his mind again. I couldn't figure out why.

Then, maybe the fifth or sixth time I had to get him something, I guess it was a Diet Coke, he pictured me cavorting with my brother. I was so nervous when I went to the table (knowing to expect something, but not knowing exactly what) that I was beyond getting angry and into the realm of tears. It reminded me of the less sophisticated tormenting I'd taken when I was in grade school.

Andy had looked up with an expectant face, and when he saw tears an amazing range of things ran across his face in quick succession: triumph, chagrin, then scalding shame.

I poured the damn coke down his shirt.

I walked right past the bar and out the back door.

"What's the matter?" Sam asked sharply. He was right on my heels.

I shook my head, not wanting to explain, and pulled an aging tissue out of my shorts pocket to mop my eyes with.

"Has he been saying ugly things to you?" Sam asked, his voice lower and angrier.

"He's been thinking them," I said helplessly, "to get a rise out of me. He knows."

"Son of a bitch," Sam said, which almost shocked me back to normal. Sam didn't curse.

Once I started crying, it seemed like I couldn't stop. I was getting my crying time done for a number of little unhappinesses.

"Just go on back in," I said, embarrassed at

my waterworks. "I'll be okay in just a minute."

I heard the back door of the bar open and shut. I figured Sam had taken me at my word. But instead, Andy Bellefleur said, "I apologize, Sookie."

"That's Miss Stackhouse to you, Andy Bellefleur," I said. "It seems to me like you better be out finding who killed Maudette and Dawn instead of playing nasty mind games with me."

I turned around and looked at the policeman. He was looking horribly embarrassed. I thought he was sincere in his shame.

Sam was swinging his arms, full of the energy of anger.

"Bellefleur, sit in someone else's area if you come back," he said, but his voice held a lot of suppressed violence.

Andy looked at Sam. He was twice as thick in the body, taller by two inches. But I would have put my money on Sam at that moment, and it seemed Andy didn't want to risk the challenge either, if only from good sense. He just nodded and walked across the parking lot to his car. The sun glinted on the blond highlights in his brown hair.

"Sookie, I'm sorry," Sam said.

"Not your fault."

"Do you want to take some time off? We're not so busy today."

"Nope. I'll finish my shift." Charlsie Tooten was getting into the swing of things, but I

165

wouldn't feel good about leaving. It was Arlene's day off.

We went back into the bar, and though several people looked at us curiously as we entered, no one asked us what had happened. There was only one couple sitting in my area, and they were busy eating and had glasses full of liquid, so they wouldn't be needing me. I began putting up wineglasses. Sam leaned against the workspace beside me.

"Is it true that Bill Compton is going to speak to the Descendants of the Glorious Dead tonight?"

"According to my grandmother."

"Are you going?"

"I hadn't planned on it." I didn't want to see Bill until he called me and made an appointment to see me.

Sam didn't say anything else then, but later in the afternoon, as I was retrieving my purse from his office, he came in and fiddled with some papers on his desk. I'd pulled out my brush and was trying to get a tangle out of my ponytail. From the way Sam dithered around, it seemed apparent that he wanted to talk to me, and I felt a wave of exasperation at the indirection men seemed to take.

Like Andy Bellefleur. He could just have asked me about my disability, instead of playing games with me.

Like Bill. He could just have stated his intentions, instead of this strange hot-cold thing.

"So?" I said, more sharply than I'd intended.

He flushed under my gaze.

"I wondered if you'd like to go to the Descendants meeting with me and have a cup of coffee afterward."

I was flabbergasted. My brush stopped in midswoop. A number of things ran through my mind, the feel of his hand when I'd held it in front of Dawn Green's duplex, the wall I'd met in his mind, the unwisdom of dating your boss.

"Sure," I said, after a notable pause.

He seemed to exhale. "Good. Then I'll pick you up at your house at seven-twenty or so. The meeting starts at seven-thirty."

"Okay. I'll see you then."

Afraid I'd do something peculiar if I stayed longer, I grabbed my purse and strode out to my car. I couldn't decide whether to giggle with glee or groan at my own idiocy.

It was five-forty-five by the time I got home. Gran already had supper on the table since she had to leave early to carry refreshments to the Descendants meeting, which was held at the Community Building.

"Wonder if he could have come if we'd had it in the fellowship hall of Good Faith Baptist?" Gran said out of the blue. But I didn't have a problem latching on to her train of thought.

"Oh, I think so," I said. "I think that idea about vampires being scared of religious items isn't true. But I haven't asked him."

"They do have a big cross hung up in there," Gran went on.

"I'll be at the meeting after all," I said. "I'm going with Sam Merlotte."

"Your boss, Sam?" Gran was very surprised.

"Yes, ma'am."

"Hmmm. Well, well." Gran began smiling while she put the plates on the table. I was trying to think of what to wear while we ate our sandwiches and fruit salad. Gran was excited about the meeting, about listening to Bill and introducing him to her friends, and now she was in outer space somewhere (probably around Venus) since I actually had a date. With a human.

"We'll be going out afterward," I said, "so I guess I'll get home maybe an hour after the meeting's over." There weren't that many places to have coffee in Bon Temps. And those restaurants weren't exactly places you'd want to linger.

"Okay, honey. You just take your time." Gran was already dressed, and after supper I helped her load up the cookie trays and the big coffee urn she'd bought for just such events. Gran had pulled her car around to the back door, which saved us a lot of steps. She was happy as she could be and fussed and chattered the whole time we were loading. This was her kind of night.

I shed my waitress clothes and got into the shower lickety-split. While I soaped up, I tried

168

to think of what to wear. Nothing black and white, that was for sure; I had gotten pretty sick of the Merlotte's waitress colors. I shaved my legs again, didn't have time to wash my hair and dry it, but I'd done it the night before. I flung open my closet and stared. Sam had seen the white flowered dress. The denim jumper wasn't nice enough for Gran's friends. Finally I yanked out some khaki slacks and a bronze silk blouse with short sleeves. I had brown leather sandals and a brown leather belt that would look good. I hung a chain around my neck, stuck in some big gold earrings, and I was ready. As if he'd timed it, Sam rang the doorbell.

There was a moment of awkwardness as I opened the door.

"You're welcome to come in, but I think we just have time —"

"I'd like to sit and visit, but I think we just have time —"

We both laughed.

I locked the door and pulled it to, and Sam hurried to open the door of his pickup. I was glad I'd worn pants, as I pictured trying to get up in the high cab in one of my shorter skirts.

"Need a boost?" he asked hopefully.

"I think I got it," I said, trying not to smile.

We were silent on the way to the Community Building, which was in the older part of Bon Temps; the part that predated the War. The structure was not antebellum, but there had actually been a building on that site that had gotten destroyed during the War, though no one seemed to have a record of what it had been.

The Descendants of the Glorious Dead were a mixed bunch. There were some very old, very fragile members, and some not quite so old and very lively members, and there were even a scattering of middle-aged men and women. But there were no young members, which Gran had often lamented, with many significant glances at me.

Mr. Sterling Norris, a longtime friend of my grandmother's and the mayor of Bon Temps, was the greeter that night, and he stood at the door shaking hands and having a little conversation with everyone who entered.

"Miss Sookie, you look prettier every day," Mr. Norris said. "And Sam, we haven't seen you in a coon's age! Sookie, is it true this vampire is a friend of yours?"

"Yes, sir."

"Can you say for sure that we're all safe?"

"Yes, I'm sure you are. He's a very nice . . . person." Being? Entity? If you like the living dead, he's pretty neat?

"If you say so," Mr. Norris said dubiously. "In my time, such a thing was just a fairy tale."

"Oh, Mr. Norris, it's still your time," I said with the cheerful smile expected of me, and he laughed and motioned us on in, which was what was expected of him. Sam took my hand

and sort of steered me to the next to last row of metal chairs, and I waved at my grandmother as we took our seats. It was just time for the meeting to start, and the room held maybe forty people, quite a gathering for Bon Temps. But Bill wasn't there.

Just then the president of Descendants, a massive, solid woman by the name of Maxine Fortenberry, came to the podium.

"Good evening! Good evening!" she boomed. "Our guest of honor has just called to say he's having car trouble and will be a few minutes late. So let's go on and have our business meeting while we're waiting for him."

The group settled down, and we got through all the boring stuff, Sam sitting beside me with his arms crossed over his chest, his right leg crossed over the left at the ankle. I was being especially careful to keep my mind guarded and face smiling, and I was a little deflated when Sam leaned slightly to me and whispered, "It's okay to relax."

"I thought I was," I whispered back.

"I don't think you know how."

I raised my eyebrows at him. I was going to have a few things to say to Mr. Merlotte after the meeting.

Just then Bill came in, and there was a moment of sheer silence as those who hadn't seen him before adjusted to his presence. If you've never been in the company of a vampire before, it's a thing you really have to get used to. Under the fluorescent lighting, Bill really looked much more unhuman than he did under the dim lighting in Merlotte's, or the equally dim lighting in his own home. There was no way he could pass for a regular guy. His pallor was very marked, of course, and the deep pools of his eyes looked darker and colder. He was wearing a lightweight medium-blue suit, and I was willing to bet that had been Gran's advice. He looked great. The dominant line of the arch of his eyebrow, the curve of his bold nose, the chiseled lips, the white hands with their long fingers and carefully trimmed nails . . . He was having an exchange with the president, and she was charmed out of her support hose by Bill's close-lipped smile.

I didn't know if Bill was casting a glamor over the whole room, or if these people were just predisposed to be interested, but the whole group hushed expectantly.

Then Bill saw me. I swear his eyebrows twitched. He gave me a little bow, and I nodded back, finding no smile in me to give him. Even in the crowd, I stood at the edge of the deep pool of his silence.

Mrs. Fortenberry introduced Bill, but I don't remember what she said or how she skirted the fact that Bill was a different kind of creature.

Then Bill began speaking. He had notes, I saw with some surprise. Beside me, Sam leaned forward, his eyes fixed on Bill's face.

". . . we didn't have any blankets and very

little food," Bill was saying calmly. "There were many deserters."

That was not a favorite fact of the Descendants, but a few of them were nodding in agreement. This account must match what they'd learned in their studies.

An ancient man in the first row raised his hand.

"Sir, did you by chance know my great-grandfather, Tolliver Humphries?"

"Yes," Bill said, after a moment. His face was unreadable. "Tolliver was my friend."

And just for a moment, there was something so tragic in his voice that I had to close my eyes.

"What was he like?" quavered the old man.

"Well, he was foolhardy, which led to his death," said Bill with a wry smile. "He was brave. He never made a cent in his life that he didn't waste."

"How did he die? Were you there?"

"Yes, I was there," said Bill wearily. "I saw him get shot by a Northern sniper in the woods about twenty miles from here. He was slow because he was starved. We all were. About the middle of the morning, a cold morning, Tolliver saw a boy in our troop get shot as he lay in poor cover in the middle of a field. The boy was not dead, but painfully wounded. But he could call to us, and he did, all morning. He called to us to help him. He knew he would die if someone didn't."

The whole room had grown so silent you could hear a pin drop.

"He screamed and he moaned. I almost shot him myself, to shut him up, because I knew to venture out to rescue him was suicide. But I could not quite bring myself to kill him. That would be murder, not war, I told myself. But later I wished I had shot him, for Tolliver was less able than I to withstand the boy's pleading. After two hours of it, he told me he planned to try to rescue the boy. I argued with him. But Tolliver told me that God wanted him to attempt it. He had been praying as we lay in the woods.

"Though I told Tolliver that God did not wish him to waste his life foolishly — that he had a wife and children praying for his safe return at home — Tolliver asked me to divert the enemy while he attempted the boy's rescue. He ran out into the field like it was a spring day and he was well rested. And he got as far as the wounded boy. But then a shot rang out, and Tolliver fell dead. And, after a time, the boy began screaming for help again."

"What happened to him?" asked Mrs. Fortenberry, her voice as quiet as she could manage to make it.

"He lived," Bill said, and there was tone to his voice that sent shivers down my spine. "He survived the day, and we were able to retrieve him that night."

Somehow those people had come alive again

as Bill spoke, and for the old man in the front row there was a memory to cherish, a memory that said much about his ancestor's character.

I don't think anyone who'd come to the meeting that night was prepared for the impact of hearing about the Civil War from a survivor. They were enthralled; they were shattered.

When Bill had answered the last question, there was thunderous applause, or at least it was as thunderous as forty people could make it. Even Sam, not Bill's biggest fan, managed to put his hands together.

Everyone wanted to have a personal word with Bill afterward except me and Sam. While the reluctant guest speaker was surrounded by Descendants, Sam and I sneaked out to Sam's pickup. We went to the Crawdad Diner, a real dive that happened to have very good food. I wasn't hungry, but Sam had key lime pie with his coffee.

"That was interesting," Sam said cautiously.

"Bill's speech? Yes," I said, just as cautiously.

"Do you have feelings for him?"

After all the indirection, Sam had decided to storm the main gate.

"Yes," I said.

"Sookie," Sam said, "you have no future with him."

"On the other hand, he's been around a while. I expect he'll be around for another few hundred years."

"You never know what's going to happen to a vampire."

I couldn't argue with that. But, as I pointed out to Sam, I couldn't know what was going to happen to me, a human, either.

We wrangled back and forth like this for too long. Finally, exasperated, I said, "What's it to you, Sam?"

His ruddy skin flushed. His bright blue eyes met mine. "I like you, Sookie. As friend or maybe something else sometime . . ."

Huh?

"I just hate to see you take a wrong turn."

I looked at him. I could feel my skeptical face forming, eyebrows drawn together, the corner of my mouth tugging up.

"Sure," I said, my voice matching my face.

"I've always liked you."

"So much that you had to wait till someone else showed an interest, before you mentioned it to me?"

"I deserve that." He seemed to be turning something over in his mind, something he wanted to say, but hadn't the resolution.

Whatever it was, he couldn't come out with it, apparently.

"Let's go," I suggested. It would be hard to turn the conversation back to neutral ground, I figured. I might as well go home.

It was a funny ride back. Sam always seemed on the verge of speaking, and then he'd shake his head and keep silent. I was so aggravated I wanted to swat him.

We got home later than I'd thought. Gran's light was on, but the rest of the house was dark. I didn't see her car, so I figured she'd parked in back to unload the leftovers right into the kitchen. The porch light was on for me.

Sam walked around and opened the pickup door, and I stepped down. But in the shadow, my foot missed the running board, and I just sort of tumbled out. Sam caught me. First his hands gripped my arms to steady me, then they just slid around me. And he kissed me.

I assumed it was going to be a little goodnight peck, but his mouth just kind of lingered. It was really more than pleasant, but suddenly my inner censor said, "This is the boss."

I gently disengaged. He was immediately aware that I was backing off, and gently slid his hands down my arms until he was just holding hands with me. We went to the door, not speaking.

"I had a good time," I said, softly. I didn't want to wake Gran, and I didn't want to sound bouncy.

"I did, too. Again sometime?"

"We'll see," I said. I really didn't know how I felt about Sam.

I waited to hear his truck turn around before I switched off the porch light and went into the house. I was unbuttoning my blouse as I walked, tired and ready for bed.

Something was wrong.

I stopped in the middle of the living room. I looked around me.

Everything looked all right, didn't it?

Yes. Everything was in its proper place.

It was the smell.

It was a sort of penny smell.

A coppery smell, sharp and salty.

The smell of blood.

It was down here with me, not upstairs where the guest bedrooms sat in neat solitude.

"Gran?" I called. I hated the quavering in my voice.

I made myself move, I made myself go to the door of her room. It was pristine. I began switching on lights as I went through the house.

My room was just as I'd left it.

The bathroom was empty.

The washroom was empty.

I switched on the last light. The kitchen was . . .

I screamed, over and over. My hands were fluttering uselessly in the air, trembling more with each scream. I heard a crash behind me, but couldn't be concerned. Then big hands gripped me and moved me, and a big body was between me and what I'd seen on the kitchen floor. I didn't recognize Bill, but he picked me up and moved me to the living room where I couldn't see any more.

"Sookie," he said harshly, "shut up! This isn't any good!"

If he'd been kind to me, I'd have kept on shrieking.

"Sorry," I said, still out of my mind. "I am acting like that boy."

He stared at me blankly.

"The one in your story," I said numbly.

"We have to call the police."

"Sure."

"We have to dial the phone."

"Wait. How did you come here?"

"Your grandmother gave me a ride home, but I insisted on coming with her first and helping her unload the car."

"So why are you still here?"

"I was waiting for you."

"So, did you see who killed her?"

"No. I went home, across the cemetery, to change."

He was wearing blue jeans and Grateful Dead T-shirt, and suddenly I began to giggle.

"That's priceless," I said, doubling over with the laughter.

And I was crying, just as suddenly. I picked up the phone and dialed 911.

Andy Bellefleur was there in five minutes.

Jason came as soon as I reached him. I tried to call him at four or five different places, and finally reached him at Merlotte's. Terry Bellefleur was bartending for Sam that night, and when he'd gotten back from telling Jason to come to his grandmother's house, I asked

179

Terry if he'd call Sam and tell him I had troubles and couldn't work for a few days.

Terry must have called Sam right away because Sam was at my house within thirty minutes, still wearing the clothes he'd worn to the meeting that night. At the sight of him I looked down, remembering unbuttoning my blouse as I walked through the living room, a fact I'd completely lost track of; but I was decent. It dawned on me that Bill must have set me to rights. I might find that embarrassing later, but at the moment I was just grateful.

So Jason came in, and when I told him Gran was dead, and dead by violence, he just looked at me. There seemed to be nothing going on behind his eyes. It was as if someone had erased his capacity for absorbing new facts. Then what I'd said sank in, and my brother sank to his knees right where he stood, and I knelt in front of him. He put his arms around me and lay his head on my shoulder, and we just stayed there for a while. We were all that was left.

Bill and Sam were out in the front yard sitting in lawn chairs, out of the way of the police. Soon Jason and I were asked to go out on the porch, at least, and we opted to sit outside, too. It was a mild evening, and I sat facing the house, all lit up like a birthday cake, and the people that came and went from it like ants who'd been allowed at the party. All this industry surrounding the tissue that

180

had been my grandmother.

"What happened?" Jason asked finally.

"I came in from the meeting," I said very slowly. "After Sam pulled off in his truck. I knew something was wrong. I looked in every room." This was the story of How I Found Grandmother Dead, the official version. "And when I got to the kitchen I saw her."

Jason turned his head very slowly so his eyes met mine.

"Tell me."

I shook my head silently. But it was his right to know. "She was beaten up, but she had tried to fight back, I think. Whoever did this cut her up some. And then strangled her, it looked like."

I could not even look at my brother's face. "It was my fault." My voice was nothing more than a whisper.

"How do you figure that?" Jason said, sounding nothing more than dull and sluggish.

"I figure someone came to kill me like they killed Maudette and Dawn, but Gran was here instead."

I could see the idea percolate in Jason's brain.

"I was supposed to be home tonight while she was at the meeting, but Sam asked me to go at the last minute. My car was here like it would be normally because we went in Sam's truck. Gran had parked her car around back while she was unloading, so it wouldn't look like she was here, just me. She had given Bill a ride home, but he helped her unload and went to change clothes. After he left, whoever it was . . . got her."

"How do we know it wasn't Bill?" Jason asked, as though Bill wasn't sitting right there beside him.

"How do we know it wasn't anyone?" I said, exasperated at my brother's slow wits. "It could be anyone, anyone we know. I don't think it was Bill. I don't think Bill killed Maudette and Dawn. And I do think whoever killed Maudette and Dawn killed Grandmother."

"Did you know," Jason said, his voice too loud, "that Grandmother left you this house all by yourself?"

It was like he'd thrown a bucket of cold water in my face. I saw Sam wince, too. Bill's eyes got darker and chillier.

"No. I just always assumed you and I would share like we did on the other one." Our parents' house, the one Jason lived in now.

"She left you all the land, too."

"Why are you saying this?" I was going to cry again, just when I'd been sure I was dry of tears now.

"She wasn't fair!" he was yelling. "It wasn't fair, and now she can't set it right!"

I began to shake. Bill pulled me out of the chair and began walking with me up and down the yard. Sam sat in front of Jason and began talking to him earnestly, his voice low and intense.

Bill's arm was around me, but I couldn't stop shaking.

"Did he mean that?" I asked, not expecting Bill to answer.

"No," he said. I looked up, surprised.

"No, he couldn't help your grandmother, and he couldn't handle the idea of someone lying in wait for you and killing her instead. So he had to get angry about something. And instead of getting angry with you for not getting killed, he's angry about things. I wouldn't let it worry me."

"I think it's pretty amazing that you're saying this," I told him bluntly.

"Oh, I took some night school courses in psychology," said Bill Compton, vampire.

And, I couldn't help thinking, hunters always study their prey. "Why would Gran leave me all this, and not Jason?"

"Maybe you'll find out later," he said, and that seemed fine to me.

Then Andy Bellefleur came out of the house and stood on the steps, looking up at the sky as if there were clues written on it.

"Compton," he called sharply.

"No," I said, and my voice came out as a growl.

I could feel Bill look down at me with the slight surprise that was a big reaction, coming from him.

"Now it's gonna happen," I said furiously.

"You *were* protecting me," he said. "You

183

thought the police would suspect me of killing those two women. That's why you wanted to be sure they were accessible to other vampires. Now you think this Bellefleur will try to blame your grandmother's death on me."

"Yes."

He took a deep breath. We were in the dark, by the trees that lined the yard. Andy bellowed Bill's name again.

"Sookie," Bill said gently, "I am sure you were the intended victim, as sure as you are."

It was kind of a shock to hear someone else say it.

"And I didn't kill them. So if the killer was the same as their killer, then I didn't do it, and he will see that. Even if he is a Bellefleur."

We began walking back into the light. I wanted none of this to be. I wanted the lights and the people to vanish, all of them, Bill, too. I wanted to be alone in the house with my grandmother, and I wanted her to look happy, as she had the last time I'd seen her.

It was futile and childish, but I could wish it nonetheless. I was lost in that dream, so lost I didn't see harm coming until it was too late.

My brother, Jason, stepped in front of me and slapped me in the face.

It was so unexpected and so painful that I lost my balance and staggered to the side, landing hard on one knee.

Jason seemed to be coming after me again, but Bill was suddenly in front of me, crouched, and his fangs were out and he was scary as hell. Sam tackled Jason and brought him down, and he may have whacked Jason's face against the ground once for good measure.

Andy Bellefleur was stunned at this unexpected display of violence. But after a second he stepped in between our two little groups on the lawn. He looked at Bill and swallowed, but he said in a steady voice, "Compton, back off. He won't hit her again."

Bill was taking deep breaths, trying to control his hunger for Jason's blood. I couldn't read his thoughts, but I could read his body language.

I couldn't exactly read Sam's thoughts, but I could tell he was very angry.

Jason was sobbing. His thoughts were a confused and tangled blue mess.

And Andy Bellefleur didn't like any of us and wished he could lock every freaking one of us up for some reason or another.

I pushed myself wearily to my feet and touched the painful spot of my cheek, using that to distract me from the pain in my heart, the dreadful grief that rolled over me.

I thought this night would never end.

The funeral was the largest ever held in Renard Parish. The minister said so. Under a brilliant early summer sky, my grandmother was buried beside my mother and father in our family plot in the ancient cemetery between the Comptons' house and Gran's house.

Jason had been right. It was my house, now. The house and the twenty acres surrounding it were mine, as were the mineral rights. Gran's money, what there was, had been divided fairly between us, and Gran had stipulated that I give Jason my half of the home our parents had lived in, if I wanted to retain full rights to her house. That was easy to do, and I didn't want any money from Jason for that half, though my lawyer looked dubious when I told him that. Jason would just blow his top if I mentioned paying me for my half; the fact that I was part-owner had never been more than a fantasy to him. Yet Gran leaving her house to me outright had come as a big shock. She had understood him better than I had.

It was lucky I had income other than from the bar, I thought heavily, trying to concentrate on something besides her loss. Paying taxes on the land and house, plus the upkeep of the house, which Gran had assumed at least partially, would really stretch my income.

"I guess you'll want to move," Maxine Fortenberry said when she was cleaning the kitchen. Maxine had brought over devilled eggs and ham salad, and she was trying to be extra helpful by scrubbing.

"No," I said, surprised.

"But honey, with it happening right here . . ." Maxine's heavy face creased with concern.

"I have far more good memories of this kitchen than bad ones," I explained.

"Oh, what a good way to look at it," she said, surprised. "Sookie, you really are smarter than anyone gives you credit for being."

"Gosh, thanks, Mrs. Fortenberry," I said, and if she heard the dry tone in my voice she didn't react. Maybe that was wise.

"Is your friend coming to the funeral?" The kitchen was very warm. Bulky, square Maxine was blotting her face with a dishtowel. The spot where Gran had fallen had been scrubbed by her friends, God bless them.

"My friend. Oh, Bill? No, he can't."

She looked at me blankly.

"We're having it in the daytime, of course."

She still didn't comprehend.

"He can't come out."

"Oh, of course!" She gave herself a light tap on the temple to indicate she was knocking sense into her head. "Silly me. Would he really fry?"

"Well, he says he would."

"You know, I'm so glad he gave that talk at the club, that has really made such a difference in making him part of the community."

I nodded, abstracted.

"There's really a lot of feeling about the murders, Sookie. There's really a lot of talk about vampires, about how they're responsible for these deaths."

I looked at her with narrowed eyes.

"Don't you go all mad on me, Sookie Stackhouse! Since Bill was so sweet about

187

telling those fascinating stories at the Descendants meeting, most people don't think he could do those awful things that were done to those women." I wondered what stories were making the rounds, and I shuddered to think. "But he's had some visitors that people didn't much like the looks of."

I wondered if she meant Malcolm, Liam, and Diane. I hadn't much liked their looks either, and I resisted the automatic impulse to defend them.

"Vampires are just as different among themselves as humans are," I said.

"That's what I told Andy Bellefleur," she said, nodding vehemently. "I said to Andy, you should go after some of those others, the ones that don't want to learn how to live with us, not like Bill Compton, who's really making an effort to settle in. He was telling me at the funeral home that he'd gotten his kitchen finished, finally."

I could only stare at her. I tried to think of what Bill might make in his kitchen. Why would he need one?

But none of the distractions worked, and finally I just realized that for a while I was going to be crying every whipstitch. And I did.

At the funeral Jason stood beside me, apparently over his surge of anger at me, apparently back in his right mind. He didn't touch me or talk to me, but he didn't hit me, either. I felt very alone. But then I realized as I looked out over the hillside that the whole town was grieving with me. There were cars as far as I could see on the narrow drives through the cemetery, there were hundreds of dark-clad folks around the funeral-home tent. Sam was there in a suit (looking quite unlike himself), and Arlene, standing by Rene, was wearing a flowered Sunday dress. Lafayette stood at the very back of the crowd, along with Terry Bellefleur and Charlsie Tooten; the bar must be closed! And all Gran's friends, all, the ones who could still walk. Mr. Norris wept openly, a snowy white handkerchief held up to his eyes. Maxine's heavy face was set in graven lines of sadness. While the minister said what he had to, while Jason and I sat alone in family area in the uneven folding chairs, I felt something in me detach and fly up, up into the blue brilliance: and I knew that whatever had happened to my grandmother, now she was at home.

The rest of the day went by in a blur, thank God. I didn't want to remember it, didn't want to even know it was happening. But one moment stood out.

Jason and I were standing by the dining room table in Gran's house, some temporary truce between us. We greeted the mourners, most of whom did their best not to stare at the bruise on my cheek.

We glided through it, Jason thinking that he would go home and have a drink after, and he wouldn't have to see me for a while and then it would be all right, and me thinking almost exactly the same thing. Except for the drink.

A well-meaning woman came up to us, the sort of woman who has thought over every ramification of a situation that was none of her business to start with.

"I am so sorry for you kids," she said, and I looked at her; for the life of me I couldn't remember her name. She was a Methodist. She had three grown children. But her name ran right out the other side of my head.

"You know it was so sad seeing you two there alone today, it made me remember your mother and father so much," she said, her face creasing into a mask of sympathy that I knew was automatic. I glanced at Jason, looked back to the woman, nodded.

"Yes," I said. But I heard her thought before she spoke, and I began to blanch.

"But where was Adele's brother today, your great uncle? Surely he's still living?"

"We're not in touch," I said, and my tone would have discouraged anyone more sensitive than this lady.

"But her only brother! Surely you . . ." and her voice died away as our combined stare finally sank home.

Several other people had commented briefly on our Uncle Bartlett's absence, but we had given the "this is family business" signals that cut them right off. This woman — what was her name? — just hadn't been as quick to read them. She'd brought a taco salad, and I planned to throw it right into the garbage when she'd left.

"We do have to tell him," Jason said quietly after she left. I put my guard up; I had no desire to know what he was thinking.

"You call him," I said.

"All right."

And that was all we said to each other for the rest of the day.

6

I stayed at home for three days after the funeral. It was too long; I needed to go back to work. But I kept thinking of things I just had to do, or so I told myself. I cleaned out Gran's room. Arlene happened to drop by, and I asked her for help, because I just couldn't be in there alone with my grandmother's things, all so familiar and imbued with her personal odor of Johnson's baby powder and Campho-Phenique.

So my friend Arlene helped me pack everything up to take to the disaster relief agency. There'd been tornadoes in northern Arkansas the past few days, and surely some person who had lost everything could use all the clothes. Gran had been smaller and thinner than I, and besides that her tastes were very different, so I wanted nothing of hers except the jewelry. She'd never worn much, but what she wore was real and precious to me.

It was amazing what Gran had managed to pack into her room. I didn't even want to think about what she'd stored in the attic: that would be dealt with later, in the fall, when the attic was bearably cool and I'd time to think.

I probably threw away more than I should have, but it made me feel efficient and strong to be doing this, and I did a drastic job of it. Arlene folded and packed, only putting aside papers and photographs, letters and bills and cancelled checks. My grandmother had never used a credit card in her life and never bought anything on time, God bless her, which made the winding-up much easier.

Arlene asked about Gran's car. It was five years old and had very little mileage. "Will you sell yours and keep hers?" she asked. "Yours is newer, but it's small."

"I hadn't thought," I said. And I found I couldn't think of it, that cleaning out the bedroom was the extent of what I could do that day.

At the end of the afternoon, the bedroom was empty of Gran. Arlene and I turned the mattress and I remade the bed out of habit. It was an old four-poster in the rice pattern. I had always thought her bedroom set was beautiful, and it occurred to me that now it was mine. I could move into the bigger bedroom and have a private bath instead of using the one in the hall.

Suddenly, that was exactly what I wanted to do. The furniture I'd been using in my bedroom had been moved over here from my parents' house when they'd died, and it was kid's furniture; overly feminine, sort of reminiscent of Barbies and sleepovers.

Not that I'd ever had many sleepovers, or been to many.

Nope, nope, nope, I wasn't going to fall into

that old pit. I was what I was, and I had a life, and I could enjoy things; the little treats that kept me going.

"I might move in here," I told Arlene as she taped a box shut.

"Isn't that a little soon?" she asked. She flushed red when she realized she'd sounded critical.

"It would be easier to be in here than be across the hall thinking about the room being empty," I said. Arlene thought that through, crouched beside the cardboard box with the roll of tape in her hand.

"I can see that," she agreed, with a nod of her flaming red head.

We loaded the cardboard boxes into Arlene's car. She had kindly agreed to drop them by the collection center on her way home, and I gratefully accepted the offer. I didn't want anyone to look at me knowingly, with pity, when I gave away my grandmother's clothes and shoes and nightgowns.

When Arlene left, I hugged her and gave her a kiss on the cheek, and she stared at me. That was outside the bounds our friendship had had up till now. She bent her head to mine and we very gently bumped foreheads.

"You crazy girl," she said, affection in her voice. "You come see us, now. Lisa's been wanting you to baby-sit again."

"You tell her Aunt Sookie said hi to her, and to Coby, too."

"I will." And Arlene sauntered off to her car, her flaming hair puffing in a waving mass above her head, her full body making her waitress outfit look like one big promise.

All my energy drained away as Arlene's car bumped down the driveway through the trees. I felt a million years old, alone and lonely. This was the way it was going to be from now on.

I didn't feel hungry, but the clock told me it was time to eat. I went into the kitchen and pulled one of the many Tupperware containers from the refrigerator. It held turkey and grape salad, and I liked it, but I sat there at the table just picking at it with a fork. I gave up, returning it to the icebox and going to the bathroom for a much-needed shower. The corners of closets are always dusty, and even a housekeeper as good as my grandmother had been had not been able to defeat that dust.

The shower felt wonderful. The hot water seemed to steam out some of my misery, and I shampooed my hair and scrubbed every inch of skin, shaving my legs and armpits. After I climbed out, I plucked my eyebrows and put on skin lotion and deodorant and a spray to untangle my hair and anything else I could lay my hands on. With my hair trailing down my back in a cascade of wet snarls, I pulled on my nightshirt, a white one with Tweety Bird on the front, and I got my comb. I'd sit in front of the television to have something to watch while I got my hair combed out, always a tedious process.

My little burst of purpose expired, and I felt almost numb.

The doorbell rang just as I was trailing into the living room with my comb in one hand and a towel in the other.

I looked through the peephole. Bill was waiting patiently on the porch.

I let him in without feeling either glad or sorry to see him.

He took me in with some surprise: the night-shirt, the wet hair, the bare feet. No makeup.

"Come in," I said.

"Are you sure?"

"Yes."

And he came in, looking around him as he always did. "What are you doing?" he asked, seeing the pile of things I'd put to one side because I thought friends of Gran's might want them: Mr. Norris might be pleased to get the framed picture of his mother and Gran's mother together, for example.

"I cleaned out the bedroom today," I said. "I think I'll move into it." Then I couldn't think of anything else to say. He turned to look at me carefully.

"Let me comb out your hair," he said.

I nodded indifferently. Bill sat on the flowered couch and indicated the old ottoman positioned in front of it. I sat down obediently, and he scooted forward a little, framing me with his thighs. Starting at the crown of my head, he began teasing the tangles out of my hair.

As always, his mental silence was a treat. Each time, it was like putting the first foot into a cool pool of water when I'd been on a long, dusty hike on a hot day.

As a bonus, Bill's long fingers seemed adept at dealing with the thick mane of my hair. I sat with my eyes closed, gradually becoming tranquil. I could feel the slight movements of his body behind me as he worked with the comb. I could almost hear his heart beating, I thought, and then realized how strange an idea that was. His heart, after all, didn't.

"I used to do this for my sister, Sarah," he murmured quietly, as if he knew how peaceful I'd gotten and was trying not to break my mood. "She had hair darker than yours, even longer. She'd never cut it. When we were children, and my mother was busy, she'd have me work on Sarah's hair."

"Was Sarah younger than you, or older?" I asked in a slow, drugged voice.

"She was younger. She was three years younger."

"Did you have other brothers or sisters?"

"My mother lost two in childbirth," he said slowly, as if he could barely remember. "I lost my brother, Robert, when he was twelve and I was eleven. He caught a fever, and it killed him. Now they would pump him full of penicillin, and he would be all right. But they couldn't then. Sarah survived the war, she and my mother, though my father died while I was soldiering; he had what I've learned since was a stroke. My wife was living with my family then, and my children . . ."

"Oh, Bill," I said sadly, almost in a whisper, for he had lost so much.

"Don't, Sookie," he said, and his voice had regained its cold clarity.

He worked on in silence for a while, until I could tell the comb was running free through my hair. He picked up the white towel I'd tossed on the arm of the couch and began to pat my hair dry, and as it dried he ran his fingers through it to give it body.

"Mmmm," I said, and as I heard it, it was no longer the sound of someone being soothed.

I could feel his cool fingers lifting the hair away from my neck and then I felt his mouth just at the nape. I couldn't speak or move. I exhaled slowly, trying not to make another sound. His lips moved to my ear, and he caught the lobe of it between his teeth. Then his tongue darted in. His arms came around me, crossing over my chest, pulling me back against him.

And for a miracle I only heard what his body was saying, not those niggling things from minds that only foul up moments like this. His body was saying something very simple.

He lifted me as easily as I'd rotate an infant. He turned me so I was facing him on his lap, my legs on either side of his. I put my arms around him and bent a little to kiss him. It went on and on, but after a while Bill settled into a rhythm with his tongue, a rhythm even someone as inexperienced as I could identify. The nightshirt slid up to the tops of my thighs. My hands began to rub his arms helplessly. Strangely, I thought of a pan of caramels my grandmother had put on the stove for a candy recipe, and I thought of the melted, warm sweet goldenness of them.

He stood up with me still wrapped around him. "Where?" he asked.

And I pointed to my grandmother's former room. He carried me in as we were, my legs locked around him, my head on his shoulder, and he lay me on the clean bed. He stood by the bed and in the moonlight coming in the unshaded windows, I saw him undress, quickly and neatly. Though I was getting great pleasure from watching him, I knew I had to do the same; but still a little embarrassed, I just drew off the nightshirt and tossed it onto the floor.

I stared at him. I'd never seen anything so beautiful or so scary in my life.

"Oh, Bill," I said anxiously, when he was beside me in the bed, "I don't want to disappoint you."

"That's not possible," he whispered. His eyes looked at my body as if it were a drink of water on a desert dune.

"I don't know much," I confessed, my voice barely audible.

"Don't worry. I know a lot." His hands began drifting over me, touching me in places I'd never been touched. I jerked with surprise, then opened myself to him.

"Will this be different from doing it with a regular guy?" I asked.

"Oh, yes."

I looked up at him questioningly.

"It'll be better," he said in my ear, and I felt a twinge of pure excitement.

A little shyly, I reached down to touch him, and he made a very human sound. After a moment, the sound became deeper.

"Now?" I asked, my voice ragged and shaking.

"Oh, yes," he said, and then he was on top of me.

A moment later he found out the true extent of my inexperience.

"You should have told me," he said, but very gently. He held himself still with an almost palpable effort.

"Oh, please don't stop!" I begged, thinking that the top would fly off my head, something drastic would happen, if he didn't go on with it.

"I have no intention of stopping," he promised a little grimly. "Sookie . . . this will hurt."

In answer, I raised myself. He made an incoherent noise and pushed into me.

I held my breath. I bit my lip. Ow, ow, ow.

"Darling," Bill said. No one had ever called me that. "How are you?" Vampire or not, he was trembling with the effort of holding back.

"Okay," I said inadequately. I was over the

sting, and I'd lose my courage if we didn't proceed. "Now," I said, and I bit him hard on the shoulder.

He gasped, and jerked, and he began moving in earnest. At first I was dazed, but I began to catch on and keep up. He found my response very exciting, and I began to feel that something was just around the corner, so to speak — something very big and good. I said, "Oh, please, Bill, please!" and dug my nails in his hips, almost there, almost there, and then a small shift in our alignment allowed him to press even more directly against me and almost before I could gather myself I was flying, flying, seeing white with gold streaks. I felt Bill's teeth against my neck, and I said, "Yes!" I felt his fangs penetrate, but it was a small pain, an exciting pain, and as he came inside me I felt him draw on the little wound.

We lay there for a long time, from time to time trembling with little aftershocks. I would never forget his taste and smell as long as I lived, I would never forget the feel of him inside me this first time — my first time, ever — I would never forget the pleasure.

Finally Bill moved to lie beside me, propped on one elbow, and he put his hand over my stomach.

"I am the first."

"Yes."

"Oh, Sookie." He bent to kiss me, his lips tracing the line of my throat.

"You could tell I don't know much," I said shyly. "But was that all right for you? I mean, about on a par with other women at least? I'll get better."

"You can get more skilled, Sookie, but you can't get any better." He kissed me on the cheek. "You're wonderful."

"Will I be sore?"

"I know you'll think this is odd, but I don't remember. The only virgin I was ever with was my wife, and that was a century and a half ago . . . yes, I recall, you will be very sore. We won't be able to make love again, for a day or two."

"Your blood heals," I observed after a little pause, feeling my cheeks redden.

In the moonlight, I could see him shift, to look at me more directly. "So it does," he said. "Would you like that?"

"Sure. Wouldn't you?"

"Yes," he breathed, and bit his own arm.

It was so sudden that I cried out, but he casually rubbed a finger in his own blood, and then before I could tense up he slid that finger up inside me. He began moving it very gently, and in a moment, sure enough, the pain was gone.

"Thanks," I said. "I'm better now."

But he didn't remove his finger.

"Oh," I said. "Would you like to do it again so soon? Can you do that?" And as his finger kept up its motion, I began to hope so.

"Look and see," he offered, a hint of amusement in his sweet dark voice.

I whispered, hardly recognizing myself, "Tell me what you want me to do."

And he did.

I went back to work the next day. No matter what Bill's healing powers were, I was a little uncomfortable, but boy, did I feel powerful. It was a totally new feeling for me. It was hard not to feel — well, cocky is surely the wrong word — maybe incredibly smug is closer.

Of course, there were the same old problems at the bar — the cacophony of voices, the buzzing of them, the persistence. But somehow I seemed better able to tone them down, to tamp them into a pocket. It was easier to keep my guard up, and I felt consequently more relaxed. Or maybe since I was more relaxed — boy, was I more relaxed — it was easier to guard? I don't know. But I felt better, and I was able to accept the condolences of the patrons with calm instead of tears.

Jason came in at lunch and had a couple of beers with his hamburger, which wasn't his normal regimen. He usually didn't drink during the work day. I knew he'd get mad if I said anything directly, so I just asked him if everything was okay.

"The chief had me in again today," he said in a low voice. He looked around to make sure no one else was listening, but the bar was sparsely filled that day since the Rotary Club was meeting at the Community Building.

"What is he asking you?" My voice was equally low.

"How often I'd seen Maudette, did I always get my gas at the place she worked. . . . Over and over and over, like I hadn't answered those questions seventy-five times. My boss is at the end of his patience, Sookie, and I don't blame him. I been gone from work at least two days, maybe three, with all the trips I been making down to the police station."

"Maybe you better get a lawyer," I said uneasily.

"That's what Rene said."

Then Rene Lenier and I saw eye to eye.

"What about Sid Matt Lancaster?" Sidney Matthew Lancaster, native son and a whiskey sour drinker, had the reputation of being the most aggressive trial lawyer in the parish. I liked him because he always treated me with respect when I served him in the bar.

"He might be my best bet." Jason looked as petulant and grim as a lovely person can. We exchanged a glance. We both knew Gran's lawyer was too old to handle the case if Jason was ever, God forbid, arrested.

Jason was far too self-absorbed to notice anything different about me, but I'd worn a white golf shirt (instead of my usual round-necked T-shirt) for the protection of its collar. Arlene was not as unaware as my brother. She'd been

204

eyeing me all morning, and by the time the three o'clock lull hit, she was pretty sure she'd got me figured out.

"Girl," she said, "you been having fun?"

I turned red as a beet. "Having fun" made my relationship with Bill lighter than it was, but it was accurate as far as it went. I didn't know whether to take the high road and say, "No, making love," or keep my mouth shut, or tell Arlene it was none of her business, or just shout, "Yes!"

"Oh, Sookie, who is the man?"

Uh-oh. "Um, well, he's not . . ."

"Not local? You dating one of those servicemen from Bossier City?"

"No," I said hesitantly.

"Sam? I've seen him looking at you."

"No."

"Who, then?"

I was acting like I was ashamed. Straighten your spine, Sookie Stackhouse, I told myself sternly. Pay the piper.

"Bill," I said, hoping against hope that she'd just say, "Oh, yeah."

"Bill," Arlene said blankly. I noticed Sam had drifted up and was listening. So was Charlsie Tooten. Even Lafayette stuck his head through the hatch.

"Bill," I said, trying to sound firm. "You know. Bill."

"Bill Auberjunois?"

"No."

"Bill . . . ?"

"Bill Compton," Sam said flatly, just as I opened my mouth to say the same thing. "Vampire Bill."

Arlene was flabbergasted, Charlsie Tooten immediately gave a little shriek, and Lafayette about dropped his bottom jaw.

"Honey, couldn't you just date a regular human fella?" Arlene asked when she got her voice back.

"A regular human fella didn't ask me out." I could feel the color fix in my cheeks. I stood there with my back straight, feeling defiant and looking it, I'm sure.

"But, sweetie," Charlsie Tooten fluted in her babyish voice, "honey . . . Bill's, ah, got that virus."

"I know that," I said, hearing the distinct edge in my voice.

"I thought you were going to say you were dating a black, but you've gone one better, ain't you, girl?" Lafayette said, picking at his fingernail polish.

Sam didn't say anything. He just stood leaning against the bar, and there was a white line around his mouth as if he were biting his cheek inside.

I stared at them all in turn, forcing them to either swallow this or spit it out.

Arlene got through it first. "All right, then. He better treat you good, or we'll get our stakes out!"

They were all able to laugh at that, albeit weakly.

"And you'll save a lot on groceries!" Lafayette pointed out.

But then in one step Sam ruined it all, that tentative acceptance, by suddenly moving to stand beside me and pull the collar of my shirt down.

You could have cut the silence of my friends with a knife.

"Oh, shit," Lafayette said, very softly.

I looked right into Sam's eyes, thinking I'd never forgive him for doing this to me.

"Don't you touch my clothes," I told him, stepping away from him and pulling the collar back straight. "Don't tend to my personal life."

"I'm scared for you, I'm worried about you," he said, as Arlene and Charlsie hastily found other things to do.

"No you're not, or not entirely. You're mad as hell. Well listen, buddy. You *never got in line.*"

And I stalked away to wipe down the formica on one of the tables. Then I collected all the salt shakers and refilled them. Then I checked the pepper shakers and the bottles of hot peppers on each table and booth, the Tabasco sauce, too. I just kept working and kept my eyes in front of me, and gradually, the atmosphere cooled down.

Sam was back in his office doing paperwork or something, I didn't care what, as long as he kept his opinions to himself. I still felt like he'd ripped the curtain off a private area of my life when he'd exposed my neck, and I hadn't forgiven him. But Arlene and Charlsie had found make-work, as I'd done, and by the time the after-work crowd began trickling in, we were once again fairly comfortable with one another.

Arlene came into the women's room with me. "Listen, Sookie, I got to ask. Are vampires all everyone says they are, in the lover department?"

I just smiled.

Bill came into the bar that evening, just after dark. I'd worked late since one of the evening waitresses had had car trouble. One minute he wasn't there, and the next minute he was, slowing down so I could see him coming. If Bill had any doubts about making our relationship public, he didn't show them. He lifted my hand and kissed it in a gesture that performed by anyone else would have seemed phony as hell. I felt the touch of his lips on the back of my hand all the way down to my toes, and I knew he could tell that.

"How are you this evening?" he whispered, and I shivered.

"A little . . ." I found I couldn't get the words out.

"You can tell me later," he suggested. "When are you through?"

"Just as soon as Susie gets here."

"Come to my house."

"Okay." I smiled up at him, feeling radiant and light-headed.

And Bill smiled back, though since my nearness had affected him, his fangs were showing, and maybe to anyone else but me the effect was a little — unsettling.

He bent to kiss me, just a light touch on the cheek, and he turned to leave. But just at that moment, the evening went all to hell.

Malcolm and Diane came in, flinging the door open as if they were making a grand entrance, and of course, they were. I wondered where Liam was. Probably parking the car. It was too much to hope they'd left him at home.

Folks in Bon Temps were getting accustomed to Bill, but the flamboyant Malcolm and the equally flamboyant Diane caused quite a stir. My first thought was that this wasn't going to help people get used to Bill and me.

Malcolm was wearing leather pants and a kind of chain-mail shirt. He looked like something on the cover of a rock album. Diane was wearing a one-piece lime green bodysuit spun out of Lycra or some other very thin, stretchy cloth. I was sure I could count her pubic hairs if I so desired. Blacks didn't come into Merlotte's much, but if any black was absolutely safe there, it was Diane. I saw Lafayette goggling through the hatch in open admiration, spiced by a dollop of fear.

The two vampires shrieked with feigned surprise when they saw Bill, like demented drunks.

As far as I could tell, Bill was not happy about their presence, but he seemed to handle their invasion calmly, as he did almost everything.

Malcolm kissed Bill on the mouth, and so did Diane. It was hard to tell which greeting was more offensive to the customers in the bar. Bill had better show distaste, and quick, I thought, if he wanted to stay in good with the human inhabitants of Bon Temps.

Bill, who was no fool, took a step back and put his arm around me, dissociating himself from the vampires and aligning himself with the humans.

"So your little waitress is still alive," Diane said, and her clear voice was audible through the whole bar. "Isn't that amazing."

"Her grandmother was murdered last week," Bill said quietly, trying to subdue Diane's desire to make a scene.

Her gorgeous lunatic brown eyes fixed on me, and I felt cold.

"Is that right?" she said and laughed.

That was it. No one would forgive her now. If Bill had been trying to find a way to entrench himself, this would be the scenario I would write. On the other hand, the disgust I could feel massing from the humans in the bar could backlash and wash over Bill as well as the renegades.

Of course . . . to Diane and her friends, Bill was the renegade.

"When's someone going to kill you, baby?"

She ran a fingernail under my chin, and I knocked her hand away.

She would have been on me if Malcolm hadn't grabbed her hand, lazily, almost effortlessly. But I saw the strain show in the way he was standing.

"Bill," he said conversationally, as if he wasn't exerting every muscle he had to keep Diane still, "I hear this town is losing its un-skilled service personnel at a terrible rate. And a little bird in Shreveport tells me you and your friend here were at Fangtasia asking questions about what vampire the murdered fang-bangers might have been with."

"You know that's for us to know, no one else," Malcolm continued, and all of a sudden his face was so serious it was truly terrifying. "Some of us don't want to go to — baseball — games and . . ." (here he was searching his memory for something disgustingly human, I could tell) "barbecues! We are Vampire!" He invested the word with majesty, with glamor, and I could tell a lot of the people in the bar were falling under his spell. Malcolm was intelligent enough to want to erase the bad impression he knew Diane had made, all the while showering contempt on those of us it had been made on.

I stomped on his instep with every ounce of weight I could muster. He showed his fangs at me. The people in the bar blinked and shook themselves.

"Why don't you just get outta here, mister," Rene said. He was slouched at the bar with his elbows flanking a beer.

There was a moment when things hung in the balance, when the bar could have turned into a bloodbath. None of my fellow humans seemed to quite comprehend how strong vampires were, or how ruthless. Bill had moved in front of me, a fact registered by every citizen in Merlotte's.

"Well, if we're not wanted . . ." Malcolm said. His thick-muscled masculinity warred with the fluting voice he suddenly affected. "These good people would like to eat meat, Diane, and do human things. By themselves. Or with our former friend Bill."

"I think the little waitress would like to do a very human thing with Bill," Diane began, when Malcolm caught her by the arm and propelled her from the room before she could cause more damage.

The entire bar seemed to shudder collectively when they were out the door, and I thought I better leave, even though Susie hadn't shown up yet. Bill waited for me outside; when I asked him why, he said he wanted to be sure they'd really left.

I followed Bill to his house, thinking we'd gotten off relatively lightly from the vampire visitation. I wondered why Diane and Malcolm had come; it seemed odd to me that they would be cruising so far from home and decide, on a whim, to drop in Merlotte's. Since they were making no real effort at assimilation, maybe they wanted to scotch Bill's prospects.

The Compton house was visibly different from the last time I'd been in, the sickening evening I'd met the other vampires.

The contractors were really coming through for Bill, whether because they were scared not to or because he was paying well, I didn't know. Maybe both. The living room was getting a new ceiling and the new wallpaper was white with a delicate flowered pattern. The hardwood floors had been cleaned, and they shone as they must have originally. Bill led me to the kitchen. It was sparse, naturally, but bright and cheerful and had a brand-new refrigerator full of bottled synthetic blood (yuck).

The downstairs bathroom was opulent.

As far as I knew, Bill never used the bathroom; at least for the primary human function. I stared around me in amazement.

The space for this grand bathroom had been achieved by including what had formerly been the pantry and about half the old kitchen.

"I like to shower," he said, pointing to a clear shower stall in one corner. It was big enough for two grownups and maybe a dwarf or two. "And I like to lie in warm water." He indicated the centerpiece of the room, a huge sort of tub surrounded by an indoor deck of cedar, with steps on two sides. There were potted plants arranged all around it. The room was as close to being in the middle of a very luxurious jungle as you could get in northern Louisiana.

"What is that?" I asked, awed.

"It's a portable spa," Bill said proudly. "It has jets you can adjust individually so each person can get the right force of water. It's a hot tub," he simplified.

"It has seats," I said, looking in. The interior was decorated around the top with green and blue tiles. There were fancy controls on the outside.

Bill turned them, and water began to surge.

"Maybe we can bathe together?" Bill suggested.

I felt my cheeks flame, and my heart began to pound a little faster.

"Maybe now?" Bill's fingers tugging at my shirt where it was tucked into my black shorts.

"Oh, well . . . maybe." I couldn't seem to look at him straight when I thought of how this — okay, man — had seen more of me than I'd ever let anyone see, including my doctor.

"Have you missed me?" he asked, his hands unbuttoning my shorts and peeling them down.

"Yes," I said promptly because I knew that to be true.

He laughed, even as he knelt to untie my Nikes. "What did you miss most, Sookie?"

"I missed your silence," I said without thinking at all.

He looked up. His fingers paused in the act of pulling the end of the bow to loosen it.

"My silence," he said.

"Not being able to hear your thoughts. You just can't imagine, Bill, how wonderful that is."

"I was thinking you'd say something else."

"Well, I missed that, too."

"Tell me about it," he invited, pulling my socks off and running his fingers up my thigh, tugging off the panties and shorts.

"Bill! I'm embarrassed," I protested.

"Sookie, don't be embarrassed with me. Least of anyone, with me." He was standing now, divesting me of my shirt and reaching behind me to unsnap my bra, running his hands over the marks the straps had made on my skin, turning his attention to my breasts. He toed off his sandals at some point.

"I'll try," I said, looking at my own toes.

"Undress me."

Now that I could do. I unbuttoned his shirt briskly and eased it out of his pants and off his shoulders. I unbuckled his belt and began to work on the waist button of his slacks. It was stiff, and I had quite a job.

I thought I was going to cry if the button didn't cooperate more. I felt clumsy and inept.

He took my hands and led them up to his chest. "Slow, Sookie, slow," he said, and his voice had gone soft and shivery. I could feel myself relaxing almost inch by inch, and I began to stroke his chest as he'd stroked mine, twining the curly hair around my fingers and gently pinching his flat nipples. His hand went behind my head and pressed gently. I hadn't known men liked that, but Bill sure did, so I paid equal attention to the other one. While I was doing that, my hands resumed work on the damn button, and this time it came undone with ease. I began pushing down his pants, sliding my fingers inside his Jockeys.

He helped me down into the spa, the water frothing around our legs.

"Shall I bathe you first?" he asked.

"No," I said breathlessly. "Give me the soap."

7

The next night Bill and I had an unsettling conversation. We were in his bed, his huge bed with the carved headboard and a brand-new Restonic mattress. His sheets were flowered like his wallpaper, and I remember wondering if he liked flowers printed on his possessions because he couldn't see the real thing, at least as they were meant to be seen . . . in the daylight.

Bill was lying on his side, looking down at me. We'd been to the movies; Bill was crazy about movies with aliens, maybe having some kindred feeling for space creatures. It had been a real shoot-em-up, with almost all the aliens being ugly, creepy, bent on killing. He'd fumed about that while he'd taken me out to eat, and then back to his place. I'd been glad when he'd suggested testing the new bed.

I was the first to lie on it with him.

He was looking at me, as he liked to do, I was learning. Maybe he was listening to my heart pounding, since he could hear things I couldn't, or maybe he was watching my pulse throb, because he could see things I couldn't, too. Our conversation had strayed from the movie we'd seen to the nearing parish elections (Bill was going to try to register to vote, absentee ballot), and then to our childhoods. I was realizing that Bill was trying desperately to remember what it had been like to be a regular person.

"Did you ever play 'show me yours' with your brother?" he asked. "They now say that's normal, but I will never forget my mother beating the tarnation out of my brother Robert after she found him in the bushes with Sarah."

"No," I said, trying to sound casual, but my face tightened, and I could feel the clenching of fear in my stomach.

"You're not telling the truth."

"Yes, I am." I kept my eyes fixed on his chin, hoping to think of some way to change the topic. But Bill was nothing if not persistent.

"Not your brother, then. Who?"

"I don't want to talk about this." My hands contracted into fists, and I could feel myself begin to shut down.

But Bill hated being evaded. He was used to people telling him whatever he wanted to know because he was used to using his glamor to get his way.

"Tell me, Sookie." His voice was coaxing, his eyes big pools of curiosity. He ran his thumb-nail down my stomach, and I shivered.

"I had a . . . funny uncle," I said, feeling the familiar tight smile stretch my lips.

He raised his dark arched brows. He hadn't heard the phrase.

I said as distantly as I could manage, "That's

an adult male relative who molests his . . . the children in the family."

His eyes began to burn. He swallowed; I could see his Adam's apple move. I grinned at him. My hands were pulling my hair back from my face. I couldn't stop it.

"And someone did this to you? How old were you?"

"Oh, it started when I was real little," and I could feel my breathing begin to speed up, my heart beat faster, the panicky traits that always came back when I remembered. My knees drew up and pressed together. "I guess I was five," I babbled, talking faster and faster, "I know you can tell, he never actually, ah, screwed me, but he did other stuff," and now my hands were shaking in front of my eyes where I held them to shield them from Bill's gaze. "And the worst thing, Bill, the worst thing," I went on, just unable to stop, "is that every time he came to visit, I always knew what he was going to do because I could read his mind! And there wasn't anything I could do to stop it!" I clamped my hands over my mouth to make myself shut up. I wasn't supposed to talk about it. I rolled over onto my stomach to conceal myself, and held my body absolutely rigid.

After a long time, I felt Bill's cool hand on my shoulder. It lay there, comforting.

"This was before your parents died?" he said in his usual calm voice. I still couldn't look at him.

"Yes."

"You told your mama? She did nothing?"

"No. She thought I was dirty minded, or that I'd found some book at the library that taught me something she didn't feel I was ready to know." I could remember her face, framed in hair about two shades darker than my medium blond. Her face pinched with distaste. She had come from a very conservative family, and any public display of affection or any mention of a subject she thought indecent was flatly discouraged.

"I wonder that she and my father seemed happy," I told my vampire. "They were so different." Then I saw how ludicrous my saying that was. I rolled over to my side. "As if we aren't," I told Bill, and tried to smile. Bill's face was quite still, but I could see a muscle in his neck jumping.

"Did you tell your father?"

"Yes, right before he died. I was too embarrassed to talk to him about it when I was younger; and Mother didn't believe me. But I couldn't stand it anymore, knowing I was going to see my great-uncle Bartlett at least two weekends out of every month when he drove up to visit."

"He still lives?"

"Uncle Bartlett? Oh, sure. He's Gran's brother, and Gran was my dad's mother. My uncle lives in Shreveport. But when Jason and I went to live with Gran, after my parents died, the first time Uncle Bartlett came to her house

I hid. When she found me and asked me why, I told her. And she believed me." I felt the relief of that day all over again, the beautiful sound of my grandmother's voice promising me I'd never have to see her brother again, that he would never never come to the house.

And he hadn't. She had cut off her own brother to protect me. He'd tried with Gran's daughter, Linda, too, when she was a small girl, but my grandmother had buried the incident in her own mind, dismissed it as something misunderstood. She had told me that she'd never left her brother alone with Linda at any time after that, had almost quit inviting him to her home, while not quite letting herself believe that he'd touched her little girl's privates.

"So he's a Stackhouse, too?"

"Oh, no. See, Gran became a Stackhouse when she married, but she was a Hale before." I wondered at having to spell this out for Bill. He was sure Southern enough, even if he was a vampire, to keep track of a simple family relationship like that.

Bill looked distant, miles away. I had put him off with my grim nasty little story, and I had chilled my own blood, that was for sure.

"Here, I'll leave," I said and slid out of bed, bending to retrieve my clothes. Quicker than I could see, he was off the bed and taking the clothes from my hands.

"Don't leave me now," he said. "Stay."

"I'm a weepy ol' thing tonight." Two tears

221

trickled down my cheeks, and I smiled at him.

His fingers wiped the tears from my face, and his tongue traced their marks.

"Stay with me till dawn," he said.

"But you have to get in your hidey hole by then."

"My what?"

"Wherever you spend the day. I don't want to know where it is!" I held up my hands to emphasize that. "But don't you have to get in there before it's even a little light?"

"Oh," he said, "I'll know. I can feel it coming."

"So you can't oversleep?"

"No."

"All right. Will you let me get some sleep?"

"Of course I will," he said with a gentlemanly bow, only a little off mark because he was naked. "In a little while." Then, as I lay down on the bed and held out my arms to him, he said, "Eventually."

Sure enough, in the morning I was in the bed by myself. I lay there for a little, thinking. I'd had little niggling thoughts from time to time, but for the first time the flaws in my relationship with the vampire hopped out of their own hidey hole and took over my brain.

I would never see Bill in the sunlight. I would never fix his breakfast, never meet him for lunch. (He could bear to watch me eat food, though he wasn't thrilled by the process, and I always had to brush my teeth afterward very thoroughly, which was a good habit anyway.)

I could never have a child by Bill, which was nice at least when you thought of not having to practice birth control, but . . .

I'd never call Bill at the office to ask him to stop on the way home for some milk. He'd never join the Rotary, or give a career speech at the high school, or coach Little League Baseball.

He'd never go to church with me.

And I knew that now, while I lay here awake — listening to the birds chirping their morning sounds and the trucks beginning to rumble down the road while all over Bon Temps people were getting up and putting on the coffee and fetching their papers and planning their day — that the creature I loved was lying somewhere in a hole underground, to all intents and purposes dead until dark.

I was so down by then that I had to think of an upside, while I cleaned up a little in the bathroom and dressed.

He seemed to genuinely care for me. It was kind of nice, but unsettling, not to know exactly how much.

Sex with him was absolutely great. I had never dreamed it would be that wonderful.

No one would mess with me while I was Bill's girlfriend. Any hands that had patted me in unwanted caresses were kept in their owners' laps, now. And if the person who'd killed my grandmother had killed her because she'd walked in on him while he was waiting for me, he wouldn't get another try at me.

And I could relax with Bill, a luxury so precious I could not put a value on it. My mind could range at will, and I would not learn anything he didn't tell me.

There was that.

It was in this kind of contemplative mood that I came down Bill's steps to my car.

To my amazement, Jason was there sitting in his pickup.

This was not exactly a happy moment. I trudged over to his window.

"I see it's true," he said. He handed me a Styrofoam cup of coffee from the Grabbit Quik. "Get in the truck with me."

I climbed in, pleased by the coffee but cautious overall. I put my guard up immediately. It slipped back into place slowly and painfully, like wiggling back into a girdle that was too tight in the first place.

"I can't say nothing," he told me. "Not after the way I lived my life these past few years. As near as I can tell, he's your first, isn't he?"

I nodded.

"He treat you good?"

I nodded again.

"I got something to tell you."

"Okay."

"Uncle Bartlett got killed last night."

I stared at him, the steam from the coffee

rising between us as I pried the lid off the cup. "He's dead," I said, trying to understand it. I'd worked hard never to think of him, and here I thought of him, and the next thing I heard, he was dead.

"Yep."

"Wow." I looked out the window at the rosy light on the horizon. I felt a surge of — freedom. The only one who remembered besides me, the only one who'd enjoyed it, who insisted to the end that I had initiated and continued the sick activities he thought were so gratifying . . . he was *dead*. I took a deep breath.

"I hope he's in hell," I said. "I hope every time he thinks of what he did to me, a demon pokes him in the butt with a pitchfork."

"God, Sookie!"

"He never messed with you."

"Damn straight!"

"Implying what?"

"Nothing, Sookie! But he never bothered anyone but you that I know of!"

"Bullshit. He molested Aunt Linda, too."

Jason's face went blank with shock. I'd finally gotten through to my brother. "Gran told you that?"

"Yes."

"She never said anything to me."

"Gran knew it was hard for you, not seeing him again when she could tell you loved him. But she couldn't let you be alone with him, because she couldn't be a hundred percent sure girls were all he wanted."

"I've seen him the past couple of years."

"You have?" This was news to me. It would have been news to Gran, too.

"Sookie, he was an old man. He was so sick. He had prostate trouble, and he was feeble, and he had to use a walker."

"That probably slowed him down chasing the five-year-olds."

"Get over it!"

"Right! Like I could!"

We glared at each other over the width of the truck seat.

"So what happened to him?" I asked finally, reluctantly.

"A burglar broke into his house last night."

"Yeah? And?"

"And broke his neck. Threw him down the stairs."

"Okay. So I know. Now I'm going home. I gotta shower and get ready for work."

"That's all you're saying?"

"What else is there to say?"

"Don't want to know about the funeral?"

"No."

"Don't want to know about his will?"

"No."

He threw up his hands. "All right," he said, as if he'd been arguing a point very hard with me and realized that I was intractable.

"What else? Anything?" I asked.

"No. Just your great-uncle dying. I thought

that was enough."

"Actually, you're right," I said, opening the truck door and sliding out. "That was enough." I raised my cup to him. "Thanks for the coffee, brother."

It wasn't till I got to work that it clicked.

I was drying a glass and really not thinking about Uncle Bartlett, and suddenly my fingers lost all strength.

"Jesus Christ, Shepherd of Judea," I said, looking down at the broken slivers of glass at my feet. "Bill had him killed."

I don't know why I was so sure I was right; but I was, the minute the idea crossed my mind. Maybe I had heard Bill dialing the phone when I was half-asleep. Maybe the expression on Bill's face when I'd finished telling him about Uncle Bartlett had rung a silent warning bell.

I wondered if Bill would pay the other vampire in money, or if he'd repay him in kind.

I got through work in a frozen state. I couldn't talk to anyone about what I was thinking, couldn't even say I was sick without someone asking me what was wrong. So I didn't speak at all, I just worked. I tuned out everything except the next order I had to fill. I drove home trying to feel just as frozen, but I had to face facts when I was alone.

I freaked out.

I had known, really I had, that Bill certainly had killed a human or two in his long, long, life. When he'd been a young vampire, when he'd needed lots of blood, before he'd gained control of his needs sufficiently to exist on a gulp here, a mouthful there, without actually killing anyone he drank from . . . he'd told me himself there'd been a death or two along the way. And he'd killed the Rattrays. But they'd have done me in that night in back of Merlotte's, without a doubt, if Bill hadn't intervened. I was naturally inclined to excuse him those deaths.

How was the murder of Uncle Bartlett different? He'd harmed me, too, dreadfully, made my already difficult childhood a true nightmare. Hadn't I been relieved, even pleased, to hear he'd been found dead? Didn't my horror at Bill's intervention reek of hypocrisy of the worst sort?

Yes. No?

Tired and incredibly confused, I sat on my front steps and waited in the darkness, my arms wrapped around my knees. The crickets were singing in the tall grass when he came, arriving so quietly and quickly I didn't hear him. One minute I was alone with the night, and the next, Bill was sitting on the steps beside me.

"What do you want to do tonight, Sookie?" His arm went around me.

"Oh, Bill." My voice was heavy with despair.

His arm dropped. I didn't look up at his face,

couldn't have seen it through the darkness, anyway.

"You should not have done it."

He didn't bother with denying it at least.

"I am glad he's dead, Bill. But I can't . . ."

"Do you think I would ever hurt you, Sookie?" His voice was quiet and rustling, like feet through dry grass.

"No. Oddly enough, I don't think you would hurt me, even if you were really mad at me."

"Then . . . ?"

"It's like dating the Godfather, Bill. I'm scared to say anything around you now. I'm not used to my problems being solved that way."

"I love you."

He'd never said it before, and I might almost have imagined it now, his voice was so low and whispery.

"Do you, Bill?" I didn't raise my face, kept my forehead pressed against my knees.

"Yes, I do."

"Then you have to let my life get lived, Bill, you can't alter it for me."

"You wanted me to alter it when the Rattrays were beating you."

"Point taken. But I can't have you trying to fine-tune my day-to-day life. I'm gonna get mad at people, people are gonna get mad at me. I can't worry about them being killed. I can't live like that, honey. You see what I'm saying?"

"Honey?" he repeated.

"I love you," I said. "I don't know why, but I do. I want to call you all those gooshy words you use when you love someone, no matter how stupid it sounds since you're a vampire. I want to tell you you're my baby, that I'll love you till we're old and gray — though that's not gonna happen. That I know you'll always be true to me — hey, that's not gonna happen either. I keep running up against a brick wall when I try to tell you I love you, Bill." I fell silent. I was all cried out.

"This crisis came sooner than I thought it would," Bill said from the darkness. The crickets had resumed their chorus, and I listened to them for a long moment.

"Yeah."

"What now, Sookie?"

"I have to have a little time."

"Before . . . ?"

"Before I decide if the love is worth the misery."

"Sookie, if you knew how different you taste, how much I want to protect you . . ."

I could tell from Bill's voice that these were very tender feelings he was sharing with me. "Oddly enough," I said, "that's what I feel about you. But I have to live here, and I have to live with myself, and I have to think about some rules we gotta get clear between us."

"So what do we do now?"

"I think. You go do whatever you were doing before we met."

"Trying to figure out if I could live mainstream. Trying to think of who I'd feed on, if I could stop drinking that damn synthetic blood."

"I know you'll — feed on someone else besides me." I was trying very hard to keep my voice level. "Please, not anyone here, not anyone I have to see. I couldn't bear it. It's not fair of me to ask, but I'm asking."

"If you won't date anyone else, won't bed anyone else."

"I won't." That seemed an easy enough promise to make.

"Will you mind if I come into the bar?"

"No. I'm not telling anyone we're apart. I'm not talking about it."

He leaned over, I could feel the pressure on my arm as his body pressed against it.

"Kiss me," he said.

I lifted my head and turned, and our lips met. It was blue fire, not orange-and-red flames, not that kind of heat: blue fire. After a second, his arms went around me. After another, my arms went around him. I began to feel boneless, limp. With a gasp, I pulled away.

"Oh, we can't, Bill."

I heard his breath draw in. "Of course not, if we're separating," he said quietly, but he didn't sound like he thought I meant it. "We should definitely not be kissing. Still less should I want to throw you back on the porch and fuck you till you faint."

231

My knees were actually shaking. His deliberately crude language, coming out in that cold sweet voice, made the longing inside me surge even higher. It took everything I had, every little scrap of self-control, to push myself up and go in the house.

But I did it.

In the following week, I began to craft a life without Gran and without Bill. I worked nights and worked hard. I was extra careful, for the first time in my life, about locks and security. There was a murderer out there, and I no longer had my powerful protector. I considered getting a dog, but couldn't decide what kind I wanted. My cat, Tina, was only protection in the sense that she always reacted when someone came very near the house.

I got calls from Gran's lawyer from time to time, informing me about the progress of winding up her estate. I got calls from Bartlett's lawyer. My great-uncle had left me twenty thousand dollars, a great sum for him. I almost turned down the legacy. But I thought again. I gave the money to the local mental health center, earmarking it for the treatment of children who were victims of molestation and rape.

They were glad to get it.

I took vitamins, loads of them, because I was a little anemic. I drank lots of fluids and ate lots of protein.

And I ate as much garlic as I wanted, something Bill hadn't been able to tolerate. He said it came out through my pores, even, when I had garlic bread with spaghetti and meat sauce one night.

I slept and slept and slept. Staying up nights after a work shift had me rest-deprived.

After three days I felt restored, physically. In fact, it seemed to me that I was a little stronger than I had been.

I began to take in what was happening around me.

The first thing I noticed was that local folks were really pissed off at the vampires who nested in Monroe. Diane, Liam, and Malcolm had been touring bars in the area, apparently trying to make it impossible for other vampires who wanted to mainstream. They'd been behaving outrageously, offensively. The three vampires made the escapades of the Louisiana Tech students look bland.

They didn't seem to ever imagine they were endangering themselves. The freedom of being out of the coffin had gone to their heads. The right to legally exist had withdrawn all their constraints, all their prudence and caution. Malcolm nipped at a bartender in Bogaloosas. Diane danced naked in Farmerville. Liam dated an underage girl in Shongaloo, and her mother, too. He took blood from both. He didn't erase the memory of either.

Rene was talking to Mike Spencer, the funeral director, in Merlotte's one Thursday night, and they hushed when I got near. Naturally, that caught my attention. So I read Mike's mind. A group of local men were thinking of burning out the Monroe vampires.

I didn't know what to do. The three were, if not exactly friends of Bill, at least sort of coreligionists. But I loathed Malcolm, Diane, and Liam just as much as anyone else. On the other hand; and boy — there always was another hand, wasn't there? — it just went against my grain to know ahead of the fact about premeditated murders and just sit on my hands.

Maybe this was all liquor talking. Just to check, I dipped into the minds of the people around me. To my dismay, many of them were thinking about torching the vampires' nest. But I couldn't track down the origin of the idea. It felt as though the poison had flowed from one mind and infected others.

There wasn't any proof, any proof at all, that Maudette and Dawn and my grandmother had been killed by a vampire. In fact, rumor had it that the coroner's report might show evidence against that. But the three vampires were behaving in such a way that people wanted to blame them for something, wanted to get rid of them, and since Maudette and Dawn were both vampire-bitten and habitues of vampire bars, well, folks just cobbled that together to pound out a conviction.

Bill came in the seventh night I'd been alone. He appeared at his table quite suddenly. He wasn't by himself. There was a boy with him, a boy who looked maybe fifteen. He was a vampire, too.

"Sookie, this is Harlen Ives from Minneapolis," Bill said, as if this were an ordinary introduction.

"Harlen," I said, and nodded. "Pleased to meet you."

"Sookie." He bobbed his head at me, too.

"Harlen is in transit from Minnesota to New Orleans," Bill said, sounding positively chatty.

"I'm going on vacation," Harlen said. "I've been wanting to visit New Orleans for years. It's just a mecca for us, you know."

"Oh . . . right," I said, trying to sound matter of fact.

"There's this number you can call," Harlen informed me. "You can stay with an actual resident, or you can rent a . . ."

"Coffin?" I asked brightly.

"Well, yes."

"How nice for you," I said, smiling for all I was worth. "What can I get you? I believe Sam has restocked the blood, Bill, if you'd like some? It's flavored A neg, or we've got the O positive."

"Oh, A negative, I think," Bill said, after he and Harlen had a silent communication.

"Coming right up!" I stomped back to the cooler behind the bar and pulled out two A neg's, popped the tops, and carted them back on a tray. I smiled the whole time, just like I used to.

"Are you all right, Sookie?" Bill asked in a more natural voice after I'd plonked their drinks down in front of them.

"Of course, Bill," I said cheerily. I wanted to break the bottle over Bill's head. Harlen, indeed. Overnight stay. Right.

"Harlen would like to drive over to visit Malcolm, later," Bill said, when I came to take the empties and ask if they wanted a refill.

"I'm sure Malcolm would love to meet Harlen," I said, trying not to sound as bitchy as I felt.

"Oh, meeting Bill has just been super," Harlen said, smiling at me, showing fangs. Harlen knew how to do bitch, all right. "But Malcolm is absolutely a legend."

"Watch out," I said to Bill. I wanted to tell him how much peril the three nesting vampires had put themselves into, but I didn't think it'd come to a head just yet. And I didn't want to spell it out because Harlen was sitting there, batting his baby blues at me and looking like a teen sex symbol. "Nobody's too happy with those three, right now," I added, after a moment. It was not an effectual warning.

Bill just looked at me, puzzled, and I spun on my heel and walked away.

I came to regret that moment, regret it bitterly.

After Bill and Harlen had left, the bar buzzed even harder with the kind of talk I'd heard from

Rene and Mike Spencer. It seemed to me like someone had been lighting fire, keeping the anger level stoked up. But for the life of me I couldn't discover who it was, though I did some random listening, both mental and physical. Jason came into the bar, and we said hello, but not much more. He hadn't forgiven me for my reaction to Uncle Bartlett's death.

He'd get over it. At least he wasn't thinking about burning anything, except maybe creating some heat in Liz Barrett's bed. Liz, even younger than me, had curly short brown hair and big brown eyes and an unexpectedly no-nonsense air about her that made me think Jason might have met his match. After I'd said good-bye to them after their pitcher of beer was empty, I realized that the anger level in the bar had escalated, that the men were really serious about doing something.

I began to be more than anxious.

As the evening wore on, the activity in the bar grew more and more frenetic. Less women, more men. More table-hopping. More drinking. Men were standing, instead of sitting. It was hard to pin down, since there wasn't any big meeting, really. It was by word-of-mouth, whispered from ear to ear. No one jumped on the bar and screamed, "Whatta ya say, boys? Are we gonna put up with those monsters in our midst? To the castle!" or anything like that. It was just that, after a time, they all began drifting out, standing in huddled groups out in the parking lot. I looked out one of the windows at them, shaking my head. This wasn't good.

Sam was uneasy, too.

"What do you think?" I asked him, and I realized this was the first time I'd spoken to him all evening, other than "Pass the pitcher," or "Give me another margarita."

"I think we've got a mob," he said. "But they'll hardly go over to Monroe now. The vampires'll be up and about until dawn."

"Where is their house, Sam?"

"I understand it's on the outskirts of Monroe on the west side — in other words, closest to us," he told me. "I don't know for sure."

I drove home after closing, half hoping I'd see Bill lurking in my driveway so I could tell him what was afoot.

But I didn't see him, and I wouldn't go to his house. After a long hesitation, I dialed his number, but got only his answering machine. I left a message. I had no idea what the three nesting vampires' phone was listed under, if they had a phone at all.

As I pulled off my shoes and removed my jewelry — all silver, take that, Bill! — I remember worrying, but I wasn't worrying enough. I went to bed and quickly to sleep in the bedroom that was now mine. The moonlight streamed in the open shades, making strange shadows on the floor. But I only stared at them for a few minutes. Bill didn't wake me that night, returning my call.

But the phone did ring, early in the morning, after daylight.

"What?" I asked, dazed, the receiver pressed to my ear. I peered at the clock. It was seven-thirty.

"They burned the vampires' house," Jason said. "I hope yours wasn't in it."

"What?" I asked again, but my voice was panicked now.

"They burned the vampires' house outside of Monroe. After sunrise. It's on Callista Street, west of Archer."

I remembered Bill saying he might take Harlen over there. Had he stayed?

"No." I said it definitely.

"Yes."

"I have to go," I said, hanging up the phone.

It smoldered in the bright sunlight. Wisps of smoke trailed up into the blue sky. Charred wood looked like alligator skin. Fire trucks and law enforcement cars were parked helter-skelter on the lawn of the two-story house. A group of the curious stood behind yellow tape.

The remains of four coffins sat side by side on the scorched grass. There was a body bag, too. I began to walk toward them, but for the longest time they seemed to be no closer; it was like one of those dreams where you can never reach your goal.

Someone grabbed my arm and tried to stop me. I can't remember what I said, but I remember a horrified face. I trudged on through the debris, inhaling the smell of burned things, wet charred things, a smell that wouldn't leave me the rest of my life.

I reached the first coffin and looked in. What was left of the lid was open to the light. The sun was coming up; any moment now it would kiss the dreadful thing resting on soggy, white silk lining.

Was it Bill? There was no way to tell. The corpse was disintegrating bit by bit even as I watched. Tiny fragments flaked off and blew into the breeze, or disappeared in a tiny puff of smoke where the sun's rays began to touch the body.

Each coffin held a similar horror.

Sam was standing by me.

"Can you call this murder, Sam?"

He shook his head. "I just don't know, Sookie. Legally, killing the vampires is murder. But you'd have to prove arson first, though I don't think that'd be very hard." We could both smell gasoline. There were men buzzing around the house, climbing here and there, yelling to each other. It didn't appear to me that these men were conducting any serious crime-scene investigation.

"But this body here, Sookie." Sam pointed to

the body bag on the grass. "This was a real human, and they have to investigate. I don't think any member of that mob ever realized there might be a human in there, ever considered anything besides what they did."

"So why are you here, Sam?"

"For you," he said simply.

"I won't know if it's Bill all day, Sam."

"Yes, I know."

"What am I supposed to do all day? How can I wait?"

"Maybe some drugs," he suggested. "What about sleeping pills or something?"

"I don't have anything like that," I said. "I've never had trouble sleeping."

This conversation was getting odder and odder, but I don't think I could have said anything else.

A big man was in front of me, the local law. He was sweating in the morning heat, and he looked like he'd been up for hours. Maybe he'd been on the night shift and had to stay on when the fire started.

When men I knew had started the fire.

"Did you know these people, miss?"

"Yes, I did. I'd met them."

"Can you identify the remains?"

"Who could identify that?" I asked incredulously.

The bodies were almost gone now, featureless and disintegrating.

He looked sick. "Yes, ma'am. But the person."

"I'll look," I said before I had time to think. The habit of being helpful was mighty hard to break.

As if he could tell I was about to change my mind, the big man knelt on the singed grass and unzipped the bag. The sooty face inside was that of a girl I'd never met. I thanked God.

"I don't know her," I said, and felt my knees give. Sam caught me before I was on the ground, and I had to lean against him.

"Poor girl," I whispered. "Sam, I don't know what to do."

The law took part of my time that day. They wanted to know everything I knew about the vampires who had owned the house, and I told them, but it didn't amount to much. Malcolm, Diane, Liam. Where they'd come from, their age, why they'd settled in Monroe, who their lawyers were; how would I know anything like that? I'd never even been to their house before.

When my questioner, whoever he was, found out that I'd met them through Bill, he wanted to know where Bill was, how he could contact him.

"He may be right there," I said, pointing to the fourth coffin. "I won't know till dark." My hand rose of its own volition and covered my mouth.

Just then one of the firemen started to laugh, and his companion, too. "Southern fried vampires!" the shorter one hooted to the man who was questioning me. "We got us some Southern fried vampires here!"

He didn't think it was so damn funny when I kicked him. Sam pulled me off and the man who'd been questioning me grabbed the fireman I'd attacked. I was screaming like a banshee and would have gone for him again if Sam had let go.

But he didn't. He dragged me toward my car, his hands just as strong as bands of iron. I had a sudden vision of how ashamed my grand-mother would have been to see me screaming at a public servant, to see me physically attack someone. The idea pricked my crazy hostility like a needle puncturing a balloon. I let Sam shove me into the passenger's seat, and when he started the car and began backing away, I let him drive me home while I sat in utter silence.

We got to my house all too soon. It was only ten o'clock in the morning. Since it was day-light savings time I had at least ten plus hours to wait.

Sam made some phone calls while I sat on the couch staring ahead of me. Five minutes had passed when he came back into the living room.

"Come on, Sookie," he said briskly. "These blinds are filthy."

"What?"

"The blinds. How could you have let them go like this?"

"What?"

"We're going to clean. Get a bucket and

some ammonia and some rags. Make some coffee."

Moving slowly and cautiously, afraid I might dry up and blow away like the bodies in the coffins, I did as he bid me.

Sam had the curtains down on the living-room windows by the time I got back with the bucket and rags.

"Where's the washing machine?"

"Back there, off the kitchen," I said, pointing.

Sam went back to the washroom with an armful of curtains. Gran had washed those not a month ago, for Bill's visit. I didn't say a word.

I lowered one of the blinds, closed it, and began washing. When the blinds were clean, we polished the windows themselves. It began raining about the middle of the morning. We couldn't get the outside. Sam got the long-handled dust mop and got the spider webs out of the corners of the high ceiling, and I wiped down the baseboards. He took down the mirror over the mantel, dusted the parts that we couldn't normally reach, and then we cleaned the mirror and rehung it. I cleaned the old marble fireplace till there wasn't a trace of winter's fire left. I got a pretty screen and put it over the fireplace, one painted with magnolia blossoms. I cleaned the television screen and had Sam lift it so I could dust underneath. I put all the movies back in their own boxes and labeled what I'd taped. I took all the cushions off the couch and vacuumed up the debris that had collected beneath them, finding a dollar and five cents in change. I vacuumed the carpet and used the dust mop on the wood floors.

We moved into the dining room and polished everything that could be polished. When the wood of the table and chairs was gleaming, Sam asked me how long it'd been since I'd done Gran's silver.

I hadn't ever polished Gran's silver. We opened the buffet to find that, yes, it certainly needed it. So into the kitchen we carried it, and we found the silver polish, and we polished away. The radio was on, but I gradually realized that Sam was turning it off every time the news began.

We cleaned all day. It rained all day. Sam only spoke to me to direct me to the next task.

I worked very hard. So did he.

By the time the light was growing dim, I had the cleanest house in Renard Parish.

Sam said, "I'm going now, Sookie. I think you want to be alone."

"Yes," I said. "I want to thank you some time, but I can't thank you now. You saved me today."

I felt his lips on my forehead and then a minute later I heard the door slam. I sat at the table while the darkness began to fill the kitchen. When I almost could not see, I went outside. I took my big flashlight.

It didn't matter that it was still raining. I had on a sleeveless denim dress and a pair of sandals, what I'd pulled on that morning after Jason had called me.

I stood in the pouring warm rain, my hair plastered to my skull and my dress clinging wetly to my skin. I turned left to the woods and began to make my way through them, slowly and carefully at first. As Sam's calming influence began to evaporate, I began to run, tearing my cheeks on branches, scratching my legs on thorny vines. I came out of the woods and began to dash through the cemetery, the beam of the flashlight bobbing before me. I had thought I was going to the house on the other side, the Compton house: but then I knew Bill must be here, somewhere in this six acres of bones and stones. I stood in the center of the oldest part of the graveyard, surrounded by monuments and modest tombstones, in the company of the dead.

I screamed, "Bill Compton! Come out now!"

I turned in circles, looking around in the near-blackness, knowing even if I couldn't see him, Bill would be able to see me, if he could see anything — if he wasn't one of those blackened, flaking atrocities I'd seen in the front yard of the house outside Monroe.

No sound. No movement except the falling of the gentle drenching rain.

"Bill! Bill! Come out!"

I felt, rather than heard, movement to my right. I turned the beam of the flashlight in that direction. The ground was buckling. As I watched, a white hand shot up from the red soil. The dirt began to heave and crumble. A figure climbed out of the ground.

"Bill?"

It moved toward me. Covered with red streaks, his hair full of dirt, Bill took a hesitant step in my direction.

I couldn't even go to him.

"Sookie," he said, very close to me, "why are you here?" For once, he sounded disoriented and uncertain.

I had to tell him, but I couldn't open my mouth.

"Sweetheart?"

I went down like a stone. I was abruptly on my knees in the sodden grass.

"What happened while I slept?" He was kneeling by me, bare and streaming with rain.

"You don't have clothes on," I murmured.

"They'd just get dirty," he said sensibly. "When I'm going to sleep in the soil, I take them off."

"Oh. Sure."

"Now you have to tell me."

"You have to not hate me."

"What have you done?"

"Oh my God, it wasn't me! But I could have warned you more, I could have grabbed you and made you listen. I tried to call you, Bill!"

"What has happened?"

I put one hand on either side of his face, touching his skin, realizing how much I would

247

have lost, how much I might yet lose.

"They're dead, Bill, the vampires from Monroe. And someone else with them."

"Harlen," he said tonelessly. "Harlen stayed over last night, he and Diane really hit it off." He waited for me to finish, his eyes fixed on mine.

"They were burned."

"On purpose."

"Yes."

He squatted beside me in the rain, in the dark, his face not visible to me. The flashlight was gripped in my hand, and all my strength had ebbed away. I could feel his anger.

I could feel his cruelty.

I could feel his hunger.

He had never been more completely vampire. There wasn't anything human in him.

He turned his face to the sky and howled.

I thought he might kill someone, the rage rolling off him was so great. And the nearest person was me.

As I comprehended my own danger, Bill gripped my upper arms. He pulled me to him, slowly. There was no point in struggling, in fact I sensed that would only excite Bill more. Bill held me about an inch from him, I could almost smell his skin, and I could feel the turmoil in him, I could taste his rage.

Directing that energy in another way might save me. I leaned that inch, put my mouth on his chest. I licked the rain off, rubbed my cheek against his nipple, pressed myself against him.

The next moment his teeth grazed my shoulder, and his body, hard and rigid and ready, shoved me so forcefully I was suddenly on my back in the mud. He slid directly into me as if he were trying to reach through me to the soil. I shrieked, and he growled in response, as though we were truly mud people, primitives from caves. My hands, gripping the flesh of his back, felt the rain pelting down and the blood under my nails, and his relentless movement. I thought I would be plowed into this mud, into my grave. His fangs sank into my neck.

Suddenly I came. Bill howled as he reached his own completion, and he collapsed on me, his fangs pulling out and his tongue cleaning the puncture marks.

I had thought he might kill me without even meaning to.

My muscles would not obey me, even if I had known what I wanted to do. Bill scooped me up. He took me to his house, pushing open the door and carrying me straight through into the large bathroom. Laying me gently on the carpet, where I spread mud and rainwater and a little streak of blood, Bill turned on the warm water in the spa, and when it was full he put me in and then got in himself. We sat on the seats, our legs trailing out in the warm frothing water that became discolored quickly.

Bill's eyes were staring miles away.

"All dead?" he said, his voice nearly inaudible.

"All dead, and a human girl, too," I said quietly.

"What have you been doing all day?"

"Cleaning. Sam made me clean my house."

"Sam," Bill said thoughtfully. "Tell me, Sookie. Can you read Sam's mind?"

"No," I confessed, suddenly exhausted. I submerged my head, and when I came up, Bill had gotten the shampoo bottle. He soaped my hair and rinsed it, combed it as he had the first time we'd made love.

"Bill, I'm sorry about your friends," I said, so exhausted I could hardly get the words out. "And I am so glad you are alive." I slid my arms around his neck and lay my head on his shoulder. It was hard as a rock. I remember Bill drying me off with a big white towel, and I remember thinking how soft the pillow was, and I remember him sliding into bed beside me and putting his arm around me. Then I fell into sleep.

In the small hours of the morning, I woke halfway to hear someone moving around the room. I must have been dreaming, and it must have been bad, because I woke with my heart racing. "Bill?" I asked, and I could hear the fear in my voice.

"What's wrong?" he asked, and I felt the bed indent as he sat on the edge.

"Are you all right?"

"Yes, I was just out walking."

"No one's out there?"

"No, sweetheart." I could hear the sound of cloth moving over skin, and then he was under the sheets with me.

"Oh, Bill, that could have been you in one of those coffins," I said, the agony still fresh in my mind.

"Sookie, did you ever think that could have been you in the body bag? What if they come here, to burn this house, at dawn?"

"You have to come to my house! They won't burn my house. You can be safe with me," I said earnestly.

"Sookie, listen: because of me you could die."

"What would I lose?" I asked, hearing the passion in my voice. "I've had the best time since I met you, the best time of my life!"

"If I die, go to Sam."

"Passing me along already?"

"Never," he said, and his smooth voice was cold. "Never." I felt his hands grip my shoulders; he was on one elbow beside me. He scooted a little closer, and I could feel the cool length of his body.

"Listen, Bill," I said. "I'm not educated, but I'm not stupid. I'm not real experienced or worldly, either, but I don't think I'm naive." I hoped he wasn't smiling in the dark. "I can make them accept you. I can."

"If anyone can, you will," he said. "I want to enter you again."

"You mean — ? Oh, yeah. I see what you mean." He'd taken my hand and guided it down to him. "I'd like that, too." And I sure would, if I could survive it after the pounding I'd taken in the graveyard. Bill had been so angry that now I felt battered. But I could also feel that liquidy warm feeling running through me, that restless excitement to which Bill had addicted me. "Honey," I said, caressing him up and down his length, "honey." I kissed him, felt his tongue in my mouth. I touched his fangs with my own tongue. "Can you do it without biting?" I whispered.

"Yes. It's just like a grand finale when I taste your blood."

"Would it be almost as good without?"

"It can never be as good without, but I don't want to weaken you."

"If you wouldn't mind," I said tentatively. "It took me a few days to feel up to par."

"I've been selfish . . . you're just so good."

"If I'm strong, it'll be even better," I suggested.

"Show me how strong you are," he said teasingly.

"Lie on your back. I'm not real sure how this works, but I know other people do it." I straddled him, heard his breathing quicken. I was glad the room was dark and outside the rain was still pouring. A flash of lightning showed

252

me his eyes, glowing. I carefully maneuvered into what I hoped was the correct position, and guided him inside me. I had great faith in instinct, and sure enough it didn't play me false.

8

Together again, my doubts at least temporarily drenched by the fear I'd felt when I'd thought I might have lost him, Bill and I settled into an uneasy routine.

If I worked nights, I would go over to Bill's house when I finished, and usually I spent the rest of the night there. If I worked days, Bill would come to my house after sunset, and we would watch TV, or go to the movies, or play Scrabble. I had to have every third night off, or Bill had to refrain from biting those nights; otherwise I began to feel weak and draggy. And there was the danger, if Bill fed on me too much . . . I kept chugging vitamins and iron until Bill complained about the flavor. Then I cut back on the iron.

When I slept at night, Bill would go do other stuff. Sometimes he read, sometimes he wandered the night; sometimes he'd go out and do my yard work under the illumination of the security lights.

If he ever took blood from anyone else, he kept it secret, and he did it far from Bon Temps, which was what I had asked.

I say this routine was uneasy because it seemed to me that we were waiting. The burning of the Monroe nest had enraged Bill and (I think) frightened him. To be so powerful when awake and so helpless when asleep had to be galling.

Both of us were wondering if public feeling against vampires would abate now that the worst troublemakers in the area were dead.

Though Bill didn't say anything directly, I knew from the course our conversation took from time to time that he was worried about my safety with the murderer of Dawn, Maudette, and my grandmother still at large.

If the men of Bon Temps and the surrounding towns thought burning out the Monroe vampires would set their minds at ease about the murders, they were wrong. Autopsy reports from the three victims finally proved they had their full complement of blood when they were killed. Furthermore, the bite marks on Maudette and Dawn had not only looked old, they were proved to be old. The cause of their deaths was strangulation. Maudette and Dawn had had sex before they'd died. And afterward.

Arlene and Charlsie and I were cautious about things like going out into the parking lot by ourselves, making sure our homes were still locked tight before we entered them, trying to notice what cars were around us as we drove. But it's hard to keep careful that way, a real strain on the nerves, and I am sure we all lapsed back into our sloppy ways. Maybe it was more excusable for Arlene and Charlsie, since they lived with other people, unlike the first two victims; Arlene with her kids (and Rene Lenier, off and on), and Charlsie with her husband, Ralph.

I was the only one who lived alone.

Jason came into the bar almost every night, and he made a point of talking to me every time. I realized he was trying to heal whatever breach lay between us, and I responded as much as I could. But Jason was drinking more, too, and his bed had as many occupants as a public toilet, though he seemed to have real feelings for Liz Barrett. We worked cautiously together on settling the business of Gran's estate and Uncle Bartlett's, though he had more to do with that than I. Uncle Bartlett had left Jason everything but my legacy.

Jason told me one night when he'd had an extra beer that he'd been back to the police station twice more, and it was driving him crazy. He'd talked to Sid Matt Lancaster, finally, and Sid Matt had advised Jason not to go to the police station any more unless Sid Matt went with him.

"How come they keep hauling you in?" I asked Jason. "There must be something you haven't told me. Andy Bellefleur hasn't kept after anybody else, and I know Dawn and Maudette both weren't too picky about who came home with them."

Jason looked mortified. I'd never seen my beautiful older brother look as embarrassed.

"Movies," he mumbled.

I bent closer to be sure I'd heard him right. "Movies?" I said, incredulously.

"Shhh," he hissed, looking guilty as hell. "We made movies."

I guess I was just as embarrassed as Jason. Sisters and brothers don't need to know everything about each other. "And you gave them a copy," I said tentatively, trying to figure out just how dumb Jason had been.

He looked off in another direction, his hazy blue eyes romantically shiny with tears.

"Moron," I said. "Even allowing for the fact that you couldn't know how this was gonna come to public light, what's gonna happen when you decide to get married? What if one of your ex-flames mails a copy of your little tango to your bride-to-be?"

"Thanks for kicking me when I'm down, Sis."

I took a deep breath. "Okay, okay. You've quit making these little videos, right?"

He nodded emphatically. I didn't believe him.

"And you told Sid Matt all about it, right?"
He nodded less firmly.

"And you think that's why Andy is on your case so much?"

"Yeah," Jason said morosely.

"So, if they test your semen and it isn't a match for what was inside Maudette and Dawn, you're clear." By now, I was as shifty-

257

faced as my brother. We had never talked about semen samples before.

"That's what Sid Matt says. I just don't trust that stuff."

My brother didn't trust the most reliable scientific evidence that could be presented in a court. "You think Andy's going to fake the results?"

"No, Andy's okay. He's just doing his job. I just don't know about that DNA stuff."

"Moron," I said, and turned away to get another pitcher of beer for four guys from Ruston, college students on a big night out in the boonies. I could only hope Sid Matt Lancaster was good at persuasion.

I spoke to Jason once more before he left Merlotte's. "Can you help me?" he asked, turning up to me a face I hardly recognized. I was standing by his table, and his date for the night had gone to the ladies' room.

My brother had never asked me for help before.

"How?"

"Can't you just read the minds of the men who come in here and find out if one of them did it?"

"That's not as easy as it sounds, Jason," I said slowly, thinking as I went along. "For one thing, the man would have to be thinking of his crime while he sat here, at the exact moment I listened in. For another thing, I can't always read clear thoughts. Some people, it's just like listening to a radio, I can hear every little thing. Other people, I just get a mass of feelings, not spelled out; it's like hearing someone talk in their sleep, see? You can hear they're talking, you can tell if they're upset or happy, but you can't hear the exact words. And then other times, I can hear a thought, but I can't trace it to its source if the room is crowded."

Jason was staring at me. It was the first time we had talked openly about my disability.

"How do you stop from going crazy?" he asked, shaking his head in amazement.

I was about to try to explain putting up my guard, but Liz Barrett returned to the table, newly lipsticked and fluffed. I watched Jason resume his woman-hunting persona like shrugging on a heavy coat, and I regretted not getting to talk to him more when he was by himself.

That night, as the staff got ready to leave, Arlene asked me if I could baby-sit for her the next evening. It would be an off-day for both of us, and she wanted to go to Shreveport with Rene to see a movie and go out to eat.

"Sure!" I said. "I haven't kept the kids in a while."

Suddenly Arlene's face froze. She half-turned to me, opened her mouth, thought the better of speaking, then thought again. "Will . . . ah . . . will Bill be there?"

"Yes, we'd planned on watching a movie. I was going to stop by the video rental place, tomorrow morning. But I'll get something for the kids to watch instead." Abruptly, I caught her meaning. "Whoa. You mean you don't want to leave the kids with me if Bill's gonna be there?" I could feel my eyes narrow to slits and my voice drop down to its angry register.

"Sookie," she began helplessly, "honey, I love you. But you can't understand, you're not a mother. I can't leave my kids with a vampire. I just can't."

"No matter that I'm there, and I love your kids, too? No matter that Bill would never in a million years harm a child." I slung my purse over my shoulder and stalked out the back door, leaving Arlene standing there looking torn. By golly, she ought to be upset!

I was a little calmer by the time I turned onto the road to go home, but I was still riled up. I was worried about Jason, miffed at Arlene, and almost permanently frosted at Sam, who was pretending these days that I was a mere acquaintance. I debated whether to just go home rather than going to Bill's; decided that was a good idea.

It was a measure of how much he worried about me that Bill was at my house about fifteen minutes after I should have been at his.

"You didn't come, you didn't call," he said quietly when I answered the door.

"I'm in a temper," I said. "A bad one."

Wisely he kept his distance.

"I apologize for making you worry," I said

after a moment. "I won't do that again." I strode away from him, toward the kitchen. He followed behind, or at least I presumed he did. Bill was so quiet you never knew until you looked.

He leaned against the door frame as I stood in the middle of the kitchen floor, wondering why I'd come in the room, feeling a rising tide of anger. I was getting pissed off all over again. I really wanted to throw something, damage something. This was not the way I'd been brought up, to give way to destructive impulses like that. I contained it, screwing my eyes shut, clenching my fists.

"I'm gonna dig a hole," I said, and I marched out the back door. I opened the door to the tool shed, removed the shovel, and stomped to the back of the yard. There was a patch back there where nothing ever grew, I don't know why. I sunk the shovel in, pushed it with my foot, came up with a hunk of soil. I kept on going. The pile of dirt grew as the hole deepened.

"I have excellent arm and shoulder muscles," I said, resting against the shovel and panting.

Bill was sitting in a lawn chair watching. He didn't say anything.

I resumed digging.

Finally, I had a really nice hole.

"Were you going to bury anything?" Bill asked, when he could tell I was done.

"No." I looked down at the cavity in the

ground. "I'm going to plant a tree."

"What kind?"

"A live oak," I said off the top of my head.

"Where can you get one?"

"At the Garden Center. I'll go sometime this week."

"They take a long time to grow."

"What difference would that make to you?" I snapped. I put the shovel up in the shed, then leaned against it, suddenly exhausted.

Bill made as if to pick me up.

"I am a *grown woman*," I snarled. "I can walk into the house on my own."

"Have I done something to you?" Bill asked. There was very little loving in his voice, and I was brought up short. I had indulged myself enough.

"I apologize," I said. "Again."

"What has made you so angry?"

I just couldn't tell him about Arlene.

"What do you do when you get mad, Bill?"

"I tear up a tree," he said. "Sometimes I hurt someone."

Digging a hole didn't seem so bad. It had been sort of constructive. But I was still wired — it was just more of a subdued buzz than a high-frequency whine. I cast around restlessly for something to affect.

Bill seemed adept at reading the symptoms. "Make love," he suggested. "Make love with me."

"I'm not in the right mood for love."

"Let me try to persuade you."

It turned out he could.

At least it wore off the excess energy of anger, but I still had a residue of sadness that sex couldn't cure. Arlene had hurt my feelings. I stared into space while Bill braided my hair, a pastime that he apparently found soothing.

Every now and then I felt like I was Bill's doll.

"Jason was in the bar tonight," I said.

"What did he want?"

Bill was too clever by far, sometimes, at reading people.

"He appealed to my mind-reading powers. He wanted me to scan the minds of the men who came into the bar until I found out who the murderer was."

"Except for a few dozen flaws, that's not a bad idea."

"You think?"

"Both your brother and I will be regarded with less suspicion if the murderer is in jail. And you'll be safe."

"That's true, but I don't know how to go about it. It would be hard, and painful, and boring, to wade through all that stuff trying to find a little bit of information, a flash of thought."

"Not any more painful or hard than being suspected of murder. You're just accustomed to keeping your gift locked up."

"Do you think so?" I began to turn to look at

his face, but he held me still so he could finish braiding. I'd never seen keeping out of people's minds as selfish, but in this case I supposed it was. I would have to invade a lot of privacy. "A detective," I murmured, trying to see myself in a better light than just nosey.

"Sookie," Bill said, and something in his voice made me take notice. "Eric has told me to bring you to Shreveport again."

It took me a second to remember who Eric was. "Oh, the big Viking vampire?"

"The very old vampire," Bill said precisely.

"You mean, he ordered you to bring me there?" I didn't like the sound of this at all. I'd been sitting on the side of the bed, Bill behind me, and now I turned to look in his face. This time he didn't stop me. I stared at Bill, seeing something in his face that I'd never seen before. "You *have* to do this," I said, appalled. I could not imagine someone giving Bill an order. "But honey, I don't want to go see Eric."

I could see that made no difference.

"What is he, the Godfather of vampires?" I asked, angry and incredulous. "Did he give you an offer you couldn't refuse?"

"He is older than me. More to the point, he is stronger."

"Nobody's stronger than you," I said stoutly.

"I wish you were right."

"So is he the head of Vampire Region Ten, or something?"

"Yes. Something like that."

Bill was always closemouthed about how vampires controlled their own affairs. That had been fine with me, until now.

"What does he want? What will happen if I don't go?"

Bill just sidestepped the first question. "He'll send someone — several someones — to get you."

"Other vampires."

"Yes." Bill's eyes were opaque, shining with his difference, brown and rich.

I tried to think this through. I wasn't used to being ordered around. I wasn't used to no choices at all. It took my thick skull several minutes to evaluate the situation.

"So, you'd feel obliged to fight them?"

"Of course. You are mine."

There was that "mine" again. It seemed he really meant it. I sure felt like whining, but I knew it wouldn't do any good.

"I guess I have to go," I said, trying not to sound bitter. "This is just plain old blackmail."

"Sookie, vampires *aren't like humans.* Eric is using the best means to achieve his goal, which is getting you to Shreveport. He didn't have to spell all this out; I understood it."

"Well, I understand it now, but I hate it. I'm between a rock and a hard place! What does he want me for, anyway?" An obvious answer popped right into my mind, and I looked at Bill, horrified. "Oh, no, I won't do that!"

"He won't have sex with you or bite you, not

without killing me." Bill's glowing face lost all vestiges of familiarity and became utterly alien.

"And he knows that," I said tentatively, "so there must be another reason he wants me in Shreveport."

"Yes," Bill agreed, "but I don't know what it is."

"Well, if it doesn't have to do with my physical charms, or the unusual quality of my blood, it must have to do with my . . . little quirk."

"Your gift."

"Right," I said, sarcasm dripping from my voice. "My precious gift." All the anger I thought I'd eased off my shoulders came back to sit like a four-hundred-pound gorilla. And I was scared to death. I wondered how Bill felt. I was even scared to ask that.

"When?" I asked instead.

"Tomorrow night."

"I guess this is the downside of nontraditional dating." I stared over Bill's shoulder at the pattern of the wallpaper my grandmother had chosen ten years ago. I promised myself that if I got through this, I would repaper.

"I love you." His voice was just a whisper.

This wasn't Bill's fault. "I love you, too," I said. I had to stop myself from begging, Please don't let the bad vampire hurt me, please don't let the vampire rape me. If I was between a rock and a hard place, Bill was doubly so. I couldn't even begin to estimate the self-control he was employing. Unless he really was calm? Could a vampire face pain and this form of helplessness without some inner turmoil?

I searched his face, the familiar clear lines and white matte complexion, the dark arches of his brows and proud line of his nose. I observed that Bill's fangs were only slightly extended, and rage and lust ran them full out.

"Tonight," he said. "Sookie . . ." His hands began urging me to lie beside him.

"What?"

"Tonight, I think, you should drink from me."

I made a face. "Ick! Don't you need all your strength for tomorrow night? I'm not hurt."

"How have you felt since you drank from me? Since I put my blood inside you?"

I mulled it over. "Good," I admitted.

"Have you been sick?"

"No, but then I almost never am."

"Have you had more energy?"

"When you weren't taking it back!" I said tartly, but I could feel my lips curve up in a little smile.

"Have you been stronger?"

"I — yes, I guess I have." I realized for the first time how extraordinary it was that I'd carried in a new chair, by myself, the week before.

"Has it been easier to control your power?"

"Yes, I did notice that." I'd written it off to increased relaxation.

"If you drink from me tonight, tomorrow

night you will have more resources."

"But you'll be weaker."

"If you don't take much, I'll recoup during the day when I sleep. And I may have to find someone else to drink from tomorrow night before we go."

My face filled with hurt. Suspecting he was doing it and knowing were sure two different things.

"Sookie, this is for us. No sex with anyone else, I promise you."

"You really think all this is necessary."

"Maybe necessary. At least helpful. And we need all the help we can get."

"Oh, all right. How do we do this?" I had only the haziest recollection of the night of the beating, and I was glad of it.

He looked at me quizzically. I had the impression he was amused. "Aren't you excited, Sookie?"

"At drinking blood from you? Excuse me, that's not my turn-on."

He shook his head, as if that was beyond his understanding. "I forget," he said simply. "I forget how it is to be otherwise. Would you prefer neck, wrist, groin?"

"Not groin," I said hastily. "I don't know, Bill. Yuck. Whichever."

"Neck," he said. "Lie on top of me, Sookie."

"That's like sex."

"It's the easiest way."

So I straddled him and gently let myself

down. This felt very peculiar. This was a position we used for lovemaking and nothing else.

"Bite, Sookie," he whispered.

"I can't do that!" I protested.

"Bite, or I'll have to use a knife."

"My teeth aren't sharp like yours."

"They're sharp enough."

"I'll hurt you."

He laughed silently. I could feel his chest moving beneath me.

"Damn." I breathed, and steeling myself, I bit his neck. I did a good job because there was no sense prolonging this. I tasted the metallic blood in my mouth. Bill groaned softly, and his hands brushed my back and continued down. His fingers found me.

I gave a gasp of shock.

"Drink," he said raggedly, and I sucked hard. He groaned, louder, deeper, and I felt him pressing against me. A little ripple of madness went through me, and I attached myself to him like a barnacle, and he entered me, began moving, his hands now gripping my hip bones. I drank and saw visions, visions all with a background of darkness, of white things coming up from the ground and going hunting, the thrill of the run through the woods, the prey panting ahead and the excitement of its fear; pursuit, legs pumping, hearing the thrumming of blood through the veins of the pursued . . .

Bill made a noise deep in his chest and convulsed inside me. I raised my head from his neck, and a wave of dark delight carried me out to sea.

This was pretty exotic stuff for a telepathic barmaid from northern Louisiana.

9

I was getting ready by sunset the next day. Bill had said he was going to feed somewhere before we went, and as upset as the idea made me, I had to agree it made sense. He was right about how I'd feel after my little informal vitamin supplement the night before, too. I felt super. I felt very strong, very alert, very quick-witted, and oddly enough, I also felt very pretty.

What would I wear for my own little interview with a vampire? I didn't want to look like I was trying to be sexy, but I didn't want to make a fool of myself by wearing a shapeless gunny-sack, either. Blue jeans seemed to be the answer, as they so often are. I put on white sandals and a pale blue scoop-neck tee. I hadn't worn it since I'd started seeing Bill because it exposed his fang marks. But Bill's "ownership" of me, I figured, could not be too strongly reinforced tonight. Remembering the cop last time checking my neck, I tucked a scarf in my purse. I thought again and added a silver necklace. I brushed my hair, which seemed at least three shades lighter, and let it ripple down my back.

Just when I was really having to struggle with picturing Bill with somebody else, he knocked.

I opened the door and we stood looking at each other for a minute. His lips had more color than normal, so he'd done it. I bit my own lips to keep from saying anything.

"You did change," he said first.

"You think anyone else'll be able to tell?" I hoped not.

"I don't know." He held out his hand, and we walked to his car. He opened my door, and I brushed by him to climb in. I stiffened.

"What's wrong?" he asked, after a moment.

"Nothing," I said, trying to keep my voice even, and I sat in the passenger's seat and stared straight ahead of me.

I told myself I might as well be mad at the cow who had given him his hamburger. But somehow the simile just didn't work.

"You smell different," I said after we'd been on the highway for a few minutes. We drove for a few minutes in silence.

"Now you know how I will feel if Eric touches you," he told me. "But I think I'll feel worse because Eric will enjoy touching you, and I didn't much enjoy my feeding."

I figured that wasn't totally, strictly, true: I know I always enjoy eating even if I'm not served my favorite food. But I appreciated the sentiment.

We didn't talk much. We were both worried about what was ahead of us. All too soon, we were parking at Fangtasia again, but this time in the back. As Bill held open the car door, I had to fight an impulse to cling to the seat and refuse to get out. Once I made myself emerge, I had another struggle involving my intense desire to hide behind Bill. I gave a kind of gasp, took his arm, and we walked to the door like we were going to a party we were anticipating with pleasure.

Bill looked down at me with approval.

I fought an urge to scowl at him.

He knocked on the metal door with FANGTASIA stencilled on it. We were in a service and delivery alley that ran behind all the stores in the little strip mall. There were several other cars parked back there, Eric's sporty red convertible among them. All the vehicles were high-priced.

You won't find a vampire in a Ford Fiesta.

Bill knocked, three quick, two spaced apart. The Secret Vampire Knock, I guess. Maybe I'd get to learn the Secret Handshake.

The beautiful blond vampire opened the door, the female who'd been at the table with Eric when I'd been to the bar before. She stood back without speaking to let us enter.

If Bill had been human, he would have protested at how tightly I was holding his hand.

The female was in front of us more quickly than my eyes could follow, and I started. Bill wasn't surprised at all, naturally. She led us through a storeroom disconcertingly similar to Merlotte's and into a little corridor. We went through the door on our right.

Eric was in the small room, his presence dominating it. Bill didn't exactly kneel to kiss his ring, but he did nod kind of deep. There was another vampire in the room, the bartender, Long Shadow; he was in fine form tonight, in a skinny-strap tee and weight-lifting pants, all in deep green.

"Bill, Sookie," Eric greeted us. "Bill, you and Sookie know Long Shadow. Sookie, you remember Pam." Pam was the blond female. "And this is Bruce."

Bruce was a human, the most frightened human I'd ever seen. I had considerable sympathy with that. Middle-aged and paunchy, Bruce had thinning dark hair that curved in stiff waves across his scalp. He was jowly and small-mouthed. He was wearing a nice suit, beige, with a white shirt and a brown-and-navy patterned tie. He was sweating heavily. He was in a straight chair across the desk from Eric. Naturally, Eric was in the power chair. Pam and Long Shadow were standing against the wall across from Eric, by the door. Bill took his place beside them, but as I moved to join him, Eric spoke again.

"Sookie, listen to Bruce."

I stood staring at Bruce for a second, waiting for him to speak, until I understood what Eric meant.

"What exactly am I listening for?" I asked, knowing my voice was sharp.

"Someone has embezzled about sixty thousand dollars from us," Eric explained.

Boy, somebody had a death wish.

"And rather than put all our human employees to death or torture, we thought perhaps you would look into their minds and tell us who it was."

He said "death or torture" as calmly as I said, "Bud or Old Milwaukee."

"And then what will you do?" I asked.

Eric seemed surprised.

"Whoever it is will give our money back," he said simply.

"And then?"

His big blue eyes narrowed as he stared at me.

"Why, if we can produce proof of the crime, we'll turn the culprit over to the police," he said smoothly.

Liar, liar, pants on fire. "I'll make a deal, Eric," I said, not bothering to smile. Winsome did not count with Eric, and he was far from any desire to jump my bones. At the moment.

He smiled, indulgently. "What would that be, Sookie?"

"If you really do turn the guilty person over to the police, I'll do this for you again, whenever you want."

Eric cocked an eyebrow.

"Yeah, I know I'd probably have to anyway. But isn't it better if I come willing, if we have good faith with each other?" I broke into a sweat. I could not believe I was bargaining with a vampire.

Eric actually seemed to be thinking that over. And suddenly, I was in his thoughts. He was thinking he could make me do what he wanted, anywhere, anytime, just by threatening Bill or some human I loved. But he wanted to mainstream, to keep as legal as he could, to keep his relations with humans aboveboard, or at least as aboveboard as vampire–human dealings could be. He didn't want to kill anyone if he didn't have to.

It was like suddenly being plunged into a pit of snakes, cold snakes, lethal snakes. It was only a flash, a slice of his mind, sort of, but it left me facing a whole new reality.

"Besides," I said quickly, before he could see I'd been inside his head, "how sure are you that the thief is a human?"

Pam and Long Shadow both moved suddenly, but Eric flooded the room with his presence, commanding them to be still.

"That's an interesting idea," he said. "Pam and Long Shadow are my partners in this bar, and if none of the humans is guilty, I guess we'll have to look at them."

"Just a thought," I said meekly, and Eric looked at me with the glacial blue eyes of a being who hardly remembers what humanity was like.

"Start now, with this man," he commanded.

I knelt by Bruce's chair, trying to decide how to proceed. I'd never tried to formalize something that was pretty chancy. Touching would help; direct contact clarified the transmission, so to speak. I took Bruce's hand, found that too personal (and too sweaty) and pushed back his coat cuff. I took hold of his wrist. I looked into his small eyes.

I didn't take the money, who took it, what crazy fool would put us in danger like this, what will Lillian do if they kill me, and Bobby and Heather, why did I work for vampires anyway, it's sheer greed, and I'm paying for it, God I'll never work for these things again how can this crazy woman find out who took the fucking money why doesn't she let go of me what is she is she a vampire, too, or some kind of demon her eyes are so strange I should have found out earlier that the money was missing and found out who took it before I even said anything to Eric . . .

"Did you take the money?" I breathed, though I was sure I already knew the answer.

"No," Bruce groaned, sweat running down his face, and his thoughts, his reaction to the question, confirmed what I'd heard already.

"Do you know who did?"

"I wish."

I stood, turned to Eric, shook my head. "Not this guy," I said.

Pam escorted poor Bruce out, brought the next interrogee.

My subject was a barmaid, dressed in trailing black with lots of cleavage on display, her ragged strawberry blond hair straggling down her back. Of course, working at Fangtasia would be a dream job for a fang-banger, and this gal had the scars to prove she enjoyed her perks. She was confident enough to grin at Eric, foolish enough to take the wooden chair with some confidence, even crossing her legs like Sharon Stone — she hoped. She was surprised to see a strange vampire and a new woman in the room, and not pleased by my presence, though Bill made her lick her lips.

"Hey, sweetie," she said to Eric, and I decided she must have no imagination at all.

"Ginger, answer this woman's questions," Eric said. His voice was like a stone wall, flat and implacable.

Ginger seemed to understand for the first time that this was a time to be serious. She crossed her ankles this time, sat with her hands on the tops of her thighs, and assumed a stern face. "Yes, master," she said, and I thought I was going to barf.

She waved an imperious hand at me, as if to say, "Begin, fellow vampire server." I reached down for her wrist, and she flung my hand away. "Don't touch me," she said, almost hissing.

It was such an extreme reaction that the vampires tensed up, and I could feel that crackling the air in the room.

"Pam, hold Ginger still," Eric commanded, and Pam appeared silently behind Ginger's chair, leaning over and putting her hands on Ginger's upper arms. You could tell Ginger struggled some because her head moved around, but Pam held her upper body in a grip that kept the girl's body absolutely immobile.

My fingers circled her wrist. "Did you take the money?" I asked, staring into Ginger's flat brown eyes.

She screamed, then, long and loud. She began to curse me. I listened to the chaos in the girl's tiny brain. It was like trying to walk over a bombed site.

"She knows who did," I said to Eric. Ginger fell silent then, though she was sobbing. "She can't say the name," I told the blond vampire. "He has bitten her." I touched the scars on Ginger's neck as if that needed more illustration. "It's some kind of compulsion," I reported, after I'd tried again. "She can't even picture him."

"Hypnosis," Pam commented. Her proximity to the frightened girl had made Pam's fangs run out. "A strong vampire."

"Bring in her closest friend," I suggested.

Ginger was shaking like a leaf by then with thoughts she was compelled not to think pressing her from their locked closet.

"Should she stay, or go?" Pam asked me directly.

"She should go. It'll only scare someone else."

I was so into this, so into openly using my strange ability, that I didn't look at Bill. I felt that somehow if I looked at him, it would weaken me. I knew where he was, that he and Long Shadow had not moved since the questioning had begun.

Pam hauled the trembling Ginger away. I don't know what she did with the barmaid, but she returned with another waitress in the same kind of clothes. This woman's name was Belinda, and she was older and wiser. Belinda had brown hair, glasses, and the sexiest pouting mouth I'd ever seen.

"Belinda, what vampire has Ginger been seeing?" Eric asked smoothly once Belinda was seated, and I was touching her. The waitress had enough sense to accept the process quietly, enough intelligence to realize she had to be honest.

"Anyone that would have her," Belinda said bluntly.

I saw an image in Belinda's mind, but she had to think the name.

"Which one from here?" I asked suddenly, and then I had the name. My eyes sought his corner before I could open my mouth, and then he was on me, Long Shadow, vaulting over the chair holding Belinda to land on top of me as I crouched in front of her. I was bowled over backward into Eric's desk, and only my upflung arms saved me from his teeth sinking into my throat and ripping it out. He bit my forearm savagely, and I screamed; at least I tried to, but with so little air left from the impact it was more like an alarmed choking noise.

I was only conscious of the heavy figure on top of me and the pain of my arm, my own fear. I hadn't been frightened that the Rats were going to kill me until almost too late, but I understood that to keep his name from leaving my lips, Long Shadow was ready to kill me instantly, and when I heard the awful noise and felt his body press even harder on me I didn't have any idea what it meant. I'd been able to see his eyes over the top of my arm. They were wide, brown, crazed, icy. Suddenly they dulled and seemed to almost flatten. Blood gushed out of Long Shadow's mouth, bathing my arm. It flowed into my open mouth, and I gagged. His teeth relaxed, and his face fell in on itself. It began to wrinkle. His eyes turned into gelatinous pools. Handfuls of his thick black hair fell on my face.

I was shocked beyond moving. Hands gripped my shoulders and began pulling me out from under the decaying corpse. I pushed with my feet to scrabble back faster.

There wasn't an odor, but there was gunk, black and streaky, and the absolute horror and disgust of watching Long Shadow deconstruct with incredible speed. There was a stake sticking out of his back. Eric stood watching, as we all were, but he had a mallet in his hand. Bill was behind me, having pulled me out from under Long Shadow. Pam was standing by the door, her hand gripping Belinda's arm. The waitress looked as rocky as I must have.

Even the gunk began to vanish in smoke. We all stood frozen until the last wisp was gone. The carpet had a kind of scorched mark on it.

"You'll have to get you an area rug," I said, completely out of the blue. Honest to God, I couldn't stand the silence any more.

"Your mouth is bloody," Eric said. All the vampires had fully extended fangs. They'd gotten pretty excited.

"He bled onto me."

"Did any go down your throat?"

"Probably. What does that mean?"

"That remains to be seen," Pam said. Her voice was dark and husky. She was eyeing Belinda in a way that would have made me distinctly nervous, but Belinda seemed to be preening, incredibly. "Usually," Pam went on, her eyes on Belinda's pouty lips, "we drink from humans, not the other way around."

Eric was looking at me with interest, the same kind of interest that Pam had in Belinda. "How do things look to you now, Sookie?" he asked in such a smooth voice you'd never think he'd just executed an old friend.

How *did* things look to me now? Brighter. Sounds were clearer, and I could hear better. I wanted to turn and look at Bill, but I was scared to take my eyes off Eric.

"Well, I guess Bill and me'll go now," I said, as if no other process was possible. "I did that for you, Eric, and now we get to go. No retaliation for Ginger and Belinda and Bruce, okay?

282

We agreed." I started toward the door with an assurance I was far from feeling. "I'll just bet you need to go see how the bar is doing, huh? Who's mixing the drinks, tonight?"

"We got a substitute," Eric said absently, his eyes never leaving my neck. "You smell different, Sookie," he murmured, taking a step closer.

"Well, remember now, Eric, we had a deal," I reminded him, my smile broad and tense, my voice snapping with good cheer. "Bill and I are going home now, aren't we?" I risked a glance behind me at Bill. My heart sank. His eyes were open wide, unblinking, his lips drawn back in a silent snarl to expose his extended fangs. His pupils were dilated enormously. He was staring at Eric.

"Pam, get out of the way," I said, quietly but sharply. Once Pam was distracted from her own blood lust, she evaluated the situation in one glance. She swung open the office door and propelled Belinda through it, stood beside it to usher us out. "Call Ginger," I suggested, and the sense of what I was saying penetrated Pam's fog of desire. "Ginger," she called hoarsely, and the blond girl stumbled from a door down the hall. "Eric wants you," Pam told her. Ginger's face lit up like she had a date with David Duchovny, and she was in the room and rubbing against Eric almost as fast as a vampire could have. As if he'd woken from a spell, Eric looked down at Ginger when she ran her hands up his chest. As he bent to kiss her, Eric looked at me over her head. "I'll see you again," he said, and I pulled Bill out the door as quick as a wink. Bill didn't want to go. It was like trying to tow a log. But once we were out in the hall he seemed to be a little more aware of the need to get out of there, and we hurried from Fangtasia and got into Bill's car.

I looked down at myself. I was bloodstained and wrinkled, and I smelled funny. Yuck. I looked over at Bill to share my disgust with him, but he was looking at me in an unmistakable way.

"No," I said forcefully. "You start this car and get out of here before anything else happens, Bill Compton. I tell you flat, I'm not in the mood."

He scooted across the seat toward me, his arms scooping me up before I could say anything else. Then his mouth was on mine, and after a second his tongue began licking the blood from my face.

I was really scared. I was also really angry. I grabbed his ears and pulled his head away from mine using every ounce of strength I possessed, which happened to be more than I thought I had.

His eyes were still like caves with ghosts dwelling in their depths.

"Bill!" I shrieked. I shook him. "Snap out of it!"

Slowly, his personality seeped back into his

eyes. He drew a shuddering sigh. He kissed me lightly on the lips.

"Okay, can we go home now?" I asked, ashamed that my voice was so quavery.

"Sure," he said, sounding none too steady himself.

"Was that like sharks scenting blood?" I asked, after a fifteen-minute silent drive that almost had us out of Shreveport.

"Good analogy."

He didn't need to apologize. He'd been doing what nature dictated, as least as natural as vampires got. He didn't bother to. I would kind of liked to have heard an apology.

"So, am I in trouble?" I asked finally. It was two in the morning, and I found the question didn't bother me as much as it should have.

"Eric will hold you to your word," Bill said. "As to whether he will leave you alone personally, I don't know. I wish . . ." but his voice trailed off. It was the first time I'd heard Bill wish for anything.

"Sixty thousand dollars isn't a lot of money to a vampire, surely," I observed. "You all seem to have plenty of money."

"Vampires rob their victims, of course," Bill said matter-of-factly. "Early on, we take the money from the corpse. Later, when we're more experienced, we can exert enough control to persuade a human to give us money willingly, then forget it's been done. Some of us hire money managers, some of us go into real estate, some of us live on the interest from our investments. Eric and Pam went in together on the bar. Eric put up most of the money, Pam the rest. They had known Long Shadow for a hundred years, and they hired him to be bartender. He betrayed them."

"Why would he steal from them?"

"He must have had some venture he needed the capital for," Bill said absently. "And he was in a mainstreaming position. He couldn't just go out and kill a bank manager after hypnotizing him and persuading the man to give him the money. So he took it from Eric."

"Wouldn't Eric have loaned it to him?"

"If Long Shadow hadn't been too proud to ask, yes," Bill said.

We had another long silence. Finally I said, "I always think of vampires as smarter than humans, but they're not, huh?"

"Not always," he agreed.

When we reached the outskirts of Bon Temps, I asked Bill to drop me off at home. He looked sideways at me, but didn't say anything. Maybe vampires were smarter than humans, after all.

10

The next day, when I was getting ready for work, I realized I was definitely off vampires for a while. Even Bill.

I was ready to remind myself I was a human.

The trouble was, I had to notice that I was a changed human.

It wasn't anything major. After the first infusion of Bill's blood on the night the Rats had beaten me, I'd felt healed, healthy, stronger. But not markedly different. Maybe more — well, sexier.

After my second draft of Bill's blood, I'd felt really strong, and I'd been braver because I'd had more confidence. I felt more secure in my sexuality and its power. It seemed apparent I was handling my disability with more aplomb and capability.

I'd had Long Shadow's blood by accident. The next morning, looking in the mirror, my teeth were whiter and sharper. My hair looked lighter and livelier, and my eyes were brighter. I looked like a poster girl for good hygiene, or some healthy cause like taking vitamins or drinking milk. The savage bite on my arm (Long Shadow's last bite on this earth, I realized) was not completely healed, but it was well on its way.

Then my purse spilled as I picked it up, and my change rolled under the couch. I held up the end of the couch with one hand while with the other I retrieved the coins.

Whoa.

I straightened and took a deep breath. At least the sunlight didn't hurt my eyes, and I didn't want to bite everyone I saw. I'd enjoyed my breakfast toast, rather than longing for tomato juice. I wasn't turning into a vampire. Maybe I was sort of an enhanced human?

Life had sure been simpler when I hadn't dated.

When I got to Merlotte's, everything was ready except for slicing the lemons and limes. We served the fruit both with mixed drinks and with tea, and I got out the cutting board and a sharp knife. Lafayette was tying on his apron as I got the lemons from the big refrigerator.

"You highlighted your hair, Sookie?"

I shook my head. Under the enveloping white apron, Lafayette was a symphony of color; he was wearing a fuschia thin-strap tee, dark purple jeans, red thong sandals, and he had sort of raspberry eye shadow on.

"It sure looks lighter," he said skeptically, raising his own plucked brows.

"I've been out in the sun a lot," I assured him. Dawn had never gotten along with Lafayette, whether because he was black or because he was gay, I didn't know . . . maybe both. Arlene and Charlsie just accepted the cook, but didn't go out of their ways to be friendly. But I'd always kind of liked Lafayette because he conducted what had to be a tough life with verve and grace.

I looked down at the cutting board. All the lemons had been quartered. All the limes had been sliced. My hand was holding the knife, and it was wet with juices. I had done it without knowing it. In about thirty seconds. I closed my eyes. My God.

When I opened them, Lafayette was staring from my face to my hands.

"Tell me I didn't just see that, girlfriend," he suggested.

"You didn't," I said. My voice was cool and level, I was surprised to note. "Excuse me, I got to put these away." I put the fruit in separate containers in the big cooler behind the bar where Sam kept the beer. When I shut the door, Sam was standing there, his arms crossed across his chest. He didn't look happy.

"Are you all right?" he asked. His bright blue eyes scanned me up and down. "You do something to your hair?" he said uncertainly.

I laughed. I realized that my guard had slid into place easily, that it didn't have to be a painful process. "Been out in the sun," I said.

"What happened to your arm?"

I looked down at my right forearm. I'd covered the bite with a bandage.

"Dog bit me."

"Had it had its shots?"

"Sure."

I looked up at Sam, not too far, and it seemed to me his wiry, curly, red-blond hair snapped with energy. It seemed to me I could hear his heart beating. I could feel his uncertainty, his desire. My body responded instantly. I focussed on his thin lips, and the rich smell of his aftershave filled my lungs. He moved two inches closer. I could feel the breath going in and out of his lungs. I knew his penis was stiffening.

Then Charlsie Tooten came in the front door and slammed it behind her. We both took a step away from each other. Thank God for Charlsie, I thought. Plump, dumb, good-natured, and hardworking, Charlsie was a dream employee. Married to Ralph, her high school sweetheart, who worked at one of the chicken processing plants, Charlsie had a girl in the eleventh grade and a married daughter. Charlsie loved to work at the bar so she could get out and see people, and she had a knack for dealing with drunks that got them out the door without a fight.

"Hi, you two!" she called cheerfully. Her dark brown hair (L'Oreal, Lafayette said) was pulled back dramatically to hang from the crown of her head in a cascade of ringlets. Her blouse was spotless and the pockets of her shorts gaped since the contents were too packed. Charlsie was wearing sheer black support hose and Keds, and her artificial nails were a sort of burgundy red.

"That girl of mine is expecting. Just call me Grandma!" she said, and I could tell Charlsie was happy as a clam. I gave her the expected hug, and Sam patted her on the shoulder. We were both glad to see her.

"When is the baby due?" I asked, and Charlsie was off and running. I didn't have to say anything for the next five minutes. Then Arlene trailed in, makeup inexpertly covering the hickeys on her neck, and she listened to everything all over again. Once my eyes met Sam's, and after a little moment, we looked away simultaneously.

Then we began serving the lunchtime crowd, and the incident was over.

Most people didn't drink much at lunchtime, maybe a beer or a glass of wine. A hefty proportion just had iced tea or water. The lunch crowd consisted of people who happened to be close to Merlotte's when the lunch hour came, people who were regulars and thought of it naturally, and the local alcoholics for whom their lunchtime drink was maybe the third or fourth. As I began to take orders, I remembered my brother's plea.

I listened in all day, and it was gruelling. I'd never spent the day listening; I'd never let my guard down for so long. Maybe it wasn't as painful as it had been; maybe I felt cooler about what I was hearing. Sheriff Bud Dearborn was sitting at a table with the mayor, my grand-mother's friend Sterling Norris. Mr. Norris patted me on the shoulder, standing up to do so, and I realized it was the first time I'd seen him since Gran's funeral.

"How are you doing, Sookie?" he asked in a sympathetic voice. He was looking poorly, him-self.

"Just great, Mr. Norris. Yourself?"

"I'm an old man, Sookie," he said with an uncertain smile. He didn't even wait for me to protest. "These murders are wearing me down. We haven't had a murder in Bon Temps since Darryl Mayhew shot Sue Mayhew. And there wasn't no mystery about that."

"That was . . . what? Six years ago?" I asked the sheriff, just to keep standing there. Mr. Norris was feeling so sad at seeing me because he was thinking my brother was going to be ar-rested for murder, for killing Maudette Pickens, and the mayor reckoned that meant Jason had most likely also killed Gran. I ducked my head to hide my eyes.

"I guess so. Let's see, I remember we were dressed up for Jean-Anne's dance recital . . . so that was . . . yes, you're right, Sookie, six years ago." The sheriff nodded at me with approval. "Jason been in today?" he asked casually, as if it were a mere afterthought.

"No, haven't seen him," I said. The sheriff told me he wanted iced tea and a hamburger; and he was thinking of the time he'd caught

Jason with his Jean-Anne, making out like crazy in the bed of Jason's pickup truck.

Oh, Lord. He was thinking Jean-Anne was lucky she hadn't been strangled. And then he had a clear thought that cut me to the quick: Sheriff Dearborn thought, These girls are all bottom-feeders, anyway.

I could read his thought in its context because the sheriff happened to be an easy scan. I could feel the nuances of the idea. He was thinking, "Low-skill jobs, no college, screwing vampires . . . bottom of the barrel."

Hurt and angry didn't begin to describe how I felt at this assessment.

I went from table to table automatically, fetching drinks and sandwiches and clearing up the remainders, working as hard as I usually did, with that awful smile stretching my face. I talked to twenty people I knew, most of whom had thoughts as innocent as the day is long. Most customers were thinking of work, or tasks they had to get done at home, or some little problem they needed to solve, like getting the Sears repairman to come work on the dishwasher or getting the house clean for weekend company.

Arlene was relieved her period had started.

Charlsie was immersed in pink glowing reflections on her shot at immortality, her grandchild. She was praying earnestly for an easy pregnancy and safe delivery for her daughter.

Lafayette was thinking that working with me

was getting spooky.

Policeman Kevin Pryor was wondering what his partner Kenya was doing on her day off. He himself was helping his mother clean out the tool shed and hating every minute of it.

I heard many comments, both aloud and unspoken, about my hair and complexion and the bandage on my arm. I seemed more desirable to more men, and one woman. Some of the guys who'd gone on the vampire burning expedition were thinking they didn't have a chance with me because of my vampire sympathies, and they were regretting their impulsive act. I marked their identities in my mind. I wasn't going to forget they could have killed my Bill, even though at the moment the rest of the vampire community was low on my list of favorite things.

Andy Bellefleur and his sister, Portia, were having lunch together, something they did at least once every week. Portia was a female version of Andy: medium height, blocky build, determined mouth and jaw. The resemblance between brother and sister favored Andy, not Portia. She was a very competent lawyer, I'd heard. I might have suggested her to Jason when he was thinking he'd need an attorney, if she'd not been female . . . and I'd been thinking about Portia's welfare more than Jason's.

Today the lawyer was feeling inwardly depressed because she was educated and made good money, but never had a date. That was her inner preoccupation.

Andy was disgusted with my continued association with Bill Compton, interested in my improved appearance, and curious about how vampires had sex. He also was feeling sorry he was probably going to arrest Jason. He was thinking that the case against Jason was not much stronger than that against several other men, but Jason was the one who looked the most scared, which meant he had something to hide. And there were the videos, which showed Jason having sex — not exactly regular, garden-variety sex — with Maudette and Dawn.

I stared at Andy while I processed his thoughts, which made him uneasy. Andy really did know what I was capable of. "Sookie, you going to get that beer?" he asked finally, waving a broad hand in the air to make sure he had my attention.

"Sure, Andy," I said absently, and got one out of the cooler. "You need any more tea, Portia?"

"No, thanks, Sookie," Portia said politely, patting her mouth with her paper napkin. Portia was remembering high school, when she would have sold her soul for a date with the gorgeous Jason Stackhouse. She was wondering what Jason was doing now, if he had a thought in his head that would interest her — maybe his body would be worth the sacrifice of intellectual companionship? So Portia hadn't seen the tapes, didn't know of their existence; Andy was being a good cop.

I tried to picture Portia with Jason, and I couldn't help smiling. That would be an experience for both of them. I wished, not for the first time, that I could plant ideas as well as reap them.

By the end of my shift, I'd learned — nothing. Except that the videos my brother had so unwisely made featured mild bondage, which caused Andy to think of the ligature marks around the victims' necks.

So, taken as a whole, letting my head open for my brother had been a futile exercise. All I'd heard tended to make me worry more and didn't supply any additional information that might help his cause.

A different crowd would come in tonight. I had never come to Merlotte's just for fun. Should I come in tonight? What would Bill do? Did I want to see him?

I felt friendless. There was no one I could talk to about Bill, no one who wouldn't be halfway shocked I was seeing him in the first place. How could I tell Arlene I was blue because Bill's vampire buddies were terrifying and ruthless, that one of them had bitten me the night before, bled into my mouth, been staked on top of me? This was not the kind of problem Arlene was equipped to handle.

I couldn't think of anyone who was.

I couldn't recall anyone dating a vampire who wasn't an indiscriminate vampire groupie, a fang-banger who would go with just any bloodsucker.

By the time I left work, my enhanced physical appearance no longer had the power to make me confident. I felt like a freak.

I puttered around the house, took a short nap, watered Gran's flowers. Toward dusk, I ate something I'd nuked in the microwave. Wavering up until the last moment about going out, I finally put on a red shirt and white slacks and some jewelry and drove back to Merlotte's.

It felt very strange entering as a customer. Sam was back behind the bar, and his eyebrows went up as he marked my entrance. Three waitresses I knew by sight were working tonight, and a different cook was grilling hamburgers, I saw through the serving hatch.

Jason was at the bar. For a wonder, the stool next to him was empty, and I eased onto it.

He turned to me with his face set for a new woman: mouth loose and smiling, eyes bright and wide. When he saw it was me, his expression underwent a comical change. "What the hell are you doing here, Sookie?" he asked, his voice indignant.

"You'd think you weren't glad to see me," I remarked. When Sam paused in front of me, I asked him for a bourbon and coke, without meeting his eyes. "I did what you told me to do, and so far nothing," I whispered to my brother. "I came in here tonight to try some more people."

"Thanks, Sookie," he said, after a long pause. "I guess I didn't realize what I was asking. Hey, is something different about your hair?"

He even paid for my drink when Sam slid it in front of me.

We didn't seem to have much to talk about, which was actually okay, since I was trying to listen to the other customers. There were a few strangers, and I scanned them first, to see if they were possible suspects. It didn't seem they were, I decided reluctantly. One was thinking hard about how much he missed his wife, and the subtext was that he was faithful to her. One was thinking about it being his first time here, and the drinks were good. Another was just concentrating on sitting up straight and hoping he could drive back to the motel.

I'd had another drink.

Jason and I had been swapping conjectures about how much the lawyer's fees would be when Gran's estate was settled. He glanced at the doorway and said, "Uh-oh."

"What?" I asked, not turning to see what he was looking at.

"Sis, the boyfriend's here. And he's not alone."

My first idea was that Bill had brought one of his fellow vampires with him, which would have been upsetting and unwise. But when I turned, I realized why Jason had sounded so angry. Bill was with a human girl. He had a grip on her arm, she was coming on to him like a whore, and his eyes were scanning the crowd. I decided he was looking for my reaction.

I got off the barstool and decided another thing.

I was drunk. I seldom drank at all, and two bourbon and cokes consumed within minutes had made me, if not knee-walking drunk, at least tipsy.

Bill's eyes met mine. He hadn't really expected to find me here. I couldn't read his mind as I had Eric's for an awful moment, but I could read his body language.

"Hey, Vampire Bill!" Jason's friend Hoyt called. Bill nodded politely in Hoyt's direction, but began to steer the girl — tiny, dark — in my direction.

I had no idea what to do.

"Sis, what's his game?" Jason said. He was working up a head of steam. "That gal's a fangbanger from Monroe. I knew her when she liked humans."

I still had no idea what to do. My hurt was overwhelming, but my pride kept trying to contain it. I had to add a dash of guilt to that emotional stew. I hadn't been where Bill had expected me to be, and I hadn't left him a note. Then again — on the other hand (my fifth or sixth) — I'd had a lot of shocks the night before at the command performance in Shreveport; and only my association with him had obliged me to go to *that* shindig.

My warring impulses held me still. I wanted

to pitch myself on her and beat the shit out of her, but I hadn't been brought up to brawl in barrooms. (I also wanted to beat the shit out of Bill, but I might as well go bang my head on the wall for the all the damage it would do him.) Then, too, I wanted to burst into tears because my feelings were hurt — but that would be weak. The best option was not to show anything because Jason was ready to launch into Bill, and all it needed was some action from me to squeeze his trigger.

Too much conflict on top of too much alcohol.

While I was enumerating all these options, Bill had approached, wending his way through the tables, with the woman in tow. I noticed the room was quieter. Instead of watching, I was being watched.

I could feel my eyes well with tears while my hands fisted. Great. The worst of both responses.

"Sookie," Bill said, "this is what Eric dropped off at my doorstep."

I could hardly understand what he was saying.

"So?" I said furiously. I looked right into the girl's eyes. They were big and dark and excited. I kept my own lids wide apart, knowing if I blinked the tears would flow.

"As a reward," Bill said. I couldn't understand how he felt about this.

"Free *beverage?*" I said, and couldn't believe

300

how venomous my voice sounded.

Jason put his hand on my shoulder. "Steady, girl," he said, his voice as low and mean as mine. "He ain't worth it."

I didn't know what Bill wasn't worth, but I was about to find out. It was almost exhilarating to have no idea what I was about to do, after a lifetime of control.

Bill was regarding me with sharp attention. Under the fluorescents over the bar, he looked remarkably white. He hadn't fed from her. And his fangs were retracted.

"Come outside and talk," he said.

"With her?" I was almost growling.

"No," he said. "With me. I have to send her back."

The distaste in his voice influenced me, and I followed Bill outside, keeping my head up and not meeting any eyes. He kept ahold of the girl's arm, and she was practically walking on her toes to keep up. I didn't know Jason was coming with us until I turned to see him behind me as we passed into the parking lot. Outside, people were coming and going, but it was marginally better than the crowded bar.

"Hi," the girl said chattily. "My name's Desiree. I think I've met you before, Jason."

"What are you doing here, Desiree?" Jason asked, his voice quiet. You could almost believe he was calm.

"Eric sent me over here to Bon Temps as a reward for Bill," she said coyly, looking at Bill from the corners of her eyes. "But he seems less than thrilled. I don't know why. I'm practically a special vintage."

"Eric?" Jason asked me.

"A vampire from Shreveport. Bar owner. Head honcho."

"He left her on my doorstep," Bill told me. "I didn't ask for her."

"What are you going to do?"

"Send her back," he said impatiently. "You and I have to talk."

I gulped. I felt my fingers uncurl.

"She needs a ride back to Monroe?" Jason asked.

Bill looked surprised. "Yes. Are you offering? I need to talk to your sister."

"Sure," Jason said, all geniality. I was instantly suspicious.

"I can't believe you're refusing me," Desiree said, looking up at Bill and pouting. "No one has ever turned me down before."

"Of course I am grateful, and I'm sure you are, as you put it, a special vintage," Bill said politely. "But I have my own wine cellar."

Little Desiree stared at him blankly for a second before comprehension slowly lit her brown eyes. "This woman yours?" she asked, jerking her head at me.

"She is."

Jason shifted nervously at Bill's flat statement.

Desiree gave me a good looking over. "She's

got funny eyes," she finally pronounced.

"She's my sister," Jason said.

"Oh. I'm sorry. You're much more . . . normal." Desiree gave Jason the up-and-down, and seemed more pleased with what she saw. "Hey, what's your last name?"

Jason took her hand and began leading her toward his pickup. "Stackhouse," he was saying, giving her the full eye treatment, as they walked away. "Maybe on the way home, you can tell me a little about what you do . . ."

I turned back to Bill, wondering what Jason's motive was for this generous act, and met Bill's gaze. It was like walking into a brick wall.

"So, you want to talk?" I asked harshly.

"Not here. Come home with me."

I scuffed the gravel with my shoe. "Not your house."

"Then yours."

"No."

He raised his arched brows. "Where then?"

Good question.

"My folks' pond." Since Jason was going to be giving Miss Dark and Tiny a ride home, he wouldn't be there.

"I'll follow you," he said briefly, and we parted to go to our respective cars.

The property where I'd spent my first few years was to the west of Bon Temps. I turned down the familiar gravel driveway and parked at the house, a modest ranch that Jason kept up pretty well. Bill emerged from his car as I slid from mine, and I motioned him to follow me. We went around the house and down the slope, following a path set with big paving stones. In a minute we were at the pond, man-made, that my dad had put in our backyard and stocked, anticipating fishing with his son in that water for years.

There was a kind of patio overlooking the water, and on one of the metal chairs was a folded blanket. Without asking me, Bill picked it up and shook it out, spreading it on the grass downslope from the patio. I sat on it reluctantly, thinking the blanket wasn't safe for the same reasons meeting him in either home wasn't safe. When I was close to Bill, what I thought about was being even closer to him.

I hugged my knees to me and stared off across the water. There was a security light on the other side of the pond, and I could see it reflected in the still water. Bill lay on his back next to me. I could feel his eyes on my face. He laced his fingers together across his ribs, ostentatiously keeping his hands to himself.

"Last night frightened you," he said neutrally.

"Weren't you just a little scared?" I asked, more quietly than I'd thought I would.

"For you. A little for myself."

I wanted to lie on my stomach but worried about getting that close to him. When I saw his skin glow in the moonlight, I yearned to touch him.

"It scared me that Eric can control our lives while we're a couple."

"Do you not want to be a couple anymore?"

The pain in my chest was so bad I put my hand over it, pressing the area above my breast.

"Sookie?" He was kneeling by me, an arm around me.

I couldn't answer. I had no breath.

"Do you love me?" he asked.

I nodded.

"Why do you talk of leaving me?"

The pain made its way out through my eyes in the form of tears.

"I'm too scared of the other vampires and the way they are. What will he ask me to do next? He'll try to make me do something else. He'll tell me he'll kill you otherwise. Or he'll threaten Jason. And he can do it."

Bill's voice was as quiet as the sound of a cricket in the grass. A month ago, I might not have been able to hear it. "Don't cry," he told me. "Sookie, I have to tell you unwelcome facts."

The only welcome thing he could have told me at that point was that Eric was dead.

"Eric is intrigued by you now. He can tell you have mental powers that most humans don't have, or ignore if they know they possess them. He anticipates your blood is rich and sweet." Bill's voice got hoarse when he said that, and I shivered. "And you're beautiful. You're even more beautiful now. He doesn't realize you have had our blood three times."

"You know that Long Shadow bled onto me?"

"Yes. I saw."

"Is there anything magic about three times?"

He laughed, that low, rumbly, rusty laugh. "No. But the more vampire blood you drink, the more desirable you become to our kind, and actually, more desirable to anyone. And Desiree thought she was a vintage! I wonder what vampire said that to her."

"One that wanted to get in her pants," I said flatly, and he laughed again. I loved to hear him laugh.

"With all this telling me how lovely I am, are you saying that Eric, like, lusts for me?"

"Yes."

"What's to stop him from taking me? You say he's stronger than you."

"Courtesy and custom, first of all."

I didn't snort, but I came close.

"Don't discount that. We're all observant of custom, we vampires. We have to live together for centuries."

"Anything else?"

"I am not as strong as Eric, but I'm not a new vampire. He might get badly hurt in a fight with me, or I might even win if I got lucky."

"Anything else?"

"Maybe," Bill said carefully, "you yourself."

"How so?"

"If you can be valuable to him otherwise, he

may leave you alone if he knows that is your sincere wish."

"But I don't want to be valuable to him! I don't want to ever see him again!"

"You promised Eric you'd help him again," Bill reminded me.

"If he turned the thief over to the police," I said. "And what did Eric do? He staked him!"

"Possibly saving your life in the process."

"Well, I found his thief!"

"Sookie, you don't know much about the world."

I stared at him, surprised. "I guess that's so."

"Things don't turn out . . . even." Bill stared out into the darkness. "Even I think sometimes I don't know much, anymore." Another gloomy pause. "I have only once before seen one vampire stake another. Eric is going beyond the limits of our world."

"So, he's not too likely to take much notice of that custom and courtesy you were bragging about earlier."

"Pam may keep him to the old ways."

"What is she to him?"

"He made her. That is, he made her vampire, centuries ago. She comes back to him from time to time and helps him do whatever he is doing at the moment. Eric's always been something of a rogue, and the older he gets the more willful he gets." Calling Eric willful seemed a huge understatement to me.

"So, have we talked our way around in circles?" I asked.

Bill seemed to be considering. "Yes," he confirmed, a tinge of regret in his voice. "You don't like associating with vampires other than myself, and I have told you we have no choice."

"How about this Desiree thing?"

"He had someone drop her off on my doorstep, hoping I would be pleased he'd sent me a pretty gift. Also, it would test my devotion to you if I drank from her. Perhaps he poisoned her blood somehow, and her blood would have weakened me. Maybe she would just have been a crack in my armor." He shrugged. "Did you think I had a date?"

"Yes." I felt my face harden, thinking about Bill walking in with the girl.

"You weren't at home. I had to come find you." His tone wasn't accusatory, but it wasn't happy, either.

"I was trying to help Jason out by listening. And I was still upset from last night."

"Are we all right now?"

"No, but we're as all right as we can get," I said. "I guess no matter who I cared for, it wouldn't always go smooth. But I hadn't counted on obstacles this drastic. There's no way you can ever outrank Eric, I guess, since age is the criterion?"

"No," said Bill. "Not outrank . . ." and he suddenly looked thoughtful. "Though there may be something I can do along those lines. I don't want to — it goes against my nature — but we would be more secure."

I let him think.

"Yes," he concluded, ending his long brood. He didn't offer to explain, and I didn't ask.

"I love you," he said, as if that was the bottom line to whatever course of action he was considering. His face loomed over me, luminous and beautiful in the half-darkness.

"I feel the same about you," I said, and put my hands against his chest so he wouldn't tempt me. "But we have too much against us right now. If we can pry Eric off our backs, that would help. And another thing, we have to stop this murder investigation. That would be a second big piece of trouble off our backs. This murderer has the deaths of your friends to answer for, and the deaths of Maudette and Dawn to answer for." I paused, took a deep breath. "And the death of my grandmother." I blinked back tears. I'd gotten adjusted to Gran not being in the house when I came home, and I was getting used to not talking to her and sharing my day with her, but every now and then I had a stab of grief so acute it robbed me of breath.

"Why do you think the same killer is responsible for the Monroe vampires being burned?"

"I think it was the murderer who planted this idea, this vigilante thing, in the men in the bar that night. I think it was the murderer who went from group to group, egging the guys on.

I've lived here all my life, and I've never seen people around here act that way. There's got to be a reason they did this time."

"He agitated them? Fomented the burning?"

"Yes."

"Listening hasn't turned up anything?"

"No," I admitted glumly. "But that's not to say tomorrow will be the same."

"You're an optimist, Sookie."

"Yes, I am. I have to be." I patted his cheek, thinking how my optimism had been justified since he had entered my life.

"You keep on listening, since you think it may be fruitful," he said. "I'll work on something else, for now. I'll see you tomorrow evening at your place, okay? I may . . . no, let me explain then."

"All right." I was curious, but Bill obviously wasn't ready to talk.

On my way home, following the taillights of Bill's car as far as my driveway, I thought of how much more frightening the past few weeks would have been if I hadn't had the security of Bill's presence. As I went cautiously down the driveway, I found myself wishing Bill hadn't felt he had to go home to make some necessary phone calls. The few nights we'd spent apart, I wouldn't say I'd been exactly writhing with fear, but I'd been very jumpy and anxious. At the house by myself, I spent lots of time going from locked window to locked door, and I wasn't used to living that way. I felt disheartened at the thought of the night ahead.

Before I got out of my car, I scanned the yard, glad I'd remembered to turn on the security lights before I left for the bar. Nothing was moving. Usually Tina came running when I'd been gone, anxious to get in the house for some cat kibble, but tonight she must be hunting in the woods.

I separated my house key from the bunch on my key ring. I dashed from the car to the front door, inserted and twisted the key in record time, and slammed and locked the door behind me. This was no way to live, I thought, shaking my head in dismay; and just as I completed that idea, something hit the front door with a thud. I shrieked before I could stop myself.

I ran for the portable phone by the couch. I punched in Bill's number as I went around the room pulling down the shades. What if the line was busy? He'd said he was going home to use the phone!

But I caught him just as he walked in the door. He sounded breathless as he picked up the receiver. "Yes?" he said. He always sounded suspicious.

"Bill," I gasped, "there's someone outside!"

He crashed the phone down. A vampire of action.

He was there in two minutes. Looking out into the yard from a slightly lifted blind, I glimpsed him coming into the yard from the woods, moving with a speed and silence a human could never equal. The relief of seeing him was overwhelming. For a second I felt ashamed at calling Bill to rescue me: I should have handled the situation myself. Then I thought, Why? When you know a practically invincible being who professes to adore you, someone so hard to kill it's next to impossible, someone preternaturally strong, that's who you're gonna call.

Bill investigated the yard and the woods, moving with a sure, silent grace. Finally he came lightly up the steps. He bent over something on the front porch. The angle was too acute, and I couldn't tell what it was. When he straightened, he had something in his hands, and he looked absolutely . . . expressionless.

This was very bad.

I went reluctantly to the front door and unlocked it. I pushed out the screen door.

Bill was holding the body of my cat.

"Tina?" I said, hearing my voice quaver and not caring at all. "Is she dead?"

Bill nodded, one little jerk of his head.

"What — how?"

"Strangled, I think."

I could feel my face crumple. Bill had to stand there holding the corpse while I cried my eyes out.

"I never got that live oak," I said, having calmed a little. I didn't sound very steady. "We can put her in that hole." So around to the backyard we went, poor Bill holding Tina, trying to look comfortable about it, and me trying not to dissolve again. Bill knelt and lay the little bundle of black fur at the bottom of my excavation. I fetched the shovel and began to fill it in, but the sight of the first dirt hitting Tina's fur undid me all over again. Silently, Bill took the shovel from my hands. I turned my back, and he finished the awful job.

"Come inside," he said gently when it was finished.

We went in the house, having to walk around to the front because I hadn't yet unlocked the back.

Bill patted me and comforted me, though I knew he hadn't ever been crazy about Tina. "God bless you, Bill," I whispered. I tightened my arms around him ferociously, in a sudden convulsion of fear that he, too, would be taken from me. When I'd gotten the sobs reduced to hiccups, I looked up, hoping I hadn't made him uncomfortable with my flood of emotion.

Bill was furious. He was staring at the wall over my shoulder, and his eyes were glowing. He was the most frightening thing I'd ever seen in my life.

"Did you find anything out in the yard?" I asked.

"No. I found traces of his presence. Some footprints, a lingering scent. Nothing you could bring into court as proof," he went on, reading my mind.

"Would you mind staying here until you have

to go to . . . get away from the sun?"

"Of course." He stared at me. He'd fully intended to do that whether or not I agreed, I could tell.

"If you still need to make phone calls, just make them here. I don't care." I meant if they were on my phone bill.

"I have a calling card," he said, once again astonishing me. Who would have thought?

I washed my face and took a Tylenol before I put on my nightgown, sadder than I'd been since Gran had been killed, and sadder in a different way. The death of a pet is naturally not in the same category as the death of a family member, I chided myself, but it didn't seem to affect my misery. I went through all the reasoning I was capable of and came no closer to any truth except the fact that I'd fed and brushed and loved Tina for four years, and I would miss her.

11

My nerves were raw the next day. When I got to work and told Arlene what had happened, she gave me a hard hug, and said, "I'd like to kill the bastard that did that to poor Tina!" Somehow, that made me feel a lot better. Charlsie was just as sympathetic, if more concerned with the shock to me rather than the agonized demise of my cat. Sam just looked grim. He thought I should call the sheriff, or Andy Bellefleur, and tell one of them what had happened. I finally did call Bud Dearborn.

"Usually these things go in cycles," Bud rumbled. "Ain't nobody else reported a pet missing or dead, though. I'm afraid it sounds like some kind a personal thing, Sookie. That vampire friend of yours, he like cats?"

I closed my eyes and breathed deeply. I was using the phone in Sam's office, and he was sitting behind the desk figuring out his next liquor order.

"Bill was at home when whoever killed Tina threw her on my porch," I said as calmly as I could. "I called him directly afterward, and he answered the phone." Sam looked up quizzically, and I rolled my eyes to let him know my opinion of the sheriff's suspicions.

"And he told you the cat was strangled," Bud

315

went on ponderously.

"Yes."

"Do you have the ligature?"

"No. I didn't even see what it was."

"What did you do with the kitty?"

"We buried her."

"Was that your idea or Mr. Compton's?"

"Mine." What else would we have done with Tina?

"We may come dig your kitty up. If we had had the ligature and the cat, maybe we could see if the method of strangulation matched the method used in killing Dawn and Maudette," Bud explained ponderously.

"I'm sorry. I didn't think about that."

"Well, it don't matter much. Without the ligature."

"Okay, good-bye." I hung up, probably applying a little more pressure than the receiver required. Sam's eyebrows lifted.

"Bud is a jerk," I told him.

"Bud's not a bad policeman," Sam said quietly. "None of us here are used to murders that are this sick."

"You're right," I admitted, after a moment. "I wasn't being fair. He just kept saying 'ligature' like he was proud he'd learned a new word. I'm sorry I got mad at him."

"You don't have to be perfect, Sookie."

"You mean I get to screw up and be less than understanding and forgiving, from time to time? Thanks, boss." I smiled at him, feeling the wry twist to my lips, and got up off the edge of his desk where I'd been propped to make my phone call. I stretched. It wasn't until I saw the way Sam's eyes drank in that stretch that I became self-conscious again. "Back to work!" I said briskly and strode out of the room, trying to make sure there wasn't a hint of sway to my hips.

"Would you keep the kids for a couple of hours this evening?" Arlene asked, a little shyly. I remembered the last time we'd talked about my keeping her kids, and I remembered the offense I'd taken at her reluctance to leave her kids with a vampire. I hadn't been thinking like a mother would think. Now, Arlene was trying to apologize.

"I'd be glad to." I waited to see if Arlene would mention Bill again, but she didn't. "When to when?"

"Well, Rene and I are gonna go to the movies in Monroe," she said. "Say, six-thirty?"

"Sure. Will they have had supper?"

"Oh, yeah, I'll feed 'em. They'll be excited to see their aunt Sookie."

"I look forward to it."

"Thanks," Arlene said. She paused, almost said something else, then appeared to think again. "See you at six-thirty."

I got home about five, most of the way driving against the sun, which was glaring like it was staring me down. I changed to a blue-and-green knit short set, brushed my hair and secured it with a banana clip. I had a sandwich, sitting uneasily by myself at the kitchen table. The house felt big and empty, and I was glad to see Rene drive up with Coby and Lisa.

"Arlene's having trouble with one of her artificial nails," he explained, looking embarrassed at having to relay this feminine problem. "And Coby and Lisa were raring to get over here." I noticed Rene was still in his work clothes — heavy boots, knife, hat, and all. Arlene wasn't going to let him take her anywhere until he showered and changed.

Coby was eight and Lisa was five, and they were hanging all over me like big earrings when Rene bent to kiss them good-bye. His affection for the kids gave Rene a big gold star in my book, and I smiled at him approvingly. I took the kids' hands to lead them back to the kitchen for some ice cream.

"We'll see you about ten-thirty, eleven," he said. "If that's all right." He put his hand on the doorknob.

"Sure," I agreed. I opened my mouth to offer to keep the kids for the night, as I'd done on previous occasions, but then I thought of Tina's limp body. I decided that tonight they'd better not stay. I raced the kids to the kitchen, and a minute or two later I heard Rene's old pickup rattling down the driveway.

I picked up Lisa. "I can hardly lift you anymore, girl, you're getting so big! And you,

Coby, you shaving yet?" We sat at the table for a good thirty minutes while the children ate ice cream and rattled off their list of achievements since we'd last visited.

Then Lisa wanted to read to me, so I got out a coloring book with the color and number words printed inside, and she read those to me with some pride. Coby, of course, had to prove he could read much better, and then they wanted to watch a favorite show. Before I knew it, it was dark.

"My friend is coming over tonight," I told them. "His name is Bill."

"Mama told us you had a special friend," Coby said. "I better like him. He better be nice to you."

"Oh, he is," I assured the boy, who had straightened and thrust out his chest, ready to defend me if my special friend wasn't nice enough in Coby's estimation.

"Does he send you flowers?" Lisa asked romantically.

"No, not yet. Maybe you can kind of hint I'd like some?"

"Ooo. Yeah, I can do that."

"Has he asked you to marry him?"

"Well, no. But I haven't asked him, either."

Naturally, Bill picked that moment to knock.

"I have company," I said, smiling, when I answered the door.

"I can hear," he said.

I took his hand and led him into the kitchen.

"Bill, this is Coby and this young woman is Lisa," I said formally.

"Good, I've been wanting to meet you," Bill said, to my surprise. "Lisa and Coby, is it all right with you if I keep company with your aunt Sookie?"

They eyed him thoughtfully. "She isn't really our aunt," Coby said, testing the waters. "She's our mom's good friend."

"Is that right?"

"Yes, and she says you don't send her flowers," Lisa said. For once, her little voice was crystal clear. I was so glad to realize that Lisa had gotten over her little problem with her *r*'s. Really.

Bill looked sideways at me. I shrugged. "Well, they asked me," I said helplessly.

"Hmmm," he said thoughtfully. "I'll have to mend my ways, Lisa. Thank you for pointing that out to me. When is Aunt Sookie's birthday, do you know?"

I could feel my face flushing. "Bill," I said sharply. "Cut it out."

"Do you know, Coby?" Bill asked the boy.

Coby shook his head, regretfully. "But I know it's in the summer because the last time Mama took Sookie to lunch in Shreveport for her birthday, it was summertime. We stayed with Rene."

"You're smart to remember that, Coby," Bill told him.

"I'm smarter than that! Guess what I learned

in school the other day." And Coby was off and running.

Lisa eyed Bill with great attention the whole time Coby spoke, and when Coby was finished, she said, "You look real white, Bill."

"Yes," he said, "that's my normal complexion."

The kids exchanged glances. I could tell they were deciding that "normal complexion" was an illness, and it wouldn't be too polite to ask more questions. Every now and then children show a certain tactfulness.

Bill, initially a little stiff, began to get more and more flexible as the evening wore on. I was ready to admit I was tired by nine, but he was still going strong with the kids when Arlene and Rene came by to pick them up at eleven.

I'd just introduced my friends to Bill, who shook their hands in an absolutely normal way, when another caller arrived.

A handsome vampire with thick black hair combed into an improbable wavy style strolled up out of the woods as Arlene was bundling the kids into the truck, and Rene and Bill were chatting. Bill waved a casual hand at the vampire, and he raised one in return, joining Bill and Rene as if he'd been expected.

From the front porch swing, I watched Bill introduce the two, and the vampire and Rene shook hands. Rene was gaping at the newcomer, and I could tell he felt he'd recognized him. Bill looked meaningfully at Rene and shook his head, and Rene's mouth closed on whatever comment he'd been going to make.

The newcomer was husky, taller than Bill, and he wore old jeans and an "I Visited Graceland" T-shirt. His heavy boots were worn at the heel. He carried a squirt bottle of synthetic blood in one hand and took a swig from time to time. Mr. Social Skills.

Maybe I'd been cued by Rene's reaction, but the more I looked at the vampire, the more familiar he seemed. I tried mentally warming up the skin tone, adding a few lines, making him stand straighter and investing his face with some liveliness.

Oh my God.

It was the man from Memphis.

Rene turned to go, and Bill began steering the newcomer up to me. From ten feet away, the vampire called, "Hey, Bill tells me someone killed your cat!" He had a heavy Southern accent.

Bill closed his eyes for a second, and I just nodded speechlessly.

"Well, I'm sorry about that. I like cats," the tall vampire said, and I clearly got the idea he didn't mean he liked to stroke their fur. I hoped the kids weren't picking up on that, but Arlene's horrified face appeared in the truck window. All the good will Bill had established had probably just gone down the drain.

Rene shook his head behind the vampire's back and climbed into the driver's seat, calling a good-bye as he started up the engine. He stuck his head out the window for a long last look at the newcomer. He must have said something to Arlene because she appeared at her window again, staring for all she was worth. I saw her mouth drop open in shock as she looked harder at the creature standing beside Bill. Her head disappeared into the truck, and I heard a screech as the truck pulled away.

"Sookie," Bill said warningly, "this is *Bubba*."

"Bubba," I repeated, not quite trusting my ears.

"Yep, Bubba," the vampire said cheerfully, goodwill radiating from his fearsome smile. "That's me. Pleased to meetcha."

I shook hands with him, making myself smile back. Good God Almighty, I never thought I'd be shaking hands with *him*. But he'd sure changed for the worse.

"Bubba, would you mind waiting here on the porch? Let me explain our arrangement to Sookie."

"That's all right with me," Bubba said casually. He settled on the swing, as happy and brainless as a clam.

We went into the living room, but not before I'd noticed that when Bubba had made his appearance, much of the night noise — bugs, frogs — had simply stopped. "I had hoped to explain this to you before Bubba got here," Bill whispered. "But I couldn't."

I said, "Is that who I think it is?"

"Yes. So now you know at least some of the sighting stories are true. But *don't* call him by his name. Call him Bubba! Something went wrong when he came over — from human to vampire — maybe it was all the chemicals in his blood."

"But he was really dead, wasn't he?"

"Not . . . quite. One of us was a morgue attendant and a big fan, and he could detect the tiny spark still left, so he brought him over, in a hurried manner."

"Brought him over?"

"Made him vampire," Bill explained. "But that was a mistake. He's never been the same from what my friends tell me. He's as smart as a tree trunk, so to make a living he does odd jobs for the rest of us. We can't have him out in public, you can see that."

I nodded, my mouth hanging open. Of course not. "Geez," I murmured, stunned at the royalty in my yard.

"So remember how stupid he is, and how impulsive . . .

don't spend time alone with him, and don't ever call him anything but Bubba. Also, he likes pets, as he told you, and a diet of their blood hasn't made him any the more reliable. Now, as to why I brought him here . . ."

I stood with my arms across my chest, waiting for Bill's explanation with some interest.

"Sweetheart, I have to go out of town for a while," Bill said.

The unexpectedness of this completely disconcerted me.

"What . . . why? No, wait. I don't need to know." I waved my hands in front of me, shooing away any implication that Bill was obligated to tell me his business.

"I'll tell you when I get back," he said firmly.

"So where does your friend — Bubba — come in?" Though I had a nasty feeling I already knew.

"Bubba is going to watch you while I'm gone," Bill said stiffly.

I raised my eyebrows.

"All right. He's not long on . . ." Bill cast around. ". . . anything," he finally admitted. "But he's strong, and he'll do what I tell him, and he'll make sure no one breaks into your house."

"He'll stay out in the woods?"

"Oh, yes," Bill said emphatically. "He's not even supposed to come up and speak to you. At dark, he'll just find a place from which he can see the house, and he'll watch all night."

I'd have to remember to close my blinds. The idea of the dim vampire peering in my windows was not edifying.

"You really think this is necessary?" I asked helplessly. "You know, I don't remember you asking me."

Bill sort of heaved, his version of taking a deep breath. "Sweetheart," he began in an overly patient voice, "I am trying very hard to get used to the way women want to be treated now. But it isn't natural to me, especially when I fear you are in danger. I'm trying to give myself peace of mind while I'm gone. I wish I didn't have to go, and it isn't what I want to do, but what I have to do, for us."

I eyed him. "I hear you," I said finally. "I'm not crazy about this, but I am afraid at night, and I guess . . . well, okay."

Frankly, I don't think it mattered a damn whether I consented or not. After all, how could I make Bubba leave if he didn't want to go? Even the law enforcement people in our little town didn't have the equipment to deal with vampires, and if they were faced with this particular vampire, they'd just stand and gape for long enough for him to tear them apart. I appreciated Bill's concern, and I figured I better have the good grace to thank him. I gave him a little hug.

"Well, if you have to go off, you just be careful while you're gone," I said, trying not to sound forlorn. "Do you have a place to stay?"

"Yes. I'll be in New Orleans. There was a room open at the Blood in the Quarter."

I'd read an article about this hotel, the first in the world that catered exclusively to vampires. It promised complete security, and so far it had delivered. It was right smack dab in the middle of the French Quarter, too. And at dusk it was absolutely surrounded by fang-bangers and tourists waiting for the vampires to come out.

I began to feel envious. Trying not to look like a wistful puppy who's being pushed back in the door when its owners leave, I yanked my smile back into place. "Well, you have a good time," I said brightly. "Got your packing done? The drive should take a few hours, and it's already dark."

"The car is ready." I understood for the first time that he had delayed leaving to spend time with me and Arlene's kids. "I had better leave." He hesitated, seemed to be searching for the right words. Then he held out his hands to me. I took them, and he pulled a little, just exerted a tiny pressure. I moved into his embrace. I rubbed my face against his shirt. My arms circled him, pressed him into me.

"I'll miss you," he said. His voice was just a breath in the air, but I heard him. I felt him kiss the top of my head, and then he stepped away from me and out the front door. I heard his voice on the front porch as he gave Bubba some last minute directions, and I heard the squeak of the swing as Bubba got up.

I didn't look out the window until I heard Bill's car going down the driveway. Then I saw Bubba sauntering into the woods. I told myself, as I took my shower, that Bill must trust Bubba since he'd left him guarding me. But I still wasn't sure who I was more afraid of: the murderer Bubba was watching for, or Bubba himself.

At work the next day, Arlene asked me why

the vampire had been at my house. I wasn't surprised that she'd brought it up.

"Well, Bill had to go out of town, and he worries, you know . . ." I was hoping to let it drop at that. But Charlsie had drifted up (we weren't at all busy: the Chamber of Commerce was having a lunch and speaker at Fins and Hooves, and the Ladies' Prayers and Potatoes group were topping their baked potatoes at old Mrs. Bellefleur's huge house). "You mean," Charlsie said with starry eyes, "that your man got you a personal bodyguard?"

I nodded reluctantly. You could put it that way.

"That's so romantic," Charlsie sighed.

You could look at it that way.

"But you should see him," Arlene told Charlsie, having held her tongue as long as she could. "He's exactly like — !"

"Oh, no, not when you talk to him," I interrupted. "He's not at all the same." That was true. "And he really doesn't like it when he hears that name."

"Oh," said Arlene in a hushed voice, as if Bubba could be listening in the broad daylight.

"I do feel safer with Bubba in the woods," I said, which was more or less true.

"Oh, he doesn't stay in the house?" Charlsie asked, clearly a little disappointed.

"God, no!" I said, then mentally apologized to God for taking his name in vain. I was having to do that a lot lately. "No, Bubba stays in the woods at night, watching the house."

"Was that true about the cats?" Arlene looked squeamish.

"He was just joking. Not a great sense of humor, huh?" I was lying through my teeth. I certainly believed Bubba enjoyed a snack of cat blood.

Arlene shook her head, unconvinced. It was time to change the subject. "Did you and Rene have fun on your evening out?" I asked.

"Rene was so good last night, wasn't he?" she said, her cheeks pink.

A much-married woman, blushing. "You tell me." Arlene enjoyed a little ribald teasing.

"Oh, you! What I mean, he was real polite to Bill and even that Bubba."

"Any reason why he wouldn't be?"

"He has kind of a problem with vampires, Sookie." Arlene shook her head. "I know, I do, too," she confessed when I looked at her with raised eyebrows. "But Rene really has some prejudice. Cindy dated a vampire for a while, and that just made Rene awful upset."

"Cindy okay?" I had a great interest in the health of someone who'd dated a vamp.

"I haven't seen her," Arlene admitted, "but Rene goes to visit every other week or so. She's doing well, she's back on the right track. She has a job in a hospital cafeteria."

Sam, who'd been standing behind the bar loading the refrigerator with bottled blood, said, "Maybe Cindy would like to move back home. Lindsey Krause quit the other shift because she's moving to Little Rock."

That certainly focussed our attention. Merlotte's was becoming seriously under-staffed. For some reason, low-level service jobs had dropped in popularity in the last couple of months.

"You interviewed anyone else?" Arlene asked.

"I'll have to go through the files," Sam said wearily. I knew that Arlene and I were the only barmaids, waitresses, servers, whatever you wanted to call us, that Sam had hung on to for more then two years. No, that wasn't true; there was Susanne Mitchell, on the other shift. Sam spent lots of time hiring and occasionally firing. "Sookie, would you have a look through the file, see if there's anyone there you know has moved, anyone already got a job, anyone you really recommend? That would save me some time."

"Sure," I said. I remembered Arlene doing the same thing a couple of years ago when Dawn had been hired. We had more ties to the community than Sam, who never seemed to join anything. Sam had been in Bon Temps for six years now, and I had never met anyone who seemed to know about Sam's life prior to his buying the bar here.

I settled down at Sam's desk with the thick file of applications. After a few minutes, I could tell I was really making a difference. I had three piles: moved, employed elsewhere, good material. Then I added a fourth and fifth stack: a pile for people I couldn't work with because I couldn't stand them, and a pile for the dead. The first form on the fifth pile had been filled out by a girl who'd died in a car accident last Christmas, and I felt sorry for her folks all over again when I saw her name at the top of the form. The other application was headed "Maudette Pickens."

Maudette had applied for a job with Sam three months before her death. I guess working at Grabbit Kwik was pretty uninspiring. When I glanced over the filled-in blanks and noticed how poor Maudette's handwriting and spelling had been, it made me feel pitiful all over again. I tried to imagine my brother thinking of having sex with this woman — and filming it — was a worthwhile way to spend his time, and I marvelled at Jason's strange mentality. I hadn't seen him since he'd driven off with Desiree. I hoped he'd gotten home in one piece. That gal was a real handful. I wished he'd settle down with Liz Barrett: she had enough backbone to hold him up, too.

Whenever I thought about my brother lately, it was to worry. If only he hadn't known Maudette and Dawn so well! Lots of men knew them both, apparently, both casually and carnally. They'd both been vampire bitten. Dawn had liked rough sex, and I didn't know Maudette's proclivities. Lots of men got gas and coffee at the Grabbit Kwik, and lots of men came in to get a drink here, too. But only my stupid brother had recorded sex with Dawn and Maudette on film.

I stared at the big plastic cup on Sam's desk, which had been full of iced tea. "The Big Kwencher from Grabbit Kwik" was written in neon orange on the side of the green cup. Sam knew them both, too. Dawn had worked for him, Maudette had applied for a job here.

Sam sure didn't like *me* dating a vampire. Maybe he didn't like *anyone* dating a vampire.

Sam walked in just then, and I jumped like I'd been doing something bad. And I had, in my book. Thinking evil of a friend was a bad thing to do.

"Which is the good pile?" he asked, but he gave me a puzzled look.

I handed him a short stack of maybe ten applications. "This gal, Amy Burley," I said, indicating the one on top, "has experience, she's only subbing at the Good Times Bar, and Charlsie used to work with her there. So you could check with Charlsie first."

"Thanks, Sookie. This'll save me some trouble."

I nodded curtly in acknowledgment.

"Are you all right?" he asked. "You seem kind of distant today."

I looked at him closely. He looked just like he always did. But his mind was closed to me. How could he do that? The only other mind completely closed to me was Bill's, because of

332

his vampire state. But Sam was sure no vampire.

"Just missing Bill," I said deliberately. Would he lecture me about the evils of dating a vampire?

Sam said, "It's daytime. He couldn't very well be here."

"Of course not," I said stiffly, and was about to add, "He's out of town." Then I asked myself if that was a smart thing to do when I had even a hint of suspicion in my heart about my boss. I left the office so abruptly that Sam stared after me in astonishment.

When I saw Arlene and Sam having a long conversation later that day, their sidelong glances told me clearly that I was the topic. Sam went back to his office looking more worried than ever. But we didn't have any more chitchat the rest of the day.

Going home that evening was hard because I knew I'd be alone until morning. When I'd been alone other evenings, I'd had the reassurance that Bill was just a phone call away. Now he wasn't. I tried to feel good about being guarded once it was dark and Bubba crawled out of whatever hole he'd slept in, but I didn't manage it.

I called Jason, but he wasn't home. I called Merlotte's, thinking he might be there, but Terry Bellefleur answered the phone and said Jason hadn't been in.

I wondered what Sam was doing tonight. I

wondered why he never seemed to date much. It wasn't for want of offers, I'd been able to observe many times.

Dawn had been especially aggressive.

That evening I couldn't think of anything that pleased me.

I began wondering if Bubba was the hitman — hitvampire? — Bill had called when he wanted Uncle Bartlett bumped off. I wondered why Bill had chosen such a dimwitted creature to guard me.

Every book I picked up seemed wrong, somehow. Every television show I tried to watch seemed completely ridiculous. I tried to read my *Time* and became incensed at the determination to commit suicide that possessed so many nations. I pitched the magazine across the room.

My mind scrabbled around like a squirrel trying to get out of a cage. It couldn't light on anything or be comfortable anywhere.

When the phone rang, I jumped a foot.

"Hello?" I said harshly.

"Jason's here now," Terry Bellefleur said. "He wants to buy you a drink."

I thought uneasily about going out to the car, now that it was dark; about coming home to an empty house, at least a house I would have to hope was empty. Then I scolded myself because, after all, there would be someone watching the house, someone very strong, if very brainless.

"Okay, I'll be there in a minute," I said.

Terry simply hung up. Mr. Chatterbox.

I pulled on a denim skirt and a yellow T-shirt and, looking both ways, crossed the yard to my car. I'd left on every outside light, and I unlocked my car and scooted inside quick as a wink. Once inside the car, I relocked my door.

This was sure no way to live.

I automatically parked in the employee lot when I got to Merlotte's. There was a dog pawing around the Dumpster, and I patted him on the head when I went in. We had to call the pound about once a week to come get some stray or dumped dogs, so many of them pregnant it just made me sick.

Terry was behind the bar.

"Hey," I said, looking around. "Where's Jason?"

"He ain't here," Terry said. "I haven't seen him this evening. I told you so on the phone."

I gaped at him. "But you called me after that and said he had come in."

"No, I didn't."

We stared at each other. Terry was having one of his bad nights, I could tell. His head was writhing around on the inside with the snakes of his army service and his battle with alcohol and drugs. On the outside, you could see he was flushed and sweating despite the air conditioning, and his movements were jerky and clumsy. Poor Terry.

"You really didn't?" I asked, in as neutral a tone as possible.

"Said so, didn't I?" His voice was belligerent.

I hoped none of the bar patrons gave Terry trouble tonight.

I backed out with a conciliatory smile.

The dog was still at the back door. He whined when he saw me.

"Are you hungry, fella?" I asked. He came right up to me, without the cringing I'd come to expect from strays. As he moved more into the light, I saw that this dog had been recently abandoned, if his glossy coat was any indicator. He was a collie, at least mostly. I started to step into the kitchen to ask whoever was cooking if they had any scraps for this guy, but then I had a better idea.

"I know bad ol' Bubba is at the house, but maybe you could come in the house with me," I said in that baby voice I use with animals when I think nobody's listening. "Can you pee outside, so we don't make a mess in the house? Hmmm, boy?"

As if he'd understood me, the collie marked the corner of the Dumpster.

"Good fella! Come for a ride?" I opened my car door, hoping he wouldn't get the seats too dirty. The dog hesitated. "Come on, sugar, I'll give you something good to eat when we get to my place, okay?" Bribery was not necessarily a bad thing.

After a couple more looks and a thorough

sniffing of my hands, the dog jumped onto the passenger seat and sat looking out the windshield like he'd committed himself to this adventure.

I told him I appreciated it, and I tickled his ears. We set off, and the dog made it clear he was used to riding.

"Now, when we get to the house, buddy," I told the collie firmly, "we're gonna make tracks for the front door, okay? There's an ogre in the woods who'd just love to eat you up."

The dog gave an excited yip.

"Well, he's not gonna get a chance," I soothed him. It sure was nice to have something to talk to. It was even nice he couldn't talk back, at least for the moment. And I didn't have to keep my guard up because he wasn't human. Relaxing. "We're gonna hurry."

"Woof," agreed my companion.

"I got to call you something," I said. "How about . . . Buffy?"

The dog growled.

"Okay. Rover?"

Whine.

"Don't like that either. Hmmm." We turned into my driveway.

"Maybe you already have a name?" I asked. "Let me check your neck." After I turned off the engine, I ran my fingers through the thick hair. Not even a flea collar. "Someone's been taking bad care of you, sweetie," I said. "But not anymore. I'll be a good mama." With that last inanity, I got my house key ready and opened my door. In a flash, the dog pushed past me and stood in the yard, looking around him alertly. He sniffed the air, and a growl rose in his throat.

"It's just the good vampire, sugar, the one that's guarding the house. You come on inside." With some constant coaxing, I got the dog to come into the house. I locked the door behind us instantly.

The dog padded all around the living room, sniffing and peering. After watching him for a minute to be sure he wasn't going to chew on anything or lift his leg, I went to the kitchen to find something for him to eat. I filled a big bowl with water. I got another plastic bowl Gran had kept lettuce in, and I put the remains of Tina's cat food and some leftover taco meat in it. I figured if you'd been starving, that would be acceptable. The dog finally worked his back to the kitchen and headed for the bowls. He sniffed at the food and raised his head to give me a long look.

"I'm sorry. I don't have any dog food. That's the best I could come up with. If you want to stay with me, I'll get some Kibbles 'N Bits." The dog stared at me for a few more seconds, then bent his head to the bowl. He ate a little meat, took a drink, and looked up at me expectantly.

"Can I call you Rex?"

A little growl.

"What about Dean?" I asked. "Dean's a nice name." A pleasant guy who helped me at a Shreveport bookstore was named Dean. His eyes looked kind of like this collie's, observant and intelligent. And Dean was a little different; I'd never met a dog named Dean. "I'll bet you're smarter than Bubba," I said thoughtfully, and the dog gave his short, sharp bark.

"Well, come on, Dean, let's get ready for bed," I said, quite enjoying having something to talk to. The dog padded after me into the bedroom, checking out all the furniture very thoroughly. I pulled off the skirt and tee, put them away, and stepped out of my panties and unhooked my bra. The dog watched me with great attention while I pulled out a clean nightgown and went into the bathroom to shower. When I stepped out, clean and soothed, Dean was sitting in the doorway, his head cocked to one side.

"That's to get clean, people like to have showers," I told him. "I know dogs don't. I guess it's a human thing." I brushed my teeth and pulled on my nightgown. "You ready for sleep, Dean?"

In answer, he jumped up on the bed, turned in a circle, and lay down.

"Hey! Wait a minute!" I'd certainly talked myself into that one. Gran would have a fit if she could know a dog was on her bed. Gran had believed animals were fine as long as they spent the night outside. Humans inside, animals outside, had been her rule. Well, now I had a vampire outside and a collie on my bed.

I said, "You get down!" and pointed at the rug.

The collie, slowly, reluctantly, descended from the bed. He eyed me reproachfully as he sat on the rug.

"You stay there," I said sternly and got in the bed. I was very tired, and not nearly so nervous now that the dog was here; though what help I expected him to be in case of an intruder, I didn't know, since he didn't know me well enough to be loyal to me. But I would accept any comfort I could find, and I began to relax into sleep. Just as I was drifting off, I felt the bed indent under the weight of the collie. A narrow tongue gave my cheek a swipe. The dog settled close to me. I turned over and patted him. It was sort of nice having him here.

The next thing I knew, it was dawn. I could hear the birds going to town outside, chirping up a storm, and it felt wonderful to be snuggled in bed. I could feel the warmth of the dog through my nightgown; I must have gotten hot during the night and thrown off the sheet. I drowsily patted the animal's head and began to stroke his fur, my fingers running idly through the thick hair. He wriggled even closer, sniffed my face, put his arm around me.

His *arm?*

I was off the bed and shrieking in one move.

In my bed, Sam propped himself on his elbows, sunny side up, and looked at me with some amusement.

"Oh, ohmyGod! Sam, how'd you get here? What are you doing? Where's Dean?" I covered my face with my hands and turned my back, but I'd certainly seen all there was to see of Sam.

"Woof," said Sam, from a human throat, and the truth stomped over me in combat boots.

I whirled back to face him, so angry I felt like I was going to blow a gasket.

"You watched me undress last night, you . . . you . . . damn dog!"

"Sookie," he said, persuasively. "Listen to me."

Another thought struck me. "Oh, Sam. Bill will kill you." I sat on the slipper chair in the corner by the bathroom door. I put my elbows on my knees and hung my head. "Oh, no," I said. "No, no, no."

He was kneeling in front of me. The wirey red-gold hair of his head was duplicated on his chest and trailed in a line down to . . . I shut my eyes again.

"Sookie, I was worried when Arlene told me you were going to be alone," Sam began.

"Didn't she tell you about Bubba?"

"Bubba?"

"This vampire Bill left watching the house."

"Oh. Yeah, she said he reminded her of some singer."

"Well, his name is Bubba. He likes to drain animals for fun."

I had the satisfaction of seeing (through my fingers) Sam turn pale.

"Well, isn't it lucky you let me in, then," he said finally.

Suddenly recalled to his guise of the night before, I said, "What are you, Sam?"

"I'm a shapeshifter. I thought it was time you knew."

"Did you have to do it quite like that?"

"Actually," he said, embarrassed, "I had planned on waking up and getting out before you opened your eyes. I just overslept. Running around on all fours kind of tires you out."

"I thought people just changed into wolves."

"Nope. I can change into anything."

I was so interested I dropped my hands and tried to just stare at his face. "How often?" I asked. "Do you get to pick?"

"I have to at the full moon," he explained. "Other times, I have to will it; it's harder and it takes longer. I turn into whatever animal I saw before I changed. So I keep a dog book open to a picture of a collie on my coffee table. Collies are big, but nonthreatening."

"So, you could be a bird?"

"Yeah, but flying is hard. I'm always scared I'm going to get fried on a power line, or fly into a window."

"Why? Why did you want me to know?"

"You seemed to handle Bill being a vampire

342

really well. In fact, you seemed to enjoy it. So I thought I would see if you could handle my . . . condition."

"But what you are," I said abruptly, off on a mental tangent, "can't be explained by a virus! I mean, you utterly change!"

He didn't say anything. He just looked at me, the eyes now blue, but just as intelligent and observant.

"Being a shapeshifter is definitely supernatural. If that is, then other things can be. So . . ." I said, slowly, carefully, "Bill hasn't got a virus at all. Being a vampire, it really can't be explained by an allergy to silver or garlic or sunlight . . . that's just so much bullshit the vampires are spreading around, propaganda, you might say . . . so they can be more easily accepted, as sufferers from a terrible disease. But really they're really . . ."

I dashed into the bathroom and threw up. Luckily, I made it to the toilet.

"Yeah," Sam said from the doorway, his voice sad. "I'm sorry, Sookie. But Bill doesn't just have a virus. He's really, really dead."

I washed my face and brushed my teeth twice. I sat down on the edge of the bed, feeling too tired to go further. Sam sat beside me. He put his arm around me comfortingly, and after a moment I nestled closer, laying my cheek in the hollow of his neck.

"You know, once I was listening to NPR," I

said, completely at random. "They were broadcasting a piece about cryogenics, about how lots of people are opting to just freeze their head because it's so much cheaper than getting your whole body frozen."

"Ummm?"

"Guess what song they played for the closing?"

"What, Sookie?"

" 'Put Your Head on My Shoulder.' "

Sam made a choking noise, then doubled over with laughter.

"Listen, Sam," I said, when he'd calmed down. "I hear what you're telling me, but I have to work this out with Bill. I love Bill. I am loyal to him. And he isn't here to give his point of view."

"Oh, this isn't about me trying to woo you away from Bill. Though that would be great." And Sam smiled his rare and brilliant smile. He seemed much more relaxed with me now that I knew his secret.

"Then what is it about?"

"This is about keeping you alive until the murderer is caught."

"So that's why you woke up naked in my bed? For my protection?"

He had the grace to look ashamed. "Well, maybe I could have planned it better. But I did think you needed someone with you, since Arlene told me Bill was out of town. I knew you wouldn't let me spend the night here as a human."

"Will you rest easy now that you know Bubba is watching the house at night?"

"Vampires are strong, and ferocious," Sam conceded. "I guess this Bubba owes Bill something, or he wouldn't be doing him a favor. Vampires aren't big on doing each other favors. They have a lot of structure in their world."

I should have paid more attention to what Sam was saying, but I was thinking I'd better not explain about Bubba's origins.

"If there's you, and Bill, I guess there must be lots of other things outside of nature," I said, realizing what a treasure trove of thought awaited me. Since I'd met Bill, I hadn't felt so much need to hoard neat things up for future contemplation, but it never hurt to be prepared. "You'll have to tell me sometime." Big Foot? The Loch Ness Monster? *I'd* always believed in the Loch Ness monster.

"Well, I guess I better be getting back home," Sam said. He looked at me hopefully. He was still naked.

"Yes, I think you better. But — oh, dang it — you . . . oh, hell." I stomped upstairs to look for some clothes. It seemed to me Jason had a couple of things in an upstairs closet he kept here for some emergency.

Sure enough, there was a pair of blue jeans and a work shirt in the first upstairs bedroom. It was already hot up there, under the tin roof, because the upstairs was on a separate thermostat. I came back down, grateful to feel the cool conditioned air.

"Here," I said, handing Sam the clothes. "I hope they fit well enough." He looked as though he wanted to start our conversation back up, but I was too aware now that I was clad in a thin nylon nightgown and he was clad in nothing at all.

"On with the clothes," I said firmly. "And you get dressed out in the living room." I shooed him out and shut the door behind him. I thought it would be insulting to lock the door, so I didn't. I did get dressed in record time, pulling on clean underwear and the denim skirt and yellow shirt I'd had on the night before. I dabbed on my makeup, put on some earrings, and brushed my hair up into a ponytail, putting a yellow squnchy over the elastic band. My morale rose as I looked in the mirror. My smile turned into a frown when I thought I heard a truck pulling into the front yard.

I came out of the bedroom like I'd been fired from a cannon, hoping like hell Sam was dressed and hiding. He'd done one better. He'd changed back into a dog. The clothes were scattered on the floor, and I swept them up and stuffed them into the closet in the hall.

"Good boy!" I said enthusiastically and scratched behind his ears. Dean responded by sticking his cold black nose up my skirt. "Now you cut that out," I said, and looked through the front window. "It's Andy Bellefleur," I told the dog.

Andy jumped out of his Dodge Ram, stretched for a long second, and headed for my front door. I opened it, Dean by my side.

I eyed Andy quizzically. "You look like you been up all night long, Andy. Can I make you some coffee?"

The dog stirred restlessly beside me.

"That would be great," he said. "Can I come in?"

"Sure." I stood aside. Dean growled.

"You got a good guard dog, there. Here, fella. Come here." Andy squatted to hold out a hand to the collie, whom I simply could not think of as Sam. Dean sniffed Andy's hand, but wouldn't give it a lick. Instead, he kept between me and Andy.

"Come on back to the kitchen," I said, and Andy stood and followed me. I had the coffee on in a jiffy and put some bread in the toaster. Assembling the cream and sugar and spoons and mugs took a few more minutes, but then I had to face why Andy was here. His face was drawn; he looked ten years older than I knew him to be. This was no courtesy call.

"Sookie, were you here last night? You didn't work?"

"No, I didn't. I was here except for a quick trip in to Merlotte's."

"Was Bill here any of that time?"

"No, he's in New Orleans. He's staying in

that new hotel in the French Quarter, the one just for vampires."

"You're sure that's where he is."

"Yes." I could feel my face tighten. The bad thing was coming.

"I've been up all night," Andy said.

"Yes."

"I've just come from another crime scene."

"Yes." I went into his mind. "Amy Burley?" I stared at his eyes, trying to make sure. "Amy who worked at the Good Times Bar?" The name at the top of yesterday's pile of prospective barmaids, the name I'd left for Sam. I looked down at the dog. He lay on the floor with his muzzle between his paws, looking as sad and stunned as I felt. He whined pathetically.

Andy's brown eyes were boring a hole in me. "How'd you know?"

"Cut the crap, Andy, you know I can read minds. I feel awful. Poor Amy. Was it like the others?"

"Yes," he said. "Yes, it was like the others. But the puncture marks were fresher."

I thought of the night Bill and I had had to go to Shreveport to answer Eric's summons. Had Amy given Bill blood that night? I couldn't even count how many days ago that had been, my schedule had been so thrown off by all the strange and terrible events of the past few weeks.

I sat down heavily in a wooden kitchen chair,

shaking my head absently for a few minutes, amazed at the turn my life had taken.

Amy Burley's life had no more turns to take. I shook the odd spell of apathy off, rose and poured the coffee.

"Bill hasn't been here since night before last," I said.

"And you were here all night?"

"Yes, I was. My dog can tell you," and I smiled down at Dean, who whined at being noticed. He came over to lay his fuzzy head on my knees while I drank my coffee. I smoothed his ears.

"Did you hear from your brother?"

"No, but I got a funny phone call, from someone who said he was at Merlotte's." After the words left my mouth I realized the caller must have been Sam, luring me over to Merlotte's so he could maneuver himself into accompanying me home. Dean yawned, a big jaw-cracking yawn that let us see every one of his white sharp teeth.

I wished I'd kept my mouth shut.

But now I had to explain the whole thing to Andy, who was slumped only half-awake in my kitchen chair, his plaid shirt wrinkled and blotched with coffee stains, his khakis shapeless through long wear. Andy was longing for bed the way a horse longs for his own stall.

"You need to get some rest," I said gently. There was something sad about Andy Bellefleur, something daunted.

"It's these murders," he said, his voice unsteady from exhaustion. "These poor women. And they were all the same in so many ways."

"Uneducated, blue-collar women who worked in bars? Didn't mind having a vampire lover from time to time?"

He nodded, his eyes drooping shut.

"Women just like me, in other words."

His eyes opened then. He was aghast at his error. "Sookie . . ."

"I understand, Andy," I said. "In some respects, we are all alike, and if you accept the attack on my grandmother as intended for me, well, I guess then I'm the only survivor."

I wondered who the murderer had left to kill. Was I the only one alive who met his criteria? That was the scariest thought I'd had all day.

Andy was practically nodding over his coffee cup.

"Why don't you go lie down in the other bedroom?" I suggested quietly. "You have to have some sleep. You're not safe to drive, I wouldn't think."

"That's kind of you," Andy said, his voice dragging. He sounded a little surprised, like kindness wasn't something he expected from me. "But I have to get home, set my alarm. I can sleep for maybe three hours."

"I promise I'll wake you up," I said. I didn't want Andy sleeping in my house, but I didn't want him to have a wreck on the way to his house, either. Old Mrs. Bellefleur would never forgive me, and probably Portia wouldn't either. "You come lie down in this room." I led him to my old bedroom. My single bed was neatly made up. "You just lie down on top of the bed, and I'll set the alarm." I did, while he watched. "Now, get a little sleep. I have one errand to run, and I'll be right back." Andy didn't offer any more resistance, but sat heavily on the bed even as I shut the door.

The dog had been padding after me while I got Andy situated, and now I said to him, in a quite different tone, "You go get dressed right *now!*"

Andy stuck his head out the bedroom door. "Sookie, who are you talking to?"

"The dog," I answered instantly. "He always gets his collar, and I put it on every day."

"Why do you ever take it off?"

"It jingles at night, keeps me up. You go to bed, now."

"All right." Looking satisfied at my explanation, Andy shut the door again.

I retrieved Jason's clothes from the closet, put them on the couch in front of the dog, and sat with my back turned. But I realized I could see in the mirror over the mantel.

The air grew hazy around the collie, seemed to hum and vibrate with energy, and then the form began to change within that electric concentration. When the haze cleared, there was Sam kneeling on the floor, buck-naked. Wow, what a bottom. I had to make myself close my eyes, tell myself repeatedly that I had not been unfaithful to Bill. Bill's butt, I told myself staunchly, was every bit as neat.

"I'm ready," Sam's voice said, so close behind me that I jumped. I stood up quickly and turned to face him, and found his face about six inches from mine.

"Sookie," he said hopefully, his hand landing on my shoulder, rubbing and caressing it.

I was angry because half of me wanted to respond.

"Listen here, buddy, you could have told me about yourself any time in the past few years. We've known each other what, four years? Or even more! And yet, Sam, despite the fact that I see you almost daily, you wait until Bill is interested in me, before you even . . ." and unable to think how to finish, I threw my hands up in the air.

Sam drew back, which was a good thing.

"I didn't see what was in front of me until I thought it might be taken away," he said, his voice quiet.

I had nothing to say to that. "Time to go home," I told him. "And we better get you there without anyone seeing you. I mean it."

This was chancy enough without some mischievous person like Rene seeing Sam in my car in the early morning and drawing wrong conclusions. And passing them on to Bill.

So off we went, Sam hunched down in the backseat. I pulled cautiously behind Merlotte's.

There was a truck there; black, with pink and aqua flames down the sides. Jason's.

"Uh-oh," I said.

"What?" Sam's voice was somewhat muffled by his position.

"Let me go look," I said, beginning to be anxious. Why would Jason park over here in the employees' parking area? And it seemed to me there was a shape in the truck.

I opened my door. I waited for the sound to alert the figure in the truck. I watched for evidence of movement. When nothing happened, I began to walk across the gravel, as frightened as I'd ever been in the light of day.

When I got closer to the window, I could see that the figure inside was Jason. He was slumped behind the wheel. I could see that his shirt was stained, that his chin was resting on his chest, that his hands were limp on the seat on either side of him, that the mark on his handsome face was a long red scratch. I could see a videotape resting on the truck dashboard, unlabelled.

"Sam," I said, hating the fear in my voice. "Please come here."

Quicker than I could believe, Sam was beside me, then reaching past me to unlatch the truck door. Since the truck had apparently been sitting there for several hours — there was dew on its hood — with the windows closed, in the early summer, the smell that rolled out was pretty strong and compounded of at least three elements: blood, sex, and liquor.

"Call the ambulance!" I said urgently as Sam reached in to feel for Jason's pulse. Sam looked at me doubtfully. "Are you sure you want to do that?" he asked.

"Of course! He's unconscious!"

"Wait, Sookie. Think about this."

And I might have reconsidered in just a minute, but at that moment Arlene pulled up in her beat-up blue Ford, and Sam sighed and went into his trailer to phone.

I was so naive. That's what comes of being a law-abiding citizen for nearly every day of my life.

I rode with Jason to the tiny local hospital, oblivious to the police looking very carefully at Jason's truck, blind to the squad car following the ambulance, totally trusting when the emergency room doctor sent me home, telling me he'd call me when Jason regained consciousness. The doctor told me, eyeing me curiously, that Jason was apparently sleeping off the effects of alcohol or drugs. But Jason had never drunk that much before, and Jason didn't use drugs: our cousin Hadley's descent into the life of the streets had made a profound impression on both of us. I told the doctor all that, and he listened, and he shooed me off.

Not knowing what to think, I went home to find that Andy Bellefleur had been roused by his pager. He'd left me a note telling me that, and nothing else. Later on, I found that he'd actually been in the hospital while I was there, and waited until I was gone out of consideration for me before he'd handcuffed Jason to the bed.

12

Sam came to give me the news about eleven o'clock. "They're going to arrest Jason as soon as he comes to, Sookie, which looks like being soon." Sam didn't tell me how he came to know this, and I didn't ask.

I stared at him, tears running down my face. Any other day, I might have thought of how plain I look when I cry, but today was not a day I cared about my outsides. I was all in a knot, frightened for Jason, sad about Amy Burley, full of anger the police were making such a stupid mistake, and underneath it all, missing my Bill.

"They think it looks like Amy Burley put up a fight. They think he got drunk after he killed her."

"Thanks, Sam, for warning me." My voice came from way faraway. "You better go to work, now."

After Sam had seen that I needed to be alone, I called information and got the number of Blood in the Quarter. I punched in the numbers, feeling somehow I was doing a bad thing, but I couldn't think how or why.

"Blooooooood . . . in the Quarter," announced a deep voice dramatically. "Your coffin away from home."

Geez. "Good morning. This is Sookie

Stackhouse calling from Bon Temps," I said politely. "I need to leave a message for Bill Compton. He's a guest there."

"Fang or human?"

"Ah . . . fang."

"Just one minute, please."

The deep voice came back on the line after a moment. "What is the message, madam?"

That gave me pause.

"Please tell Mr. Compton that . . . my brother has been arrested, and I would appreciate it if he could come home as soon as his business is completed."

"I have that down." The sound of scribbling. "And your name again?"

"Stackhouse. Sookie Stackhouse."

"All right, miss. I'll see to it that he gets your message."

"Thanks."

And that was the only action I could think of to take, until I realized it would be much more practical to call Sid Matt Lancaster. He did his best to sound appalled to hear Jason was going to be arrested, said he'd hurry over to the hospital as soon as he got out of court that afternoon, and that he'd report back to me.

I drove back to the hospital to see if they'd let me sit with Jason until he became conscious. They wouldn't. I wondered if he was already conscious, and they weren't telling me. I saw Andy Bellefleur at the other end of the hall, and he turned and walked the other way.

Damn coward.

I went home because I couldn't think of anything to do. I realized it wasn't a workday for me anyway, and that was a good thing, though I didn't really care too much at that point. It occurred to me that I wasn't handling this as well as I ought, that I had been much steadier when Gran had died.

But that had been a finite situation. We would bury Gran, her killer would be arrested, we would go on. If the police seriously believed that Jason had killed Gran in addition to the other women, then the world was such a bad and chancy place that I wanted no part of it.

But I realized, as I sat and looked in front of me that long, long afternoon, that it was naivete like that that had led to Jason's arrest. If I'd just gotten him into Sam's trailer and cleaned him up, hidden the film until I found out what it contained, above all not called the ambulance . . . that had been what Sam had been thinking when he'd looked at me so doubtfully. However, Arlene's arrival had kind of wiped out my options.

I thought the phone would start ringing as soon as people heard.

But no one called.

They didn't know what to say.

Sid Matt Lancaster came about four-thirty.

Without any preliminary, he told me, "They've arrested him. For first-degree murder."

I closed my eyes. When I opened them, Sid was regarding me with a shrewd expression on his mild face. His conservative black-framed glasses magnified his muddy brown eyes, and his jowls and sharp nose made him look a little like a bloodhound.

"What does he say?" I asked.

"He says that he was with Amy last night."

I sighed.

"He says they went to bed together, that he had been with Amy before. He says he hadn't seen Amy in a long time, that the last time they were together Amy was acting jealous about the other women he was seeing, really angry. So he was surprised when she approached him last night in Good Times. Jason says Amy acted funny all night, like she had an agenda he didn't know about. He remembers having sex with her, he remembers them lying in bed having a drink afterward, then he remembers nothing until he woke up in the hospital."

"He was set up," I said firmly, thinking I sounded exactly like a bad made-for-TV movie.

"Of course." Sid Matt's eyes were as steady and assured as if he'd been at Amy Burley's place last night.

Hell, maybe he had.

"Listen, Sid Matt." I leaned forward and made him meet my eyes. "Even if I could somehow believe that Jason had killed Amy, and Dawn, and Maudette, I could never believe he would raise his finger to hurt my grandmother."

"All right, then." Sid Matt prepared to meet my thoughts, fair and square, his entire body proclaimed it. "Miss Sookie, let's just assume for a minute that Jason did have some kind of involvement in those deaths. Perhaps, the police might think, your friend Bill Compton killed your grandmother since she was keeping you two apart."

I tried to give the appearance of considering this piece of idiocy. "Well, Sid Matt, my grandmother liked Bill, and she was pleased I was seeing him."

Until he put his game face back on, I saw stark disbelief in the lawyer's eyes. He wouldn't be at all happy if his daughter was seeing a vampire. He couldn't imagine a responsible parent being anything but appalled. And he couldn't imagine trying to convince a jury that my grandmother had been pleased I was dating a guy who wasn't even alive, and furthermore was over a hundred years older than me.

Those were Sid Matt's thoughts.

"Have you met Bill?" I asked.

He was taken aback. "No," he admitted. "You know, Miss Sookie, I'm not for this vampire stuff. I think it's taking a chink out of a wall we should keep built up, a wall between us and the so-called virus-infected. I think God intended that wall to be there, and I for one will hold up my section."

"The problem with that, Sid Matt, is that I personally was created straddling that wall." After a lifetime of keeping my mouth shut about my "gift," I found that if it would help Jason, I'd shake it in anybody's face.

"Well," Sid Matt said bravely, pushing his glasses up on the bridge of his sharp nose, "I am sure the Good Lord gave you this problem I've heard about for a reason. You have to learn how to use it for his glory."

No one had ever quite put it that way. That was an idea to chew over when I had time.

"I've made us stray from the subject, I'm afraid, and I know your time is valuable." I gathered my thoughts. "I want Jason out on bail. There is nothing but circumstantial evidence tying him to Amy's murder, am I right?"

"He's admitted to being with the victim right before the murder, and the videotape, one of the cops hinted to me pretty strongly, shows your brother having sex with the victim. The time and date on the film indicate it was made in the hours before her death, if not minutes."

Damn Jason's peculiar bedroom preferences. "Jason doesn't drink much at all. He smelled of liquor in the truck. I think it was just spilled over him. I think a test will prove that. Maybe Amy gave him some narcotic in the drink she fixed him."

"Why would she do that?"

"Because, like so many women, she was mad at Jason because she wanted him so much. My brother is able to date almost anyone he wants. No, I'm using that euphemism."

Sid Matt looked surprised I knew the word.

"He could go to bed with almost anyone he wanted. A dream life, most guys would think." Weariness descended on me like fog. "Now there he sits in the jail."

"You think another man did this to him? Framed him for this murder?"

"Yes, I do." I leaned forward, trying to persuade this skeptical lawyer by the force of my own belief. "Someone envious of him. Someone who knows his schedule, who kills these women when Jason's off work. Someone who knows Jason had had sex with these gals. Someone who knows he likes to make tapes."

"Could be almost anyone," Jason's lawyer said practically.

"Yep," I said sadly. "Even if Jason was nice enough to keep quiet about exactly who he'd been with, all anyone'd have to do is see who he left a bar with at closing time. Just being observant, maybe having asked about the tapes on a visit to his house . . ." My brother might be somewhat immoral, but I didn't think he'd show those videos to anyone else. He might tell another man that he liked to make the videos, though. "So this man, whoever he is, made some kind of deal with Amy, knowing she was mad at Jason. Maybe he told her he was going to play a practical joke on Jason or something."

"Your brother's never been arrested before,"

Sid Matt observed.

"No." Though it had been a near thing, a couple of times, to hear Jason tell it.

"No record, upstanding member of the community, steady job. There may be a chance I can get him out on bail. But if he runs, you'll lose everything."

It truly had never occurred to me that Jason might skip bail. I didn't know anything about arranging for bail, and I didn't know what I'd have to do, but I wanted Jason out of that jail. Somehow, staying in jail until the legal processes had been gone through before the trial . . . somehow, that would make him look guiltier.

"You find out about it and let me know what I have to do," I said. "In the meantime, can I go see him?"

"He'd rather you didn't," Sid Matt said.

That hurt dreadfully. "Why?" I asked, trying really hard not to tear up again.

"He's ashamed," said the lawyer.

The thought of Jason feeling shame was fascinating.

"So," I said, trying to move along, suddenly tired of this unsatisfactory meeting. "You'll call me when I can actually do something?"

Sid Matt nodded, his jowls trembling slightly with the movement. I made him uneasy. He sure was glad to be leaving me.

The lawyer drove off in his pickup, clapping a cowboy hat on his head when he was still in sight.

When it was full dark, I went out to check on Bubba. He was sitting under a pin oak, bottles of blood lined up beside him, empties on one side, fulls on the other.

I had a flashlight, and though I knew Bubba was there, it was still a shock to see him in the beam of light. I shook my head. Something really had gone wrong when Bubba "came over," no doubt about it. I was sincerely glad I couldn't read Bubba's thoughts. His eyes were crazy as hell.

"Hey, sugar," he said, his Southern accent as thick as syrup. "How you doing? You come to keep me company?"

"I just wanted to make sure you were comfortable," I said.

"Well, I could think of places I'd be more comfortable, but since you're Bill's girl, I ain't about to talk about them."

"Good," I said firmly.

"Any cats around here? I'm getting mighty tired of this bottled stuff."

"No cats. I'm sure Bill will be back soon, and then you can go home." I started back toward the house, not feeling comfortable enough in Bubba's presence to prolong the conversation, if you could call it that. I wondered what thoughts Bubba had during his long watchful nights; I wondered if he remembered his past.

"What about that dog?" he called after me.

"He went home," I called back over my shoulder.

"Too bad," Bubba said to himself, so softly I almost didn't hear him.

I got ready for bed. I watched television. I ate some ice cream, and I even chopped up a Heath Bar for a topping. None of my usual comfort things seemed to work tonight. My brother was in jail, my boyfriend was in New Orleans, my grandmother was dead, and someone had murdered my cat. I felt lonely and sorry for myself all the way around.

Sometimes you just have to roll in it.

Bill didn't return my call.

That added fuel to the flame of my misery. He'd probably found some accommodating whore in New Orleans, or some fang-banger, like the ones who hung around Blood in the Quarter every night, hoping for a vampire "date."

If I were a drinking woman, I would have gotten drunk. If I'd been a casual woman, I would have called lovely JB du Rone and had sex with him. But I'm not anything so dramatic or drastic, so I just ate ice cream and watched old movies on TV. By an eerie coincidence, *Blue Hawaii* was on.

I finally went to bed about midnight.

A shriek outside my bedroom window woke me up. I sat up straight in bed. I heard thumps, and thuds, and finally a voice I was sure was Bubba's shouting, "Come back here, sucker!"

When I hadn't heard anything in a couple of minutes, I pulled on a bathrobe and went to the front door. The yard, lit by the security light, was empty. Then I glimpsed movement to the left, and when I stuck my head out the door, I saw Bubba, trudging back to his hideout.

"What happened?" I called softly.

Bubba changed direction and slouched over to the porch.

"Sure enough, some sumbitch, scuse me, was sneaking around the house," Bubba said. His brown eyes were glowing, and he looked more like his former self. "I heard him minutes before he got here, and I thought I'd catch ahold of him. But he cut through the woods to the road, and he had a truck parked there."

"Did you get a look?"

"Not enough of one to describe him," Bubba said shamefacedly. "He was driving a pickup, but I couldn't even tell what color it was. Dark."

"You saved me, though," I said, hoping my very real gratitude showed in my voice. I felt a swell of love for Bill, who had arranged my protection. Even Bubba looked better than he had before. "Thanks, Bubba."

"Aw, think nothing of it," he said graciously, and for that moment he stood up straight, kind of tossed his head back, had that sleepy smile on his face . . . it *was* him, and I'd opened my mouth to say his name, when Bill's warning came back to shut my mouth.

Jason made bail the next day.

It cost a fortune. I signed what Sid Matt told me to, though mostly the collateral was Jason's house and truck and his fishing boat. If Jason had ever been arrested before, even for jaywalking, I don't think he would have been permitted to post bond.

I was standing on the courthouse steps wearing my horrible, sober, navy blue suit in the heat of the late morning. Sweat trickled down my face and ran between my lips in that nasty way that makes you want to go jump in the shower. Jason stopped in front of me. I hadn't been sure he would speak. His face was years older. Real trouble had come to sit on his shoulder, real trouble that would not go away or ease up, like grief did.

"I can't talk to you about this," he said, so softly I could barely hear him. "You know it wasn't me. I've never been violent beyond a fight or two in a parking lot over some woman."

I touched his shoulder, let my hand drop when he didn't respond. "I never thought it was you. I never will. I'm sorry I was fool enough to call 911 yesterday. If I'd realized that wasn't your blood, I'd have taken you into Sam's trailer and cleaned you up and burned the tape. I was just so scared that was your blood." And I felt my eyes fill. This was no time to cry, though, and I tightened up all over, feeling my face tense. Jason's mind was a mess, like a mental pigsty. In it bubbled an unhealthy brew compounded of regrets, shame at his

367

sexual habits being made public, guilt that he didn't feel worse about Amy being killed, horror that anyone in the town would think he'd killed his own grandmother while lying in wait for his sister.

"We'll get through this," I said helplessly.

"We'll get through this," he repeated, trying to make his voice sound strong and assured. But I thought it would be awhile, a long while, before Jason's assurance, that golden certainty that had made him irresistible, returned to his posture and his face and his speech.

Maybe it never would.

We parted there, at the courthouse. We had nothing more to say.

I sat in the bar all day, looking at the men who came in, reading their minds. Not one of them was thinking of how he'd killed four women and gotten away with it so far. At lunchtime Hoyt and Rene walked in the door and walked back out when they saw me sitting. Too embarrassing for them, I guess.

Finally, Sam made me leave. He said I was so creepy that I was driving away any customers who might give me useful information.

I trudged out the door and into the glaring sun. It was about to set. I thought about Bubba, about Bill, about all those creatures that were coming out of their deep sleep to walk the surface of the earth.

I stopped at the Grabbit Kwik to buy some milk for my morning cereal. The new clerk was a kid with pimples and a huge Adam's apple, who stared at me eagerly as if he was trying to make a print in his head of how I looked, the sister of a murderer. I could tell he could hardly wait for me to leave the store so he could use the phone to call his girlfriend. He was wishing he could see the puncture marks on my neck. He was wondering if there was any way he could find out how vampires did it.

This was the kind of trash I had to listen to, day in, day out. No matter how hard I concentrated on something else, no matter how high I kept my guard, how broad I kept my smile, it seeped through.

I reached home just when it was getting dark. After putting away the milk and taking off my suit, I put on a pair of shorts and a black Garth Brooks T-shirt and tried to think of some goal for the evening. I couldn't settle down enough to read; and I needed to go to the library and change my books anyway, which would be a real ordeal under the circumstances. Nothing on TV was good, at least tonight. I thought I might watch *Braveheart* again: Mel Gibson in a kilt is always a mood raiser. But it was just too bloody for my frame of mind. I couldn't bear for that gal to get her throat cut again, even though I knew when to cover my eyes.

I'd gone into the bathroom to wash off my sweaty makeup when, over the sound of the running water, I thought I heard a yowl outside.

I turned the faucets off. I stood still, almost feeling my antenna twitch, I was listening so intently. What . . . ? Water from my wet face trickled onto my T-shirt.

No sound. No sound at all.

I crept toward the front door because it was closest to Bubba's watch point in the woods.

I opened the door a little. I yelled, "Bubba?"

No answer.

I tried again.

It seemed to me even the locusts and toads were holding their breaths. The night was so silent it might hold anything. Something was prowling out there, in the darkness.

I tried to think, but my heart was hammering so hard it interfered with the process.

Call the police, first.

I found that was not an option. The phone was dead.

So I could either wait in this house for trouble to come to me, or I could go out into the woods.

That was a tough one. I bit into my lower lip while I went around the house turning out the lamps, trying to map out a course of action. The house provided some protection: locks, walls, nooks, and crannies. But I knew any really determined person could get in, and then I would be trapped.

Okay. How could I get outside without being seen? I turned off the outside lights, for a start. The back door was closer to the woods, so that was the better choice. I knew the woods pretty well. I should be able to hide in them until daylight. I could go over to Bill's house, maybe; surely his phone was working, and I had a key.

Or I could try to get to my car and start it. But that pinned me down to a particular place for particular seconds.

No, the woods seemed the better choice to me.

In one of my pockets I tucked Bill's key and a pocketknife of my grandfather's that Gran had kept in the living-room table drawer, handy for opening packages. I tucked a tiny flashlight in the other pocket. Gran kept an old rifle in the coat closet by the front door. It had been my dad's when he was little, and she mostly had used it for shooting snakes; well, I had me a snake to shoot. I hated the damn rifle, hated the thought of using it, but now seemed to be the time.

It wasn't there.

I could hardly believe my senses. I felt all through the closet.

He'd been in my house!

But it hadn't been broken into.

Someone I'd invited in. Who'd been here? I tried to list them all as I went to the back door, my sneakers retied so they wouldn't have any spare shoelaces to step on. I skinned my hair into a ponytail sloppily, almost one handed, so it wouldn't get in my face, and twisted a rubber band around it. But all the time I thought about the stolen rifle.

Who'd been in my house? Bill, Jason, Arlene, Rene, the kids, Andy Bellefleur, Sam, Sid Matt; I was sure I'd left them all alone for a minute or two, perhaps long enough to stick the rifle outside to retrieve later.

Then I remembered the day of the funeral. Almost everyone I knew had been in and out of the house when Gran had died, and I couldn't remember if I'd seen the rifle since then. But it would have been hard to have casually strolled out of the crowded, busy house with a rifle. And if it had vanished then, I thought I would have noticed its absence by now. In fact, I was almost sure I would have.

I had to shove that aside now and concentrate on outwitting whatever was out there in the dark.

I opened the back door. I duckwalked out, keeping as low as I could, and gently eased the door nearly shut behind me. Rather than use the steps, I straightened one leg and tapped the ground while squatting on the porch; I shifted my weight to it, pulled the other leg behind me. I crouched again. This was a lot like playing hide and seek with Jason in the woods when we were kids.

I prayed I was not playing hide and seek with Jason again.

I used the tub full of flowers that Gran had planted as cover first, then I crept to her car, my second goal. I looked up in the sky. The moon was new, and since the night was clear the stars were out. The air was heavy with humidity, and it was still hot. My arms were slick with sweat in minutes.

Next step, from the car to the mimosa tree.

I wasn't as quiet this time. I tripped over a stump and hit the ground hard. I bit the inside of my mouth to keep from crying out. Pain shot through my leg and hip, and I knew the edges of the ragged stump had scraped my thigh pretty severely. Why hadn't I come out and sawed that stump off clean? Gran had asked Jason to do it, but he'd never found the time.

I heard, sensed, movement. Throwing caution to the winds, I leaped up and dashed for the trees. Someone crashed through the edge of the woods to my right and headed for me. But I knew where I was going, and in a vault that amazed me, I'd seized the low branch of our favorite childhood climbing tree and pulled myself up. If I lived until the next day, I'd have severely strained muscles, but it would be worth it. I balanced on the branch, trying to keep my breathing quiet, when I wanted to pant and groan like a dog dreaming.

I wished this were a dream. Yet here I undeniably was, Sookie Stackhouse, waitress and mind reader, sitting on a branch in the woods in the dead of night, armed with nothing more than a pocket knife.

Movement below me; a man glided through the woods. He had a length of cord hanging from one wrist. Oh, Jesus. Though the moon was almost full, his head stayed stubbornly in the shadow of the tree, and I couldn't tell who it was. He passed underneath without seeing me.

When he was out of sight, I breathed again. As quietly as I could, I scrambled down. I began working my way through the woods to the road. It would take awhile, but if I could get to the road maybe I could flag someone down. Then I thought of how seldom the road got traveled; it might be better to work my way across the cemetery to Bill's house. I thought of the cemetery at night, of the murderer looking for me, and I shivered all over.

Being even more scared was pointless. I had to concentrate on the here and now. I watched every foot placement, moving slowly. A fall would be noisy in this undergrowth, and he'd be on me in a minute.

I found the dead cat about ten yards south east of my perching tree. The cat's throat was a gaping wound. I couldn't even tell what color its fur had been in the bleaching effect of the moonlight, but the dark splotches around the little corpse were surely blood. After five more feet of stealthy movement, I found Bubba. He was unconscious or dead. With a vampire it was hard to tell the difference. But with no stake through his heart, and his head still on, I could hope he was only unconscious.

Someone had brought Bubba a drugged cat,

I figured. Someone who had known Bubba was guarding me and had heard of Bubba's penchant for draining cats.

I heard a crackle behind me. The snap of a twig. I glided into the shadow of the nearest large tree. I was mad, mad and scared, and I wondered if I would die this night.

I might not have the rifle, but I had a built-in tool. I closed my eyes and reached out with my mind.

Dark tangle, red, black. Hate.

I flinched. But this was necessary, this was my only protection. I let down every shred of defense.

Into my head poured images that made me sick, made me terrified. Dawn, asking someone to punch her, then finding out that he'd got one of her hose in his hand, was stretching it between his fingers, preparing to tighten it around her neck. A flash of Maudette, naked and begging. A woman I'd never seen, her bare back to me, bruises and welts covering it. Then my grandmother — my grandmother — in our familiar kitchen, angry and fighting for her life.

I was paralyzed by the shock of it, the horror of it. Whose thoughts were these? I had an image of Arlene's kids, playing on my living room floor; I saw myself, and I didn't look like the person I saw in my own mirror. I had huge holes in my neck, and I was lewd; I had a knowing leer on my face, and I patted the inside of my thigh suggestively.

I was in the mind of Rene Lenier. This was how Rene saw me.

Rene was mad.

Now I knew why I'd never been able to read his thoughts explicitly; he kept them in a secret hole, a place in his mind he kept hidden and separate from his conscious self.

He was seeing an outline behind a tree now and wondering if it looked like the outline of a woman.

He was seeing me.

I bolted and ran west toward the cemetery. I couldn't listen to his head anymore, because my own head was focused so fixedly on running, dodging the obstacles of trees, bushes, fallen limbs, a little gully where rain had collected. My strong legs pumped, my arms swung, and my breath sounded like the wheezing of a bagpipe.

I broke from the woods and was in the cemetery. The oldest portion of the graveyard was farther north toward Bill's house, and it had the best places of concealment. I bounded over headstones, the modern kind, set almost flush with the ground, no good for hiding. I leaped over Gran's grave, the earth still raw, no stone yet. Her killer followed me. I turned to look, to see how close he was, like a fool, and in the moonlight I saw Rene's rough head of hair clearly as he gained on me.

I ran down into the gentle bowl the cemetery formed, then began sprinting up the other side.

When I thought there were enough large head-stones and statues between me and Rene, I dodged behind a tall granite column topped with a cross. I remained standing, flattening myself against the cold hardness of the stone. I clamped a hand across my own mouth to silence my sobbing effort to get air in my lungs. I made myself calm enough to try to listen to Rene; but his thoughts were not even coherent enough to decipher, except the rage he felt. Then a clear concept presented itself.

"Your sister," I yelled. "Is Cindy still alive, Rene?"

"Bitch!" he screamed, and I knew in that second that the first woman to die had been Rene's sister, the one who liked vampires, the one he was supposedly still visiting from time to time, according to Arlene. Rene had killed Cindy, his waitress sister, while she was still wearing her pink-and-white hospital cafeteria uniform. He'd strangled her with her apron strings. And he'd had sex with her, after she was dead. She'd sunk so low, she wouldn't mind her own brother, he'd thought, as much as he was capable of thinking. Anyone who'd let a vampire do that deserved to die. And he'd hidden her body from shame. The others weren't his flesh and blood; it had been all right to let them lie.

I'd gotten sucked down into Rene's sick interior like a twig dragged down by a whirlpool, and it made me stagger. When I came back into my own head, he was on me. He hit me in the face as hard as he could, and he expected me to go down. The blow broke my nose and hurt so bad I almost blanked out, but I didn't collapse. I hit him back. My lack of experience made my blow ineffectual. I just thumped him in the ribs, and he grunted, but in the next instant he retaliated.

His fist broke my collarbone. But I didn't fall.

He hadn't known how strong I was. In the moonlight, his face was shocked when I fought back, and I thanked the vampire blood I'd taken. I thought of my brave grandmother, and I launched myself at him, grabbing him by the ears and attempting to hit his head against the granite column. His hands shot up to grip my forearms, and he tried to pull me away so I'd loose my grip. Finally he succeeded, but I could tell from his eyes he was surprised and more on guard. I tried to knee him, but he anticipated me, twisting just far enough away to dodge me. While I was off-balance, he pushed, and I hit the ground with a teeth-chattering thud.

Then he was straddling me. But he'd dropped the cord in our struggle, and while he held my neck with one hand, he was groping with the other for his method of choice. My right arm was pinned, but my left was free, and I struck and clawed at him. He had to ignore this, had to look for the strangling cord because that was part of his ritual. My scrabbling hand encountered a familiar shape.

Rene, in his work clothes, was still wearing his knife on his belt. I yanked the snap open and pulled the knife from its sheath, and while he was still thinking, "I should have taken that off," I sank the knife into the soft flesh of his waist, angling up. And I pulled it out.

He screamed, then.

He staggered to his feet, twisting his upper torso sideways, trying with both hands to stanch the blood that was pouring from the wound.

I scuttered backward, getting up, trying to put distance between myself and man who was a monster just as surely as Bill was.

Rene screamed. "Aw, Jesus, woman! What you done to me? Oh, God, it hurts!"

That was rich.

He was scared now, frightened of discovery, of an end to his games, of an end to his vengeance.

"Girls like you deserve to die," he snarled. "I can feel you in my head, you freak!"

"Who's the freak around here?" I hissed. "Die, you bastard."

I didn't know I had it in me. I stood by the headstone in a crouch, the bloody knife still clutched in my hand, waiting for him to charge me again.

He staggered in circles, and I watched, my face stony. I closed my mind to him, to his feeling his death crawl up behind him. I stood ready to knife him a second time when he fell to the ground. When I was sure he couldn't move, I went to Bill's house, but I didn't run. I told myself it was because I couldn't: but I'm not sure. I kept seeing my grandmother, encapsuled in Rene's memory forever, fighting for her life in her own house.

I fished Bill's key out of my pocket, almost amazed it was still there.

I turned it somehow, staggered into the big living room, felt for the phone. My fingers touched the buttons, managed to figure out which was the nine and where the one was. I pushed the numbers hard enough to make them beep, and then, without warning, I checked out of consciousness.

I knew I was in the hospital: I was surrounded by the clean smell of hospital sheets.

The next thing I knew was that I hurt all over.

And someone was in the room with me. I opened my eyes, not without effort.

Andy Bellefleur. His square face was even more fatigued than the last time I'd seen him.

"Can you hear me?" he said.

I nodded, just a tiny movement, but even that sent a wave of pain through my head.

"We got him," he said, and then he proceeded to tell me a lot more, but I fell back asleep.

It was daylight when I woke again, and this

time, I seemed to be much more alert.

Someone in the room.

"Who's here?" I said, and my voice came out in a painful rasp.

Kevin rose from the chair in the corner, rolling a crossword puzzle magazine and sticking it into his uniform pocket.

"Where's Kenya?" I whispered.

He grinned at me unexpectedly. "She was here for a couple of hours," he explained. "She'll be back soon. I spelled her for lunch."

His thin face and body formed one lean line of approval. "You are one tough lady," he told me.

"I don't feel tough," I managed.

"You got hurt," he told me as if I didn't know that.

"Rene."

"We found him out in the cemetery," Kevin assured me. "You stuck him pretty good. But he was still conscious, and he told us he'd been trying to kill you."

"Good."

"He was real sorry he hadn't finished the job. I can't believe he spilled the beans like that, but he was some kind of hurting and he was some kind of scared, by the time we got to him. He told us the whole thing was your fault because you wouldn't just lie down to die like the others. He said it must run in your genes, because your grandmother . . ." Here Kevin stopped short, aware that he was on upsetting ground.

"She fought, too," I whispered.

Kenya came in then, massive, impassive, and holding a steaming Styrofoam cup of coffee.

"She's awake," Kevin said, beaming at his partner.

"Good." Kenya sounded less overjoyed about it. "She say what happened? Maybe we should call Andy."

"Yeah, that's what he said to do. But he's just been asleep four hours."

"The man said call."

Kevin shrugged, went to the phone at the side of the bed. I eased off into a doze as I heard him speaking, but I could hear him murmur with Kenya as they waited. He was talking about his hunting dogs. Kenya, I guess, was listening.

Andy came in, I could feel his thoughts, the pattern of his brain. His solid presence came to roost by my bed. I opened my eyes as he was bending to look at me. We exchanged a long stare.

Two pair of feet in regulation shoes moved out into the hall.

"He's still alive," Andy said abruptly. "And he won't stop talking."

I made the briefest motion of my head, indicating a nod, I hoped.

"He says this goes back to his sister, who was seeing a vampire. She evidently got so low on blood that Rene thought she'd turn into a vamp herself if he didn't stop her. He gave her an ul-

382

timatum, one evening in her apartment. She talked back, said she wouldn't give up her lover. She was tying her apron around her, getting ready to go to work as they were arguing. He yanked it off her, strangled her . . . did other stuff."

Andy looked a little sick.

"I know," I whispered.

"It seems to me," Andy began again, "that somehow he decided he'd feel justified in doing that horrible thing if he convinced himself that everyone in his sister's situation deserved to die. In fact, the murders here are very similar to two in Shreveport that haven't been solved up until now, and we're expecting Rene to touch on those while he's rambling along. If he makes it."

I could feel my lips pressing together in horrified sympathy for those other poor women.

"Can you tell me what happened to you?" Andy asked quietly. "Go slow, take your time, and keep your voice down to a whisper. Your throat is badly bruised."

I had figured that out for myself, thanks very much. I murmured my account of the evening, and I didn't leave anything out. Andy had switched on a little tape recorder after asking me if that was all right. He placed it on the pillow close to my mouth when I indicated the device was okay with me, so he'd have the whole story.

"Mr. Compton still out of town?" he asked

me, after I'd finished.

"New Orleans," I whispered, barely able to speak.

"We'll look in Rene's house for the rifle, now that we know it's yours. It'll be a nice piece of corroborative evidence."

Then a gleaming young woman in white came into the room, looked at my face, and told Andy he'd have to come back some other time.

He nodded at me, gave me an awkward pat on the hand, and left. He gave the doctor a backward glance of admiration. She was sure worth admiring, but she was also wearing a wedding ring, so Andy was once again too late.

She thought he seemed too serious and grim.

I didn't want to hear this.

But I didn't have enough energy to keep everyone out of my head.

"Miss Stackhouse, how are you feeling?" the young woman asked a little too loudly. She was brunette and lean, with wide brown eyes and a full mouth.

"Like hell," I whispered.

"I can imagine," she said, nodding repeatedly while looking me over. I somehow didn't think she could. I was willing to bet she'd never been beaten up by a multiple murderer in a grave-yard.

"You just lost your grandmother, too, didn't you?" she asked sympathetically. I nodded, just a fraction of an inch.

"My husband died about six months ago," she said. "I know about grief. It's tough being brave, isn't it?"

Well, well, well. I let my expression ask a question.

"He had cancer," she explained. I tried to look my condolences without moving anything, which was nearly impossible.

"Well," she said, standing upright, returning to her brisk manner, "Miss Stackhouse, you're sure gonna live. You have a broken collarbone, and two broken ribs, and a broken nose."

Shepherd of Judea! No wonder I felt bad.

"Your face and neck are severely bruised. Of course, you could tell your throat was hurt."

I was trying to imagine what I looked like. Good thing I didn't have a mirror handy.

"And you have lots of relatively minor bruises and cuts on your legs and arms." She smiled. "Your stomach is fine, and your feet!"

Hohoho. Very funny.

"I have prescribed pain medication for you, so when you start feeling bad, just ring for the nurse."

A visitor stuck his head in the door behind her. She turned, blocking my view, and said, "Hello?"

"This Sookie's room?"

"Yes, I was just finishing her examination. You can come in." The doctor (whose name was Sonntag, by her nameplate) looked questioningly at me to get my permission, and I managed a tiny "Sure."

JB du Rone drifted to my bedside, looking as lovely as the cover model on a romance novel. His tawny hair gleamed under the fluorescent lights, his eyes were just the same color, and his sleeveless shirt showed muscle definition that might have been chiseled with a — well, with a chisel. He was looking down at me, and Dr. Sonntag was drinking him in.

"Hey, Sookie, you feelin' all right?" he asked. He lay a finger gently on my cheek. He kissed an unbruised spot on my forehead.

"Thanks," I whispered. "I'll be okay. Meet my doctor."

JB turned his wide eyes on Dr. Sonntag, who practically tripped over her own feet to introduce herself.

"Doctors weren't this pretty when I was getting my shots," JB said sincerely and simply.

"You haven't been to a doctor since you were a kid?" Dr. Sonntag said, amazed.

"I never get sick." He beamed at her. "Strong as an ox."

And the brain of one. But Dr. Sonntag probably had smarts enough for two.

She couldn't think of any reason for lingering, though she cast a wistful glance over her shoulder as she left.

JB bent down to me and said earnestly, "Can I bring you anything, Sookie? Nabs or something?"

The thought of trying to eat crackers made

tears come to my eyes. "No thanks," I breathed. "The doctor's a widow."

You could change subjects on JB without him wondering why.

"Wow," he said, impressed. "She's smart and single."

I wiggled my eyebrows in a significant way.

"You think I oughtta ask her out?" JB looked as thoughtful as it was possible for him to be. "That might be a good idea." He smiled down at me. "Long as *you* won't date me, Sookie. You're always number one to me. You just crook your little finger, and I'll come running."

What a sweet guy. I didn't believe in his devotion for a minute, but I did believe he knew how to make a woman feel good, even if she was as sure as I was that I looked breathtakingly bad. I felt pretty bad, too. Where were those pain pills? I tried to smile at JB.

"You're hurting," he said. "I'll send the nurse down here."

Oh, good. The reach to the little button had seemed longer and longer as I tried to get my arm to move.

He kissed me again as he left and said, "I'll go track that doctor of yours down, Sookie. I better ask her some more questions about your recovery."

After the nurse injected some stuff into my IV drip, I was just looking forward to feeling no pain when the door opened again.

My brother came in. He stood by my bed for

a long time, staring at my face. He said finally, heavily, "I talked to the doctor for a minute before she left for the cafeteria with JB. She told me what-all was wrong with you." He walked away from me, took a turn around the room, came back. More staring. "You look like hell."

"Thanks," I whispered.

"Oh, yeah, your throat. I forgot."

He started to pat me, thought the better of it.

"Listen, Sis, I gotta say thank you, but it's got me down that you stood in for me when it came time to fight."

If I could have, I'd have kicked him.

Stood in for him, hell.

"I owe you big, Sis. I was so dumb, thinking Rene was a good friend."

Betrayed. He felt betrayed.

Then Arlene came in, to make things just peachy keen.

She was a mess. Her hair was in a red tangle, she had no makeup, and her clothes were chosen at random. I'd never seen Arlene without her hair curled and her makeup loud and bright.

She looked down at me — boy, would I be glad when I could stand up again — and for a second her face was hard as granite, but when she really took in my face, she began to crumble.

"I was so mad at you, I didn't believe it, but now that I'm seeing you and what he did . . . oh, Sookie, can you ever forgive me?"

Geez, I wanted her out of here. I tried to tele-graph this to Jason, and for once I got through, because he put an arm around her shoulders and led her out. Arlene was sobbing before she reached the door. "I didn't know . . ." she said, barely coherent. "I just didn't know!"

"Hell, neither did I," Jason said heavily.

I took a nap after trying to ingest some deli-cious green gelatin.

My big excitement of the afternoon was walking to the bathroom, more or less by my-self. I sat in the chair for ten minutes, after which I was more than ready to get back in bed. I looked in the mirror concealed in the rolling table and was very sorry I had.

I was running a little temperature, just enough to make me shivery and tender-skinned. My face was blue and gray and my nose was swollen double. My right eye was puffy and almost closed. I shuddered, and even that hurt. My legs . . . oh, hell, I didn't even want to check. I lay back very carefully and wanted this day to be over. Probably four days from now I'd feel just great. Work! When could I go back to work?

A little knock at the door distracted me. An-other damn visitor. Well, this was someone I didn't know. An older lady with blue hair and red-framed glasses wheeled in a cart. She was wearing the yellow smock the hospital volun-teers called Sunshine Ladies had to don when they were working.

The cart was covered with flowers for the patients in this wing.

"I'm delivering you a load of best wishes!" the lady said cheerfully.

I smiled, but the effect must have been ghastly because her own cheer wavered a little.

"These are for you," she said, lifting a potted plant decorated with a red ribbon. "Here's the card, honey. Let's see, these are for you, too . . ." This was an arrangement of cut flowers, featuring pink rosebuds and pink carnations and white baby's breath. She plucked the card from that bowl, too. Surveying the cart, she said, "Now, aren't you the lucky one! Here are some more for you!!"

The focus of the third floral tribute was a bizarre red flower I'd never seen before, surrounded by a host of other, more familiar blooms. I looked at this one doubtfully. The Sunshine Lady dutifully presented me with the card from the plastic prongs.

After she'd smiled her way out of the room, I opened the little envelopes. It was easier to move when I was in a better mood, I noticed wryly.

The potted plant was from Sam and "all your coworkers at Merlotte's" read the card, but it was written in Sam's handwriting. I touched the glossy leaves and wondered where I'd put it when I took it home. The cut flowers were from Sid Matt Lancaster and Elva Deene Lancaster — pooey. The arrangement centered with the peculiar red blossom (I decided that somehow the flower looked almost obscene, like a lady's private part) was definitely the most interesting of the three. I opened the card with some curiosity. It bore only a signature, "Eric."

That was all I needed. How the hell had he heard I was in the hospital? Why hadn't I heard from Bill?

After some delicious red gelatin for supper, I focused on the television for a couple of hours, since I hadn't anything to read, even if my eyes had been up to it. My bruises grew more charming every hour, and I felt weary to my bones, despite the fact that I'd only walked once to the bathroom and twice around my room. I switched off the television and turned onto my side. I fell asleep, and in my dreams the pain from my body seeped in and made me have nightmares. I ran in my dreams, ran through the cemetery, afraid for my life, falling over stones, into open graves, encountering all the people I knew who lay there: my father and mother, my grandmother, Maudette Pickens, Dawn Green, even a childhood friend who'd been killed in a hunting accident. I was looking for a particular headstone; if I found it, I was home free. They would all go back into their graves and leave me alone. I ran from this one to that one, putting my hand on each one, hoping it would be the right stone. I whimpered.

"Sweetheart, you're safe," came a familiar cool voice.

"Bill," I muttered. I turned to face a stone I hadn't yet touched. When I lay my fingers on it, they traced the letters "William Erasmus Compton." As if I'd been dashed with cold water, my eyes flew open, I drew in a breath to scream, and my throat gave a great throb of pain. I choked on the extra air, and the pain of the coughing, which pretty much hurt every single thing I'd broken, completed my awakening. A hand slipped under my cheek, the cool fingers feeling wonderfully good against my hot skin. I tried not to whimper, but a little noise made its way through my teeth.

"Turn to the light, darling," Bill said, his voice very light and casual.

I'd been sleeping with my back to the light the nurse had left on, the one in the bathroom. Now I rolled obediently to my back and looked up at my vampire.

Bill hissed.

"I'll kill him," he said, with a simple certainty that chilled me to the bone.

There was enough tension in the room to send a fleet of the nervous running for their tranquilizers.

"Hi, Bill," I croaked. "Glad to see you, too. Where you been so long? Thanks for returning all my calls."

That brought him up short. He blinked. I could feel him making an effort to calm himself.

"Sookie," he said. "I didn't call because I

wanted to tell you in person what has happened." I couldn't read the expression on his face. If I'd had to take a shot, I would've said he looked proud of himself.

He paused, scanned all visible portions of me.

"This doesn't hurt," I croaked obligingly, extending my hand to him. He kissed that, lingered over it in a way that sent a faint tingle through my body. Believe me, a faint tingle was more than I'd thought I was capable of.

"Tell me what has been done to you," he commanded.

"Then lean down so I can whisper. This really hurts."

He pulled a chair close to the bed, lowered the bed rail, and lay his chin on his folded arms. His face was maybe four inches from mine.

"Your nose is broken," he observed.

I rolled my eyes. "Glad you spotted that," I whispered. "I'll tell the doctor when she comes in."

His gaze narrowed. "Stop trying to deflect me."

"Okay. Nose broken, two ribs, a collarbone."

But Bill wanted to examine me all over, and he pulled the sheet down. My mortification was complete. Of course, I was wearing an awful hospital gown, in itself a downer, and I hadn't bathed properly, and my face was several different shades, and my hair hadn't been brushed.

"I want to take you home," he announced, after he'd run his hands all over and minutely examined each scrape and cut. The Vampire Physician.

I motioned with my hand to make him bend down. "No," I breathed. I pointed to the drip bag. He eyed it with some suspicion, but of course he had to know what one was.

"I can take it out," he said.

I shook my head vehemently.

"You don't want me to take care of you?"

I puffed out my breath in exasperation, which hurt like hell.

I made a writing motion with my hand, and Bill searched the drawers until he found a notepad. Oddly enough, he had a pen. I wrote, "They'll let me out of the hospital tomorrow if my fever doesn't go high."

"Who'll take you home?" he asked. He was standing by the bed again, and looking down at me with stern disapproval, like a teacher whose best pupil happens to be chronically tardy.

"I'll get them to call Jason, or Charlsie Tooten," I wrote. If things had been different, I would have written Arlene's name automatically.

"I'll be there at dark," he said.

I looked up into his pale face, the clear whites of his eyes almost shining in the gloomy room.

"I'll heal you," he offered. "Let me give you some blood."

I remembered the way my hair had lightened, remembered that I was almost twice as strong as I'd ever been. I shook my head.

"Why not?" he said, as if he'd offered me a drink of water when I was thirsty and I'd said no. I thought maybe I'd hurt his feelings.

I took his hand and guided it to my mouth. I kissed the palm gently. I held the hand to my better cheek.

"People notice I am changing," I wrote, after a moment. "I notice I am changing."

He bowed his head for a moment, and then looked at me sadly.

"You know what happened?" I wrote.

"Bubba told me part of it," he said, and his face grew scary as he mentioned the half-witted vampire. "Sam told me the rest, and I went to the police department and read the police reports."

"Andy let you do that?" I scribbled.

"No one knew I was there," he said carelessly.

I tried to imagine that, and it gave me the creeps.

I gave him a disapproving look.

"Tell me what happened in New Orleans," I wrote. I was beginning to feel sleepy again.

"You will have to know a little about us," he said hesitantly.

"Woo woo, secret vampire stuff!!" I croaked.

It was his turn to give me disapproving.

"We're a little organized," he told me. "I was

trying to think of ways to keep us safe from Eric." Involuntarily, I looked at the red flower arrangement.

"I knew if I were an official, like Eric, it would be much more difficult for him to interfere with my private life."

I looked encouraging, or at least I tried to.

"So I attended the regional meeting, and though I have never been involved in our politics, I ran for an office. And, through some concentrated lobbying, I won!"

This was absolutely amazing. Bill was a *union rep?* I wondered about the concentrated lobbying, too. Did that mean Bill had killed all the opposition? Or that he'd bought the voters a bottle of A positive apiece?

"What is your job?" I wrote slowly, imagining Bill sitting in a meeting. I tried to look proud, which seemed to be what Bill was looking for.

"I'm the Fifth Area investigator," he said. "I'll tell you what that means when you're home. I don't want to wear you out."

I nodded, beaming at him. I sure hoped he didn't take it into his head to ask me who all the flowers were from. I wondered if I had to write Eric a thank-you note. I wondered why my mind was going off on all these tangents. Must be the pain medication.

I gestured to Bill to draw close. He did, his face resting on the bed next to mine. "Don't kill Rene," I whispered.

He looked cold, colder, coldest.

"I may have already done the job. He's in intensive care. But even if he lives, there's been enough murder. Let the law do it. I don't want any more witchhunts coming after you. I want us to have peace." It was becoming very difficult to talk. I took his hand in both of mine, held it again to my least-bruised cheek. Suddenly, how much I had missed him became a solid lump lodged in my chest, and I held out my arms. He sat carefully on the edge of the bed, and leaning toward me, he carefully, carefully, slid his arms under me and pulled me up to him, a fraction of an inch at a time, to give me time to tell him if it hurt.

"I won't kill him," Bill said finally, into my ear.

"Sweetheart," I breathed, knowing his sharp hearing could pick it up. "I missed you." I heard his quick sigh, and his arms tightened a little, his hands began their gentle stroking down my back. "I wonder how quickly you can heal," he said, "without my help?"

"Oh, I'll try to hurry," I whispered. "I'll bet I surprise the doctor as it is."

A collie trotted down the corridor, looked in the open door, said, "Rowwf," and trotted away. Astonished, Bill turned to glance out into the corridor. Oh, yeah, it was the full moon, tonight — I could see it out of the window. I could see something else, too. A white face appeared out of the blackness and floated between me and the moon. It was a handsome face, framed by long golden hair. Eric the Vampire grinned at me and gradually disappeared from my view. He was flying.

"Soon we'll be back to normal," Bill said, laying me down gently so he could switch out the light in the bathroom. He glowed in the dark.

"Right," I whispered. "Yeah. Back to normal."

We hope you have enjoyed this Large Print book. Other Thorndike, Wheeler or Chivers Press Large Print books are available at your library or directly from the publishers.

For more information about current and upcoming titles, please call or write, without obligation, to:

Publisher
Thorndike Press
295 Kennedy Memorial Drive
Waterville, ME   04901
Tel. (800) 223-1244

Or visit our Web site at:
www.gale.com/thorndike
www.gale.com/wheeler

OR

Chivers Large Print
published by BBC Audiobooks Ltd
St James House, The Square
Lower Bristol Road
Bath BA2 3SB
England
Tel. +44(0) 800 136919
email: bbcaudiobooks@bbc.co.uk
www.bbcaudiobooks.co.uk

All our Large Print titles are designed for easy reading, and all our books are made to last.